End

MEETING AGENDA

FROM THE OFFICE OF JAE LEE

En(DEAR)
Be(LIE)ve
(SIGN)ificant
(GOOD)bye
Un(LIKE)ly
(QUEST)ion
(MEET)ing
Bl(INK)
St(ART)
Be(TROTH)ed
Mis(TAKE)
Hi(STORY)
No(THING)
(WED)ge
Admi(RING)
(FUN)ction
(FOREVER)lasting
Birth(DAY)
Misunder(STAND)
(CAT)astrophe
(FLIP)ping
(ENGAGE)ment
(DIS)aster
Over(HEARD)
Inti(MATE)
(FAKE)r
(CAN)cer
(PROMISE)d
Mis(COMMUNICATIONS)
At(TEMPT)
D(ATE)
(SPARK)ling
Loop(HOLES)
(CARE)ssing
Re(UNITE)d
A(LONE)
(SWEET)heart
(SHOW)er
(LONG)ing
(SPELL)bound
(SIGN)ificant
(DISAPPOINT)ment
(VOW)el
(RUN)away
(HONOR)ary
(SOFT)en
(WARM)th
Cl(AIM)
(BEGIN)nings
(TEMPT)ation
(CLING)ing
(KIND)ling
(SLOW)burn
Cli(MAX)
(BOSS)y
Epilogue

LUMINOUS INDUSTRIES

FROM THE OFFICE OF JAE LEE

DATE JUNE 24TH, 2024

FROM JAE LEE

ADDRESSED TO LUMINOUS EMPLOYEES

SUBJECT TEIF PROJECT

To all the frenemies: this one's for you. May your coffee always be lukewarm, your Wi-Fi perpetually spotty, and your memory of us vivid enough that you one day beg for our forgiveness. Here's to bridges burnt and lessons learned—cheers!

Jae Lee

LUMINOUS INDUSTRIES

HUMAN RESOURCES

DATE JUNE 24TH, 2024
FROM HUMAN RESOURCES
ADDRESSED TO VERENA WILLIAMS
SUBJECT TEIF PROJECT

Please be advised that during office hours, the only approved playlist is the "Luminous Industries Focus Mix," available on the company drive. Adherence to this policy ensures a calm and productive work environment. Failure to comply may result in disciplinary action.

Best regards,
Karen Smith
Human Resources Department
Luminous Industries

1

EN(DEAR)

VERENA

Jae Lee always left his office door ajar, an irritating invitation to his daily surveillance party over my desk. It was his way of ensuring that no stapler went unpressed, no Post-it note unstuck, all under his vigilant gaze. As I nudged the door open wider, I saw him entrenched behind his paper barricades, his hair as unruly as his obsession with micromanagement.

I placed the quinoa chicken breakfast bowl—his latest health craze—beside him. "I moved your four to five," I said, leaning against the cool metal of his desk, the casual barrier between his world and mine. "Oh, and there's a fire to put out regarding the Eastside project." I glanced at my watch, its sleek design matching the cold ethos of Luminous Industries. "You have, what, twenty-three minutes until showtime with the project managers?" My tone hovered between helpful and sardonic, a reminder that despite the early hour, some of us were already balancing the scales of this empire.

Our firm, specializing in cutting-edge architectural designs and innovative building solutions, was headquartered in the bustling heart of New York. Jae, momentarily shifting his attention from the intricate schematics before him, was buried in designs for the next big innovation. Barely acknowledging my presence, he muttered, "Tie," tossing the word out like a royal decree rather than a simple request, his gaze glued to the organized pandemonium of papers. As the CEO, his mind constantly toggled between managing multi-million dollar projects, strategizing new product launches, and overseeing the construction of cutting-edge facilities.

As I moved closer, the stubble on his jaw caught my eye—a minor rebellion against his own unrelenting standards. His suit, however, screamed control, every line and stitch meticulously calculated, much like the man himself.

Ambitious and driven, Jae navigated a world of patents, blueprints, and billion-dollar deals with ease. Yet somewhere beneath that crisp exterior, a hint of warmth lingered, reserved for those he deemed worthy of seeing it. His mind was a constant storm of innovation and strategy, shaping the future one calculated move at a time.

Jae popped up from his paper fortress, and I sprang into action, straightening his tie with the precision of a bomb defuser. If he was going to nitpick my every move, I might as well return the favor.

He finally looked up, our eyes locking in that loaded silence. His deep brown eyes, framed by impeccably groomed eyebrows and a strong jawline, still held that spark that once lured me here—a spark that now felt more like a challenge. His features, striking and precise like a model's, conveyed an intensity that dared me to keep pace in this persistent game. In that fleeting moment, entire strategies were born and decisions sealed, all without a word.

"Anything else?" His voice, usually carrying the weight of big decisions, softened slightly—a small acknowledgment of my role.

"Just the usual fires to put out," I quipped, my tone light despite the constant rush of beating deadlines and outpacing rivals. "Try to eat before your breakfast turns into a science project."

"No time," he shot back, already halfway to the door, his presence a whirlwind that seemed to suck the air from the room. "Legal's a disaster. We're on double time now. Adjust the temperature in the conference room; I think I'm getting sick." His urgency was a clear signal—fall in line or fall behind.

I kept pace, phone glued to one hand and my iPad in the other.

"Make sure the conference room's hot, the coffee's hotter, and for the love of God, check the projector," I barked into the phone to the legal secretary, who was probably already under ten cups of caffeine herself.

In the sauna that was our conference room, Jae was turning up the heat even more. His voice cut through the air. "We need a solution, now!" he demanded. The legal team looked like they'd rather be anywhere but the firing line.

The debacle of the day? A patent mess. Some rival thought they could claim something we'd been babying for months. The table was a disaster zone of schematics and legal documents, each one screaming for salvation.

Jae planted himself at the head of it all, more dictator than director. "Why is no one answering me?" he growled, his impatience snapping through the room like a live wire.

A lawyer, clutching papers that shook like a leaf in a hurricane, tried to interject, "We're reviewing every angle, but—"

"But nothing," Jae interrupted, his voice sharp. "Time's running out."

Standing there, watching my once-best-friend-now-boss manhandle what used to be our dream team, I couldn't help but reminisce about the good old days when the biggest decision we had to make was whose turn it was to buy beer.

Now? I was juggling his demands like flaming torches, wondering when *assistant* had become synonymous with errand bitch.

I leaned in, tablet in hand. "Here's the latest from our patent counsel," I whispered, sliding the digital peace pipe across to Jae without missing a beat.

He gave me a quick nod, a flicker of recognition, then zeroed in on the screen. "Good, keep digging. Verena, let's move." His tone was all business, but there was a hint of the old camaraderie in that brief eye contact.

We power walked to the elevator, Jae leading by half a step, already strategizing the next chess move in his head. "What's next?" he fired off without breaking stride.

As we stepped into the elevator, I handed him the phone, all prepped and ready to switch gears. "Project managers next. Oh, and your aunt's flight just touched down. I've arranged for her pickup, and your penthouse is all set for her visit."

He took the phone, already dialing his aunt. His CEO armor slipped for a moment, revealing the nephew beneath. As he switched to Korean, his voice softened, the edges blurring into something gentler. I assumed he was being nice. He only reserved that courtesy for her these days. If I had to guess, he was saying something like, *"Hello, Auntie, how was your flight? I'll see you tonight."* It was like watching the Grinch's heart grow—brief but unmistakably there. That fleeting softness, a rare crack in his corporate facade, reminded me there was a heart beating under that suit after all.

Watching Jae switch from corporate shark to doting nephew was jarring. For a second, I saw the old Jae—the college buddy whose laugh was easy and whose eyes weren't shadowed by a NASDAQ's worth of stress. Now, I wasn't sure what we were. Pals? Co-workers? Chess pieces in a game where the kings and pawns wore the same suits?

After the call, the curtain fell quickly, and CEO Jae was back, the familial warmth fading as fast as it had appeared. "We have a tight schedule today," he clipped, the earlier softness gone. "Book my aunt a spa day for tomorrow, will you? She needs to relax."

The way he switched gears wasn't new, but it stung a bit more each time. Here we were, side by side but worlds apart, running on the fumes of a friendship that used to fuel our dreams. Now, I was just keeping the engine running while he steered us into the future.

"Of course," I said, tapping into my tablet, already plotting the next move in the day's itinerary. "And since your aunt loves catching up with my mom, how about I book them a lunch date at El Centro on Ninth Avenue?"

Jae laughed, a rare sound these days. "Jennifer loves that place. But make sure we have a driver lined up. When your mother and my aunt get together, they usually enjoy way too many margaritas."

"Good point," I replied, smiling. It was a brief, genuine moment of connection, a nod to the personal lives we occasionally remembered we had.

As we power walked to the project managers' meeting, the unrelenting pace of the day was briefly interrupted by the sound of Jae's stomach complaining—apparently, it hadn't gotten the memo about his no-breakfast policy.

"You should have eaten breakfast," I chided lightly, diving into my purse and pulling out a protein bar. I always kept a stash, knowing Jae's eating habits were as sporadic as our emergency meetings.

He grabbed it with a brisk "Thanks," his mind already a thousand tasks ahead.

Upon entering the meeting room, Jae swooped into his throne at the head of the table, transitioning into the persona of Luminous's autocratic ruler with the ease of a seasoned actor. "Eastside project," he began, sweeping his gaze across the room, "why are we behind?"

A brave manager started to spell out the hurdles, "The budget's tight, and—"

But Jae, ever the fan of curt interruptions, cut in, "I don't want excuses." His laser focus then zeroed in on me. "Verena, where do we stand?"

There I was, tablet in hand, the modern-day shield against corporate chaos, ready to navigate us back on track. "Here's the breakdown. We can reallocate resources from—" Suddenly, my trusty digital sidekick decided to take a nap. Right there. In the heat of battle. Perfect.

I tapped the screen with a frenzy that would've impressed a Morse code operator, while a low-key panic party started in my gut. "Just a moment," I muttered, trying to sound like I had this under control— spoiler: I did not. The tablet, traitor that it was, remained unresponsive.

Jae's patience, always more of a napkin-thin veneer, finally snapped. "Verena!" His voice cracked, cutting through the thick air of the meeting room, broadcasting his annoyance loud and clear. "We absolutely do not have time for this kind of hold-up. Get it together, now."

The atmosphere in the room turned heavier than my last date's overuse of cologne. As everyone's eyes ping-ponged between Jae and me, I forced an apologetic smile.

"I'm sorry," I muttered. "I'll handle it immediately." But really, what I wanted was to handle that malfunctioning tablet like a frisbee, aimed straight at his head. In my mind, I pictured it—a perfect throw, slow-mo, maybe even set to some triumphant music. Of course, in reality, I was just apologizing for both the tech fail and the sad decline of our once epic friendship.

Just as I was bracing for another round of corporate gladiatorial combat, a knock at the door threw a wrench into the gears. Another assistant timidly popped her head in, her smile faltering as she took in the frosty atmosphere. "Uh, you've got a delivery," she stammered, her eyes darting nervously between Jae and me.

Jae's irritation bubbled over. "What now? Why are you interrupting this meeting?" he snapped.

The assistant edged into the room, clutching a bouquet of flowers like a lifeline.

"What the hell is that?" Jae asked.

"It was a delivery, sir," she said softly.

"And you thought interrupting my meeting for a delivery was necessary? Verena, how many times have I told you to make sure everyone understands the importance of not interrupting my meetings!?"

"Uh, these are for Verena for, uh, her birthday," she mumbled, clearly wishing she could melt into the floor.

I accepted the bouquet with a tight smile, turning the moment into a tiny life raft in an ocean of awkwardness.

Jae's eyebrows shot up in surprise. "It's your birthday?" His voice held a blend of disbelief and annoyance, as if birthdays were items on a meeting agenda he'd overlooked.

"Yeah, it's today," I replied, the irony not lost on me. "Even got a heartfelt note from you," I added, waving the card for him to see.

His reaction held a pinch of guilt, but we both knew this was just part of the dance—the assistant choreographing her own birthday surprises because, well, that's what assistants do.

I flipped open the card attached to the flowers, glancing at the neat script that looked suspiciously like my own handwriting—because it was. "Dear Verena, Happy Birthday. Sincerely, Jae," I read. It was a bit too formal, a bit too impersonal, but perfectly in line with the role of an assistant who's left to remember her own birthday.

For a moment, the room was silent, everyone unsure how to react. I looked up at Jae, his stern expression softening just a fraction, a flicker of something human beneath the corporate armor. The absurdity of it all hit me like a wave, and I let out a small, bitter laugh. "Thank you, Jae," I said. "I appreciate the thoughtful gesture."

The tension in the room cracked slightly, the flowers a strange, poignant reminder of what once was and what had become. As Jae's eyes met mine, I saw a glimmer of the friend I used to know, buried deep under the weight of responsibilities and expectations. But then his gaze drifted, locking onto the sprawl of papers covering the conference room table.

"In the future, please don't waste precious time on such trivial things," Jae said, making my stomach sink. Was he serious? Not only did I have to send myself flowers, I had to make sure they were delivered in a way that didn't piss him off.

"Alright, back to business," he commanded. "We need to solve this Eastside project issue immediately."

As the meeting resumed, I clutched the bouquet a little tighter.

"Right. Business. Of course." Each word was a punch.

As the tablet rebooted with the gusto of a Monday morning, Jae was quick to shelve the birthday buzz. "That's enough distractions for today," he declared, like we could just mute the awkward.

In the future, please don't waste precious time on such trivial things...

So I was trivial to Jae? I gave him ten years of my life at this stupid job, and he couldn't even acknowledge me for five seconds?

The old Jae would have taken me to dinner or made me a card. He would have cut class with me.

In the future, please don't waste precious time on such trivial things...

How many damn times did I waste my precious time on trivial shit for Jae? The meticulous errands, the late night synergy calls. I was always going above and beyond for this man, and he couldn't even give me the bare minimum.

A sharp thought hit me. Here we were, waltzing through a corporate tango, but I was done dancing to this tune.

This was a building resentment. The kind that only needed a small chip to shatter the glass ceiling of this whole damn building.

The clock ticked, each sound a reminder of our partnership that had downgraded to a transaction.

Amidst the chatter of strategies and half-baked plans, a lightbulb moment—brighter than my future at this company—flashed before me. My best friend—no, my boss, my frenemy—forgot my birthday.

This job was never supposed to be my forever. Ten years ago, my best friend hired me to be his assistant. Something temporary until I got my writing career off the ground.

But I was still here.

And if I didn't leave soon, I never would.

In the future, please don't waste precious time on such trivial things...

I was wasting my life, my patience, my talents, and my soul at this damn office.

Today, I would cut the cord. Today, I'd hand in my resignation. No more wondering if I was a friend or just the calendar keeper. Today, I'd make it official.

As I looked around the room, I knew it was time to swipe left on this corporate drama. My heart pounded as I stood up, the bouquet clutched in my hand, and took a deep breath. This was it.

"Jae," I said, my voice steady but resolute, "we need to talk."

The room fell silent, all eyes on us. Jae's gaze met mine, confusion flickering across his face. But I had already made up my mind. This was the end of one chapter and the start of another.

"Fine," he gritted. "Schedule it for this evening."

2

BE(LIE)VE

VERENA

As the day was winding down, fate had its own dramatic twist lined up, courtesy of the ever-chaotic Luminous. Just as I was gearing up for a low-key birthday dinner, Jae burst through like a hurricane. "We have a meeting tonight with a potential partner."

I paused, the sting of disappointment sharp. "But my birthday dinner with Mom, Luke, and Laura..." I started, my voice heavy with letdown. "And I told you, we need to talk."

"No time, Verena," he insisted, practically already out the door. "Jennifer will understand, and as for Luke, you know I've never liked him. I don't understand why you continue to entertain a friendship with that man child."

I grumbled to myself. Why Jae had such an issue with Luke was beyond my pay grade. I stopped trying to understand it years ago.

But, fuck, what about my birthday dinner?

As we made a mad dash from the office, I dialed my mom, the guilt tightening in my stomach. "Mom, hey. I...I can't make it tonight," I stumbled over the words, dreading her response.

"Again, Verena?" Her tone was a mix of disappointment and dry wit. "What's it this time? Another last-minute rescue mission for Sir Demands-a-Lot?"

"Yeah, Mom, I'm really sorry. A meeting just came up, and Jae is adamant."

"Seriously? I stood in line for your favorite Tres Leches Cake at the corner bakery!" she huffed, her voice carrying the familiar edge of exasperation that came from years of dealing with hospital emergencies and family dramas.

I winced, preparing for the inevitable mom lecture. "I know, Mom, and I'm so sorry. It's just—"

"Just what? On Christmas, you ran out on dinner. Thanksgiving, you jetted off to London. And now, your birthday? Honey, I love Jae, but you're not running a charity for overworked bosses. He needs to learn that you have a life, too."

I could almost see her rolling her eyes, one hand probably on her hip, the other likely gesturing animatedly as she spoke.

"Mom, it's complicated..."

"Complicated? Sweetie, life is complicated, but you can't keep letting him walk all over you. Friends don't use friends as their all-access help pass," she said, her voice softening but still carrying that no-nonsense edge that only a retired nurse from New Jersey could master.

She had a point. But he wasn't my friend. Not anymore. He was...

"He's my boss, Mom. We'll really talk about this soon, just not tonight," I managed.

As I walked to the car, her words echoed in my mind. She wasn't going to let this go easily, and she was right. I needed to stand up for myself.

"You need to stand up for yourself," she reiterated, almost reading my thoughts. "Also, I got your calendar invite to lunch with Binna. Is he going to spend time with her while she visits, or does he expect us to keep her entertained?"

"You love Auntie Binna."

"I do. But that boy needs to spend time with his family, too," she replied, a hint of a smile creeping into her voice. "He needs to realize the world doesn't revolve around him."

I chuckled, feeling a bit of the tension ease. "Thanks, Mom. I'll make it up to you, I promise. Maybe a spa day this weekend?"

"Now you're talking," she said, her tone brightening. "And tell Jae he owes me a dinner. I'll give him a piece of my mind about stealing my daughter on her birthday."

"I will," I laughed. "Love you, Mom."

"Love you too, honey. And remember, take care of yourself," she finished, her voice a comforting blend of strength and nurturing.

Her words lingered as I hung up, a small comfort amidst the whirlwind that was my life with Jae. As I reached the car and climbed in, I couldn't shake the feeling that this would be the last time I let him derail my plans so easily.

Jae's personal driver sped off, and the air was electric with all the things we weren't saying.

"About your birthday..." Jae began, his voice softer, almost apologetic.

"It's fine," I cut in, trying to keep the disappointment from my voice as I stared out the window, watching the city lights blur past.

"Maybe tomorrow we can hit up The Carb Apothecary? Your favorite, right?"

I sighed. "That was the plan for tonight. But now? Doesn't seem worth it."

He didn't give up. "Okay, what about that movie you wanted to see this weekend?"

I couldn't contain a short, humorless laugh, flipping open my iPad. "Really, Jae? Let's see. You've got the charity gala on Saturday night, your infamous networking brunch early Sunday," I started, my fingers swiping through his calendar with practiced ease.

He tried to interject, "Well, the gala's—"

I cut him off. "And then there's the strategy meeting with the design team, lunch with the board members, that interview with *Tech Today*, the conference call with Berlin, reviewing the quarterly financials, the product development debrief, not to mention your personal training session, and oh, let's not forget the live Q&A you promised on social media."

He opened his mouth, perhaps to argue or make excuses, but nothing came out.

"See?" I pressed on, the list of commitments hanging between us like a verdict. "You're too busy for me. For anything that's not work."

Jae's silence was heavy, loaded with unspoken truths we both knew but had never dared to acknowledge. The car ride continued, the distance of the journey mirroring the gap that had formed between us —not just in plans, but in what we had become to each other.

"By the way," I added, "I reached out to Catherine Giles to be your date for the gala. You liked her last time, right?"

"Why don't you go with me?" His suggestion caught me off guard.

"I have plans," I said flatly. "And she's a better fit." I didn't dare say that I needed a break from him, and the idea of a calm Saturday night seemed like heaven.

"I really am sorry about your birthday. Things have been busy lately," he offered, sincerity in his voice.

"It's no problem, Jae. I know how busy you are. I manage your schedule, remember?" My response was light, but it carried the significance of our changed dynamic. "Let's just meet with the potential partner, hmm?" I proposed, steering us back to professional waters.

"Thank you, Verena. I can always count on you."

Pretty soon he'd have to lean on someone else.

The sleek black leather seats and the soft purr of the engine contrasted sharply with the upheaval in my mind. Jae's focus was already shifting, his mind whirring with the next item on his endless to-do list. The brief moment of attempted camaraderie evaporated as quickly as it had come. The city sped by, a blur of neon lights and honking horns, as we plunged back into the uncompromising grind of our lives at Luminous Industries.

"Tonight, we need to talk," I stated firmly.

"Why can't we talk now?" Jae countered, confusion and a hint of concern lacing his question.

I glanced at my iPad, pulling up his meticulously managed schedule. "As you requested, I penciled in a formal meeting on your schedule for after our dinner with the client and before your driver takes you home. We can do it then."

"We can still talk now. It's not that rigid of an appointment, Verena. Since when do you schedule simple conversations with me?"

"I've been doing it for a while," I admitted, tapping on the screen to highlight our meetings in purple. "See?" I showed him the calendar. He leaned over to look, his expression shifting from confusion to a frown. He could see the little minutes of our friendship clear as day.

Remind Jae that Auntie is visiting this week.

Talk to Jae about the house plants in his office.

Tell Jae that his date for the gala is confirmed.

"I've been scheduling us since last year. It was more efficient that way," I explained.

"Oh." He paused, absorbing the information. "Well, tell me now. We still have some time until we get to the restaurant."

"Let's just wait," I insisted, feeling that the gravity of what I had to say deserved its own space, not a hurried conversation in his town car. Plus, I didn't want the awkwardness of a long dinner to follow after it.

He sighed, a sound of resignation. "Fine, we'll wait. But, Verena, you know you can talk to me about anything, anytime, right?"

I nodded, a lump forming in my throat. "Sure. We'll talk tonight."

The car sped through the bustling streets of New York, the city lights casting fleeting shadows across our faces. The ride continued in silence, both of us lost in our thoughts, the impending conversation hanging over us like a cloud.

As we neared the restaurant, the atmosphere in the car grew heavier. Jae's gaze was fixed on the window, his mind likely already shifting to the upcoming meeting, while I grappled with the words I needed to say.

When we finally pulled up to the elegant facade of the restaurant, Jae turned to me, his expression unreadable. "I need the quarterly reports after dinner. It might be a late night."

I stared at him.

"I know it's your birthday," he added, almost as an afterthought, "but after the meeting, we might have to go to my house to get it all done."

I nodded. "I'll have everything ready."

He softened slightly, offering a small concession. "I'll order your favorite dessert and maybe we can get some beer. An all-nighter like we used to do."

The attempt at nostalgia did little to lighten the load. As we walked toward the entrance, his steps quickened, leaving me trailing behind.

Tonight would change everything between us.

As I followed him inside, a sense of resolve settled over me. Tonight, I would finally say what needed to be said, no matter the outcome.

As we entered the restaurant, I knew that this was the beginning of the end.

3

(SIGN)IFICANT

JAE

I realized I needed a second assistant—someone tasked solely with reminding me of my first assistant's birthday. As ridiculous as it sounds, that day's oversight shone a harsh light on a truth I'd been too preoccupied to see. Verena, my steadfast right hand and the person who had been by my side since our college days, had slowly faded into the background of my ever-demanding schedule.

When Verena's English degree didn't open the doors she had hoped it would, offering her a job seemed like the natural thing to do. Her intelligence, wit, and uncanny ability to navigate complex situations had always impressed me. She had a knack for making sense of it all, foreseeing problems before they arose, and finding solutions that seemed to elude everyone else. She became an integral part of my life and, eventually, of Luminous.

Verena was indispensable—no question about it. Her efficiency and reliability made it easy to overlook the fact that she had her own needs, her own life.

The realization was a mild inconvenience.

I could reassure her.

I could fix *anything*.

Maybe offer her a bonus or a Saturday excursion. Last time, I took her with me to Tokyo. I had a trip to London planned; she'd probably enjoy that.

Sure, I had the company to run, millions—no, *billions*—of dollars at stake, and my eyes set on conquering new markets. But even I had to admit that Verena's role had become crucial. Without her, the well-oiled machine that was Luminous would have ground to a halt.

But it was an easy fix. I could make it better. I *always* made it better.

As I looked at her now, efficiently coordinating yet another impossibly complex day, I felt a rare twinge of something close to regret. She deserved more than my oversight and neglect. She deserved acknowledgment, appreciation, and, above all, respect.

Tonight, however, was not the night for sentimentality. We had a potential investor to impress, and distractions were not an option. I would make it up to her—just not tonight. Business came first.

Walking into the private room of the five-star restaurant, I couldn't help but notice the ease with which Verena adapted to the ever-changing demands of our work. Her brown hair cascaded over her shoulders, catching the soft, ambient lighting of the luxurious dining room. Dressed in a sleek, tailored blazer and pants, she exuded an effortless elegance that always seemed to draw stares from patrons and staff alike.

I signaled to the maître d', who nodded and brought over a bottle of their finest wine. As he poured, I glanced at Verena, who was busy setting up the presentation. "Make sure we have all the materials ready for the pitch during dinner," I commanded, trying to shift our focus to the task at hand. "It needs to be perfect."

Verena flashed me a look, half-amused, half-exasperated, her green eyes sparkling. "Jae, it's already taken care of. Presentation's updated, financials reviewed, and your notes are highlighted."

Her preparedness impressed me. "You're always three steps ahead, aren't you?" I remarked, a note of genuine admiration slipping into my voice despite my efforts to maintain my usual authoritative demeanor.

"That's the plan," she replied, her tone light but carrying an edge of seriousness. Her efficiency was one of the many reasons I relied on her so heavily, yet it was also a reminder of how much I had come to take her for granted.

As we settled into the private room, I looked at her again. Verena was no longer just my assistant; she was the linchpin holding my chaotic world together. And as I watched her handle everything with such grace and competence, I felt like I had overlooked something crucial.

The door swung open, and Mr. Harrison, a distinguished man in his fifties with an air of sophistication, walked in. His suit and polished demeanor spoke of old money and meticulous taste.

I stood, extending a confident hand. "Mr. Harrison, welcome. I'm Jae Lee, CEO of Luminous. It's a pleasure to meet you." My appearance was as calculated as my business strategies—perfectly tailored charcoal suit, crisp white shirt, and a navy tie that spoke of understated elegance. My dark hair was styled with precision, and I knew my presence commanded attention.

Mr. Harrison shook my hand firmly, his eyes assessing me with keen interest. "Pleasure's all mine, Jae. I've heard great things about your firm."

"Thank you," I replied, gesturing for him to take a seat. "We have a lot to discuss tonight, and I'm confident you'll be impressed with what we have to offer."

Mr. Harrison settled into the plush chair across from me, his gaze firm. He was a man used to high-stakes negotiations, and tonight was no different. I could feel the weight of his expectations, but I thrived under pressure.

Luminous was my brainchild, a company I had built from the ground up with drive and a vision for creating iconic structures that defined city skylines. Our latest project, a cutting-edge eco-friendly skyscraper, was poised to set new standards in sustainable architecture. It was a bold endeavor, designed to be a landmark in New York City, highlighting innovative green technologies and state-of-the-art design.

As I began the pitch, my mind briefly flickered to my background. Born to immigrant parents who owned a small construction business, I had seen firsthand the hard work and determination it took to succeed in this industry. I had taken that foundation and transformed it into a billion-dollar empire, driven by an unyielding pursuit of excellence and a refusal to accept anything less than perfection.

"Mr. Harrison, at Luminous Industries, we don't just build structures, we create landmarks," I began, my voice carrying the conviction of someone who knew his worth. "Our latest project is designed to be the pinnacle of sustainable architecture, integrating the latest in green technology with unparalleled aesthetic appeal. This skyscraper will not only redefine the skyline but also set a new benchmark for eco-friendly construction."

Mr. Harrison nodded, clearly intrigued. "I've seen some of your past projects, Jae. Your firm's reputation for innovation is impressive. Tell me more about the sustainability aspects."

I leaned forward, the flicker of a smile playing on my lips. "We've incorporated solar panels, wind turbines, and rainwater harvesting systems into the design. The building's facade is made of photovoltaic glass, which generates energy while providing natural light. Additionally, the structure uses advanced insulation techniques to minimize energy consumption. This project isn't just about building a skyscraper; it's about creating a sustainable future."

As I clicked through the slides on my tablet, showcasing past detailed blueprints and financial projections, Mr. Harrison's interest deepened. But then, disaster struck. My tablet froze. The screen went blank, and no amount of tapping or swiping brought it back to life.

Panic surged through me, but I couldn't let it show. Not in front of the client. "Uh, as you can see," I stammered, trying to recover, "we have a very strong financial track record..."

Mr. Harrison's eyebrows knitted together in confusion. "These figures don't seem to align with what I've heard."

Verena, sensing the impending disaster, smoothly interjected. "Mr. Harrison, if I may," she said, her voice calm and authoritative. "There seems to be a technical issue. Allow me to correct it."

She quickly accessed her own tablet, and within moments, the correct slide appeared on the screen. "Here are the accurate financials," she continued, seamlessly taking over. "As you can see, our growth trajectory has been consistent, and our budgets are solid."

Mr. Harrison's frown eased as he reviewed the corrected data. "Ah, yes. This makes much more sense. Thank you, Miss."

"No problem," she replied with a professional smile. "I always have a backup."

The irony wasn't lost on me. Earlier in the day, I had no grace for her technical mishap, and now here she was, saving me from a potentially deal-breaking error.

As the presentation continued, Verena and I worked in tandem, her expertise and my vision combining to create a compelling case for Luminous. By the end of the dinner, Mr. Harrison seemed impressed, his initial doubts forgotten.

"Well, Jae," he said, standing up and shaking my hand once more, "you've got yourself a deal. I'll have my people contact yours to finalize the details."

"Thank you, Mr. Harrison," I replied, masking my earlier embarrassment with a broad smile. "We look forward to working with you."

As Mr. Harrison left, I turned to Verena. "Nice save," I said, trying to sound appreciative, though my pride was still stinging.

She shrugged, a hint of amusement in her eyes. "Just doing my job, Jae."

We walked out of the restaurant together, the night air cool against my skin. The bustling streets of New York City created a cacophony of sounds around us, a stark contrast to the quiet intensity of our private dining room. "Let's go to my house to work on the follow-up," I suggested, eager to shift back to familiar ground.

Verena stopped, turning to face me, her expression resolute. "I won't be going to your house tonight, Mr. Lee. It's time for that talk."

4

(GOOD)BYE

VERENA

Jae's attempt at gratitude fell flat, a feeble attempt to bridge the widening gap between us. "Thanks, Verena. Really."

"For what?" I asked, my voice edged with frustration as I turned to face him. The strain of the day etched lines of sarcasm into my words.

"For handling all of this with such grace," he offered, a poor plaster over the crack in our dynamic.

I couldn't help the laughter that bubbled up, bitter and sharp. "It's what I do, right?" I retorted, my smile tight and devoid of any real humor. "Put out your fires, handle your schedule? Drop everything for you?" Each word was a pinpoint strike on the pretense we'd maintained for so long.

Jae opened his mouth to respond, perhaps to defend or to deflect, but I wasn't interested in hearing more excuses or platitudes. I turned on my heel, marching toward the car with a purpose, leaving him standing amidst the throng of travelers, a silent witness to my departure.

Each step felt like shedding a layer of the persona I had built—the ever-reliable, ever-present assistant, always ready to dive into the fray for Luminous, for Jae. But no more. This was the moment of reckoning, the climax of years spent in the shadows of greatness, years of my needs and desires being systematically overshadowed by the demands of a job that had consumed my identity. The realization was sharp, a clarity that cut through the fog of obligation and loyalty that had clouded my judgment.

As I slid into the car, the finality of the moment settled in. This wasn't just another task to be checked off my endless list. This was my exit, a step into the unknown, propelled by the recognition of my worth beyond the confines of my role as Jae's assistant.

Jae's voice cut through the tension, a tentative olive branch extended in the midst of our silent battlefield. "I know you're mad about your birthday," he began, his tone a blend of caution and genuine concern. "I shouldn't have asked you to work late, but this was a big opportunity."

"Mad?" I echoed, my words sharp, a defensive barrier rising instinctively. "Mr. Lee, of course not. It would be unprofessional to be mad. I'm doing my job, sir. If there's something I've done wrong, please, enlighten me." My voice, cool and collected, belied the turmoil within, a storm of emotions I refused to unleash. There was power in containing my rage. In controlling it.

He sighed, a sound of frustration and maybe a hint of sadness. "Come on, Verena. I know you're upset. Remember college? You used to yank on my ear and drag me around campus whenever you were pissed at me. Just let me have it so we can get this over with."

I scoffed, the absurdity of the situation not lost on me. "I'm so sorry, Mr. Lee, but I think we need to stick to the agenda." My response was curt, the formal address a pointed reminder of the line that had been drawn between us.

"Stop with the *Mr. Lee* thing; it's pissing me off," he countered, the frustration now evident in his voice.

"I'm sorry, Mr. Lee," I repeated, my tone unwavering, a clear indication that the professional veneer would remain intact.

His next question was almost a whisper, a sign that the layers of our professional dynamic were peeling away, leaving the raw, unresolved heart of our relationship exposed. "What did you want to talk about?"

I checked my watch; it was time for our scheduled meeting, a fixture in our relationship that had become as routine as it was essential. "You're right, Mr. Lee. It's time for our scheduled meeting. I have five things on the agenda," I started, my voice steady despite the storm inside.

As I navigated through the list of updates, my voice steady, I noticed Jae's reactions—a blend of surprise and something that might have been gratitude once. "I've sent over the notes from our meeting with Mr. Harrison," I started, keeping my tone professional, detached. "His concerns are highlighted for legal review."

"Mm-hmm," Jae interjected, a standard reply that felt devoid of warmth.

"And the patent issue has been resolved. Plus, I've drafted and sent the cease and desist to our competitors over their false claims," I continued, ticking off each item with precision.

"Good job," he repeated, his voice flat, the phrase echoing in the space between us.

"I've gathered a resolution team to address the problem with the project managers to figure out why they are behind schedule," I replied.

Then, as if sensing my growing detachment, Jae leaned forward, his voice sharpening. "I need a solution, Verena. Not just updates."

"Of course, Mr. Lee," I replied, my response automatic, a shield raised against the vulnerability of our fraying connection. The formality of his title, once unheard of in our conversations, now hung heavily in the air, a barrier as tangible as the walls of the car enclosing us.

A sigh escaped him as he rubbed his temples. "Once again, stop with the *Mr. Lee*, Verena. It's like you're talking to a stranger."

"Apologies for the formality, Mr. Lee," I persisted, the address a deliberate choice, a line drawn. The once seamless blend of our professional and personal lives had unraveled, leaving us tangled in the remnants of a partnership that had once felt unbreakable.

And then, the moment of truth, a cliff I had been inching towards without fully realizing the depth of the fall. "I also just emailed you my letter of resignation," I announced, the words tumbling out into the space between us, heavy with finality. My gaze shifted away from him, unable to bear witness to his reaction, a mix of shock and confusion I wasn't sure I could face.

In the suffocating silence of the car, I finally voiced the decision that had been crystallizing within me, my tone clipped, the epitome of professional detachment. "Mr. Lee, I have decided to resign from my position at Luminous. I will remain for one month to ensure a seamless transition, assist in hiring my replacement, and oversee their training."

Jae's reaction was a blend of shock and disbelief, his words tumbling out in a rush. "What the fuck, Verena? Resign? Just like that?"

"Indeed, Mr. Lee," I continued, my voice unwavering, each word meticulously chosen to underscore the professional boundary I was enforcing. "I've also prepared a job posting for your review. Upon your approval, I intend to proceed with the posting."

"After everything we've done here? You're just going to leave?"

"My decision is final," I stated firmly, refusing to be drawn into emotional turmoil. "I believe this to be in the best interest of both my professional development and the continued success of Luminous."

He was searching for a foothold in a conversation that was slipping away from him. "But why, Verena? We can fix whatever is wrong. Do you want a raise? More vacation days—"

I cut him off before he could continue, my tone as cool and collected as ever. "I appreciate your concern, Mr. Lee, but my decision stands. I have outlined the necessary steps for my departure in the memo attached to the job posting."

"Stop calling me Mr. Lee!" he finally exploded, the strain breaking through his shock. "What the hell happened to us, Verena?"

I paused, allowing myself a moment to look at him directly, to let the full significance of my decision—and our fractured friendship— sink in. "We ceased to be *us* the moment professional demands overtook personal regard, Mr. Lee. I'm merely acting in accordance with the current dynamic."

Before he could muster another response, the car came to a halt in front of the office. I stepped out, leaving behind the shell of a relationship that had once meant the world to me. "Goodbye. I wish Luminous all the best."

As I walked away, the door closing with a soft thud behind me, the finality of my actions settled in. I had not only resigned from a job, but had also closed a chapter on a friendship that had been eroded by years of neglect, hidden under the guise of professionalism.

The office lights glowed in the night, a beacon of what had been and what could have been. As I walked down the bustling street, each step taking me further from Jae and Luminous, I felt a strange combination of liberation and sorrow.

The conversation, however, was far from over. It was merely the beginning of a reckoning that would redefine us both.

5

UN(LIKE)LY

VERENA

Eleven Years Ago

I bounced out of my creative writing class, the crisp fall air waking me up faster than my third cup of coffee that morning. Our campus at Rutgers was charming in that small-town, postcard-perfect way, but what I loved most was that we were just a train ride away from the magic of Manhattan.

My notebook, filled with half-finished stories and random doodles, was clutched to my chest as I headed toward the coffee cart. Coffee was my post-class ritual and, let's be honest, my lifeline. As I approached, I saw Jae leaning against a lamppost, looking like he walked out of an Abercrombie & Fitch ad. His dark hair fell perfectly into his eyes, which were focused on his phone.

Jae was an architecture major, and the dude could draw like Michelangelo. He was tall, handsome, and had this quiet confidence that made people gravitate toward him. It didn't hurt that he had the body of a Greek god, but hey, that's just a bonus.

He looked up as I approached, flashing me a grin that could probably stop traffic. He held up a finger, signaling for me to hang on.

"Is that Auntie?" I squealed. "Tell her I said hi and that I had that hot TA in class again and—"

Jae rolled his eyes, still smiling. "Call her yourself," he mouthed before turning back to his phone. "Yes, Auntie. I'll tell her," he said into the phone, his voice dripping with affection.

I crossed my arms, waiting impatiently. Finally, he glanced at me, his smile widening. "Vee says hi."

I could hear her delighted voice faintly through the phone, and it made me smile. Auntie was like a second mom to me.

"Auntie says we need to come home one weekend for dinner before she moves back to Korea," Jae relayed.

"Tell her I'd love that," I said eagerly.

Jae nodded and finished his conversation, then slipped his phone into his pocket. "She keeps teasing me that we're dating. Maybe this dinner will finally convince her we're just friends."

"She's been teasing you about that for years," I said with a laugh. "Ever since that first weekend I went home with you and she cooked us that massive feast."

"Yeah," Jae said, grinning at the memory. "She wouldn't let you leave the table until you tried everything."

"The food coma was worth it," I replied, reaching the coffee cart and ordering my usual double-shot latte. Jae got his black coffee, and we found a bench to sit on.

"So, how's the latest creative writing assignment going?" Jae asked, raising an eyebrow.

I groaned dramatically. "Ugh, don't even get me started. We're supposed to write a modern retelling of a classic fairy tale, and I'm stuck. I've got nothing."

"Nothing at all?" Jae asked, amused. "Come on, Vee, you're always full of ideas."

"Yeah, well, not this time," I sighed, taking a sip of my coffee. "I'm thinking about turning Sleeping Beauty *into a story about a girl who's in a perpetual nap because she's so overwhelmed by life. But it feels too...depressing."*

Jae chuckled, shaking his head. "You'll figure it out. You always do."

"What about you?" I asked, changing the subject. "How's your latest project coming along?"

He sighed, running a hand through his thick, dark hair, the kind that always looked perfectly tousled. "We're designing a sustainable community center. It's supposed to be this innovative, eco-friendly space that brings people together. But my professor keeps shooting down my ideas." His frustration was evident in the crease between his eyebrows, and I couldn't help but notice how his eyes, deep and expressive, seemed even more intense when he was worked up. There was something undeniably attractive about his passion, something that made my heart skip a beat despite knowing he was my best friend.

I nodded sympathetically. "Sounds frustrating."

"It is," Jae admitted. "But I'll keep at it. Just need to find the right angle."

Our banter was easy, comfortable. We had known each other since freshman year, and over the years, our friendship had only grown stronger. Our relationship was built on a foundation of late-night study sessions, spontaneous trips to the city, and countless hours spent exploring every corner of Manhattan.

I remembered that first weekend Jae invited me home with him. His aunt had been teasing him nonstop about having a secret girlfriend, and he wanted to prove that we were just friends. Auntie welcomed me with open arms, and Jae and I connected in a way that solidified our friendship forever. We spent that weekend exploring, eating our weight in food, and talking about everything from our hopes and dreams to our fears and failures. Since then, Jae and I had been inseparable.

And now, with Auntie moving back to Korea, it felt like the end of an era. But I knew that no matter where life took us, Jae and I would always be best friends.

"I can't believe she's moving," I said, shaking my head.

Jae sighed, rubbing the back of his neck. "Yeah, she's been talking about it for a while now. Guess it's finally happening."

"But why now?" I asked, curiosity piqued. "She seems so settled here."

Jae took a deep breath, clearly trying to find the right words. "When my parents died, Auntie dropped everything to come take care of me. I was only fifteen and she thought moving to another country would be more than I could handle. She was engaged at the time."

"Wait, what? She had a fiancé?" I blinked in surprise. "Why didn't you ever mention that?"

"Yeah," Jae said. "Her fiancé didn't want to move to the States, and she couldn't leave me. So she broke it off and came here. She sacrificed so much."

"Wow," I said, feeling a pang of sympathy. "She never talks about that."

"She's not one to dwell on the past," Jae said, staring at his coffee cup. "But now she's ready to go home. She misses her family, her friends. And honestly, she deserves to live her life for herself."

"Absolutely," I agreed, thinking about Auntie and all she'd done. "She's a superhero."

Jae's eyes grew distant as he continued. "I used to spend my summers in Korea when my parents were alive. We'd visit Auntie and the rest of the family there. Those were the best times. The food, the culture, the way everyone came together..."

"Sounds like one big family reunion," I said, picturing it in my head.

"It was," Jae said, a hint of a smile on his lips. "After my parents died, everything changed. Auntie became my rock. She took care of me, made sure I never felt alone. I owe her everything."

I nudged his shoulder. "Promise me we'll visit her in Korea. I've always wanted to go."

Jae chuckled, but there was a hint of sadness in his eyes that he couldn't quite hide. "You got it. We'll make it happen."

As much as he tried to play it cool, I could tell the idea of Auntie moving back to Korea weighed heavily on him. The place held happy memories from his childhood, but it also reminded him of all he had lost. His parents, who had taken him to Korea every summer before they passed away, and the life he once knew before everything changed.

We settled into a comfortable silence for a moment, the noise of the campus bustling around us. I watched a group of students arguing about which was the best coffee shop nearby, and then turned my attention back to Jae.

"So Auntie still believes we're secretly dating?" I broke the silence, smirking.

Jae laughed, the sound rich and warm. He shook his head, the corners of *his eyes crinkling. "I told her we're just friends, but she insists we have chemistry."*

"Well, she's not wrong about the chemistry," I teased, nudging him playfully with my shoulder. The touch lingered longer than necessary, and I could feel the warmth radiating off him.

Jae rolled his eyes, but the grin on his face gave him away. "You're impossible."

"And you love it," I shot back, sticking out my tongue.

"Yeah, yeah," he said, shaking his head with a smile. His eyes flickered to my mouth briefly before meeting my gaze again, and for a moment, the air between us felt charged with something unspoken.

I shifted feeling a sudden flush creep up my neck. "Anyway, it's not like I can help it if I'm this charming."

"Oh, is that what we're calling it now?" Jae leaned in closer, his voice dropping to a playful whisper. "I thought it was just you being a pain in my ass."

I laughed, swatting at his arm, but my heart was racing. His nearness, the way his eyes sparkled with mischief, the subtle tension—it was all making it hard to think straight. "Well, if I'm such a pain, why do you keep hanging out with me?"

"Maybe I like the pain," he said, his voice teasing but his eyes holding a hint of something deeper. He reached out and tucked a loose strand of hair behind my ear, the touch sending a shiver down my spine.

I swallowed, suddenly hyperaware of how close we were. "Careful, Jae. Someone might think you actually enjoy my company."

He smirked, leaning back but still keeping his gaze locked on mine. "Someone might think that."

Our playful banter hung in the air, the underlying tension making it hard to breathe. It was awkward, this dance we did around our feelings, neither of us willing to take the first step. But in moments like this, when the world seemed to fade away and it was just us, it was hard to ignore the sparks.

I cleared my throat, trying to shake off the strange, almost electric feeling that had settled between us. "So, um, about that project of yours. Need any help?"

Jae blinked, then chuckled, the tension easing a bit. "Yeah, actually. I could use another pair of eyes on it. You free later?"

"Always," I said, offering him a genuine smile. "Anything for my best friend." I reached over and squeezed his hand. "Speaking of, I know you don't like talking about your feelings," I started, giving him a sidelong glance.

"Feelings? What are those?" Jae quipped, his grin widening.

"Seriously, Jae," I said. "I know you're probably scared that Auntie is leaving and you'll be alone."

He scoffed, shaking his head. "Scared? Me? Nah."

"I'm just saying, you aren't alone. I'm here," I insisted, squeezing his hand again.

"Oh great, the one person who makes me carry their books," he bantered back, giving me a playful nudge.

"Seriously," I repeated, giving him a look that was half-stern, half-amused. "And I can introduce you to my mom. She likes to adopt strays."

"Oh joy," he said, rolling his eyes again. "I've heard your stories about her. I'm not sure I need another mom in my life. I've managed to avoid it for three years."

I laughed, the sound light and easy. "She's not that bad. Just a bit intrusive. Actually, she and Auntie would probably be best friends."

Jae raised an eyebrow. "You think?"

"Totally. Let's get them together," I suggested.

Jae pretended to think about it, then nodded. "Alright, fine. But if she tries to adopt me, I'm holding you responsible."

"Deal," I said. "You're not getting rid of me that easily."

"Wouldn't dream of it," he replied, giving my arm a squeeze.

As we finished our coffee, I couldn't help but feel grateful for our bond. No matter how much things changed, I knew Jae and I would always have each other to lean on.

"Okay, enough sappy stuff," I said, standing up and stretching. "Walk me to my next class?"

"Only if you carry my books," Jae quipped, standing up and slinging his backpack over one shoulder.

"Nice try," I shot back, poking him in the ribs. "But I'll let you carry mine."

He groaned dramatically. "You're lucky I like you, Vee."

"Like? You love me," I teased, linking my arm with his as we started walking. "According to Auntie, we're practically married."

"Yeah, yeah," Jae said, laughing. "Just don't let it go to your head."

6

(QUEST)ION

VERENA

lick—the lock to my New York apartment echoed, sounding like my sanity snapping. My heart was doing the cha-cha-cha because I'd just flung my career out the window with all the subtlety of a circus elephant. "I quit my job," I whispered, the words tasting strange, like they belonged to someone else. Maybe if I screamed it from the rooftop of my Manhattan apartment building, it would feel real. Verena Williams, the perpetual planner, had just made an impromptu life choice.

I mean, was it impromptu, though? I'd been daydreaming about it for years. I once even ordered a cake that said *I Quit*. I never gave it to Jae, though. Instead, I ate it while sobbing at my desk. It was one of those decisions that had been building up, but I never had the balls to actually do it.

Until today.

I guess getting older gave you less fucks.

I flicked on the lights and—bam! My Zen, minimalist apartment had transformed into party central. Balloons bobbed around like tipsy guests, streamers dangled with careless abandon, and right in the middle of it all was my mom, decked out in what could only be described as fashion anarchy. "Happy birthday, baby!" she exclaimed, a vortex of sparkles and enthusiastic prints.

Her eyes glowed with mischievous delight, echoing the shimmer of her chaotic ensemble. Her hair, once dark, now boasted smears of gray she wore like a crown, styled wildly as if she had just spun through a windstorm of joy.

"Oh wow, a surprise party...and I just quit my job." The words slipped out before I could stop them. Maybe saying it out loud was my way of proving it really happened.

"Wh-what?" Mom asked.

I scanned the room, catching sight of my two best friends. Laura, my quirky neighbor and confidante, stood frozen mid-bite, a bright pink cupcake clutched in her hand. Her blonde hair was piled into a messy bun, frosting smudged on her lip. She wore a bright yellow sundress that clashed wonderfully with the cupcake, making her look like a walking, talking burst of sunshine caught in a moment of paused confusion. Her eyes were wide as saucers, clearly torn between celebrating and comforting.

Then there was Luke, my childhood partner in countless escapades. His real name was Lucia, but only his mom called him that. He was your classic Jersey Italian, with dark curls that refused to be tamed and a naturally tanned complexion. In the middle of offering me a colorful balloon, his actions halted as my words hung in the air. The balloon slipped from his grip, floating upward in a lazy, almost comical spiral until it met its dramatic end with a sharp pop against the ceiling. The sound filled the room, mirroring the shock of my announcement with perfect, unintended timing.

"You did what?" they exclaimed in unison, a chorus of surprise that would've been comical under different circumstances.

"I quit," I reiterated, the words feeling more real with each repetition. "Handed in my resignation."

Luke recovered first, his initial shock morphing into an intrigued smirk. "You quit your job? Like, for real quit?"

Laura, setting her cupcake aside as if it suddenly held the answers to life's questions, rushed toward me. "When did this happen? What made you decide right now?"

My mom, always quick to the punch with the practicalities of life, chimed in with a dose of reality. "Verena, how are you going to pay your rent?"

The questions flew fast and thick, a barrage that felt like being pecked by a very concerned, very nosy flock of birds.

"Yeah, I really did it," I said, trying to wrangle my emotions. "Today. Just felt like now or never, you know? And, well, I don't have a grand plan." I glanced at Laura, whose follow-your-bliss philosophy suddenly seemed very relevant. "I've got some savings, but not a treasure chest."

Luke let out a low whistle, shaking his head with a mix of admiration and disbelief. "Man, Vee, that's bold. And totally unlike you. But hey, if you're looking for a new adventure, my company's hiring."

I raised an eyebrow, unable to suppress a laugh. "Yeah? Remind me again, what exactly do you do? You change jobs so often I can barely keep up." Last month he was a bartender; the month before, he did food deliveries. The man had an engineering degree but hated structure.

He grinned, a sheepish look on his face. "Well, technically, right now I'm a Waste Management Specialist. But let's be real, I deal with the city's garbage. Pays well, though."

Laura giggled. "Yeah, Vee, you should totally go work with Luke. Nothing like bonding over bags of trash and the sweet smell of rotting leftovers. Are you planning romantic drives with Vee in your garbage truck, Luke?"

Laura liked to tease Luke for his...well...obvious crush on me. I mostly ignored it.

Luke shrugged, his dark curls bouncing. "Hey now, it's a dirty job, but someone's gotta do it. Plus, the overtime is killer. Think about it— city benefits, hazard pay, and the glamorous life of waste disposal."

I laughed, shaking my head. "Thanks for the offer, Luke. I'll keep that in mind if my dreams of becoming a bestselling author don't pan out."

He shot me a thumbs-up, still grinning. "Anytime, Vee. Just think about it—you, me, and a mountain of garbage. What could be better?"

Laura changed the subject. "This is huge, Vee. I bet Jae is freaking the fuck out. Do you think he's"—she paused—"drowning his sorrows in green smoothies and spreadsheets?"

"He's probably writing passive aggressive emails," I deadpanned.

My mom sighed. "I'm happy for you but also slightly freaking out. Anyone else?"

Luke sprang into action, a playful grin on his face. "I'm getting the booze." He winked and headed to the kitchen.

Laura leaped up, grabbing a fork with a dramatic flourish. "We're eating this cake barbarian style—no slices. Just dig in. It's a metaphor for your new life, Vee. Sweet and messy, eh?"

My mom, ever practical, declared, "I'm getting your laptop. We're job hunting tonight!" She bustled off to my bedroom.

I couldn't help but laugh, the absurdity and warmth of the moment washing over me. "You all hated my job more than I did."

"Duh," they chimed in unison.

Laura set her cupcake aside with a flourish. "That job was sucking the life out of you, and not even in a glamorous, vampire kind of way."

Luke nodded vigorously, handing me a balloon from the bunch. "Every time we talked, it was like listening to a robot reboot. I missed my adventurous friend who'd rather scale mountains than corporate ladders."

My mom returned with my laptop, her eyes twinkling with determination. "I've watched you trade your spark for stability for too long. It's time to find something that makes you come alive again. And you're not getting any younger. I want to be a grandmother eventually."

I ignored that statement, but she wasn't wrong. My job made it impossible to date.

Laura, forking a generous portion of cake, started, "Remember that time Jae made you pick out suits for his date? And you had to lug around like fifteen bags of clothes through the mall?"

Luke, returning with a triumphant clink of beer bottles, cut in. "Oh, and let's not forget the Tokyo trip. You got food poisoning, and Jae was too busy with back-to-back meetings to even check on you."

I defended weakly, "Well, he couldn't really skip them. They were important—"

My mom, laptop now humming to life on the coffee table, interrupted, "Important? More important than my second wedding? You missed that because of work." She paused for effect, her voice taking on a mock solemnity as she continued, "And my divorce party. And your brother's baptism."

"Mom, your chihuahua does not count as my brother," I retorted, unable to suppress a grin.

"He is your dog brother, no matter what you say," she shot back, the hint of a smile betraying her feigned sternness.

I burst into laughter. "You're the only person I know who would baptize a chihuahua, Mom."

"Either way, you missed it," she sighed dramatically, "and it was very important to both of us. More important than my wedding and divorce party combined."

We all giggled, mouths full of cake.

My mom, her expression easing, paused from the laughter. "You know, I've always had a soft spot for Jae." She sighed, absently stirring her drink. "And now I have lunch with his aunt tomorrow. This is going to be awkward. What am I supposed to say?"

"Just act clueless," I suggested, half joking.

She chuckled ruefully. "I can't lie to save my life, honey." Her tone shifted, more serious now. "But honestly, he's changed since his company took off. I don't like how he's been treating you."

Laura, ever the voice of reason, piped up, "You know what they say, never mix friends and business."

Luke, always the joker, grinned. "Well, I guess working with me is off the table, then."

"Yeah," I agreed, feeling an ache at the truth of it. "Working with him completely ruined our friendship. Being his assistant, especially when he's this world-renowned CEO...it just became about taking care of him. And along the way, he stopped respecting me. We stopped being friends, and that's the whole reason I wanted to work with him in the first place."

My mom reached across, squeezing my hand. "I'm sorry, honey. But maybe this is for the best. It's time for a change. What do you really want to do?"

I hesitated, the enormity of the question and the crossroads before me suddenly very real. "I don't know. I mean, I went to school for creative writing. I always thought I'd have written my first book by now. The plan was to make money and write on the side, but there was never any time for that."

Laura leaned in, her eyes shining with excitement. "Well, you have time now. What if we move in together? I have a spare bedroom. It'd stretch your savings and give you time to write. Maybe even get a part-time job that's less demanding."

The thought was terrifying and thrilling all at once. "I don't know. Starting over at thirty-two? Shouldn't I be more...settled? Have a 401K and health insurance?"

My mom nodded thoughtfully. "Stability is important, but cutting expenses while you figure things out...that's smart."

Luke chimed in, "My place is always open, too. You wouldn't have to pay rent."

The room went quiet, all eyes on me, my mom giving me a knowing nudge. I knew what she was hinting at—Luke's long-standing crush, an unspoken thread woven through our years of friendship.

Absolutely not. Eventually, he'd figure out that I was the same girl who saw him through his awkward phase, but until then, I just had to evade and distract.

"I don't know, guys," I murmured. "Everything just happened so fast. I need to figure it out."

My mom, grounding us in the moment, clapped her hands gently. "Okay, let's just take a minute to pause and really celebrate your birthday—and the fact that you're free now. We have time."

"Yes, I have time," I echoed. "I told him I'd stay on for a month to train whoever takes over. Gives me a moment to breathe and plan my next steps."

She nodded understandingly. "Okay, so there's a window to figure things out. That's good."

I sighed, the reality of the situation settling in. "Yeah. Though, working alongside him for another month? I just know he's going to be pissed." The words hung in the air, a cloud of impending doom. "Or... do you think he'll be...okay?"

Laura and Luke exchanged a glance, a silent conversation passing between them before they looked back at me.

"Verena," Laura started, hesitant, "do you want us to be honest with you, or do you want the comforting lies?"

"Great," I muttered, the sarcasm dripping from my voice as I slumped back against the couch, a sense of foreboding washing over me. The realization that the next month could very well be a torturous dance of awkwardness and tension loomed large.

"The next month is going to be hell," I said finally, the words a quiet admission of the challenge I faced. But in the eyes of my friends and family, there was an unspoken promise—a vow that no matter what the next month held, I wouldn't have to face it alone.

7

(MEET)ING

JAE

Eleven Years Ago

Meeting Verena's mom shouldn't have been that big of a deal. I mean, she's just my best friend's mom. So why was I wearing a suit and clutching flowers like some nervous kid on prom night?

Auntie stood beside me, waiting at the front door, a serene smile on her face. "You look good, Jae. Stop looking so terrified. She'll love you."

I forced a smile back at her. Auntie was leaving for Korea next week, and this dinner had been planned for months. Jennifer, Verena's mom, had insisted on meeting Auntie, planning an elaborate dinner that would probably put most Michelin-starred restaurants to shame. Of course, Auntie had to bring a dish of her own, as if challenging Jennifer's hospitality to a friendly duel.

The door swung open, and Jennifer appeared, a whirlwind of energy. "Jae! Binna! Welcome!" She immediately hugged Auntie, pulling her inside. "You must be Binna. I've heard so much about you!"

Auntie smiled warmly. "All good things, I hope."

Jennifer laughed. "Oh, absolutely. And thank you for bringing a dish. I can't wait to see how it stacks up against my cooking."

As they bantered like old friends, Jennifer turned to me. "And you must be

Jae! My goodness, look at you, all dressed up like you're meeting the Queen. You're overdressed for a simple family dinner, dear." She took the flowers from my hand, her touch light but assertive. "And these! How lovely! You shouldn't have, really. But they'll look perfect on the table. Come in, come in."

I felt my face heat up, embarrassment creeping up my neck. "Thank you, Mrs. Williams."

"Oh, please, call me Jennifer," she said. "Mrs. Williams was two husbands ago."

I glanced at Auntie, who gave me an encouraging nod. "Yes, Jennifer," I corrected myself, feeling slightly more at ease.

Jennifer ushered us inside, her presence filling the space with warmth and chatter. "The table's all set, but I could use a hand with the final touches. Jae, would you mind helping out in the kitchen? Everything's ready, just needs to be put on the table."

"Of course," I said, eager to make a good impression.

The interior of Jennifer's home was cozy and inviting, filled with the rich aroma of home-cooked food. Family photos lined the walls, and a large, friendly-looking chihuahua barked from the living room, its tiny body shaking with effort.

"Oh, don't mind Muffin," Jennifer said, waving off the dog's noise. "He's just excited to meet new people."

As I set the table, I couldn't help but glance around, taking in the details. There were quirky and mismatched elements everywhere. Nothing flowed or made sense, but it looked authentically real.

The front door opened again, and I turned to see Verena walk in, looking radiant as always. My heart did its usual flip at the sight of her, but then my gaze shifted to the guy beside her. Dark curly hair, a confident smirk that I instantly disliked.

"Jae, this is Luke," Verena said, introducing him. "Luke's my neighbor and best friend."

I forced a smile, sizing him up. He was taller than me, with a build that suggested he spent a lot of time in the gym. His clothes were casual but stylish, like he was trying just hard enough without making it obvious. I remembered Verena mentioning he was studying engineering in Jersey but also that he never really stuck to anything, always changing his mind.

Luke extended a hand, his grin widening. "Nice to meet you, Jae. Verena's told me a lot about you."

"Likewise," I said, shaking his hand. His grip was firm, almost a challenge in itself. I matched it, refusing to let him get the upper hand.

"So, the famous best friend, huh?" I said, forcing a laugh. "What about me, Vee? I thought I was the best friend."

"You're both my best friends. There's enough of me to go around."

Luke chuckled, but I could see the competitive glint in his eyes. "Yeah, Jae, I guess you'll have to share."

"Share, huh?" I replied, arching an eyebrow. "I guess that's fine, as long as you know I'm the one who gets the late-night calls and emergency donut runs."

Verena laughed, nudging me with her elbow. "Stop it, both of you. Let's just enjoy dinner, okay?"

Jennifer walked in, her hands on her hips, surveying the room. "Luke, be a dear and make the salad, would you?"

Luke immediately sprang into action, striding to the kitchen with a confidence that grated on my nerves. "Sure thing," he called back, already grabbing ingredients from the fridge. He moved around the kitchen with an ease that spoke of familiarity, tossing a wink at Jennifer as he started chopping vegetables. "You still keep the salad spinner in the same place, right?" he asked with a grin.

Jennifer laughed. "Of course. Haven't changed a thing since you were in high school."

Luke laughed, glancing over at Verena. "Remember those cooking disasters in home ec? You always managed to burn the cookies, no matter what."

Verena chuckled. "Those ovens were cursed, I swear."

"Or maybe you just can't bake," Luke teased, and they both laughed, a shared memory flickering between them. I clenched my jaw, forcing a smile. I didn't like how comfortable he was here, how well he knew Jennifer and Verena's history.

Auntie and Jennifer sat down at the kitchen table, settling into a comfortable banter. I hovered nearby, setting the table, but their conversation drew me in.

"My ex-husband was so dull," Jennifer said. "You could tell him the sky was falling, and he'd probably just shrug and ask what's for dinner."

Auntie Binna chuckled, shaking her head. "Men can be like that sometimes. My ex-fiancé was no better. He'd rather spend hours tinkering with his car than have a meaningful conversation."

Jennifer leaned in, a mischievous glint in her eye. "Oh, I've got a story for you."

Auntie laughed. "I'm ready."

Jennifer grinned, launching into her tale. "We went to the movies to see Pearl Harbor. But it was the hottest summer on record, and the theater was packed. The body heat was real, and I'm no skinny Minnie. Some serious forced proximity happened. Poor Walter was up against a human furnace."

Auntie's eyes sparkled with amusement. "Go on."

Jennifer's hands animated the story as she spoke. "During one of the really gut-wrenching scenes, I hear Walter sniffling. He wipes his face, and I'm thinking, Aww, he's so sensitive and kind, and we're having this vulnerable moment. We're finally bonding."

She paused, drawing out the suspense. "So, I lean over and whisper, 'Walter, dear, are you crying?' Ready to give him a tissue and have an insightful discussion about the moment on the way home."

Auntie leaned in closer, already giggling.

"Without missing a beat, he goes, 'No, I'm sweating my ass off, can you scoot over?'"

The room filled with laughter, and I couldn't help but join in, the sound of their amusement warming the atmosphere.

Auntie wiped a tear of laughter from her eye. "Jennifer, that is priceless. I can just see it."

Jennifer nodded, her laughter subsiding. "Yeah, well, I thought we were having this deep moment. Turns out he was just trying not to melt."

Auntie leaned back, a thoughtful smile on her face. "You know, Jennifer, that reminds me of the time I broke off my engagement in a furniture store."

I perked up at this, pulling up a chair to listen. Auntie rarely talked about this part of her past, and hearing her laugh about it now was both surprising and comforting.

"Oh, you have to tell us this one," Jennifer said.

Auntie chuckled. "Well, I was already conflicted about whether I should bring Jae to Korea or come here to the States. My fiancé at the time was no help, always criticizing my decisions. One day, we were at this furniture store, and he kept saying he didn't like the couches I was picking."

I couldn't help but laugh, imagining Auntie in a showdown over sofas. She continued, her voice animated with the memory.

"He kept saying, 'This one's too modern,' or 'That one's too colorful.' Finally, I just snapped. I turned to him in the middle of the store and said, 'If you can't love the couches I love, then you can't love me! We're done!'"

Jennifer giggled. "Oh my God, Binna, you didn't!"

"I did!" Auntie said, her laughter mingling with Jennifer's. "Right there in the store. The poor sales clerk didn't know what to do. My fiancé was stunned, just standing there with his mouth open."

Verena and I exchanged amused glances, and I could see the admiration in her eyes for Auntie's boldness.

Jennifer wiped a tear from her eye. "That's hilarious. You broke off an engagement over a couch."

Auntie grinned. "Well, it wasn't really about the couch. It was about realizing that if he couldn't support my choices, big or small, then he wasn't the right partner for me. And honestly, it made the decision to come here and take care of Jae so much clearer."

A wave of gratitude washed over me. Auntie had sacrificed so much to raise me after my parents passed away. This story, as funny as it was, highlighted just how much she had given up.

Verena reached over and squeezed my hand. "Your Auntie is amazing."

"I know," I said, my voice thick with emotion. "She really is."

Jennifer leaned forward, looking between Auntie and me. "You two are lucky to have each other. Family is everything."

I smiled at my aunt, and my gaze drifted—overlooking fucking Luke, of course—and when my gaze landed on Vee, I thought yeah, it really is.

8

BL(INK)

JAE

The city lights blurred outside my penthouse windows. With each step I took, pacing back and forth, Verena's resignation consumed my thoughts. Normally, she'd be here, her presence a calm in the corporate storm, effortlessly steering my world away from turmoil. But tonight, she was the epicenter of the storm.

I picked up my phone, the device feeling foreign in my hand without Verena on the other end. The first call was to John, my head of legal. His name flashed on the screen like an accusation. "John, this is Jae," I snapped, my voice a sharp command, each word a hammer strike. "I need legal in my office at eight a.m. sharp tomorrow. No excuses. Be prepared for crisis resolution. Bring all employee contracts. Prepare for a long day." The line went dead, my decree delivered.

Next was Susan from Human Resources. "Susan, it's Jae. I need you and your team on standby. Be in a meeting with legal at eight a.m. sharp. It's going to be a long day." The routine calls, once effortlessly managed through Verena's meticulous organization, now felt like trying to remember how to ride a bike. You knew how, but it had been a few years since I'd even had time for a joy ride, let alone the need to do it.

After I hung up, the silence of the room closed in, punctuated only by my own harsh breathing. Normally, Verena would have handled all this. But she was the conflict that needed resolution. The irony wasn't lost on me.

I was prepared to comb through her employment contract for a loophole. Anything to keep her tethered to me, to the company.

I would bind her to us legally if I had to.

Then convince her to stay.

The thought sparked a vindictive satisfaction within me. She thought she could just walk away? Not a chance.

I didn't lose.

My musings were interrupted by the sound of the door opening gently. Auntie stepped into the room, her petite frame and silver-streaked hair a stark contrast to the cold, sleek lines of my penthouse. Her presence was a blend of tenderness and resilience, a testament to the strength she had shown through the years. She approached softly, cautiously, her steps light as if she were walking on the thin ice of my temper.

"What's wrong?" she asked, her voice carrying the warmth and concern that had been a balm in the years since my parents' passing. Her inquiry pulled me from my thoughts, grounding me back in the present.

"Verena put in her resignation," I admitted, the words feeling like ash in my mouth.

"Oh, really?" Her casual response, laden with an undercurrent of surprise, grated on me. "Good for her."

"No," I snapped. "Not good for her. I need her. She's the best at her job. She knows what she's doing."

A spark of recognition flickered in Auntie's eyes. "She can finally write that book!"

"No. No, no, no." My denial came too quickly, too forcefully. "I can't do my job without her," I protested, trying to keep my voice even.

"Huh, I see," Auntie said, her voice rich with unspoken understanding.

"You're having lunch with Verena's mother tomorrow. Be sure to mention this is a terrible mistake." I stopped, mid-turn, the frustration and fear of losing Verena bubbling to the surface. "I need you to talk to

Verena's mother about convincing her to stay. Remind her of the benefits, the steady income... It's important."

Auntie's expression softened, a hint of nostalgia lighting up her features. "Oh, I miss Jennifer. Haven't seen her in ages. I'm really looking forward to it," she said with a smirk. Then, her brow furrowed slightly in thought. "Should have gotten her a gift. It's been too long since we last saw each other."

She looked at me. "But hey, maybe I can just give her a photo of you pouting. That's priceless."

I shook my head, trying to stay focused on the task at hand, despite the conversation's drift. "I think Verena already got a gift you can give her. She always thinks ahead." How long had she been planning to quit? Why didn't she give me a heads-up?

Auntie laughed, a sound both warm and wistful. "That girl, always thinking of everything. Did you know she put my favorite skincare products in the guest bathroom?" Her voice carried a mix of admiration and slight exasperation. "She even made sure my favorite restaurant delivered lunch to the car when I arrived. Can't stand airplane food with my restricted diet. I was famished after the long flight."

A twinge of something deep and unsettling stirred within me.

Verena's thoughtfulness wasn't just limited to me. It extended to those I cared about.

She was more than just an assistant.

She was the glue holding pieces of my life together I didn't even realize were coming apart.

And I was about to lose her.

Not a chance.

Shaking off the feeling, I pressed on, "I need you to tell her mom that leaving the company is a mistake. Jennifer gets through to her better than anyone else. She'll talk some sense into her."

Auntie's expression changed, warmth fading. "Jae, that's not the right approach. If Verena decided to quit, it means she's unhappy. We should be helping her find her bliss."

"Unhappy? With me?" I retorted. "We're best friends. Working together is amazing. We travel, we do fun things. It's been great for her."

Auntie raised an eyebrow, her look cutting right through my defenses. "Maybe it's great for you," she said, sarcasm lacing her voice, "but have you ever considered if it's truly what Verena wants?"

The question hung in the air like an unwelcome guest. My justifications sounded weaker with each word I uttered. Auntie's insinuation—that my view of our working relationship was clouded by my own selfish desires—was a bitter pill I refused to swallow.

"No," I declared, my tone sharp but lacking real conviction. "Verena loves her job."

Yet, even as the words left my mouth, a sliver of doubt crept in. Verena's resignation wasn't a spur-of-the-moment decision; it was a clear message that she needed more, something different. Auntie's gentle probing had peeled back a layer of truth I wasn't prepared to confront—that in my arrogance, I had taken Verena's loyalty and happiness for granted.

I clenched my jaw, unwilling to admit fault. "She's fine," I added, as if saying it firmly enough could make it true.

Auntie's response was just as firm. "This might be good for her. You didn't think she would be your assistant forever, did you? What if she wants more from life? A husband? Kids?"

The suggestion hit a nerve, igniting a fire within me. "Absolutely not! She can have more while still working for me. Actually, no, she can't." My own words echoed with the confusion and desperation roiling inside me.

Auntie's knowing look was infuriatingly perceptive. In her eyes, I didn't see the unflappable CEO of an empire, but a man on the brink of losing the one person who had become his anchor in a sea of relentless demands and expectations.

"By the way, how long are you staying?" I asked. "I need to check my calendar to see if we can spend time together, but I'm pretty busy right now. You mentioned six months; you can stay at one of my other properties if it's a long-term visit."

Auntie's demeanor shifted, the usual spark in her eyes dimming as she took a deep breath. The room seemed to grow quieter, the air thick with unspoken tension.

"Listen, darling," she began, her tone uncharacteristically serious. "There's something I need to tell you."

I raised an eyebrow, my curiosity piqued but tinged with impatience. "I don't have much time to talk. I need to figure out Verena's employment contract and—"

Her eyes narrowed slightly, a flash of the old sass returning. "Oh, I wouldn't dare take up too much of your precious time, Mr. Important CEO." She paused, her gaze softening. "But this is something you need to hear."

I folded my arms. "Alright, I'm listening."

She took another breath, her voice steady but laced with an underlying tremor. "The cancer came back."

The words hit me like a sledgehammer, knocking the breath out of me. For a moment, I just stared at her, my mind grappling with the gravity of what she'd said. Auntie, the unshakable pillar of my life, was facing something I couldn't control, couldn't fix.

"I know I promised I wouldn't leave you alone," she continued. "But it looks like I might not be able to keep that promise."

Her words settled between us, heavy and ominous. My arrogant facade began to crack, a cold fear creeping into the corners of my mind. For the first time in a long while, I felt truly powerless.

I cleared my throat, trying to regain some semblance of control. "How long?" I asked, my voice sounding foreign to my own ears.

She shrugged, a small, sad smile playing on her lips. "Long enough to see you get your act together, I hope."

The room was silent, the reality of the situation sinking in. For once, my position, my power, meant nothing. It was just Auntie and me, facing an uncertain future.

"That's why I came here," Auntie explained, a fragile smile touching her lips. "I'm going to need some help towards the end." The vulnerability in her admission was something new, a side of her I'd never seen.

"What do you mean?" The question escaped me before I could temper it with the gravity the moment deserved, my mind reeling from the implications.

"You know how it goes. Three years ago, we thought we got it all, but it's like the neighborhood stray. Give it a little food, and it always comes back. There's a doctor here, but most of my options revolve around comfort care this time," she said, her pragmatism laced with a poignant acceptance of her reality. "So, I really need you to promise me that you're going to do everything you can to not be lonely anymore. I'm here because I don't want you to be so isolated."

Auntie's eyes locked onto mine. "I know you think you can handle everything on your own," she continued. "But this...this is different. You need to let people in, Jae. You can't do it all by yourself."

I opened my mouth to argue, to insist that I was perfectly fine on my own, but the look in her eyes stopped me. For once, my usual bravado felt like a flimsy shield against the raw truth she was laying bare.

"I don't want you to be like me," she added softly. "Alone when it matters most."

Her words, each one delivered with a deliberate emphasis, struck a chord deep within me. The enormity of her situation, her bravery in facing it, and her concern for me amidst her own battle—it was overwhelming.

Auntie's revelation about her condition was a seismic shift in the landscape of my reality, forcing me to confront not just the impending loss of the last of my family but the seclusion of my existence she sought to shield me from.

"I bought a one-way ticket," she said, attempting a lighthearted tone that fell flat. "I'm here to see you get your life in order before I kick the bucket."

I clenched my fists, frustration bubbling up. "Auntie, what are you talking about?"

She sighed, a fragile smile touching her lips. "Well, for starters, your home is boring," she said, trying to keep things light. "You need to learn how to cook, and I have to find you a wife."

I stared at her. "Really? You just said the cancer came back, and you want to talk about my dating life?"

She nodded, her smile growing more genuine. "Yes, because I want to leave this world knowing you're okay. I can't have my favorite nephew all alone, clueless in the kitchen, and buried in work."

A bitter laugh escaped me. "So, your master plan is to turn me into a cooking, wife-hunting CEO?"

She chuckled, the sound both comforting and heartbreaking. "Exactly. Maybe I'll even get to see you whip up something edible before I go. And who knows, maybe I'll set you up on a few dates."

"Auntie…" I began. "This isn't a joke."

She reached out, placing a hand on mine. "I know, Jae. But humor is how I cope. And right now, I need to focus on the future—your future. I want to leave this world knowing you're not just surviving, but living."

I swallowed hard, the lump in my throat making it difficult to speak. "I don't know if I can do this without you."

Her grip tightened, her eyes sparkling with the determination that had always defined her. "You're stronger than you think, Jae. And you won't be without me. I'll be right here," she said, tapping her heart. "But promise me you'll try."

I nodded, a mix of emotions swirling inside me. "I promise," I managed, the words barely a whisper, but a vow nonetheless.

"And who knows," she added with a mischievous grin, "maybe you'll actually find someone who can tolerate your bossy, arrogant self."

Despite everything, I found myself smiling. "If you say so, Auntie. If you say so."

9

ST(ART)

JAE

Graduation was a blur of caps, gowns, and the bittersweet taste of endings and beginnings. I'd just completed the paperwork to start my own architecture business, and as a nod to my parents, I named it after their construction company: Luminous. My parents had built that company from the ground up, and now, with my degree in hand, I was determined to carry on their legacy. I even landed my first job, a small but promising project to design a library.

To celebrate—or maybe just to blow off some steam—I decided to drop by the bar where Verena worked. I hated that place. Not because of the ambiance, which was actually decent, but because it made her wear those ridiculous short shorts, and guys were constantly hitting on her. Every time I walked in there, the possessive edge I felt was unsettling. I tried to convince myself it was just protective friendship, but deep down, I knew it was something more.

Not that I'd ever admit it.

The place was buzzing, as usual. Neon lights flickered overhead, casting a colorful glow over the worn-out booths and polished bar. The air was thick with the smell of beer and fried food, and the sound of laughter and clinking *glasses filled the room. I pushed through the crowd, my eyes scanning for Verena. The bartender, Tony, spotted me first.*

"Hey, Jae!" Tony called out, wiping down the bar. "Back again? You sure you're not here more for the company than the drinks?"

I smirked. "You caught me. I'm here for Verena. Where is she?"

Tony chuckled, nodding toward the far end of the bar. "Same place as always, fending off the guys."

"Thanks, Tony," I said, making my way over.

I spotted her at the far end, expertly balancing a tray of drinks. Even in that stupid uniform, she looked incredible. Her long dark hair was pulled into a high ponytail, and her shorts rode up in a way that made my blood boil. I couldn't help but notice how the guys at the bar were eyeing her like she was the last cold drink on a hot day. One guy in particular was leaning over the bar, clearly hitting on her.

Great. Just what I needed.

As I approached, I caught the tail end of their conversation.

"Come on, sweetheart. Give me your number. We could have a great time," the guy was saying, his voice dripping with sleaze.

Verena's polite smile was starting to strain. "I'm working. How about you just enjoy your drink?"

"Come on, baby!"

Without thinking, I stepped in, placing myself between Verena and the guy. "She said she's working, asshole. Why don't you get lost before I make you?"

The guy looked up at me, clearly annoyed. "Who the hell are you?"

"Her friend," I said, my voice low and firm. "Fuck off."

The guy scoffed but decided not to press the issue. He muttered something under his breath and slunk away, leaving me alone with Verena.

"Jae," she hissed, clearly annoyed. "You can't keep doing that. You're going to get me fired."

"Good," I shot back. "You shouldn't be working here anyway."

She rolled her eyes, crossing her arms over her chest, which accentuated her—nope, not going there. Best friend. She's my best fucking friend. "And where exactly am I supposed to work, huh? Writing a book doesn't exactly pay the bills."

"That's why I'm here," I said, leaning against the bar. "I've got my first job with Luminous, and I need help. Come work for me."

Verena laughed, shaking her head. "You can't afford me."

"I'm serious, Vee. I need an assistant. Someone I can trust. And you need a job that doesn't involve wearing short shorts and dealing with drunk idiots."

She arched an eyebrow, clearly unconvinced. "I don't think so, Jae."

I smirked, a plan forming in my mind. "How about this: we play a game of darts. If I win, you come work for me. If you win, I'll drop it."

Verena eyed me suspiciously. "You're not going to let this go, are you?"

"Not a chance."

She sighed, but I could see the hint of a smile tugging at her lips. "Fine. But don't cry when I beat you."

We moved over to the dartboard, and a small crowd gathered, sensing a challenge. Verena grabbed the darts, her competitive spirit kicking in. "Ladies first," she said with a playful glint in her eye.

"By all means," I replied, stepping back to watch. My eyes couldn't help but follow the curve of her hips, the way her shorts clung to her ass. It was infuriating how effortlessly she made that damn uniform look good. Focus, Jae. This is business.

She took her first shot, landing impressively close to the bullseye. I whistled. "Not bad, Vee. Not bad at all."

"Don't sound so surprised," she shot back.

I took my turn, managing to match her score. We went back and forth, the tension growing with each throw. Every time we passed the darts, our fingers brushed, sending jolts of electricity through me. I tried to focus on the game, but all I could think about was how good she looked and how much I hated the way those guys were staring at her.

"So, why should I leave this wonderful job and work for you?" she asked with a smirk, lining up her next shot.

"Let's see," I said, stepping closer, my breath brushing against her ear. "For starters, you'd get to spend all your spare time with your best friend."

She rolled her eyes, and threw her dart, hitting just shy of the bullseye. "Not bad," I said, taking the darts from her, letting my fingers linger on hers a moment longer. "You'd also get to avoid dealing with creeps hitting on you all night."

"Oh, so you're going to be my personal bodyguard now?" she teased, watching as I lined up my shot.

"Something like that," I said, throwing the dart. It landed close to the bullseye, but not quite there. She raised an eyebrow, impressed.

"Nice try," she said, taking the darts from me. Our fingers brushed again, and I felt that familiar jolt. "What else?"

"You'd get to go on business trips with me," I said, leaning in close as she prepared to throw. "Imagine all the late nights, just you and me, working together."

She snorted, trying to hide her smile. "Yeah, right. You just want someone to carry your bags."

"Guilty," I admitted with a grin. "But seriously, you'd be amazing."

She threw her dart, hitting just outside the bullseye again. "Still not convinced," she said.

"How about this," I said, my voice low and teasing as I stepped up to the line. "If you work for me, I'll buy you all your favorite dinners. Every night."

She laughed, the sound light and musical. "You're really pulling out all the stops, aren't you?"

"Desperate times," I said, throwing my dart. It landed just shy of the bullseye again, and I cursed under my breath.

"Alright, last round," she said. "Give me your best offer."

I leaned in close as she lined up her throw. "You know you love me, Vee," I whispered. "You can't resist."

Her hand wavered slightly, and she threw the dart, missing the bullseye by a fraction. She turned to glare at me, but there was no real heat in it. "Cheater."

"Just giving you some incentive," I replied, grinning. I lined up my shot, feeling the weight of her gaze on me. This was it. I needed to win this.

I took a deep breath and threw the dart. It flew straight and true, landing perfectly in the bullseye. The small crowd erupted in cheers, and I turned to Verena, a triumphant smile on my face.

"Looks like you're coming to work for me," I said, my voice smug but my heart pounding.

Verena shook her head, laughing. "You're impossible, you know that?"

"Yeah, but you love it," I teased back. It was our thing we'd always said to one another. But today, what felt impossible was my growing attraction to her. "If you were really worried about losing your job, you wouldn't be playing darts during your shift."

She playfully shoved me, her touch sending a thrill through me. "Fine, you win this round. But I'll make your life hell as your assistant."

"Looking forward to it," I said, my tone light but my thoughts swirling. This was going to be interesting. Very interesting.

10

BE(TROTH)ED

VERENA

Sitting at my desk with the uneasy feeling of being a spy in enemy territory, I couldn't help but let my gaze drift over to Jae's office. The blinds were closed tight, a surefire sign that the legal and HR teams were probably drawing up battle plans instead of mere contracts. Jae hadn't so much as looked in my direction, a clear indicator of the impending storm. Under the force of his silence, I found myself tapping my heel against the floor, hoping someone, anyone, would decode my distress signal.

The usual flurry of tasks Jae would have me juggle was conspicuously absent today. He had practically erected a Do Not Disturb sign the size of a billboard over his office door. The one fleeting glimpse I caught of him earlier had done nothing to ease my nerves; if anything, the bags under his eyes and his tight-lipped expression were a testament to the severity of the situation.

When the door to Jae's office finally opened, releasing the legal and HR team like a flock of pigeons startled by a car alarm, I nearly jumped out of my skin. Their hurried exit did nothing to soothe my fraying nerves.

"Verena, come to my office. Immediately." Jae's voice was sharp.

With a deep breath that did little to steady my racing heart, I made my way to his office, half expecting to find a gladiator arena instead of the familiar workspace. "Okay," I managed to squeak out, my voice betraying the false bravado I was desperately clinging to.

As I entered, Jae motioned for me to take a seat, his demeanor as welcoming as a tax audit. He slid a document across the table with all the casualness of someone handing over a ticking time bomb. "Here's your contract," he announced.

My eyes scanned the document, trying to make sense of the legal gibberish that seemed designed to confuse rather than clarify. Jae cleared his throat, launching into an explanation.

"According to Clause 6.72 of Section four," he began, his tone taking on the cadence of a lawyer who had memorized the entire legal code for fun, "you possess proprietary information on Project Eagle Stone, an ongoing venture of paramount importance to our strategic objectives. Given the project's current status—specifically, its deviation from the projected timeline due to unforeseen complications in the deployment phase—your departure would precipitate a significant disruption to its successful completion."

I blinked, trying to process the verbal labyrinth he'd just constructed. "Wait, what the hell are you talking about, Jae?" I asked, half expecting him to pull out a whiteboard and start drawing diagrams.

He plowed on, undeterred. "Furthermore, your intimate familiarity with the project's inner workings and the consequential potential for competitive disadvantage necessitate the enforcement of the six-month notice period stipulated by your contract, thereby legally binding you to continue your employment until such a time as Project Eagle Stone reaches a satisfactory conclusion."

"Six months?" His words shocked me out of the daze his speech had induced. "You can't be serious. I can't stay here for another six months!"

"Unfortunately, the contractual obligations as outlined are unequivocal," he replied, his expression as rigid as his tone. "The continuation of your tenure is not only advisable but mandated."

"Are you kidding me?" I could feel my frustration boiling over, the absurdity of the situation reaching peak levels. "I cannot stay here for another six months, Jae. I'm at my wit's end."

His next question caught me off guard, a slight crack in his CEO armor. "Is it really that bad?"

The room was charged with conflict, an invisible chasm widening between us. Here we were, caught in a standoff not just over contractual obligations but over the very nature of our working relationship. His long-winded, jargon-filled spiel, designed to bewilder rather than explain, had done its job, leaving me more confused and frustrated than before.

"Bad?" I scoffed. I reached into my briefcase and pulled out the most incriminating piece of evidence I possessed—a well-worn notebook, its pages a testament to the insanity that had become my everyday life. Flipping it open, I prepared to unleash the full extent of my grievances, each entry meticulously noted with times, dates, and locations—a chronicle of absurdity that would make any sane person question the nature of their employment.

"Ah, here's a memorable one," I started, the sarcasm in my voice sharp enough to cut glass. "February fourteenth, 9:32 a.m., you had me charter a private jet because you needed to pick up a specific type of tulips for Auntie—tulips, Jae, from the Netherlands—because apparently, they *signify a deep and ancient bond* in some book you read."

I glanced up to see Jae's reaction, but before he could speak, I plunged forward. "Oh, and let's not overlook April seventh, 11:17 p.m., when you made me coordinate a midnight meeting in Tokyo. You insisted I sit through a three-hour dinner with a man who thought business negotiations included proposing a strategic marriage alliance."

Jae opened his mouth, likely to mount some defense, but I was having none of it. "And before you say anything," I cut him off, flipping to another page, "do you remember August twenty-third? When you sent me on a wild goose chase across three states to secure a limited edition gaming console? Because you needed it for a potential business partner's kid, and it had to be delivered personally by me to demonstrate the company's commitment to personal relationships."

His expression faltered. "Is that what you've been scribbling in your notepad? Grievances against me?" he asked, a note of incredulity in his voice.

I met his gaze squarely, my frustration unabated. "This is the fourth notebook, Jae. The fourth!" I emphasized the weight of those countless, ludicrous tasks bearing down on me once more.

"The fourth?" he echoed.

"Yes, the fourth!" I exclaimed, my voice rising in pitch. "Every absurd request, every over-the-top demand. Do you want to hear about the time you had me arrange a private viewing of the Crown Jewels because you were considering incorporating regal elements into the company's branding?"

I didn't wait for his response, too caught up in the absurdity of it all.

"And don't even get me started on the number of personal dates I've had to cancel because of your whims," I continued, my voice gaining momentum like a runaway train. Flipping through the pages of my notebook, I found the section I'd dedicated to the personal sacrifices I'd made at the altar of Jae's convenience. "Let's take a walk down memory lane, shall we?

"September fourth with Tony Martinez. We planned an arcade date, something I was genuinely looking forward to. But no, I had to leave in the middle of it because you decided you needed an emergency meeting about...what was it again? Oh, yes, the urgent redesign of the company logo that couldn't possibly wait until morning."

"I hated him," Jae cut in. "Never liked his smile. Too smarmy."

"October twenty-second with Nathan Thompson. We had tickets to the premiere of the movie we'd been dying to see for months. But guess what? I had to bail because you thought it was the perfect time to fly to Los Angeles for a spontaneous brand synergy meeting."

"He was weird. Never trust a guy who calls himself Nate."

"January fifteenth with Michael Reed. Dinner at his place, meeting his sister who was visiting from out of town. But oh, I received a text from you saying you felt a sudden inspiration for a new project and needed me there to brainstorm."

"That guy was a bore. Tried to talk to me about wine for half an hour once."

"Thanksgiving with Peter Nguyen. I was at dinner with his family, Jae. His family. And I had to leave because you thought that was the ideal moment to renegotiate the terms of a deal that was perfectly fine."

"He was too nice. People like that always have something to hide."

"August twenty-first with Ryan Kim. A hiking trip we'd planned for weeks. Canceled because you believed we needed to 'seize the day' and review every contract in the third quarter by hand."

"I hated him. His cologne was way too strong."

"You're ludicrous," I shot back, exasperation and disbelief mingling in my voice. The realization that my personal life had been steamrolled by Jae's capricious demands was both infuriating and sadly comical.

The room was charged with the tension of our confrontation, years of frustration and missed opportunities hanging heavy between us. As I closed the notebook, the symbol of all my grievances, the absurdity of the situation couldn't be clearer. My role had morphed from a professional partnership into a bizarre, one-sided dynamic where my personal happiness was repeatedly sacrificed for Jae's whims.

Pointing directly at him, I let out a challenge. "If you think for one second I'm staying here for six months, you are out of your mind."

Jae's response was cold and calculated, a severe departure from the tension-fueled argument we'd been having. "Well, then I hope you're prepared to pay me half a million dollars in damages, because that's what you'll be responsible for if you leave beforehand."

I gasped in shock. "Half a million? After everything I've done for you, you're willing to sue me for half a million in damages?"

"Yes," he affirmed, his tone unwavering, "and I will win. My legal team is confident in that."

"You are ridiculous," I shot back, the words tasting bitter on my tongue, the incredulity of the situation wrapping around me like a vise.

In a moment charged with an intensity that seemed to warp the very air around us, Jae stormed over to me. The distance closed between us in seconds, and he got in my face, the tension a living entity that buzzed with electricity. My heart hammered in my chest as I looked into his eyes—eyes that seemed to be searching mine for something unfathomable.

His gaze flickered down to my lips, back up to my eyes, a silent question hanging between us, the atmosphere thick with unspoken possibilities. The world seemed to hold its breath, waiting for his next words, waiting for the crackle of the air around us to ignite into an inferno.

"But I do have a way," he finally said, his voice a low murmur that seemed to vibrate through the very ground beneath us. "I'll forgive it, and I won't make you stay six months if you do one thing for me."

The proposition hung in the air, a sword suspended by a thread so thin it was nearly invisible. My heart raced, my thoughts a whirlwind of confusion and disbelief. "What?" The word barely escaped as a whisper, my defenses crumbling.

And then he delivered the words that would change everything.

"Marry me."

11

MIS(TAKE)

VERENA

"Marry you?!" I blurted out, my voice ringing with disbelief and a sharp edge of sarcasm. "I should call your doctor for a referral, because you've obviously lost your mind."

Jae didn't even flinch. His expression was steel, all business. "We're going to lunch. I don't want to discuss this here," he stated firmly, his grip on my wrist unyielding as he practically dragged me from his office. The sharp tug was more than just physical; it was a jolt back to our complicated reality, a reminder of the force Jae could exert without even seeming to try.

As we made our way through the office, I could feel the weight of every curious glance from our coworkers. Their eyes followed us as Jae's hand, wrapped securely around my wrist, felt like a shackle I couldn't shake. The murmurs began as soon as we passed, their whispers trailing us like shadows as we got on the elevator.

Once in the sushi restaurant next door, Jae marched me straight to a secluded booth in the back corner, away from the prying eyes and within the quiet confines where we could speak freely. He finally released my wrist as we slid into the booth, the abrupt absence of his touch leaving a strange, tingling sensation on my skin.

As I sat across from him, the distance between us felt charged, thick with unspoken words and the heavy beat of my racing heart.

"Jae, seriously, what's going on with you?" I demanded, my tone a mix of concern and lingering frustration. "This isn't like you. What kind of joke is this?"

He looked away, his jaw tightening. "Auntie's cancer is back." His voice was low, strained.

The news hit me hard. I couldn't even process it. "What?" I whispered, my throat closing up as tears sprang to my eyes, unbidden. My heart sank.

"She's going to stay here so I can take care of her," he continued, his gaze distant, as if he were already bracing himself for the ordeal ahead.

I tried to process the information, but it felt like the ground had been pulled out from under me. Auntie had always been a constant, a pillar of warmth and love in our lives. The thought of her battling cancer again was almost too much to bear. I blinked rapidly, willing the tears to stop, but they came anyway, streaming down my cheeks in silent testament to the heartbreak I felt.

My voice trembled as I spoke, "How...how bad is it?"

He finally met my eyes, and the pain there was unmistakable. "It's not good," he admitted, his own voice breaking.

I reached out, covering his hand with mine, feeling like his friend for the first time in a long while. "I'll help, whatever you need."

Jae's eyes met mine again, this time clouded with a sadness that cut right through the firm facade he had upheld moments earlier. "It's bad, Verena," he murmured, the weight of his aunt's illness sinking his voice to a whisper. "It's...it's everywhere, and it's aggressive."

I swallowed hard, the reality of his words lodging in my throat. "Oh, Jae, I...I'm so sorry."

He nodded slowly, his hand turning under mine to give a gentle squeeze, an acknowledgment of our shared past and the layers of complicated history between us. "I need to make sure she's comfortable, happy. She's worried about me, about what happens after... She doesn't want me to be alone." His voice cracked on the last word, a snap in his usually composed demeanor.

"So you thought…"

"We could get married," he finished for me.

"That's a bit extreme, don't you think?" I tried to lighten the mood, but my attempt felt flat even to my own ears.

"It's not just for her," he admitted, looking away. "It's for me too. I don't want to be alone in this. And I know it's a lot to ask, Verena, but—"

"Jae, she's your only family left," I cut in, my mind racing as I thought about his parents, long gone, and how he had always leaned on his aunt for support. The thought of him facing everything alone was more painful than I anticipated. "I understand why she's worried, but—"

He looked back at me, his eyes pleading. "She's always seen you as family too. Remember how she used to talk about wanting us to end up together when we were in college? This would mean the world to her, to see us united, even if it's just for a while."

I sighed. "Jae, pretending to be married won't fix the real problems. And it won't ease the pain of…of what's coming."

"But it could give her peace, Verena. Isn't it worth it if we can give her that?" His gaze was steady, earnest, seeking not just my agreement but my support.

I paused, considering his words, the depth of his desperation, and the genuine fear of loss that shadowed his features. It wasn't just about fulfilling a dying wish; it was about him grasping for a lifeline in a sea of uncertainty.

"Let's think this through, Jae. Really think about what this means for us, for her, for the future." I squeezed his hand, signaling not just my concern for his aunt but also for him, my once closest friend now looking so lost.

"It's just marriage, Verena," he shot back, his tone flippant but his eyes betraying his anxiety.

The importance of his proposal, the urgency and desperation behind it, left me reeling. "Jae, *just marriage*? I can help, but why do we have to get married?"

He leaned back, a half smirk playing on his lips. "Come on, we can do what they do in dramas. Have a contract marriage and amicably divorce when it's over. I'll even throw in a dramatic soundtrack and a slow-motion running scene for authenticity."

I was unable to suppress a reluctant smile. "Really, Jae? We're going to reenact one of Auntie's favorite soap operas? What's next, amnesia and a long-lost twin?"

"Why not? Might as well go all in," he replied, shrugging nonchalantly. "But seriously, Verena, it would give her peace. And I need this. I need you."

"No, Jae. The goal is to escape from you, not entangle myself further." My tone was light, teasing, despite the gravity of his proposal.

"But you want to quit, right? Focus on your writing? That's your dream." He leaned forward, his gaze intense. "Think about it. No day job, just you and your words. And all you have to do is play my adoring wife for a bit."

I leaned across the table, fixing Jae with a pointed look. "So, let me get this straight, Jae. You want me to upgrade from managing your professional life to managing your personal life too? From executive assistant to executive wife—what's next, coordinating your socks with your mood swings?"

Jae's defensive reply was tinged with his usual dry humor. "Well, you're very good at managing, Verena. I thought you'd appreciate the promotion."

I scoffed, shaking my head. "Oh, right, a promotion. Because being your fake wife just screams career advancement. And here I was, thinking I could finally enjoy my alone time without someone asking me to schedule their tooth brushing."

He folded his arms, a smirk playing on his lips. "It's not like you don't already handle everything for me. Plus, you love organizing. You'd be living your dream."

"Jae, being your wife—fake or not—sounds a lot like I'd be working twenty-four seven," I shot back, my tone dripping with sarcasm. "And honestly, the thought of having to sync my bathroom breaks with your conference calls? Pass."

Jae chuckled, clearly enjoying our banter despite the seriousness of his proposal. "Come on, Verena. Think of it as…immersive role-playing. You love a good drama, and what's more dramatic than pretending to be married to me?"

I rolled my eyes, the absurdity of the situation washing over me yet again. "Yeah, a drama where I play the pitiful wife who has to listen to you drone on about your day. And let's not forget the thrilling episode where I pretend to be interested in your golf scores."

Jae leaned forward, his tone mock-serious. "You'd get to share in all the perks, too. My charming company, my bank card. Plus, I promise to upgrade your title to Chief Life Organizer if it makes you feel any better."

I laughed despite myself, the tension easing slightly. "Wow, how can I refuse such a generous offer? Do I also get hazard pay for every family dinner where I convincingly call you honey without cringing?"

"Absolutely," Jae quipped. "And let's not forget the bonus for every time you manage to keep a straight face while my aunt discusses our non-existent future children."

I let out a genuine laugh, one that felt strangely liberating amidst the tension. It was a rare moment, reminiscent of easier times. Jae's expression softened, a flicker of nostalgia passing over his features.

"It's been a while since we laughed like this," he noted, the corners of his eyes crinkling slightly.

The warmth of the moment faded as quickly as it came, and my voice took on a sharper edge, the lingering bitterness finding its way back. "Yeah, well, it's been a while since I've felt like your friend, Jae. Not just an extension of your office."

He looked taken aback, but he didn't interrupt, allowing the weight of my words to hang between us.

"Look, Jae, I will help Auntie and be there for her. You know I love her like my own family. I promise." My tone softened with sincerity as I mentioned his aunt, but then it hardened again as I addressed his proposal. "But I can't do this insane idea of a fake marriage. It's just too much."

Jae's expression shifted, the business side of him coming to the forefront as he considered my refusal. "Then I guess you'll be working for me for six months," he said flatly, a hint of resignation lacing his tone.

A spark of defiance lit within me, bolstered by the absurdity of his backup plan. "Well then, I guess I'm going to be the worst employee you've ever had."

"Oh, really?"

"Yes," I retorted confidently.

"Good luck with that," he shot back, the corner of his mouth twitching in amusement.

I glanced at my watch, feigning nonchalance. "It's my lunch hour. I don't feel like eating sushi, so I guess you'll have to do without me."

"But we need to discuss my schedule for the day," Jae insisted, starting to list off a series of meetings, calls, and decisions that supposedly couldn't wait. "There's the conference call at two, the budget review at three, and—"

"Hmm. Nah." I cut him off with a dismissive wave, standing up from the booth. "I'm going to visit Auntie. She's probably done having lunch with my mom by now."

Jae's face showed a flicker of frustration, masked quickly by his usual composed exterior. "You're really going to leave me to handle all this alone?"

"Looks like you'll have to manage your own crises today, Jae," I quipped, stepping away from the table. "Consider it practice for when I'm not around to bail you out."

He watched me for a moment, then a sly grin spread across his face. "You think you're pretty clever, don't you?"

I shrugged, feigning innocence. "I don't know about clever, but I am on lunch break. And last I checked, that means no bosses, no schedules, just me time."

He scoffed. "You haven't taken a legitimate lunch break in years."

I crossed my arms over my chest. "And that, Jae, is the problem."

12

HI(STORY)

VERENA

The familiar hum of the city buzzed beneath me as I approached Jae's luxury penthouse atop one of New York's skyscrapers. I'd been here countless times, but today felt different—a blend of dread and determination stirred in me as the doorman greeted me with his usual warmth.

"Hey, Eddie." I smiled, stepping into the shade of the grand lobby.

"Miss Williams!" Eddie's face brightened as he held the door open for me. "How you been? Also, the grandkids loved that cake you got them. They're growing too fast!"

"That's what they do best," I laughed, the familiarity of our exchange providing a brief comfort. "Keep an eye on them; they'll be graduating college before you know it."

"Tell me about it!" he chuckled, shaking his head.

I waved goodbye and made my way to the private elevator, punching in the code to Jae's apartment without a second thought—my own birthday, a number I'd never forget, especially not when it'd been repurposed as a security code for something as impersonal as an apartment entry.

The elevator dinged softly, announcing my arrival at the top floor. As the doors slid open, the expansive living area of Jae's penthouse came into view, bathed in the soft glow of the afternoon sun filtering through large windows that offered a panoramic view of the bustling city below.

Auntie was on the couch, a bottle of wine by her side, looking as regal and composed as ever despite the circumstances. She glanced up, her eyes softening when she saw me.

Without a word, I walked over, took the bottle from the table, and took a long drink directly from it, not bothering with a glass. She watched me, her expression unreadable.

"You know?" She finally broke the silence.

"I know," I replied softly.

Setting the bottle down, I joined her on the couch and lay my head in her lap, the floodgates opening as tears began to stream down my face. She stroked my hair gently, a comforting presence as always.

"I know," she said, her voice thick with emotion. "The last time I was sick, you cried like this too...I remember."

Lying there, in the quiet comfort of her lap, surrounded by the luxury that felt both familiar and foreign, I let the tears flow.

Auntie gazed at me with a mixture of strength and sorrow that seemed to deepen the lines around her eyes. "When did you find out?" I asked, my voice barely a whisper.

"Three weeks ago. I booked my flight immediately. I wanted to spend time with Jae." Her voice softened as she continued, her eyes distant. "You really start to care about time when you realize how little of it you have left. I should have visited more."

I shook my head. "He should have visited *you* more."

She sighed, a long, weary breath. "Jae doesn't like coming to Korea. Not after his parents died. Too many memories in those walls from summer vacations and holidays. Some people like to settle in their memories; some run from them. My nephew is a runner."

"So, how bad is it?" I dared to ask, though part of me feared her answer.

Her gaze met mine, unflinching. "I'm dying, dear."

The starkness of her words hung in the air, burdensome and

undeniable. I swallowed hard, my mind scrambling. "I don't know what to do, what to say…"

"You know, grief and death, they don't wait for us to be ready. They come suddenly, and they don't pause—not even while we're healing, not even while we're just sitting here, trying to make sense of it all."

Auntie's expression held a resolute calm as I asked the next inevitable question. "Are you getting any treatment?"

She shook her head. "And be sick with the little time I have left? I've done the chemo thing before, and I don't want to be miserable." Her eyes met mine, filled with a serene acceptance that I found both heartbreaking and courageous.

"So, what do you want to do?" I asked, my voice soft, not wanting to disturb the fragile peace she seemed to have found.

Her response was immediate, her focus sharp. "Make sure Jae is okay." She glanced around the expansive room, her gaze lingering on the cold, modern decor. "This house has no warmth, you know? He's working himself to death in this glass tower. I need to know that he'll be okay."

Her words stirred something within me. I thought about his desperate request for a fake marriage, how outlandish it seemed but how it now made a sad kind of sense.

Auntie continued, her voice lowering, "I was always comforted by the fact that I knew he had you. But I think he ruined that." There was a note of regret in her voice, a mournful acknowledgment of the strained threads between Jae and me.

I remained silent, letting her words sink in. The truth in them was filled with years of unspoken fears and quiet hopes. I didn't respond, but her insight echoed loudly in the space between us, filling the room with more than just the chill of its decor.

I felt my heart break a little more. It wasn't just about the cancer or the absurd marriage proposal. It was about everything—every moment of joy and frustration that had led us here, to this place of raw, unfiltered truth.

Auntie shifted slightly, a glimmer of mischief lighting up her eyes.

"Remember the last time I visited?" she asked, her voice tinged with nostalgia.

"Yes," I nodded, recalling the memory fondly.

She leaned back, a smile spreading across her face as she reminisced about the day Jae had taken us to a vineyard. "He was so bogged down with conference calls on my birthday that you and I ended up getting drunk together."

Her laugh was light, but her eyes held a warmth that filled the room.

"Jae has a collection of very expensive wine, you know," I said.

Then, almost conspiratorially, she spoke. "I want to get very drunk with you."

I couldn't help but laugh along with her. Despite the circumstances, Auntie had always maintained her sass and dignity, becoming a figure in my life that somehow kept me connected to Jae, even when he drove me mad. "Well, I know where he keeps the most pricey bottles," I confessed, standing up from the couch.

I moved towards Jae's well-stocked wine cellar, and once I selected a particularly expensive-looking bottle, I returned to the living room, popping the cork with a sense of ceremony.

"I'm not going back to the office today," I declared, pouring us each a generous glass. "I'm getting drunk with you."

Auntie raised her glass, her smile wide and genuinely happy. "To making memories," she toasted, her voice strong despite everything.

"To making memories," I echoed, clinking my glass against hers, settling in for an afternoon of shared stories, laughter, and a bit of rebellious indulgence, all while the world outside continued unaware of the little oasis of joy we'd created in a corner of Jae's penthouse.

13

NO(THING)

JAE

Nine years ago

My business was just starting, but it was already growing faster than I'd ever imagined. Every day brought new work requests. People loved what I did, and I loved working with Vee. She was incredible, truly helping to shape Luminous into what it was becoming. Together, we were unstoppable.

I was at my desk, surrounded by blueprints and sketches, when my phone rang. Glancing at the screen, I saw Auntie's name. I answered quickly, eager to hear her voice.

"Hi, Auntie," I said, leaning back in my chair.

"Jae! How are you doing?" Her voice was warm, but there was a rough edge to it, followed by a cough.

"I'm good. Busy, but good," I replied. Her coughing made me sit up straighter. "Auntie, are you sick?"

"No, no," she insisted, though her voice was strained. "Just a cold."

I frowned, not convinced. "Are you sure you're okay?"

"I'm fine, Jae. Just tired. How's Verena?" she asked, deftly changing the subject.

"She's doing good," I said, a smile creeping into my voice. "Working hard, as always."

"When are you coming home to visit?" Auntie pressed.

"Work's been crazy, Auntie. I've got so much going on," I began.

"That's good. But don't forget to take breaks. Vee wants to visit," she said softly. "It would be good for you both."

Verena always had a way of getting me to do things I wouldn't normally consider. "Alright, once things settle down, I'll come visit."

"Good," Auntie said. "Take care of yourself, Jae."

"I will. You too, Auntie."

The call ended and Verena walked into my office, juggling a stack of papers. She was a whirlwind of efficiency, but she always had time to fuck with me.

"Hey, boss," Verena said with a grin, dropping the papers onto my desk. "Got a minute?"

"For you? Always," I replied, leaning back in my chair to get a better look at her. She was wearing a fitted blouse and a pencil skirt that hugged her curves just right. Her hair was pulled back in a messy bun, a few loose strands framing her face. My eyes traced the line of her neck, lingering on the delicate curve where her shoulder met her collarbone.

"Busy day?" I asked, my gaze following her every move.

"You know it," she said, rolling her eyes. "We've got three new projects coming in, and everyone wants them yesterday."

I chuckled, trying to focus on her words and not the way her lips moved. "Sounds about right. What would I do without you?"

"Crash and burn, probably," she teased, leaning over my desk to point out some details on a blueprint. Her scent—vanilla and something floral—filled my senses, making my head swim. The proximity made my pulse quicken. I could feel the warmth radiating from her, and it took every ounce of self-control not to reach out and touch her.

"Speaking of crashing and burning, have you eaten today?" she asked, raising an eyebrow. Her fingers brushed against mine as she moved a paper aside, sending a jolt of electricity through me.

"Uh, no," I admitted. "Haven't had time."

She shook her head. "Jae, you need to take care of yourself."

"Don't worry, I've got you to keep me in line," I said, giving her a playful wink, trying to ignore how I imagined keeping her in line. In the bedroom.

No.

Best friend.

Best friend.

Best fucking friend.

She laughed, the sound like music to my ears. "Yeah, yeah. You know, you're lucky I haven't found another job yet."

"You wouldn't dare," I said, standing up and walking around the desk to stand beside her. The air felt charged between us. "Who else would put up with my shit?"

"Good point," she said, looking up at me with a smirk. Her eyes sparkled with amusement, but there was something else there, something that made my heart beat a little faster. "But seriously, take a break. Eat something."

I nodded, knowing she was right. "Alright, Mom," I teased, earning a playful shove that sent a thrill through me.

"Watch it, boss. I can still quit," she warned.

"Not a chance," I said, my tone softening. "I'd be lost without you."

She held my gaze for a moment, and the air between us seemed to thicken with unspoken words. I felt a pull towards her, an urge to close the distance and finally say what I'd been feeling for so long. Her lips parted slightly, and for a heartbeat, I imagined leaning in, tasting the sweetness of her kiss. But then she broke the moment, turning to grab another stack of papers.

"Let's get through these, and then maybe later we can grab some lunch," she suggested, her voice all business again. I couldn't help but notice how her fingers trembled ever so slightly as she handled the documents.

"Sounds like a plan," I agreed, though my thoughts were still lingering on that brief, intense moment. Her proximity made it hard to think straight.

As we worked side by side, the familiar rhythm of our banter and shared focus on the projects brought a sense of comfort. Her presence was a balm to my scattered thoughts, her laughter a constant reminder of why I needed her in my life. But underneath it all, I couldn't shake the feeling that things were changing. The growing demands of the business and my evolving feelings for Verena were all coming to a head.

One thing was clear: I needed to find a way to balance it all without *losing the people who mattered most to me. And that started with taking care of myself and being honest about what I wanted—both in business and in my personal life.*

"Jae," Verena said, pulling me out of my thoughts. "Are you okay? You seem a bit off." Her voice was gentle, laced with concern. Her hand rested lightly on my arm, the touch sending warmth through my body.

I forced a smile, trying to push aside the turmoil inside. "Yeah, just thinking about some stuff. I'll be fine."

She studied me for a moment, her eyes searching mine. "I'm here for you, Jae."

"Yeah, I know," I said, my voice softening. "Thanks, Vee."

As we continued to work, I couldn't help but feel grateful for her presence. She was my rock, my confidante, and the person who kept me grounded. And as much as I tried to deny it, she was also the person I was falling for, more and more each day.

14

(WED)GE

JAE

After what was undeniably the worst day at work, I stormed into my penthouse. My mind was a chaotic mess. Without Verena to keep me on track, I was juggling too many plates, and today, they all shattered. Her absence revealed how much I depended on her, a reality I had never acknowledged. The idea of finding a replacement hung over me, but I doubted anyone could ever truly fill her shoes.

Stepping into my penthouse, I froze. Auntie was dancing on my pristine white couch, a glass of $700-a-bottle wine in hand, sloshing it around while belting out some K-pop tune. And Verena—hell, she looked good. Her usually strict ponytail was gone, her hair cascading down her shoulders. She had unbuttoned her top just enough to reveal the lace of her bra, and her pencil skirt was replaced by my gray sweats, rolled at the waist.

"My assistant is very drunk," I muttered, amusement and surprise bubbling up. I couldn't remember the last time I'd seen Verena let loose like this.

Auntie caught sight of me and paused mid-twirl, a wide, tipsy grin spreading across her face. "Oh, Jae is home!" she announced, like I was the guest of honor at a party.

"Apparently so," I remarked dryly. I took a moment to take in the scene, the sheer absurdity of it all. The two most important women in my life were completely dismantling the orderly environment I had meticulously maintained.

Verena looked up, her eyes widening as if she had forgotten I might come home. Her cheeks were flushed—from alcohol, dancing, or both. She straightened up, futilely trying to smooth down my borrowed sweats.

"Auntie was just showing me some of her old dance moves," she slurred, attempting decorum. "We decided to...uh, sample your wine collection. Hope that's okay."

I raised an eyebrow, a reluctant smile tugging at my lips. "Sampling, huh? That bottle was a Château something-or-other. Worth more than a small car."

Auntie giggled, swaying slightly on the couch. "Oh, it's just grape juice, Jae. Very expensive grape juice."

I shook my head, my initial irritation fading as I took in their carefree expressions. It was rare to see Verena so unguarded, so...happy. And Auntie, despite everything, was clearly enjoying what little time she felt she had left.

"Looks like I missed the party," I said, moving further into the room. The tension from my day began to dissolve, replaced by a warmth that only this kind of genuine human connection could foster.

"Yeah, but it's not over yet," Verena replied, patting the couch next to her. "Come join us, boss. You look like you could use a drink."

"I can't," I said sharply. "I have work to do since you abandoned me today, and it was a clusterfuck."

At my words, the playful smile vanished from Verena's face, her eyes hardening as the warm atmosphere chilled. Auntie mumbled something about going to bed and shuffled out of the room, leaving us in sudden, uncomfortable silence.

"Oh, you always have to work," Verena shot back, bitterness lacing her words. "You don't even say 'Honey, I'm home.'" Her mocking tone dripped with sarcasm.

"I wouldn't have to work tonight if you did your job," I retorted, my frustration bubbling over.

"I do three jobs," she snapped, her voice rising as she stumbled closer. Her hands gripped my cheeks, pulling my face toward hers. "It pisses me off how serious you look when you work. Some of the women say it looks sexy."

Verena's fingers tightened on my cheeks, her face inches from mine, her breath tinged with the scent of expensive wine. "Yeah, they whisper about it, Jae. About how serious you look, like you're going to conquer the world or burn it down. They think it's hot." She spat the last word as if it were an accusation.

"Does it?" I challenged, unable to resist pushing her buttons despite the tension strung tight between us. "Does it look sexy to you?"

Her eyes flicked down to my lips briefly before flashing back to mine again, her expression defiant. "No, it doesn't. It looks lonely. It looks like you're just...missing life."

I let out a humorless chuckle, her words striking closer to home than I wanted to admit. "Maybe I am missing life, Verena. Maybe I'm just trying to keep everything together, ever think of that?" My voice rose, anger and desperation lacing each word.

"And maybe you're not the only one keeping things together," she shot back, her voice thick with emotion. "Maybe I'm tired, Jae. Tired of always being the one who has to be strong, who has to pick up after your messes, who has to—"

I cut her off, my patience snapping. "So what, you want a medal? For doing the job you're paid to do?" The words were out before I could stop them, and I regretted them instantly. But the dam had broken, and years of unspoken frustrations were spilling out unchecked.

Verena's hands dropped from my face, and she took a step back, as if I'd physically pushed her. "I don't want a medal, Jae. I want a friend. I want the guy I used to know who didn't put work before everything else. But that guy's gone, isn't he? Buried under all your contracts and meetings."

I scoffed, the tension between us crackling. "So now it's my fault you're unhappy? You think I enjoy this? I do what I have to for this empire."

"And what about you?" she demanded, her eyes burning with intensity. "What do you do for you? Or is there nothing left of the Jae who used to laugh, who used to care about more than just the bottom line?"

For a moment, we stood there. My jaw tightened, unable to form a response, as the truth of her accusations settled deep.

She stared at my lips, her gaze drunk and unfocused, then shook her head slowly. Her hands forced the corners of my mouth into a smile. "There he is. There's my Jae."

Her balance faltered, and she nearly toppled over. Instinctively, I caught her, lifting her effortlessly. In one fluid motion, I threw her over my shoulder and carried her to my bedroom. It had been ages since our last drunken college sleepover, but some habits—like how easily she fit against me—didn't fade.

I tossed her gently onto the bed, where she landed with a soft pout. As I began to loosen my tie, her voice cut through the silence, heavier now. "She's really dying, Jae. And it hurts...more than anything I've ever felt."

I paused, the tie hanging loose around my neck. The room felt colder, emptier.

"I hate that you make me pity you when I'm supposed to leave you," she murmured, her eyes glistening with unshed tears.

I knelt beside the bed, my hand brushing a stray lock of hair from her face. "I normally don't like pity, but I'll take it," I whispered, my own voice rough with emotion.

Knowing how she hated her hair touching her neck when she slept, I began to gently gather her locks into a loose bun. Then I grabbed a pair of socks from the dresser. She hated cold feet.

Once she was settled and seemed more comfortable, I climbed onto the bed beside her, powering up my laptop. The soft glow of the screen cast shadows across the room as I began to work, stealing glances at her. There, in the dim light, with her resting next to me, the weight of everything we were facing—of everything that might soon change—settled heavily on my shoulders. But for now, she was here, and that had to be enough.

15

ADMI(RING)

VERENA

Waking up with the familiar crush of a hangover pressing against my temples, I made a mental note—again—that drinking was a truly terrible hobby. The pros? Dubious at best. The cons? A laundry list that started with a pounding headache and ended somewhere around mortifying nudity. And speaking of nudity, I had done it again.

As the fog of sleep cleared, I realized with a sinking feeling that I had stripped off every stitch of clothing in the night. I was as naked as the day I was born, lying under the soft duvet of what was unmistakably Jae's bed. Jae, who was currently asleep beside me, blissfully unaware of the naked truth—literally, in this case—next to him.

Why did I do this? Why was my drunken alter ego a nudist? Every time I got past a certain point with alcohol, I just wanted to strip away all constraints. It made sense at the time, apparently. The breeze against your skin, the freedom, the sheer rebellion of it—exhilarating.

Until the morning after.

Peeking over at Jae, I noticed his peaceful expression, the kind that made him look less like the corporate automaton he usually was and more like the college boy I remembered. The boy who had once hosted

a pajama party that strictly banned actual pajamas. The irony wasn't lost on me.

Just as I was about to make a smooth, stealthy escape from Jae's bed, disaster—or perhaps fate—decided to intervene. Jae shifted in his sleep, his arm snaking out with surprising quickness for a man usually slow to rouse. Before I could utter a word or make another move, he pulled me close, my very naked body now pressed firmly against his.

The awkwardness of the situation was palpable, like being caught singing an embarrassing pop song at a traffic light by the driver next to you—only a thousand times worse because, well, nudity.

There I was, skin against skin, trying not to acknowledge how warm and reassuring his body felt against mine. My mind, traitorous thing that it was, couldn't help but notice just how handsome he looked up close, with his disheveled hair. The morning light softened his usually sharp features, highlighting his annoyingly perfect jawline.

As much as I wanted to pull away and protect what was left of my dignity, there was an undeniable thrill to the warmth and solidity of his embrace. The same arms that had thrown me over his shoulder last night now held me in a protective cocoon that felt both right and wildly inappropriate.

The sexual tension simmered, a silent yet screaming presence in the room. It was like someone had dialed the awkward meter up to ten and then snapped the knob off for good measure. Every rational part of me screamed that I should extricate myself from this compromising position, but the part of me that had always harbored a maybe-sort-of-kind-of attraction to Jae found itself inconveniently enjoying the closeness.

And then, as if the universe hadn't already thrown enough awkwardness my way, I felt it. His morning wood. Yep, right there, a most unwelcome guest making its presence known in a very compromising locale.

Each time I attempted a subtle wiggle to extricate myself from this rather prickly situation, it just seemed to nestle in closer. It was like playing musical chairs, but the music was a slow, torturous grind, and there was only one chair—me.

Just as I was debating whether I could possibly shimmy out of his grip without further embarrassing body contact, Jae groaned, a sound that seemed to vibrate through my entire body.

I froze, holding my breath, praying to every deity I could think of that he might think this was all a dream. Maybe he'd just roll over, mumble something about coffee, and let me escape to a cold shower and a strong coffee. But no, the universe apparently had a different plan, and I was now part of this script whether I liked it or not.

Then, just when I thought my morning couldn't get any more terrible, the worst happened. Auntie, bless her soul, decided it was the perfect moment to waltz in with a tray of water, likely assuming she'd find us groggily nursing hangovers, not...this.

Her entrance was anything but quiet. The door swung open with a cheery "Rise and shine—" which cut off into a shriek as the tray clattered to the floor, glasses shattering like my last shreds of dignity. The noise and sudden commotion jolted Jae awake.

In a panic that matched the pitch of Auntie's shriek, Jae flung the bedding aside in a wild, sweeping motion that would have been comical if not for the dire consequences. Suddenly, everything was on display: me, stark naked; him, shirtless; and both of us in a decidedly compromising position.

My instincts kicked into overdrive. Unfortunately, they were the clumsy, uncoordinated instincts. I flailed, attempting to cover myself and escape the bed simultaneously, which resulted in me tumbling off the mattress in a graceless heap. I landed face down, ass up—a position that had its contexts, but greeting my best friend's aunt was definitely not one of them.

"Ah, this is not—It's not what it looks like!" I sputtered from the floor, the words muffled by the carpet and my acute embarrassment.

Jae, equally flustered, scrambled for the bedding, his attempts to cover us both only half-successful as he managed to throw a pillow in my direction instead of anything remotely useful like a blanket. "Auntie, I can explain," he stammered, his face the picture of mortification.

Auntie, recovering from her initial shock, her eyes wide and undoubtedly registering more than anyone wanted before breakfast, clutched at her chest. "I just came to bring water..." Her voice trailed off as she backed slowly out of the room, her eyes still locked on the havoc in front of her.

I grabbed the pillow, pressing it against myself like a makeshift shield, my cheeks burning hotter than the sun. From my awkward sprawl on the floor, I shot Jae a look that could only be described as *this is your fault* mixed with a plea for assistance.

There was a long, painful silence filled with the sounds of our ragged breathing and my heart hammering against my ribs. Finally, with a groan, I pushed myself up, ready to face the fallout of what would undoubtedly be an unforgettable breakfast conversation.

As I scrambled to my feet, still clutching the pillow to my front, Jae did the unthinkable. He looked between me and his still-recovering aunt and blurted out, "We're engaged."

The words hung in the air, ludicrous and heavy. My jaw dropped, my grip on the pillow loosened, and all I could do was stare at him in disbelief. Engaged? As in, planning to marry? My brain was too scrambled to form a coherent response.

Auntie, however, recovered from her shock much faster than I did, and her reaction was not at all what I expected. She squealed—a high-pitched sound of delight—and clapped her hands together. "Oh, get dressed! Oh my gosh, we can talk about this at breakfast!"

She hustled out of the room, her earlier shock replaced with bubbly excitement, leaving a trail of enthusiastic murmurs behind her.

And she probably shouldn't have left. Because when I saw Jae's triumphant smirk as he tossed me his shirt, I made the decision to kill him.

I was going to fucking *murder* Jae fucking Lee.

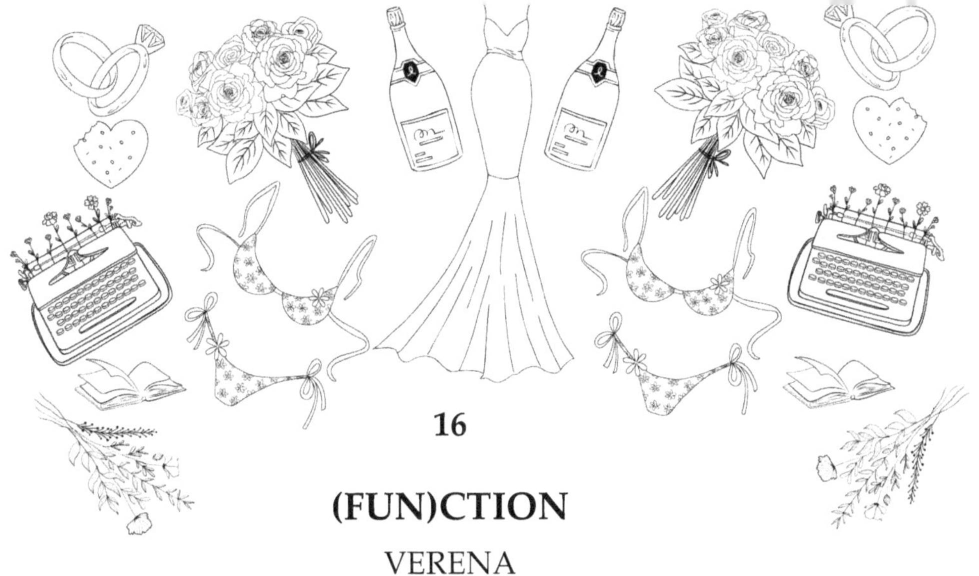

16

(FUN)CTION

VERENA

Ordinarily, breakfast with Auntie was a joyous occasion, steeped in the rich aromas of kimchi, fluffy rice, and sizzling fish—staples of her legendary Korean culinary repertoire. Today, however, as we gathered around her lavish spread, the air was as thick with sesame oil as it was with duplicity.

Auntie was practically vibrating with excitement, her eyes sparkling as she looked from Jae to me and back again. I, on the other hand, wanted to murder Jae for the lie he'd so casually thrown into the room. The only reason he was still alive was because I hadn't worked out my alibi.

How was I supposed to enjoy my seaweed soup with his impromptu engagement hanging over us?

As we settled into breakfast, the spicy scent of kimchi filled the air, mingling with the heavy anticipation of Auntie's impending questions. She looked at us, her eyes alight with curiosity and something akin to mischief. "So, when did all this start?" she asked, her voice eager.

I parted my lips to set the record straight—that there was no whirlwind romance, no secret lovers' saga to recount. But before the truth could tumble out, Jae cut in with the authoritative tone he reserved for board meetings and quarterly reports.

"We've been seeing each other secretly for quite some time," Jae declared, sending me a quick glance that practically dared me to contradict him.

Under the table, my hand found his thigh, pinching it hard enough to grind gears. His only reaction was a slight stiffening of his smile, which Auntie must have interpreted as a flutter of romantic nerves.

Auntie clapped her hands delightedly. "Oh, that's wonderful! And here I thought you two were just good friends! When did the sparks start flying?"

Jae, unfazed by the pain—or perhaps spurred on by it—continued weaving his web of deceit. "Well, it's hard to pinpoint the exact moment when friendship turned into something more," he said, his voice smooth as silk. I had to resist the urge to roll my eyes.

"Was it during the company retreat last spring?" he mused aloud, as if recalling a fond memory. "You know, where Verena heroically saved that presentation."

I choked on my tea. Jae was the one that fucked up that presentation in the first place but blamed it all on me. I was still pissed off about that.

"Yes. I was just smitten," Jae lied, effortlessly.

Auntie was eating it up, leaning in closer. "Oh, tell me more! Did you two sneak away for secret rendezvous? Have clandestine meetings?"

"It wasn't quite like the movies, Auntie," Jae said, chuckling. "We're professionals. But yes, we found moments for ourselves, didn't we, Verena?" His gaze locked on mine, challenging.

Trying to keep my composure, I managed a tight-lipped smile. "Yes, moments," I echoed hollowly, my voice nearly a whisper. Beneath the table, my pinching had turned into a full-blown assault on Jae's leg, each word he spoke earning him a new bruise.

Auntie, oblivious to the silent battle raging under the dining table, clapped her hands joyfully. "And now you're engaged! What a story to tell the grandchildren!"

Jae nodded solemnly, the picture of a devoted fiancé—if one

ignored the slight grimace from my relentless pinching. "Absolutely, Auntie. It's been quite the romantic journey."

Auntie's eyes sparkled with understanding, her nod slow and sage-like. "So that's why you quit," she murmured, piecing together her own version of our non-existent love story. "You're ready to take the relationship to the next level and don't want the conflict of interest."

Jae, with his impeccable timing and unshakeable composure, leaned into the moment with all the charm of a seasoned actor. "Exactly," he agreed, his voice rich with feigned emotion. "We just couldn't keep our love a secret any longer."

He squeezed my hand dramatically, securing it within his own as if sealing our intertwined fates right there at the breakfast table. I tried to reclaim my hand, not ready to be an accessory to his fabrications, but his grip was firm, unyielding.

"We've been juggling our professional and personal lives separately for too long," Jae continued, his eyes on Auntie but his words clearly meant for battle.

I opened my mouth, ready to interject, to set the record straight that my resignation was about personal growth, not about cultivating some secret romance. But before I could get a word out, Jae was digging a deeper grave for the both of us.

"And Verena, she's just been so amazing through it all," he gushed, turning to give me a look filled with mock adoration that might have fooled anyone who didn't know him as well as I did. "Haven't you, baby?" he added, turning back to Auntie before I could respond.

And I hated that he called me baby.

Mostly because he knew I had a weakness for men who called me pet names.

I gritted my teeth, a smile plastered on my face that I hoped looked loving instead of lethal. "Oh, absolutely," I managed, my tone dripping with a sarcasm that thankfully went unnoticed by Auntie.

"She loves me so much she decided it was best to remove any professional conflicts that could jeopardize our future together," Jae declared grandly, launching into a soliloquy that would have made

Shakespeare think twice. "I was upset at first. I mean, no one can do the job like Vee can. But I see now that it's for the best."

Each word was a nail in the coffin of my patience. I tried again to speak, to cut through his elaborately spun web of lies. "Actually, Auntie, the thing is—" I started, only for Jae to cut across me smoothly.

"And you know, it's been such a relief," Jae interjected, his smile unwavering as he steamrolled over my attempts to clarify. "To finally be open with our love. To not have to hide behind closed doors or sneak around corners or steal kisses in the stairwell."

Auntie clasped her hands together, completely taken in. "Oh, how romantic! Stealing kisses in the stairwell, oh my!"

As I looked across the table at Auntie, her hopeful gaze locking onto mine, the weight of the moment settled heavily on my shoulders. Her eyes, shimmering with unshed tears, were filled with a profound relief that pierced right through the facade we had concocted. "I was so worried you'd be alone," she whispered, her voice fragile, betraying the depth of her concern for Jae.

Those simple, heartfelt words echoed in my ears, reverberating through the carefully constructed walls I'd put up around myself. Here was a woman who loved her nephew so profoundly that the mere idea of his loneliness could bring her to tears. And here I was, on the verge of toppling the one thing that brought her comfort during her final days.

The air thickened around us, charged with unspoken truths and the palpable relief radiating from Auntie. The happiness that lit her face at the thought of Jae not having to face the world alone after she was gone was both beautiful and heartbreaking.

In that stretched-out moment, the clarity of what was at stake crystallized within me. How could I, in good conscience, strip away this newfound peace from a dying woman? She was holding onto the thought of Jae's happiness as a beacon through her pain.

So, as I felt Jae's expectant gaze on me, waiting to see if I'd expose our ruse, I made a choice.

I tightened my grip on his hand, an unspoken truce forming between us under the table.

My nod was slow, deliberate.

"Yes, Auntie," I echoed my earlier lie with a newfound resolve, "we didn't want to worry you until we were sure."

The lie tasted bitter on my tongue, but the smile I offered her was tender, crafted from a genuine desire to protect her from any further pain. Her smile in return was radiant, sweeping away any remnants of doubt about our deception. She reached across the table, covering both our hands with her own. "Oh, I am just so relieved." She sighed, a contented exhale that seemed to take the weight of the world off her shoulders.

As we cleared the breakfast dishes, Auntie's excitement bubbled over into planning mode. "So, when's the wedding?" she chirped, almost bouncing on her feet with anticipation.

Jae, always quick on his feet, replied with a grin, "Well, we got engaged last night."

Auntie's brow furrowed. "Last night?"

I chimed in with a playful smirk, "He just sprung it on me. Right there." I pointed at the spot beside the couch, dramatizing the spontaneity of it all.

Auntie clucked her tongue disapprovingly. "This won't do, Jae. You have to make it romantic. We're redoing this."

Jae tried to salvage his approach, "Auntie, Verena isn't someone that likes frills. Right?" He looked at me, hoping for some backup.

I paused, a mischievous idea forming. "Actually," I began, drawing out the moment, "I want a big proposal."

Auntie's face lit up. "See? You can't just spring it on her like this. I'll help you."

Before I knew it, Auntie was ushering me out of Jae's penthouse, her arm looped through mine as she whispered conspiratorially about flowers, locations, and flash mobs. "We're going to make it the proposal of a lifetime," she promised, her enthusiasm infectious.

As I glanced back over my shoulder, Jae's face was a picture of horror at the looming spectacle Auntie envisioned. The door closed behind us, leaving him to ponder the grand romantic gesture that was now expected of him. It wasn't until I was in the elevator that the truth hit me.

Fuck.

Jae won.

I was fake engaged to him.

<h1 style="text-align:center">17</h1>

(FOREVER)LASTING

VERENA

Stepping into Jae's office, I was immediately hit by the icy atmosphere that mirrored his demeanor. Undeterred, I tossed my bag onto his pristine desk, sending his neatly arranged pens scattering.

"Planning to camp here, Verena?" Jae raised an eyebrow, looking at the bag as if it personally offended him.

"Just making myself comfortable for the absurdity ahead," I replied, sinking into a chair and propping my feet on his desk, right next to the financial reports I knew he hadn't finished yet.

It had been a week since Auntie threatened me with a massive engagement plan, and I'd been looking over my shoulder for a public proposal ever since. I'd refused to come to the office and finish my handover because I was terrified Jae would do it here.

But I couldn't avoid him today.

No, we had a contract to sign.

He sighed, swiping my feet off his desk and straightening the papers. Before he could launch into his usual reprimand, the door swung open and in breezed his new assistant. Dressed in a skirt that was undeniably too short for corporate decorum and a smile that stretched wide enough to include everyone but somehow felt meant just for Jae, she was the human equivalent of a sunbeam—albeit one designed to blind.

"Mr. Lee, I've brought the revised contract drafts you asked for," she chimed, placing the documents a little too close to his hand on the desk.

Jae barely acknowledged her, his eyes cold and calculating. "About time," he muttered, snatching the papers without so much as a thank you. He glanced at me, his expression hardening. "Unlike some people, at least she knows how to do her job."

"I don't work here anymore, Jae," I argued.

He ignored me. "Thank you, Mina. That'll be all for now," Jae responded smoothly, not missing a beat.

Mina lingered a moment longer than necessary, batting her eyes in a way that made mine involuntarily roll. "If you need anything else, just buzz me," she said, her tone dripping with implications.

As the door clicked shut behind her, I turned to Jae, arching an eyebrow. "Is that my replacement? She's...enthusiastic."

Jae picked up the papers, his smirk betraying his amusement. "Definitely better at following instructions than you ever were. Less sarcastic."

I snorted. "I'm surprised you found someone so quickly. She's flirty."

He leaned back in his chair. "Competence isn't as rare as you think, Verena. You were just...expendable."

I scowled at him, my irritation bubbling just beneath the surface. "You're just pissed I wouldn't come in yesterday for your meeting with the project managers."

"It was a shit show without you." His tone was more resigned than angry, a subtle fracture in his usually impervious facade.

"Well, it looks like you found someone to help you," I said with a forced smile, gesturing towards the pile of documents scattered haphazardly across his once impeccably organized desk.

He scoffed, running a hand through his perfectly styled hair, the stress evident in the tension of his shoulders. "Help? If you can call it that. I swear, the interns are practically useless. They can't even collect documents without fucking everything up. I spent half the night fixing their mess."

"Sounds like you're struggling," I replied, unable to hide the amusement in my voice. "Maybe you should consider being nicer to people. Might make them more willing to help."

He leaned forward, eyes blazing. "You think this is funny? I had to deal with Daniels's complete incompetence during the presentation. He couldn't even answer basic questions about the project scope. It was embarrassing."

I shrugged. "Maybe if you were a bit more approachable, people wouldn't be so scared of making mistakes around you."

His glare intensified. "Approachable? This is business, not a damn therapy session. And speaking of mistakes, do you know how many contracts I had to personally review because no one else could get them right? I've barely slept in days, Verena."

"Well, you wanted to show that you could handle everything without me," I said, enjoying the sight of him unraveling. "How's that working out for you?"

He stood up, towering over his desk, his usual air of superiority crumbling. "Fine. You want to hear it? Everything has gone to shit without you. The office is in chaos. Projects are delayed, the staff is demoralized, and I'm on the verge of losing a major client because no one can keep up with the workload."

I blinked, taken aback by his sudden honesty. "You're really struggling, huh?"

"Struggling doesn't begin to cover it," he admitted, his voice dropping to a rough whisper. "I'm drowning here, Verena. Every time I think I've put out one fire, another one starts. And all I can think about is how much smoother everything ran when you were here."

My heart softened slightly at his confession, but I wasn't about to let him off the hook that easily. "So, what are you going to do about it?"

He sighed, sinking back into his chair. "I don't know. Beg you to come back? Offer you a raise? Hell, I'll even throw in extra vacation days if that's what it takes. Just...I need you here."

"Unfortunately, my schedule is booked. I don't know if you heard this, but I recently got engaged. I just have too much on my plate," I replied sarcastically. "Mina has got it under control. And she likes you, so I suppose you'll find your groove soon."

"Since you made it abundantly clear you won't be going back to work after I forced the engagement—very inconvenient, by the way— you didn't assist in the handover."

"Tough shit," I retorted, leaning back in the chair.

"She came from another department," he explained, as if that justified the rapid recruitment. "And yes, she likes me."

"She's like every other woman in the city," I muttered under my breath.

Jae leaned forward, his eyes gleaming with the challenge. "Jealous, Verena?"

"Why would I be jealous of your fan club?" I scoffed. "I'm more concerned about how you'll survive when she figures out you're not as charming as your balance sheets suggest."

"That's where you're wrong," Jae countered, leaning back with a smug grin. "I am exactly as charming as my balance sheets suggest. Perhaps even more."

"You're unlikable," I shot back. "And your new assistant will learn that soon enough."

Jae's laugh was cold and sharp. "We'll see. Maybe she'll last longer than you did."

"Maybe she will. But she won't put up with half as much of your shit as I did."

He smirked. "Let's get this over with. First clause: the living arrangement. Try to keep up, Verena. I don't have time for drawn-out negotiations."

"Oh, joy," I muttered, crossing my arms. "Hit me with it."

"We need to cohabitate," Jae stated, as if discussing the weather rather than proposing we share living quarters. "It lends authenticity."

"In what universe do you think living with you is going to make this easier?"

"In a universe where you keep your clothes in my closet and we convince everyone we're madly in love," he retorted, his tone dripping with dry sarcasm.

"*Mad* is the operative word here," I said, shaking my head. "Fine, but we set ground rules. Once Auntie is asleep, I move to the guest room."

Jae scribbled down the note, then looked up. "Afraid you won't be able to resist my charms up close?"

"More like afraid I'll smother you with a pillow in your sleep," I said. "Next clause?"

"Duration of the engagement. I say one year," he proposed, tapping his pen against the notepad.

"One year? Have you lost your mind?" I leaned forward, glaring at him. "Six months, Jae, I can't fake it for longer without risking my sanity."

"Nine months," he countered. "Compromise, and it gives us enough time to stage a dramatic breakup."

"Fine, but we're doing this my way. No over-the-top romantic gestures that'll make me gag. We keep it believable, but low-key."

Jae made a note, then hesitated. "Public appearances?"

"Minimum and always mutually agreed upon beforehand. And if you drag me to one of your charity galas, you owe me a new dress. Something expensive."

He chuckled. "Agreed. But you have to dance at least one slow dance with me. For appearances, you know."

I rolled my eyes. "Only if you promise not to step on my feet."

"Noted. Now, about your mother…"

I sighed deeply. "Let me figure out how to break it to her. I'm not sure how I'll convince her I've been dating you, considering she's heard me complain every day for years."

Jae paused, pen mid-air. "Need me to go with you to sell the story of our happy relationship?"

"And be an accessory to murder? I don't think so."

Jae made a note, then looked up with that calculated calm he mastered so well. "Public displays of affection," he continued, tapping his pen against the desk. "Necessary for a convincing engagement, wouldn't you say?"

I grimaced. "Fine, but let's lay down some ground rules. Hand-holding is tolerable. Occasional pecks are acceptable."

Jae's smirk reappeared. "What about a passionate kiss? For believability?"

"No tongue," I said immediately.

"Where's the passion in that?" Jae teased.

"In your imagination, where it belongs," I retorted. "And keep your hands north of the equator, buddy."

"No southern excursions, got it. Anything else, Your Highness?"

"And you can't treat me like your assistant," I added, my tone firm. This was a big one for me. I didn't quit my job just to do the exact same thing without a salary. "I'm not managing your schedule, picking up your sushi, or making your dentist appointments anymore."

Jae's eyebrows shot up. "But who will ensure my teeth are sparkling and my calendar is flawless?"

"You will," I said flatly. "It's high time you learned how to use Google Calendar and the phone."

"But I'm terrible at it," he protested.

"Tragic," I replied, not missing a beat. "Maybe Mina can help. Isn't handling your...logistics part of her charm offensive?"

He sighed dramatically. "Fine, no assistant duties. What about emergencies? Can I call you if there's a crisis?"

"Only if the world is ending," I said.

Jae chuckled, nodding in defeat. "Noted. Anything else?"

"No treating me like an intern either. I don't fetch coffee, dry cleaning, or your associates' approval."

"Understood. So, how should I treat you?" His tone was teasing but edged with genuine curiosity.

"Like a fiancée who wants to marry you, then kill you for your money," I shot back with a smirk. "Speaking of money, don't try to pay me to be your fiancée. I don't want to feel like a lady of the night."

"Who even says that?"

"I'm serious, Jae. I'll use the time to figure out what I'm doing with my life, but don't try to write me a check. That would just make me feel...icky."

"Done. But keep my card for emergencies and for convincing people. Auntie would think it's weird if my fiancée wasn't taken care of."

I nodded. "I'll happily buy overpriced coffee on your dime, Mr. Lee. Oh! And you can't fall in love with me," I added, only half-joking. "This is professional."

Jae put down his pen and leaned back, folding his arms and studying me with a playful tilt of his head. "I thought that was assumed."

"I just want to be extra clear."

He raised an eyebrow. "You think I'd fall in love with you?"

"It's a common hazard in fake engagements," I said, trying to keep the mood light, though my heart wasn't quite in it. "Seen enough movies to know how this goes."

Jae laughed, that rich, infuriating sound that filled his office. "I'll add it to the contract. 'Party A hereby agrees not to fall in love with Party B. Penalty for breach: immediate termination of the engagement and forfeiture of all rights to Party B's excellent hugs.'"

"Make sure it's legally binding," I quipped, standing up and gathering my things. "And send me a draft for review. I have amendments."

"Will do," Jae replied while standing to walk me to the door.

"Look at us, negotiating like civilized people. It's almost like we're friends again."

Jae's response was instant, his voice tinged with surprise. "I didn't realize we ever stopped being friends."

"Really, Jae? You hadn't noticed?"

"No, really. When did we stop?" he asked, his tone serious now.

"A long time ago," I said, letting the weight of those words hang between us. "And now we're not just not-friends, we're fake fiancés. From frenemies to fiancés, what a leap."

"Frenemies?" Jae repeated, the word rolling off his tongue as if tasting it for the first time.

I nodded. "For six months, I gave you decaf." I giggled, thinking back to all of his yawns during meetings.

His jaw dropped, a look of comical betrayal crossing his face. "That's why I've been so sleepy? What else did you do?"

With a shrug and a smirk, I leaned back slightly. "Let's see, there was the time I signed you up for that newsletter you hate. You know, the one about mail order brides."

Jae groaned, recalling the daily influx of emails he'd complained about for weeks. "That was you?"

"And I may have told the dry cleaners to add extra starch to your shirts. A lot extra." I grinned, enjoying the confession more than I probably should have.

Jae ran a hand through his hair, a smile slowly spreading across his face despite the revelations. "You're terrible," he said.

"I am," I agreed. "But you should probably get used to it. You've got six more months of my terrible company."

"Nine months," he reiterated. "I guess I'll have to find some way to make it bearable."

"Good luck with that," I said playfully as I walked away, leaving Jae with a challenge he seemed only too happy to accept.

18

BIRTH(DAY)

VERENA

Eight Years Ago

I glanced at my watch for the tenth time, the seconds ticking by. An hour late. I tried to keep my disappointment at bay, but it was hard. Today was Jae's birthday, and I had gone all out to plan a surprise dinner for him at his favorite restaurant. The staff had even set up a table in the corner with balloons and a birthday banner. I'd been looking forward to this for weeks, knowing how busy Jae had been with work.

Since Luminous had taken off, we'd been swamped with projects. Two years in, and we were already designing multiple buildings, with fifty employees under our belt. Jae had changed a bit too. The once laid-back guy I'd known in college had become a bit of a workaholic. It wasn't necessarily a bad thing—his dedication was admirable—but it also meant he was more often than not glued to his desk or running from one meeting to another.

Finally, the door swung open, and Jae walked in, looking frazzled but undeniably handsome. His dark hair was tousled, and he still wore his work clothes—black slacks and a crisp white shirt with the sleeves rolled up. He spotted me, and his face lit up with a sheepish grin.

"Verena, I'm so sorry I'm late," he said, sliding into the seat across from

125

me. "I got a call just as I was leaving from TherTech; you know how much that damn lady can talk. She's driving me nuts."

"It's okay," I said. "I figured you were busy. I'm just glad you're here now."

He reached across the table and squeezed my hand. "I really am sorry, Vee. You went to all this trouble for my birthday, and I almost blew it."

I shrugged, trying to brush it off. "Let's just enjoy the dinner, okay? I ordered your favorite."

As if on cue, the waiter brought over a platter of grilled steak and roasted vegetables. Jae's eyes lit up at the sight, and I felt a little better. Maybe this dinner would still be good.

"How's everything?" I asked, trying to keep my tone light. "I see you every day, but I feel like all we talk about is work."

Jae took a bite of steak, savoring it before responding. "Yeah, it's been nuts. Did I tell you about the new project we landed? It's a complete redesign of the old rec center downtown. I've been buried in blueprints."

"That sounds exciting. But I meant how are you doing? Outside of work?"

He looked at me, a bit startled by the question. "Oh, um, Auntie's coming to visit next month. She's been wanting to check in and make sure I'm eating well, taking care of myself, all the typical."

I smiled. "She's always good at keeping you grounded. It'll be nice to see her."

"Yeah." He nodded. "And your mom asked if we could help her with the garden this weekend, but I don't think I'll be able to make it. I've got a ton of prep to do for the presentation on Monday."

I shrugged, trying to brush it off. "I'll go help her out. We'll manage."

He reached across the table, squeezing my hand. "I'm really sorry, Vee. I know you wanted us to do that together."

"It's fine," I said, forcing a smile. "Really."

We settled into an uneasy silence. The food was delicious, but I could barely taste it. My mind was too occupied with the realization that work was starting to consume Jae entirely, leaving little room for anything else.

"So," I said, trying to steer the conversation to lighter territory. "Any other non-work-related news?"

"Not much. How about you?"

I sighed. "I'm still looking for an apartment. The places in my budget are all either too small or in terrible condition."

"Oh!" Jae interrupted, his eyes lighting up with excitement. "I have a pitch for an apartment building renovation. Complete overhaul. We need to plan for that. Who knows, maybe you could live there, hmm? I'll work it into the contract."

I forced another smile, trying to match his enthusiasm. "That sounds great, Jae. But I need something now. Not in six months."

"Right, right," Jae said, his excitement dimming slightly. "I just thought it'd be perfect for you. You'd get first dibs on the best unit."

"Yeah, it would be," I said softly, looking down at my plate. "But I can't wait that long."

"Just move in with me."

I blinked, momentarily caught off guard. "Uh, what?"

Jae leaned forward, his eyes sparkling with the enthusiasm of his idea. "Think about it. We work together all the time, have late nights. It'd be great. Less time traveling back and forth."

I laughed, trying to deflect the sudden tension his suggestion brought. "Jae, you're my best friend, but living with you? You're so...meticulous. You'd probably label my cereal boxes."

"C'mon, it wouldn't be that bad," he teased, a smirk playing on his lips. "You might actually learn to appreciate my organization skills."

I shook my head, unable to hide my grin. "Yeah, right. I'd probably drive you nuts with my mess."

"Maybe," he said, chuckling. "But it'd be worth it. We could share meals, talk about work without having to call each other all the time. And I'd make sure you get the best room."

"Is that a bribe?" I raised an eyebrow, trying to keep the tone light despite the fluttering in my stomach.

He leaned back, crossing his arms with a mock-serious expression. "Absolutely. It'll be awesome, and you won't have to pay rent. Think about it —pizza nights, movie marathons. You know you love hanging out with me."

I snorted. "I can't just mooch off of you, Jae. I don't think it's a good idea."

His smile faded, replaced by a vulnerability I rarely saw. "Why not?"

I hesitated, searching for the right words. "I just think...it might complicate things. We already spend so much time together at work."

He frowned, a hint of hurt flashing in his eyes. "Complicate things how? We're best friends, Vee. What's wrong with living together?"

I sighed, trying to soothe the rising tension. "It's not about that. It's about needing some space, you know? A place to unwind and recharge without... without work constantly looming over us."

Jae's expression hardened slightly, his defensiveness kicking in. "So what, you're saying I'd be a burden?"

"No, of course not," I quickly interjected, reaching out to touch his hand. "It's just...we both need a break sometimes. And I don't want us to get on each other's nerves."

He pulled his hand back, crossing his arms again. "You think I'd get on your nerves?"

I could see the walls going up, the familiar mask of indifference slipping into place. "Jae, that's not what I'm saying."

"Then what are you saying?" he pressed, his tone sharper than before. "Because it sounds like you don't want to be around me more than you have to."

"That's not it at all," I insisted, frustration creeping into my voice. "I just think it's healthy to have some boundaries. To keep work and personal life separate."

He huffed, looking away. "Maybe I don't want to keep them separate."

The admission hung in the air, heavy with unspoken meaning. I bit my lip, unsure how to navigate the sudden shift. "Jae..."

"Forget it," he muttered, his jaw tight. "I was just trying to help."

"I know," I said softly. "And I appreciate it. Really. But I think we need to find balance first."

He didn't respond, his gaze fixed on some distant point beyond our table. The silence stretched, fraught with unspoken emotions. I wanted to reach out, to tell him that I understood, that I felt the same way. But the words caught in my throat, tangled with my own fears and doubts.

Finally, Jae sighed, the tension easing from his shoulders. "Fine. I get it."

We ate in relative silence after that, the clinking of cutlery and muted conversations around us filling the void. I was acutely aware of every moment that passed, feeling the weight of our earlier conversation still hanging in the air. Jae seemed lost in his thoughts, occasionally glancing up at me with an unreadable expression.

As if sensing the tension, the waiter arrived with the cake I had requested. It was a small, beautifully decorated chocolate cake with "Happy Birthday Jae" written in elegant script. Candles flickered on top, casting a warm glow across the table.

I tried to lighten the mood, putting on my best smile. "Make a wish, birthday boy," I said, my voice attempting cheerfulness.

Jae looked at the cake, then at me, his eyes locking with mine. The intensity of his gaze made my heart skip a beat. There was something there, something deep and unspoken, that made the air between us crackle with tension.

After a moment, he blew out the candles, the flames flickering out in a puff of smoke.

I clapped softly, trying to keep the atmosphere light. "What did you wish for?"

He gave me a half smile, but it didn't reach his eyes. "I can't tell you, or it won't come true."

"That's the rule, huh?" I teased, trying to bring back our usual flirty banter.

"Yup," he said, leaning back in his chair. "Besides, I don't want any cake. You eat it."

I frowned, feeling a pang of disappointment. "But it's your birthday cake."

He shrugged, looking almost apologetic. "I just don't have much of an appetite right now. You enjoy it."

I hesitated, then nodded, cutting a slice of the cake and taking a bite. The rich chocolate melted in my mouth, but it tasted bittersweet in the current atmosphere. I glanced at Jae, hoping to find a way to bridge the gap that had formed between us.

Just then, his phone buzzed. He glanced at the screen, his expression tightening. "I need to take this," he said, standing up and stepping away from the table.

As he walked off, talking into the phone, I felt a mix of frustration and sadness. This dinner was supposed to be a celebration, a chance for us to reconnect. But instead, it had turned into another reminder of how work was consuming him, pulling him away from everything else.

I took another bite of the cake, trying to focus on the sweetness instead of the growing ache in my chest. Jae's voice drifted back to me, low and urgent as he discussed something with whoever was on the other end of the line.

I couldn't help but wonder if this was how it was always going to be—me waiting, hoping for a moment of his time, while he was constantly pulled away by the demands of his growing business. The thought was almost too much to bear, and I blinked back the sting of tears.

When Jae finally returned, he looked even more exhausted than before. "Sorry about that," he said, sliding back into his seat. "Just some urgent work stuff."

I forced a smile, pushing the rest of the cake towards him. "It's okay. Here, at least have a bite of your cake."

He took the fork from me, cutting a small piece and eating it. "Thanks, Vee. For everything."

"You're welcome," I said softly, wishing things could be different. Wishing that for once, work wouldn't come between us. But even as we sat there, I knew that this was the reality of our lives now—me constantly trying to reach him, and him always just out of reach.

19

MISUNDER(STAND)

VERENA

The rattling of the subway tracks was like a metronome, keeping time with the pounding of my heart. Riding the train from New York to Jersey was a regular part of my routine since I visited Mom often, but today, the trip felt unusually grave. I clutched my phone in one hand, the other gripping the cold metal pole, my mind spinning with how I was going to break the news to her.

I had texted Laura and Luke to meet me there for moral support. A part of me feared this revelation would be rough, and I wanted allies—just in case. Laura always knew how to handle my mom, while Luke could defuse any tension with his humor.

"Almost there," I muttered to myself, the words swallowed by the noise of the train. The dingy walls of the tunnel flickered past, and I took a deep breath, steeling myself for what was to come.

When the train finally pulled into the station, I hustled out with the rest of the crowd. The familiar, comforting scent of Jersey air—part greenery, part car exhaust—greeted me as I emerged onto the street. Mom's house was only a short walk away, nestled in a cozy neighborhood with tree-lined streets and charming, if slightly worn, houses.

Mom's house was my sanctuary growing up—a place of affection and love, where the kitchen always smelled of home-cooked meals and the walls were filled with laughter. I walked up the path, noticing the meticulous garden Mom tended to religiously, the flowers a riot of color against the green lawn. I took a deep breath and opened the door, the scent of my favorite foods wafting through the air—a sure sign she was already in host mode.

"Mom, I'm here!" I called out, shrugging off my coat and hanging it on the familiar hook by the door. The sound of clattering dishes from the kitchen told me she was putting the finishing touches on our meal.

"In the kitchen, sweetheart!" she replied, her voice welcoming. I stepped inside, the sight of her bustling around the kitchen filling me with nostalgia and dread.

"Hey, Mom," I said, giving her a quick hug. "Thanks for making all my favorites."

"Anything for you, honey," she said, beaming. "Now, tell me what's got you so worked up that you needed reinforcements." Her eyes flicked to the living room where Laura and Luke were already making themselves comfortable.

"Verena, you know the last time you needed backup, we ended up bailing you out after the whole male stripper incident," Luke teased, grinning widely as he lounged on the couch.

"You promised never to bring that up again!" I joked.

"We just want to know why we're here. Is it 'strippers at the office' bad or 'burning down the kitchen' bad?" Laura asked with a grin.

"It's not bad. Just an announcement."

As we moved to the kitchen table, I glanced around the room, taking in the familiar surroundings that always brought a sense of comfort. The kitchen was a perfect blend of cozy and chaotic—mom's penchant for eclectic decor evident in the mismatched chairs around the vintage wooden table. The walls were a soft pastel yellow, adorned with framed family photos and quirky knickknacks she had collected over the years.

Her chihuahua, Muffin, came in through the doggie door—barely. He was so fat from all the food mom gave him he waddled everywhere, too tired and old to greet me.

"Alright, everyone, let's sit down and eat before the food gets cold," I said, motioning for everyone to take a seat.

As we all settled in, Mom looked at me with an expectant gaze, her eyes narrowing slightly. "Just spit it out, Verena. You already quit your job; what else could there be?"

I took a deep breath, my heart pounding in my chest. This was it, the moment of truth. "I'm dating Jae."

There was a beat of silence, the room suddenly feeling a lot smaller. The anticipation hung heavy in the air, my mother's eyes widening in disbelief. Then, to my complete surprise, she burst out laughing. Not just a chuckle, but a full, hearty laugh that echoed off the walls. She laughed so hard, tears formed at the corners of her eyes, and she had to clutch her stomach.

"Yeah right, okay," she said between giggles, wiping her eyes. "Tell me the truth now, Verena."

I stared at her, bewildered. "Mom, I am telling the truth."

Her laughter subsided into sporadic giggles, and she looked at me, still incredulous. "You're serious? You, dating that arrogant CEO who can barely remember to say *please* and *thank you*? Verena, come on."

"Dead serious," I replied, my insides twisting with nerves.

She shook her head, a skeptical smile still playing on her lips. "So, what? He suddenly developed a personality overnight? Or did you finally lose a bet?"

My friends exchanged amused glances, clearly enjoying the spectacle.

"I'm serious, Mom," I insisted. "Jae and I are dating. It's been a few months now."

Her laughter faded into a disbelieving chuckle as she took in my serious expression. "You mean to tell me that, after all these years of complaining about that man, you're now dating him? I don't believe it."

Luke puffed out his chest, looking as macho as he could manage. "He's not your type."

I arched an eyebrow, amused. "Oh really? And how do you know my type?"

Luke blushed, scratching the back of his neck awkwardly. "I pay attention. You like them...uh...tall, with dark hair, a bit scruffy but in a ruggedly handsome way. Preferably wearing a flannel shirt and those well-worn jeans that look like they've seen some actual work. Oh, and a pair of beat-up boots that have clearly walked through a few adventures."

I looked at him, taking in his current outfit—a perfect match to the description he just gave. He wore a red flannel shirt rolled up at the sleeves, jeans that had definitely seen better days, and his old brown boots that had been through countless escapades with me.

Laura snorted, nearly choking on her drink. "Wow, Luke, way to subtly describe yourself."

"Smooth," Mom added.

Luke's blush deepened, and he shot me a sheepish grin. "Well, I guess I know your type better than I thought."

I shook my head, chuckling. "Nice try, Luke. But Jae...he surprised me. It's more about who he is, not just what he looks like."

"Yeah, sure," Luke mumbled, still looking embarrassed but managing a smile.

Mom leaned forward, narrowing her eyes suspiciously. "Okay, spill. What's the real secret?"

I sighed, feeling the pressure of their skepticism. "That is the secret, Mom."

Mom crossed her arms. "No, really."

I nodded, trying to appear earnest. "Really."

She glanced at Laura, a knowing look passing between them. "I think we need to take her to the hospital. She's clearly delusional."

"No, seriously. We've been dating in secret for a while. Working for him was hurting our relationship."

Laura deadpanned, "Because he's such an asshole?"

Mom nodded aggressively, her eyes wide with agreement. "Exactly! He's always seemed so...demanding."

I rolled my eyes, exasperated but amused. "He's not that bad, guys. He's just...driven."

Luke snorted. "Driven? That's one way to put it."

I could feel my mom's gaze bore into me. "You tell me everything,

Vee, and you expect me to believe you've been secretly dating him for months?"

I nodded slowly, trying to appear confident.

"So, you've been lying to me?" she pressed, her voice rising with incredulity. "Why would you tell me how awful he is if you're dating him? What's really going on, Vee?"

I squirmed under their collective stare. Their judgment was almost unbearable. I couldn't tell them the truth, not just because my mom wouldn't approve but also because I'd signed an ironclad NDA. "I just wasn't ready," I finally said, shrugging helplessly. "I knew how you felt about him."

"Damn right," Mom retorted, her eyes narrowing. She launched into a rant about how Jae treated me, her voice rising with each accusation. "He bosses you around, expects you to be at his beck and call, and never shows any appreciation! And now you're dating him?"

Laura jumped in, shaking her head. "This is a terrible idea, Vee. You deserve so much better than Jae."

Luke, usually the jokester, looked vulnerable, his eyes filled with genuine concern. "Why would you want someone who treats you like shit, Verena? It doesn't make sense."

I could feel the frustration building, the pressure of their expectations and my own guilt. I stood abruptly, my chair scraping loudly against the floor. "We're dating. End of story." Grabbing a breadstick from the table, I stormed out of the house, ignoring their calls for me to come back.

The cool air hit my face as I stepped outside, the anger and sadness swirling inside me like a storm. How had I ended up here, caught in this web of lies? Pissed at Jae for putting me in this situation, and even more pissed at myself for agreeing to it, I walked briskly down the sidewalk, fuming.

Then I saw it—a small, scrappy cat sitting by the side of the road, looking up at me with big, hopeful eyes. Its orange fur was matted and dirty, and it looked like it had been through a rough time. "Great," I muttered, bending down to scratch its head. "Just what I need right now."

The cat rubbed against my hand, purring softly. Despite my frustration, I felt a pang of pity for the little creature. It was as lost and stuck as I felt. The parallel struck me hard, and for a moment, I just sat there, stroking the cat and thinking about the mess my life had become.

"You know what?" I said aloud, scooping the cat up into my arms. "If Jae is going to control my life, I might as well make it as difficult as possible for him."

The cat nestled into my arms, purring even louder, and I felt a surprising sense of comfort from its presence. As I stood up, I realized this small act of defiance—adopting a stray cat—was a tiny step towards reclaiming some control over my own life.

With the cat cradled in my arms, I headed back toward the subway station. My mind was a whirlwind of thoughts and emotions. This whole thing had been a terrible idea. I was mad at Jae for putting me in this position, sad that I was now fighting with my mom and best friends, and frustrated that I felt so trapped.

As the train rattled along the tracks, I glanced down at the cat, who had settled comfortably in my lap. "Guess we're stuck together now," I said softly, feeling a tiny flicker of resolve. "Let's see how Jae likes dealing with us both."

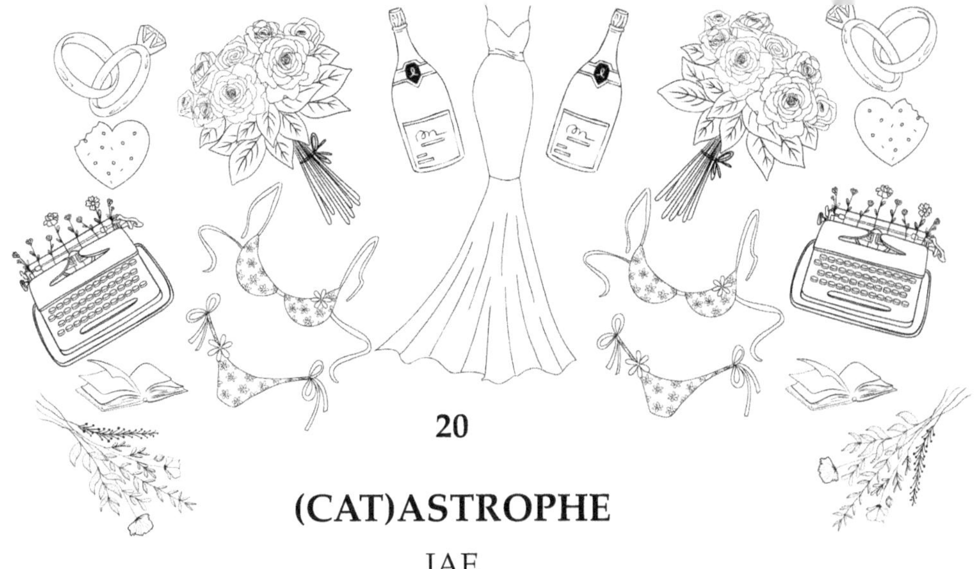

20

(CAT)ASTROPHE

JAE

Stepping into my penthouse after a grueling day, I expected the usual sanctuary of silence and order. Instead, chaos greeted me. Verena stood in the middle of my living room, cradling a scrappy-looking cat, surrounded by a mountain of suitcases.

"What the fuck is a cat doing in my house?" I demanded, my voice slicing through the air.

"Jae, meet Mina," she said, her grin wide and unapologetic.

I raised an eyebrow, incredulous. "Mina? You named that thing after my assistant?"

Verena smirked. "A unique choice, don't you think?"

I sneezed, once, twice, then glared at her, my patience wearing thin.

Auntie, lounging comfortably on the couch, clapped her hands in delight. "She's so cute!"

This was not how I envisioned my evening.

Before I could respond, the cat leaped out of Verena's arms, darting across the room. Auntie immediately got up, laughing as she scooped up the furball. "Oh, she's adorable! Come here, Mina."

I watched the scene unfold. This was my life now, it seemed— turmoil wrapped in affection, pushing my limits every damn day.

I turned my attention back to Verena, ready to launch into a tirade, but my words caught in my throat. She stood there in short shorts that flaunted her long, toned legs and a crop top that revealed a tantalizing sliver of her stomach. Her hair was pulled up into a high ponytail, and that infuriating, confident smirk played on her lips. She looked like trouble wrapped in sunshine, the kind of woman who could make a man forget his own name.

"Are you serious?" I finally managed to say, trying to keep my eyes from lingering too long on her bare skin. "You brought a cat into my house?"

"What's the matter, Jae? Afraid of a little fur?" she taunted.

"Afraid of a lot of fur," I corrected, rubbing my temples as the first tickle of an allergic reaction began to set in. "I told you, I'm allergic to cats."

Verena's smirk widened. "Oh, did you? I must have missed that memo."

"Are you trying to Pavlov's dog me into sneezing every time I see my assistant at work?" I asked, glaring at her.

She just laughed, and I couldn't decide whether to be more irritated by the cat or by the fact that, despite my best efforts not to find her attractive, she was still the most captivating thing in the room. "That would be really manipulative and downright diabolical."

"Exactly," I muttered, sneezing again. "And you're loving every minute of this, aren't you?"

"Absolutely," she said with a grin. "This is payback for all those late-night calls and unreasonable demands."

"Great. I've got a diabolical fiancée, a cat anarchist, and a penthouse full of suitcases. I didn't realize you'd bring so much when I suggested you move in. Anything else you want to spring on me?"

"I was thinking Mina looked lonely and needed a brother or sister kitten..."

My nose twitched, and I felt another sneeze coming on. "Verena..."

"Relax," she said, waving a hand dismissively before stepping closer and lowering her voice so only I could hear. "Mina is part of the act. Makes our relationship more believable. Plus, she needed a home."

A violent sneeze erupted from me, followed by another. My eyes started to itch, and I knew I was in for a long night.

"See? You're already adjusting," Verena said with a wicked smile, clearly enjoying my discomfort.

I turned to Auntie, hoping for some backup. "Auntie, please, you can't seriously think this is a good idea. I'm allergic."

Auntie beamed at me, clearly oblivious to my suffering. "Oh, Jae, it's perfect! I'll send you to an acupuncturist, and you'll be right as rain. Plus, I think having a little snuggly cat would be great for me."

Verena shrugged. "Looks like you're outvoted. Sucks when someone makes decisions for you, huh?"

I sighed, resigning myself to the inevitable. "Fine. But the cat stays in one part of the house."

"Deal," Verena said, her smile widening. "And I'll take care of all its needs."

Just then, Mina leaped onto a bookshelf, sending a framed photo crashing to the ground. Auntie laughed, clearly delighted by the cat's antics, while I could feel my patience fraying.

"Mina!" I barked, trying to maintain some semblance of control. The cat merely flicked its tail and sauntered off, completely unimpressed by my authority.

I stared after the cat, realizing that this tiny creature, much like Verena, had waltzed into my life and upended my carefully constructed world.

Verena chuckled, crossing her arms. "Looks like you're not the boss here, after all."

"Oh, I'm still the boss," I countered, my voice firm despite the tickle in my throat. "And as boss, I declare that you need to keep this cat under control."

Verena saluted mockingly. "Yes, Mr. Lee."

We spent the next hour chasing after Mina, who seemed to take great pleasure in causing as much mayhem as possible. Every time we thought we had her cornered, she darted off to another part of the penthouse, knocking over expensive decor and sending me into another fit of sneezing. Verena was laughing so hard she could barely stand.

"Okay, this has to stop," I said between sneezes, glaring at Mina, who was now perched on top of a tall bookshelf, her tail flicking.

Verena, still chuckling, wiped tears from her eyes. "Come on, Jae. She's just exploring."

"Exploring or redecorating," I grumbled.

Verena's laughter only intensified, and despite the irritation clawing at my sinuses, I watched her. The way she moved, the way she laughed —it was a distraction I didn't need but couldn't resist. The cat, the disarray, Verena herself—they were all tests of my patience, but damn if they didn't make life a hell of a lot more interesting. It was…nice having a full house. I just wished we didn't have a cat.

Verena stepped closer to the bookshelf, trying to coax Mina down. "Here, kitty, kitty. Come on, Mina. Let's get down from there."

Mina meowed defiantly, refusing to budge. Verena sighed and reached up, her fingers just barely grazing the cat's fur.

"Hold on, I'll get her," I said, moving to stand behind Verena. "Just be careful. If she jumps, she could hurt herself."

As I moved closer, Verena stretched up, her back pressing against my chest. My breath caught, acutely aware of her proximity. Her body fit against mine, every inch aligning perfectly. The curve of her ass. The intoxicating scent of her perfume. She wobbled slightly, and in an instant, lost her balance and started to fall back.

Instinctively, I reached out and caught her, pulling her against me. "I got you," I muttered, my grip firm and possessive.

Verena spun around in my arms, her face inches from mine, her breath warm against my skin. I stared down at her.

Verena Williams had kissable lips. Plush. Naturally pink. So fucking soft. And I probably could have kissed her. She was just right there.

But just as I leaned in, Mina let out a loud, impatient meow, breaking the spell. Verena and I both snapped back to reality, the moment shattered by the cat's interruption.

Verena quickly stepped back, her cheeks flushed. "Uh, thanks for catching me," she said, her voice husky.

"Yeah, whatever," I muttered, clearing my throat and trying to shake off the lingering effect of almost kissing her. "We need to get that damn cat down."

"Right," Verena said, her focus shifting back to Mina. "Come on, Mina. Let's get you somewhere safe."

With more effort than it should have taken, we finally managed to coax Mina down and corral her into the guest room, securing her in a makeshift play area. My irritation simmered beneath the surface, but my fascination with those damn lips was undeniable.

"See? That wasn't so bad," she teased, wiping tears from her eyes again.

I shot her a glare, though I couldn't help the twitch of a smile. "Not so bad? My house is a disaster, and I'm pretty sure I'm going to need antihistamines just to survive the night."

Verena patted my shoulder. "Welcome to life with a cat. It's good for you. Builds character."

"Character," I muttered, shaking my head. "I have enough character, thank you very much."

We went back into the living room, and Auntie, still beaming, suddenly looked around. "Verena, did you bring all those suitcases?"

Verena nodded. "Yep. Figured I'd move in now and make myself at home."

"Wonderful!" Auntie exclaimed. "I've always thought this place needed a woman's touch."

I looked around, suddenly noticing the subtle changes. The sterile, modern decor was softened by cozy throws, a few colorful pillows, and —was that a scented candle? The smell of vanilla was both overwhelming and strangely homey.

"You redecorated?" I asked, my voice rising with disbelief.

Verena shrugged, nonchalant. "Just a few touches. To make it feel more like home."

"Home?" I echoed, another sneeze erupting. "This is my home, and it was perfectly fine the way it was."

Verena smirked, unfazed by my indignation. "Well, now it's our home. I have a few more things I want to put up. Let me grab them out of the guest room."

I opened my mouth in horror, hoping to stop her from letting the feline demon out of her cage, but Mina darted out of the guest room the second Verena disappeared to get her things. The damn cat knocked over a stack of books, and I could feel my blood pressure rising.

"Verena!" I barked, my patience stretched thin. She appeared in the doorway with a box, completely oblivious to the pandemonium unfolding. Verena giggled as she showed us more decorative touches, pulling out items one by one, holding each one up for me to see. The first was a gaudy ceramic cat, painted in vibrant colors with a tail that looked like it might wag any second.

"Really?" I asked, raising an eyebrow.

"What's wrong with it?" Verena countered, placing the ceramic cat on the mantle where a priceless sculpture had once stood.

I gritted my teeth. "It's...unique."

She pulled out a bright pink throw pillow with glittery sequins, tossing it onto the pristine white couch. "How about this one?"

I felt my eye twitch. "It's certainly...colorful."

Then she revealed a garish neon sign that read "Live, Laugh, Love" and hung it above the entryway. "This is a classic."

I couldn't hold back any longer. "Are you trying to drive me insane?"

Verena turned to me, feigning innocence. "What? You don't like it? It's very...homey."

I sneezed again, a violent, unstoppable sneeze that echoed through the room. "I'm going to take an allergy pill."

As I turned to leave, Verena called after me. "Hey, Jae, you sure you're not just allergic to good taste?"

I shot her a look that could have melted steel. "If by 'good taste' you mean tacky decor and hyperactive cats, then yes, I might be."

She just laughed, clearly enjoying my discomfort. "Don't worry, you'll get used to it. Maybe Mina can help you develop an appreciation for the finer things in life."

"Like fur-covered furniture and constant sneezing?" I muttered, heading towards the bathroom.

Verena's voice followed me. "Exactly!"

I could hear Auntie chuckling in the background, thoroughly entertained by our banter. "You two are quite the pair. It's nice to have some life in this house."

I swallowed an allergy pill, hoping it would kick in before I succumbed to another round of sneezing. As I walked back into the living room, I saw Verena pulling out a hideous floral rug and unrolling it in the center of the room.

"Oh, come on!" I exclaimed. "Not the rug!"

Verena looked up, batting her eyelashes. "What? It ties the room together."

"It ties the room together like a hostage," I grumbled, but there was a small part of me that couldn't help but admire her tenacity.

Mina jumped onto the newly placed rug, purring contentedly. Verena beamed. "See? Mina loves it."

"Great," I said dryly. "At least someone does."

21

(FLIP)PING
VERENA

Seven Years Ago

I wanted to quit. It wasn't a fleeting thought or a moment of frustration; it was a persistent itch that I couldn't scratch away. Every time I sat down to write, my phone would ring with yet another task from Jae. The company had grown exponentially, and with that growth came an avalanche of demands. I felt like I was drowning in responsibilities that seemed endless and overwhelming.

Jae had been invited to a gala, and he had been a grumpy asshole about it all week. Barking orders about his tux, what time he had to arrive, and the speech he practiced daily. I knew it was a big ordeal for him. The company had grown even more. We'd moved into a new building, and he just kept needing more, more, more.

I was at my desk, picking things up, preparing for yet another late night. On top of the gala he wanted me to handle, there was also a crisis response I needed to negotiate. I was buried under a mountain of tasks, trying to keep my head above water. Jae had always been demanding, but this was different. He wasn't the friend I used to stay up late with, brainstorming ideas and laughing over takeout. Lately, he felt more like my boss than my friend, and it hurt. I wanted to be there for him, to support him through this critical time, but it was becoming increasingly difficult. The constant pressure and his relentless demands were taking their toll on me.

The worst part was that I understood why he was like this. The company was his dream, a way to honor his parents' legacy, and I respected that. But somewhere along the line, he had forgotten that I was more than just his assistant. I was supposed to be his partner, his confidante. Now, I felt like I was drowning in his expectations.

As I shuffled through the endless stack of papers on my desk, trying to prioritize the most urgent tasks, I couldn't shake the feeling of resentment that was growing inside me. It wasn't just about the work. It was about him not seeing me, not appreciating me. I missed the old Jae, the one who would have noticed how overwhelmed I was and offered to help.

But that Jae was gone, replaced by a workaholic who only saw the bottom line. He walked past my desk, paused, and gave me a look that made my stomach drop. "What are you still doing here?" he asked, his voice laced with irritation.

I blinked, looking up from my computer. "Uh, working?"

Jae's frown deepened. "Shouldn't you be getting ready?"

I quickly grabbed my calendar, flipping through the pages, my heart racing. Had I forgotten something? The days were becoming too short, and everything was blurring together. "No, did I miss something?"

Jae's frustration bubbled over. "The gala is tonight, Verena."

I sighed inwardly, trying to keep my patience. "Jae, I already have everything planned. Your tux is ready, your car picks you up in two hours, the hairstylist will be at your apartment. I even coordinated with Senator Greene's daughter to be your date—"

He cut me off, his voice sharp and angry. "I thought you were going."

I stared at him blankly. "You never said I was going. You said your date has to be someone respectable. You said, 'I want our outfits to coordinate,' so I reached out to your contacts and—"

"I was talking about you, Verena," he interrupted, his tone making it clear he thought I was an idiot.

"Well, that would have been nice to know," I shot back, feeling my own frustration rise. "But you gave me a list of everything I needed to do to make *you ready. I couldn't even go if I wanted to. It was hard finding you a date; you can't cancel on her now."*

"It didn't once occur to you that you were going with me?" Jae's voice was a mix of disbelief and anger.

"No, you weren't very clear about that," I replied, crossing my arms.

Jae's face reddened with anger. "You don't want to go with me, do you?" His voice was quieter now, almost hurt.

"Of course, I do," I said, my frustration bubbling over. "I just have a lot of other tasks, and you didn't tell me."

"You should have known," he snapped, his eyes flashing with anger. "You should have told me."

"Told you what?" I demanded, standing up from my desk. "That you need to be clear about what you want? That I can't read your mind?"

"Yes, damn it!" Jae exploded, his hands clenched into fists. "You should have known that I wanted you there with me. This is a really big event and I need you there by my side."

I stared at him, my heart pounding. This was more than just a misunderstanding. This was the beginning of something breaking between us. "I'm not a mind reader, Jae," I said quietly. "And I'm not a machine. I can't do everything."

His face contorted with anger and something else—something that looked like regret. "Fine," he said, grabbing a notepad and scribbling furiously. "Add these to your list." He shoved the paper at me and stormed off.

I looked down at the new tasks, my hands shaking. This was too much. I couldn't keep up with his constant demands. I wanted to scream, to tell him how unfair he was being, but I bit my tongue. I had work to do.

As I ticked off the items on the never-ending list, my mind wandered back to the early days of the company. It had been just the two of us, working late nights fueled by takeout and ambition. We had been a team. But now, it felt like I was just another cog in the machine he was building.

I couldn't help but feel a pang of hurt. Was I just his assistant now? Had he forgotten everything we had been through together? Every accomplishment, every late-night brainstorming session, every moment of triumph and failure. I shook my head, trying to push those thoughts away. I needed to focus.

Hours passed, and I was still at my desk, hunched over my work. The office was silent except for the soft hum of the air conditioning and the occasional rustle of paper. I checked my watch, realizing how late it was. The gala would be starting soon, and Jae would be there, looking polished and perfect, while I was stuck here, buried in work.

The phone rang, snapping me out of my thoughts. I picked it up, expecting another task, but it was Jae.

"Verena, where are you?"

I took a deep inhale. "At the office, finishing up the list you gave me."

There was a pause on the other end. "I'm sorry," he finally said, his voice softer. "I didn't mean to snap at you. It's just...this gala is important, and I wanted you to be there."

I closed my eyes, leaning back in my chair. "I know, Jae. But you didn't tell me that. You just gave me orders. I can't read your mind."

"I know," he sighed. "I'll make it up to you, I promise."

I wanted to believe him, but I was too tired to argue. "Okay," I said quietly.

"Get some rest," he said. "I'll see you tomorrow."

"Goodnight, Jae," I replied, hanging up the phone.

I sat there for a moment, staring at the list in front of me. Maybe tomorrow would be different. Maybe he would start seeing me as more than just his assistant. But as I gathered my things and headed home, I couldn't shake the feeling that things were changing. And I wasn't sure if it was for the better.

22

(ENGAGE)MENT

VERENA

As I stepped into the grand event hall, regret washed over me. The place looked more like a venue for the Oscars than, well, whatever the hell it was supposed to be. Jae's proposal, if I had to guess. Chandeliers cast glittering light onto a sea of formally dressed guests, and my stomach sank as I glanced down at my outfit: jeans and a chic, casual top. I'd thought this would be low-key, but Jae clearly had other ideas.

"You're late," Jae snapped as soon as I approached him, his eyes narrowing.

"Well, I didn't know the entire office was waiting for me," I retorted, irritation bubbling beneath my forced smile.

"Of course the whole office is here," he replied, his tone dripping with condescension. "Along with editors from *Forbes*, *The New York Times*, and *Wall Street Journal*."

I glanced around, feeling the weight of countless eyes on me. "You could have warned me. I would have prepared."

Jae's gaze flicked up and down my outfit. "You certainly don't look like you dressed up for the occasion."

I clenched my fists, my temper rising. "I wasn't aware of what this was. A heads-up would have been nice."

How had I ended up here? It all started with an invite from Jae, delivered in his usual no-nonsense style. A simple, elegant card that read "Please join me tonight at 7 PM." No dress code. No information. Just a town car parked outside his penthouse. He'd made it sound like a casual get-together. I'd figured it was just the public display of our engagement that Auntie was forcing on Jae. Maybe dinner at her favorite restaurant. If I could go back in time, I'd take back all my teasing about wanting a spectacle. I just wanted to make him sweat, not orchestrate an actual engagement party.

Now, I was standing in a room full of people, feeling like I'd stumbled into someone else's fairy-tale nightmare.

"Jae, what the hell is this?" I hissed, sidling up to him as discreetly as possible. He looked impeccable, of course, in a tailored tuxedo that screamed powerful CEO.

"Surprise," he said, flashing me that infuriatingly smug smile.

"Are you going to propose to me in front of everyone? And you invited newspapers?" I demanded.

"I'm a very influential person, Verena. They'll want exclusives, and it's a good PR opportunity. They'll even feature my new project," he said, completely unfazed.

I stared in disbelief.

Jae shrugged, looking unapologetically pleased with himself. "I thought it would be a good idea to show everyone how serious we are."

"I'm *serious*ly going to strangle you in your sleep."

Before I could press him further, a familiar figure approached us. Mina, Jae's new assistant, sashayed over in a cocktail dress that hugged her curves. She looked me up and down, barely concealing her disdain.

"Mr. Lee, the champagne is ready for the toast," she said. Then, she looked down her nose at me. "And the dress you prepared for Miss Williams is ready."

"Wait, you got me a dress?" I asked, unable to hide my surprise.

Jae had that infuriatingly smug look. "Of course. I couldn't have you looking bad for all the press releases. Now, go get dressed."

I rolled my eyes but couldn't suppress a small smile as I headed to the dressing room Mina gestured to, where the dress was waiting.

Hanging on a sleek hanger, it was a stunning piece: an elegant black evening gown with intricate beading along the bodice and a deep, daring neckline. The fabric was smooth and luxurious, hugging my curves in all the right places while still leaving a little to the imagination.

Slipping into the dress, I admired the way it transformed me. I felt powerful, confident, and, dare I say, beautiful. After a few adjustments and a quick touch-up to my makeup, I made my way back to the event hall, nerves tingling with anticipation.

Jae looked up as I entered, his eyes widening slightly. He stood slowly, taking in the sight of me from head to toe, his gaze intense and filled with unspoken tension. For a moment, the air between us crackled with electricity.

"You look nice," he said finally, his voice low and rough, a compliment that felt more intimate than any he'd ever given me before.

Mina was at his side in an instant. "Verena, your mother has arrived with *friends*."

I glared at Jae. "Wait. You invited my mother?!" I exclaimed, my voice a mix of disbelief and horror.

He smiled, still unfazed. "Of course. It's a family event, after all."

I turned to see my mom entering the hall, looking as if she'd rather be anywhere else. She was dressed similarly to what I wore before—jeans and a casual top—which only added to her displeasure. Flanking her were Laura and Luke, both dressed down and equally annoyed.

"Mom," I started, trying to figure out how to smooth over the mess Jae had created.

"Verena," she said, barely acknowledging Jae.

I forced a smile. "You look nice," I said, each word going up in pitch.

"I didn't realize what sort of party I was attending. We got some vague invite, and a damn limo showed up at our door."

Jae smiled. "Only the best for you, Jennifer."

My mother could have burned him with her gaze as she poked his chest. "Don't start with me, Lee. What's going on? Why did you bring us here? What are your intentions with my daughter?"

"If you just give me a moment, everything will make sense," Jae replied with a cocky smile.

Oh my God. No.

Mina handed him a microphone.

"Why does he have a microphone?" Laura asked.

Luke looked like he was going to vomit.

Auntie stepped up, resplendent in a shimmering emerald gown, complemented by the streaks of silver in her hair. Her dress, adorned with intricate beadwork, sparkled under the chandeliers, exuding an air of timeless grace. She moved with the poise of someone who was always the center of attention but carried none of the arrogance.

With a warm smile, Auntie enveloped my mom in a hug, completely oblivious to the tension crackling in the air. My mom looked slightly out of place amidst the sea of formality, yet she returned Auntie's embrace with genuine affection.

"Auntie, it's so good to see you," my mom said, her voice tinged with warmth despite the underlying discomfort.

"It's wonderful to see you too, Jennifer," Auntie replied. "I'm so glad you could make it."

Meanwhile, Jae took the mic, clearing his throat and straightening his jacket. He looked every bit the powerful CEO, with his tailored tuxedo and commanding presence. But I knew him well enough to see the faint nervousness in his eyes, a subtle flicker that only someone who truly knew him would catch.

"Good evening, everyone," Jae began, his voice commanding attention across the room. "Thank you all for coming tonight. I have an important announcement to make."

I stood there, feeling like I was watching a car crash in slow motion. Jae had never been one for grand romantic gestures, and I had a sinking feeling this was going to be painfully awkward.

"Our engagement," he continued, "is not just a personal milestone but a strategic alliance. In business, as in life, choosing the right partner is crucial for success. Verena and I have built a solid foundation over the years, collaborating and achieving together."

Oh God, he's turning this into a business presentation. I glanced around, seeing the puzzled expressions on the faces of our guests. Mom's scowl deepened, Laura rolled her eyes, and Luke looked like he was about to drag me out of here.

"In both our personal and professional lives, trust, respect, and shared goals are essential. Verena embodies these qualities, making her the ideal partner for both my life and my ventures," Jae concluded, his voice confident.

I could see Laura mouthing "What the hell?" to Luke, who clenched his fists at his side.

Jae turned to me, and I could see the determination in his eyes. He got down on one knee, holding out a small velvet box. "Verena, will you marry me?"

There was a beat of silence, the tension thick enough to cut with a knife. I glanced around at the expectant faces, feeling trapped. Backing out now would make things even worse.

"Sure," I said, trying to sound enthusiastic but knowing it came off as resigned.

Jae's eyes flickered with irritation, but he forced a smile, the kind that didn't reach his eyes. He grabbed my hand a little too firmly and slipped the ring onto my finger. It didn't fit. It was too small, pinching my skin uncomfortably.

"Hold still," he muttered through gritted teeth, shoving the ring further.

I winced. The ring itself was garish, an oversized diamond surrounded by an overabundance of tiny stones, more of a display of wealth than a symbol of love. It didn't look cute or elegant; it looked like something chosen to impress an audience rather than the person who had to wear it.

"Perfect, just perfect," I muttered under my breath, the sarcasm thick.

Jae's forced smile didn't falter, but I could see the tightness in his jaw. He leaned in close, his voice a low whisper meant only for me. "Smile, Verena. Don't ruin this."

Forcing a smile, I turned to face the crowd, my hand throbbing from the tight ring. This was not how I imagined our engagement would be, and the reality was starting to feel more like a nightmare than a dream.

"You call this an engagement? You're proposing to my daughter like she's an assistant signing a contract?" Mom's voice sliced through the moment, her eyes blazing with anger as she looked at Jae.

Jae's expression hardened, his irritation barely concealed. "Jennifer, I assure you, my intentions are entirely sincere," he replied. "This is how serious matters are handled in my world."

Mom pushed through the crowd, her face a mask of fury. "Are you insane?" she demanded, her voice cutting through the murmurs of the guests. "You haven't been dating nearly long enough. You didn't even ask for my blessing!"

Jae rolled his eyes. "Jennifer, we don't need your blessing. This is our decision."

Mom's eyes blazed with anger as she turned to me. "Verena, what is going on? This is ridiculous."

Before I could answer, Auntie stepped in, her voice overly cheerful. "Okay, let's get the mother of the bride a drink!" She gently but firmly steered Mom away from us, trying to defuse the situation.

Jae and I plastered on our best fake smiles and turned to face the crowd.

Jae leaned in, his voice low and commanding. "Keep that smile on, Verena. We need to show them we're strong and united."

I forced a brighter smile. "Lead the way, Mr. CEO," I replied, the sarcasm barely masked.

We moved through the sea of guests, exchanging pleasantries with practiced politeness. Jae's grip on my hand was firm, almost possessive, as if reminding me who was in control. The guests buzzed with excitement, their eyes flitting between us and the spectacle we had become.

"So, Verena," one of Jae's colleagues said, raising an eyebrow. "How did Jae finally convince you to say yes?"

"Oh, you know," I said breezily, "he wore me down with his relentless charm and impeccable organizational skills."

Jae shot me a sharp look, his eyes flashing with annoyance. "And

Verena's dedication and patience won me over," he added, his voice edged with a warning.

As we moved to the next group of guests, Jae leaned in close again. "Could you at least try to sound convincing?" he hissed.

"I'm doing my best," I shot back through clenched teeth. "This whole thing is your fault."

"My fault?" he whispered harshly. "You're the one who insisted on a spectacle."

"I was joking!" I retorted, maintaining my smile as we greeted another couple. "You should have known that."

"Clearly, our communication needs work," Jae muttered, his jaw tight.

Before I could respond, the emcee's voice boomed through the hall. "Ladies and gentlemen, our lovely couple will now share their first dance as an engaged pair!"

The crowd applauded, and I felt a sinking feeling in my stomach. Jae led me to the dance floor, his grip never loosening, and we took our positions, trying to ignore the sea of eyes watching our every move.

As the music started, Jae pulled me closer. "Just follow my lead," he said softly, his tone leaving no room for argument.

"I'm trying," I whispered back, my nerves making my movements stiff.

We swayed awkwardly to the music, our bodies close but our minds miles apart. The crowd watched, and I could see my mom's disapproving glare from the corner of my eye.

"You're stepping on my toes," I muttered, trying to keep my tone light.

"Then keep up," Jae replied sharply, adjusting his grip.

The song ended, and the emcee's voice rang out again. "And now, a kiss to seal the deal!"

The crowd erupted into chants of "Kiss! Kiss! Kiss!" I felt my face flush, and I glanced at Jae, who looked equally uncomfortable.

"Well, here goes nothing," he said, leaning in, his expression unyielding.

Our lips met awkwardly, a stiff and uncomfortable touch that lacked any real passion or connection. It was everything our engagement wasn't supposed to be.

As we pulled away, both of us blushing furiously, I avoided eye contact with anyone, focusing on the floor instead.

"That was terrible," Jae muttered.

"No kidding," I replied, trying to keep my voice steady.

Jae sighed, a deep, resigned sound. "Fuck it," he said abruptly, grabbing my wrist.

"Jae, what are you—" I started, but he was already pulling me off the dance floor.

Ignoring the confused stares and whispers, he dragged me through the maze of guests and into a dark, narrow hallway. Before I could protest further, he yanked open the door to a supply closet and pulled me inside, shutting the door firmly behind us.

The sudden silence was jarring. The small, dimly lit space was filled with shelves of cleaning supplies and a faint smell of disinfectant. I could feel Jae's breath, warm and unsteady, on my face.

"What the hell are you doing?" I hissed, trying to pull my wrist free from his grip.

"Fixing this goddamn train wreck," he snarled, his voice low and intense. He released my wrist with a huff, running a hand through his hair in frustration.

I took a step back, crossing my arms over my chest. "And you think dragging me into a supply closet is going to help?"

He leaned against the door, his eyes boring into mine. "I needed to get us away from them. All those prying eyes and their damn expectations. We need to talk."

"Talk?" I echoed, incredulous. "You think now is the time for a heart-to-heart?"

Jae's gaze didn't soften, the tension in his posture unyielding. "Verena, I know this is a mess. But we have to figure it out. We have to make this work. For Auntie, for your mother, for...me."

A flicker of something—hope, maybe?—stirred at his words, but it was quickly smothered by the overwhelming frustration and confusion of the night. "Jae, I don't know how to pretend anymore. I don't know how to act like this is real when it's not."

He stepped closer, his eyes intense, almost desperate. "Then let's stop pretending. Just for a moment. Let's just be...us."

And with those words, Jae grabbed my cheeks roughly and slammed his lips to mine.

LUMINOUS INDUSTRIES

FROM THE OFFICE OF JAE LEE

DATE   JUNE 24TH, 2024
FROM   JAE LEE
ADDRESSED TO   LUMINOUS EMPLOYEES
SUBJECT   TEIF PROJECT

HR didn't approve this, but let's be clear—no one tells Jae Lee what to do. I've built an empire my way, and I'm not letting a few objections stop me from delivering the best.

Erotic audio artist Apogee_Aligned has brought my vision to life, creating an immersive experience that will pull you into the next scene with incredible *sound effects.*

Whimpers...
Panting...
Dirty talk...

Want to experience it? Just provide your email, and we'll send you the link. Trust me, you won't want to miss this.

Best,
Jae Lee

Jae Lee

23

(DIS)ASTER

JAE

The instant our lips collided, the world ceased to exist. Her lips, soft and warm, tasted like pure insanity.

Regret hit me like a ton of bricks. Not because it was bad —I don't do bad decisions. No, I regretted it because I was kissing her in a damn supply closet when I needed a bed to fully unleash everything I craved to do to her.

My hands gripped her waist, yanking her closer, demanding more of her against me.

"Oh, fuck," I muttered against her mouth, the curse slipping out before I could stop it.

Verena's hands clamped onto my shoulders, her body curving into mine, responding to my touch.

"Goddamn, have you always tasted this good? Felt this good?" I whispered harshly, my voice trembling with desperation.

She moaned softly, the sound shooting straight through me, igniting a fire I couldn't control.

I needed more.

I needed all of her. My hands roamed her back, pulling her even closer until there was no space left between us.

I couldn't get enough. Not nearly enough. And I always got what I wanted.

In a swift motion, I pressed her against the wall, my body pinning hers in place. The feel of her against me, her warmth, her scent—it was overwhelming.

I was lost in her, completely and utterly lost.

"Oh. *Oh*," I exhaled, my lips trailing down her neck, tasting the salt of her skin. "Verena, please..."

Her fingers tangled in my hair, pulling me closer, and I could feel her heartbeat racing against my chest.

"We should stop," she whispered.

I pulled back slightly, just enough to look into her eyes. They were dark, filled with a mix of emotions that mirrored my own. I was drowning in them, in her.

I leaned in, capturing her lips again, pouring every ounce of my desperation, longing, and need into the kiss.

I'd buried the hope of this ever happening again so deep inside that I forgot to consider it would feel this fucking good. And now that I started, I couldn't—wouldn't—stop.

"Fuck, I need you," I whispered against her mouth, my hands sliding over her shoulders, feeling the warmth of her skin.

She arched into me, her nails digging into my shoulders, and I knew she felt it too. She had to, right? How fucking *perfect* we were together.

"Jae," she panted, her voice a soft, urgent plea.

I kissed her harder, deeper, losing myself in her entirely.

"Oh, fuck, you're so soft," I muttered, my voice breaking with the intensity of my need. "Fuck, Verena, I had no idea."

Her hands roamed over my back. "We need to stop," she whispered, her voice shaky with desire.

"Please, don't," I begged, my lips moving against her neck, tasting her skin. "Just a little more. Let me feel you, Verena."

I pressed her harder against the wall, my hands exploring every inch of her body. "I...I need..." I murmured, my breath hot in her ear. "I need to practice, to learn every part of you."

Her resolve weakened as I kissed her again, more urgently. "Please, baby, let me," I whispered. I felt her shudder beneath my touch, her resistance melting away. "Just a little more."

She pulled back slightly, her eyes meeting mine, and for a moment, everything was still.

"Jae, I...I think we've practiced enough," she said, her voice soft and filled with something I couldn't quite name.

I cleared my throat, trying to steady my racing heart. "No. I want to get this right," I said, the words sounding hollow even to my own ears. "So it looks real."

But my actions betrayed me. My hands trembled as they cupped her face, my lips moving against hers with a desperation I couldn't hide. When did she start feeling so good? Why did I crave her sighs, her moans, my name on her lips? I thought I forced these feelings down years ago.

Her taste was driving me insane.

I was the master of control, yet she unraveled me. The world at my feet, but here, pressed against her, I was powerless.

"Just practice," I muttered, my voice breaking with need. "But fuck, Verena, we...we have to practice more."

Verena nodded. "Just practice."

But as I kissed her neck, the soft skin under her ear, she let out a soft sigh that was fucking *addictive*.

I didn't think she'd ever respond to me that way.

The sound was like a drug, making me crave more, making me desperate to hear it again. "What can I do to make you sigh like that again?" I demanded, my voice low and rough.

"Hmm?" She was teasing, but I had no patience for games right now.

"That fucking sigh, Verena. Tell me how I can make you do it again." My tone was harsh, almost a growl, the need in me barely contained.

She stilled. "My...neck," she whispered, her voice trembling.

I smirked, my lips curving against her skin. "Yes, baby," I muttered, before my mouth found the sensitive spot on her neck again, determined to draw out those sweet sounds until I was a puddle at her feet.

My thigh slipped between her legs. When she whimpered, that soft, breathless sound, a groan tore from my lips.

"This isn't enough," I growled, my voice rough with need.

"I think we're done," she snapped. I felt her squirm on my thigh as she spoke.

"Like fucking hell we are. It's not real," I said, my voice rough with need. "So don't stop now."

I reached for her dress, pulling it up so I could touch what I really wanted to.

"Jae?" she asked, sounding uncertain.

"I just...need to know how you feel. Need to touch you. So I can..."

So I can do what? This wasn't practice anymore. It wasn't like I was training to fuck her with an audience—because fuck that. But the thought of walking through that room, her pleasure on my fingers... fuck, fuck, FUCK.

I'd get on my knees and beg for a chance if she'd let me.

"Hurry up and fucking touch me then, Jae," she growled, her voice laced with anger and challenge.

Shock coursed through me, freezing me in place. She saw my hesitation and pushed harder.

"It's not real, right? So if you need to figure out what I sound like when I come to make this bullshit more believable, then be a man and fucking touch me," she said.

Adrenaline surged through my veins as I fumbled with her dress, inching it up. With shaking fingers, I reached for her, my heart pounding in my chest.

I slid my hand past her panties. My thumb brushed against her, and she let out a soft sigh, the sound like music to my ears.

She leaned closer, her lips grazing mine. "You just needed to know how I feel, huh?"

I smiled weakly, my heart hammering in my chest. "I'm fucking practicing, Vee."

"Then practice harder. Rub my clit like you mean it, Jae, or I'm done."

I smirked at her demand, but my hand didn't falter. I knew this was far from practice, and I was more than happy to go all in. My fingers danced over her, teasing and tempting, driving her crazy. I could feel her heat, her pulse, her desire. It was intoxicating.

Verena's hands found their way to my hair again, gripping tight as I continued to explore her. "Jae, please..." she moaned, her voice desperate.

Her pleas only fueled me further, and I thrust my fingers deeper, finding that sweet spot that made her squirm.

"Oh God, that's it," she gasped, her legs trembling. "Don't stop."

Like hell I was going to stop. My fingers moved faster, harder. I could feel her body tightening, her breaths becoming shallow and ragged.

"I'm close, Jae," she whispered, her voice barely audible.

"Fuck, Verena, I need to hear you say my name when you come," I demanded. "You're mine right now. Give it to me."

My fingers worked her relentlessly, the need to see her unravel consuming me. "Please, Verena," I begged, my tone both commanding and desperate. "Let go. I need to feel you fall apart for me."

I continued to touch her, my fingers moving in a frenzied dance.

"I'm there," she cried out, her body trembling with pleasure. "I'm going to come. Please don't stop."

I didn't stop. I couldn't stop. My fingers kept thrusting until she reached the edge.

Her body convulsed, her moans filling the room as she came hard against my hand. I felt her heat flood my fingers, the sensation unlike anything I'd ever experienced. Her eyes rolled back, her back bowed, and those plush lips parted in pure ecstasy.

Fuck yeah, I made her come.

I made Verena Williams come all over my fucking palm.

I couldn't wait to fuck her. I couldn't wait to slide right inside her, to claim her completely.

My frantic hands reached for my belt, but she stopped me with a cruel, icy gaze. "Practice is over," she said, her voice cold and cutting.

"Wh-what?" I stammered, disbelief hitting me.

"I don't need to fuck you to convince those people out there, Jae," she rasped.

Desperation clawed at me. For the first time in years, I found myself begging. "P-please, Verena."

Her lips parted in surprise. "Are you really begging right now?"

"Please," I begged, the word escaping as a low, desperate whimper. I had never felt so on edge, so utterly at the mercy of my need for her. I was left bare, craving her touch, her approval. "I need you. Don't stop now. Please, Verena."

"Jae," she whispered, her voice trembling. "We need to go."

Voices outside the closet reminded me of the reality beyond our heated moment. People were looking for us, murmuring and calling our names.

I cursed, the frustration and desperation boiling over. "Please," I repeated, grabbing her hand and pressing it against my aching arousal. I couldn't help it. I needed her to understand, to feel what she was doing to me.

"Are you alright?" she asked, her voice filled with a mix of concern and disbelief.

My eyes closed, my mouth parting as another whimper escaped me. Her touch, even through the fabric of my pants, was electric. I had never ached this much for anyone. I moved her hand, just slightly. Just enough friction to—

"Fuckkk, Verena," I whispered, my voice breaking. "I've never needed anything like this before."

Her hand cupped me gently, and I shuddered, pressing into her touch.

And then I did something I really hadn't done in years.

I came in my pants.

From one touch.

One fucking touch, and I lost it. Unbelievable.

She looked down at the wet spot on my pants, her expression a mix of surprise and...pure elation.

"You're gonna walk out of here like that, boss?"

Her words snapped me out of my haze. Anger and embarrassment warred within me. "We're leaving," I said, my voice harsher than I intended. "This was just practice."

"Practice?" she repeated, a smirk playing on her lips. "Sure didn't feel like practice to me."

"What the fuck happened?" I demanded, trying to regain control over the situation and my own body.

She shrugged, nonchalant. "You're really going to ask that with cum dripping down your leg?"

"This was really us just getting comfortable with one another," I insisted, though my voice wavered with doubt.

She nodded, her smirk widening. "It definitely won't happen again."

Desperation clawed at my chest. I grabbed her arm, pulling her close. "It won't?"

"This was a one-time thing," she said, her tone firm and final.

"Really?" I asked, my voice betraying my need.

"Stop pouting," she said, her eyes dancing with amusement.

I schooled my face, forcing a stern expression. "I'm not fucking pouting."

"Sure, Jae. Whatever you say."

I shoved her against the wall, my hands trembling as I fixed her dress, trying to erase the evidence of our heated moment. "There. Fixed," I muttered.

She watched me. "You okay?"

"I'm fine," I snapped, but we both knew I was lying. "This was just practice."

"Just practice," she echoed, her voice soft but teasing.

I stormed out of the closet, leaving her behind, my mind a whirlwind of frustration and desire. I needed to get a grip. This was supposed to be just practice, but fuck...we had to practice more.

24

OVER(HEARD)

JAE

Six Years Ago

I was standing on the cusp of greatness, the empire I'd built from the ground up like a testament to my brilliance. Verena Williams had been by my side for every step of it, or so I thought. I'd assumed that bringing her into my world, giving her a key role in my company, would naturally draw her closer to me. But for the past year, every attempt I made to include her in my life outside of work—dinners, galas, even a simple coffee —she brushed off with some excuse or another. It was infuriating. How could I romance her if she wouldn't even give me a chance?

I stalked through the halls of Luminous, my presence commanding, my suit a perfectly tailored extension of my power. I was unstoppable, and it was time Verena saw me for what I was—a man worthy of her. The thought solidified as I made my way toward my office, but then I heard voices from the break room.

I paused, recognizing Verena's voice, sharp and unfiltered. "He's insufferable," she was saying. My steps halted, curiosity piqued. "Always demanding more, never satisfied. It's like working for a machine. Jae is driving me insane!"

The words stung more than I'd anticipated. Her coworker's voice, a *woman whose name I didn't care to remember, chimed in. "But you're his best friend! And he's so hot. Are you seriously telling me nothing's ever happened between you two?"*

Verena's laugh was cold, dismissive. "Best friend? You've got to be kidding me. Nothing's ever happened and nothing ever will. The person he is today is so not my type. I'm not interested in men who think they own the world and everyone in it."

Her words hit. I stood frozen, the reality of her rejection crashing over me. I was alone in a way I hadn't fully understood until that moment. The empire, the power, the success—none of it mattered if she didn't see me beyond the CEO title. I felt sick, a hollow ache settling in my chest.

Her coworker, sensing an opening, leaned in. "But, Verena, you've spent so much time together. There has to be something there. You've never even been tempted?"

"Sure, he's attractive in that arrogant, power-hungry way, but that's not my type. I need someone who sees me, not just another piece in their game."

"But he's done so much for you, hasn't he? Promoted you, trusted you with major projects. That has to count for something."

"Professional respect, maybe," Verena replied, her tone clipped. "There's no warmth, no real connection. Everything is transactional with him."

I clenched my fists, struggling to keep my composure. Each word was a dagger, slicing through the carefully constructed image I had of our relationship. The way she spoke about me, it was as if I was nothing more than a tyrant, a figurehead without a heart.

"Still," the coworker persisted, "you have to admit, he's got that...allure. The power, the control. Doesn't that do anything for you?"

Verena's laugh was sharper this time, almost cruel. "Allure? Please. If I ever fell for him, I'd be an idiot. He'd probably propose to me over a conference call with legal on the other line."

The coworker giggled, but the sound grated on me. "So you've never once thought about it? About what it might be like to be with him?"

"Honestly? No. I don't want someone who sees relationships as another business deal. I want someone who's present, who cares about more than just their next conquest."

Her words reverberated through me, echoing the fears I'd tried so hard to suppress. I'd thought my actions, my efforts to include her, would show her how much she meant to me. But she didn't see it. She didn't see me. To her, I was just a powerful, overbearing boss.

I couldn't listen anymore. As I stormed away, I made a decision. If Verena wanted a boss, she'd get one. I was done pining over someone who obviously would never see me the way I saw her. My feelings were a liability, a weakness I could no longer afford.

I straightened, the mask of the arrogant, untouchable CEO sliding back into place. From this point forward, Verena was just another employee. I'd still keep her close—I couldn't imagine my life without her presence—but I was done loving her. She'd never reciprocate, and I wasn't about to beg for scraps of her attention.

I marched back to my office, each step reaffirming my resolve. The softness I'd felt for her hardened into steel. I would bury these feelings deep, where they couldn't hurt me anymore. Verena would see the full extent of my ambition, my power. She'd get her boss, and nothing more.

I sat behind my desk, the city sprawled beneath me like a conquered realm. My empire was intact, my position unchallenged. But the man behind the success, the one who'd been ready to give his heart to a woman who didn't want it, he was gone. I was Jae Lee, CEO of Luminous, and I didn't have time for love.

If Verena thought I was insufferable before, she hadn't seen anything yet.

25

INTI(MATE)

VERENA

Lying in bed with Jae wasn't a new experience. We'd been through the wringer together over the years—sleeping next to each other in libraries during finals, collapsing onto a single bed after exhausting work trips, and even passing out beside each other after too many drinks at college parties. Seriously, our history was littered with mundane, non-romantic nights spent in close quarters.

But sleeping beside him after getting off in a supply closet at our totally fake engagement party while he was begging for more? Yeah, this was fucking awkward.

To make matters worse, Auntie was currently staying with us. Sneaking off to the guest room while she roamed around the three-story penthouse wasn't an option. So here I was, lying next to Jae in the master bedroom, wishing I could disappear.

"This is weird," I whispered, staring up at the ceiling, my voice barely audible in the dark.

"Just go to bed, Verena," Jae muttered beside me, irritation dripping from his words.

"Why are you grumpy?" I turned my head to look at him, but all I could see was his silhouette.

"I don't like being next to you either," he snapped, his tone harsh and dismissive.

"Oh, please," I scoffed. "I'm a much better sleeper than you. You hog the covers and talk in your sleep."

Jae dragged his hands down his face, clearly exasperated. "That's not what I mean, Vee. Go to sleep."

"You set this up," I shot back. "I'm the only one allowed to complain."

He cursed under his breath, and before I could react, he pulled me close, his grip firm and unyielding. My body stiffened as I felt the unmistakable hardness pressing against my thigh.

"I'm allowed to complain because I've been like this since the engagement party," he growled, his voice a mixture of frustration and raw need.

A laugh bubbled up before I could stop it. "Maybe you should call your doctor. Isn't there a warning about erections lasting more than six hours?"

"This isn't funny, Verena."

"Sure it is," I said, struggling to maintain a straight face. "I mean, it's a little funny. Didn't you already...you know...finish? In your, uh, pants?"

His grip on me tightened, and I could feel the tension radiating from him. "You are not allowed to ever mention that again. I'm serious, Vee."

"So am I," I replied, my voice softening slightly. "Why is *he* back?"

"He? As in my cock?"

A shiver traveled down my spine at that filthy word. "Yeah. Why is your eager little buddy back?"

"Don't ever call my *cock* an eager little buddy again, and because every time I close my eyes, all I can see is you. And then it just gets worse."

"This was your brilliant idea, remember?" I reminded him. "Now you have to deal with the consequences."

"God, you're impossible," he muttered, but there was no real anger in his voice. Instead, he sounded almost...resigned.

I shifted slightly, trying to find a more comfortable position. "Just go to sleep, Jae. We'll figure it out in the morning."

"Fine," he grumbled, loosening his hold on me just enough to allow some space. "But if I die of frustration, it's on you."

"Deal," I whispered, closing my eyes and willing sleep to come.

Ha. Come. Like I came all over his palm. God, why was I thinking about orgasms again?

"Stop thinking about it," Jae said, his voice tight with irritation. How the fuck did he always know what I was thinking?

"*You* stop thinking about it," I shot back, unable to keep the edge out of my voice. "And stop reading my mind."

"Hard to do when you're squirming. Maybe we just need to get it out of our system," he suggested, his tone shifting to something more desperate. "Do it again to prove that it was just a heat-of-the-moment kind of thing."

I opened my eyes and turned to face him, taking in his silhouette in the dim light. He was shirtless, his chest rising and falling with each frustrated breath. The shadows highlighted the definition of his muscles, and the moonlight streaming through the window made his eyes look darker, more intense.

"While your aunt is somewhere in the house? I don't think so."

He sighed, the sound heavy with frustration. "My penthouse is three floors, and it's four in the morning. She's fast asleep on the top floor, far away from us. You didn't care who was nearby when I got you off at the engagement party."

"That was different. You ambushed me."

"Just let me see if it was a fluke," he said, his voice dropping to a husky whisper. "Maybe we just need to prove to ourselves that it was a one-time thing."

"Absolutely not," I replied, trying to sound firm.

He shifted closer, his body heat making the already small space between us feel even more intimate. "Think of it as...testing a theory."

"The fact that you're trying to convince yourself that you couldn't possibly be attracted to me is offensive, Jae."

He chuckled softly. "I already knew I was attracted to you. It's your reaction to me that I want to test."

I couldn't even form words. I had to practically choke down the shock that traveled up my throat. "Excuse me?"

"You heard me. Don't make me say it again. Please, let me test it out."

"You're begging again," I said, my voice barely above a whisper.

His hand found my waist, fingers curling around my hip. His touch was gentle but firm. "Verena. Just once more. Let me see if it's real."

I could feel the tension radiating off him, the desperation in his touch. We were inches from giving in, the air between us thick and suffocating. His eyes locked onto mine, dark and intense, and he hovered over my lips, so close that I could feel the warmth of his breath mingling with mine.

"Please," he whispered again, his voice trembling. "I need to know."

He inched closer, his lips almost brushing mine. The raw need in his eyes made my heart race. His other hand slid up my side, fingers splayed across my ribs, pulling me even closer. His touch was electric, each point of contact sparking a fire that spread through my entire body.

"Jae," I murmured, but it was more of a sigh, my resolve weakening with every passing second.

"Vee, just let me..." he whispered, his voice breaking. He leaned in, his lips just a hair's breadth away from mine.

When his lips finally met mine in a tentative kiss, the sensation sent a shockwave through me, and I felt my body responding instinctively. His grip on my waist tightened, pulling me flush against him. His kiss deepened, growing more urgent, more desperate. He tasted like mint and something uniquely Jae, and it was...hell...it was *fucked up*.

Jae was an asshole.

My best friend. No—*my frenemy.*

He broke the kiss just long enough to murmur, "Verena," his voice a low, needy whimper.

My heart pounded in my chest as he moved his lips to my neck, kissing and nipping at the sensitive skin there. Every touch, every kiss was a plea, a desperate attempt to convince me. His hand slid over my nightgown, fingers tracing the curve of my waist, and I could feel the heat of his palm searing into my skin.

His mouth found its way back to mine, and he kissed me harder, more insistently.

Just as I was about to give in completely, I remembered that this was the man that tricked me, tortured me, and made me miserable.

I shoved him away, breaking the kiss with a gasp.

Jae stared at me, his eyes wide with shock and frustration, his chest heaving. "Verena!" he begged, his voice hoarse. "Just let me...test this theory a little more."

"Absolutely not," I repeated, my own voice shaky but resolute. The tension between us was nearly unbearable, but I couldn't let him have this control. Not like this. Not when it felt so dangerously real. "I had a hard night with my mom getting pissed at me. I don't want to deal with this."

He sighed deeply, pulling back. "Well, mentioning your mother officially killed my boner." I laughed despite myself, the tension breaking for a moment. "How pissed was she?"

"Very. I think she dated a guy in the mafia once. You should be very concerned about her connections, Jae."

He chuckled, the sound low and rough in the quiet room. "Great. Something else to worry about."

"We'll be fine. Or she'll just kill you. No big deal. I mean. You *did* spring a full public proposal on her just days after I told her we were *dating*."

"Did she say anything else to you?" Jae asked, his voice still rugged with leftover frustration.

"No, luckily I was able to escape before she could corner me, but I have about four hundred missed calls. I'm sure she'll show up here at your house soon. We really have to figure this out, or I'm going to have to tell her the truth, Jae. She's not buying it."

"What did you tell her about me to make her hate me so much?" Jae's brow furrowed, a hint of genuine curiosity in his tone. "Your mom used to love me."

I sighed, feeling the weight of the explanation I knew I had to give. "It's not just me complaining about a boss, Jae. My mom witnessed it. All the times you called me in during holidays, family gatherings, special events."

Jae interrupted, a defensive edge to his voice. "Yeah? Well, maybe you should have invited me over for Christmas morning."

"What?" I asked, taken aback by the unexpected response.

He shook his head, rolling his eyes. "Nothing."

"No, tell me," I insisted.

Jae exhaled sharply, his shoulders slumping. "You know, sometimes I wished you'd invite your best friend over for the holidays, Vee. A few years ago, you stopped including me. I have no one. Auntie was all the way in Korea. My parents are gone. And every holiday, I was left alone in this big, empty house." His voice grew softer, more vulnerable. "But I guess you didn't want to invite your boss to Thanksgiving dinner or Christmas morning."

His words hit me, a pang of guilt and sadness settling in my chest. "Jae, I...I didn't know you felt that way."

He rolled over, his back to me, his voice now just a whisper. "Yeah, well, I didn't want to be alone, Vee. So I came up with bullshit excuses to make you work on the holidays. I'm sorry, but that's the truth."

I reached out instinctively, but hesitated, my hand hovering just above his shoulder. "Jae, I...I'm so sorry. I didn't realize. You should have said something."

"Goodnight, Verena," he muttered, his voice tight.

I stared at his back, feeling a lump forming in my throat. I wanted to say something, to comfort him, to apologize for not seeing the loneliness he had been hiding behind his demanding exterior. But the words wouldn't come. Instead, I lay there in the dark, the significance of his confession pressing down on me, making it impossible to sleep.

My mind raced, replaying every holiday, every missed invitation, every time I had cursed him for ruining my plans without considering why he might have done it. The realization that Jae had been using work as an excuse to avoid being alone hit me hard. And suddenly, all the anger I had felt toward him seemed misplaced, replaced by a deep sense of regret.

I wanted to reach out, to touch his shoulder, to let him know that I understood now. But I hesitated, afraid that my touch might make things worse. Instead, I lay there, staring at the ceiling, feeling the distance between us more acutely than ever.

"Jae," I whispered, my voice barely audible in the darkness. "I'm sorry."

He didn't respond, and I wasn't sure if he had heard me or if he was already asleep. But the silence that followed felt heavy, filled with unspoken words and unresolved feelings. I knew that things between us had shifted, that the barriers we had built over the years were beginning to crumble. And as I lay there, the warmth of his body just inches away, I realized that maybe, just maybe, there was a chance for us to bridge the gap that had grown between us.

26

(FAKE)R

VERENA

The luxurious sheets tangled around me as I rolled over, stretching out across Jae's bed. It felt strange being here, especially after the mess we'd gotten ourselves into. I could hear noises from the kitchen—clattering and what sounded like a frustrated mutter. Curiosity piqued, I slipped out of bed, padding softly towards the source of the commotion.

Leaning against the doorway, I took in the sight of Jae attempting to make breakfast. Pancake batter was splattered everywhere, and he was fumbling with a spatula, looking incredibly out of his element. His bare chest glistened with a light sheen of sweat, muscles flexing as he moved. The sight was almost too much to handle, especially after everything that had happened yesterday.

"You don't know how to cook," I stated, amused at the sight.

Jae glanced up, his dark eyes locking onto mine with a mix of frustration and something else—something hotter, more intense. "I'm trying, okay? Auntie says I need to make more effort for you."

I couldn't help but laugh. "You'd rather poke an eye out than be forced to cook. It's a waste of your precious time."

He rolled his eyes, turning back to the skillet and attempting to flip a pancake. It landed half on, half off the skillet, looking more like a mess than a meal.

"How'd you sleep?" he asked, his eyes trailing over me as I stretched, my silk nightgown riding up slightly.

"Fine," I replied, enjoying the way his gaze lingered on me. "You?"

"Not great," he admitted, his eyes snapping back up to meet mine. "I want to add a clause to the contract."

I raised an eyebrow, intrigued. "What clause?"

"You need different pajamas."

I looked down at my nightgown, arching a brow. "What's wrong with this?"

He cleared his throat, his eyes flicking away and then back to mine, filled with a heat that was impossible to ignore. "Pants. You need pants and a long sleeve shirt."

I snorted, unable to hide my amusement. "Whatever."

But as I walked closer, passing by him to get a glass of water, I felt his hand gently brush against my arm. I turned to face him, noticing the way his eyes darkened, his voice dropping to a husky whisper.

"Please," he said, the word filled with a desperate edge. "Change clothes."

I enjoyed the power I seemed to have over him. "Since when are you so...?"

He swallowed hard, his eyes locked onto mine. "So what?"

I leaned in slightly, my voice a teasing whisper. "Distracted."

His jaw clenched, and I saw a muscle twitch in his neck. "You have no idea."

I stepped even closer, our bodies nearly touching. "I think I have some idea."

Jae let out a frustrated groan, running a hand through his hair. "I can't concentrate when you wear that."

I smirked, feeling a thrill at his admission. "Maybe you just need more practice."

He inhaled sharply, his eyes following every movement I made. "Verena..."

Before he could say more, Auntie came down the stairs, her face lighting up as she saw us. "Aww, you're cooking, Jae!"

Jae forced a smile, stepping back slightly. "Just trying to be helpful."

Auntie beamed, patting his shoulder. "Such a good boy."

I stifled a laugh as Jae's jaw tightened. The smell of burning pancakes filled the air, and I quickly moved to open a window.

"Maybe I should take over before you set off the smoke alarm," I teased, pushing him gently aside.

"Be my guest," he muttered, stepping back and crossing his arms. "Just don't burn the place down."

As I salvaged what I could from the pancake disaster, Auntie sat at the table, clearly pleased with the domestic scene. "It's so nice to see you two working together."

"Yeah, teamwork makes the dream work," I quipped, placing a somewhat edible-looking pancake on a plate.

Jae watched me, a small smile tugging at his lips despite his earlier frustration. "I think it's safe to say cooking isn't my strong suit."

I laughed, shaking my head. "You think?"

Auntie clapped her hands, her eyes twinkling. "You should ask Jennifer to teach you, that way the two of you can bond."

"It's gonna take a lot more than cooking lessons," I muttered.

Auntie either ignored me or didn't hear me, because she changed the subject. "This reminds me of when you two came to visit me that summer you were in college. Always bickering but inseparable."

Jae and I exchanged a glance, and for a moment, it felt almost normal. Almost like the old days before things got complicated.

Auntie sighed contentedly. "I'm so proud of you two. Seeing you in love like this is everything I ever hoped for."

Jae's eyes met mine, and there was a flicker of something—maybe guilt, maybe something else. "Yeah," he said softly. "In love."

I turned away, focusing on flipping another pancake. The lines between what was real and what was pretend were blurring dangerously.

"So," I said, trying to lighten the mood. "What's on the agenda for today?"

Auntie perked up. "Shopping! I want to buy Verena some cute new outfits. Jae, you're coming with us."

Jae's eyes widened. "Today?"

"Yes, today!" Auntie insisted. "No time like the present."

I shot Jae a look. "Guess we're going shopping."

He sighed, resigning himself to the plan. "Fine. But I'm not trying on anything ridiculous."

Auntie patted his arm. "Don't worry, dear. You'll look dashing in whatever we find."

Just as we were about to finish cooking breakfast, the doorbell rang. Jae opened it to reveal his new assistant, Mina, standing there with a stack of documents. She was dressed to the nines in a short dress that screamed "look at me."

"Oh yay, Mina's here," I said sarcastically, and as if summoned, our rescue cat, also named Mina, came bolting from whatever depths of hell she was hiding in and ran into the kitchen.

The assistant, Mina, stepped inside, her eyes widening as she took in the chaotic scene. "Good morning, Jae," she purred, her gaze lingering on him before flicking to me. "I brought those urgent documents you needed."

Auntie, ever the gracious host, ushered her in. "Come in, dear. Have some breakfast."

The *cat* Mina, seizing the moment, leaped onto the kitchen counter, her tail flicking dangerously close to the pancake batter. Jae sneezed violently, the sound startling everyone.

"Mina!" Jae barked, both at the cat and the assistant, though only one of them seemed to notice. The cat stared back defiantly, while Assistant Mina looked confused.

"Did I come at a bad time?" she asked, her voice full of false sweetness. Her gaze lingered on him, clearly appreciating the view. Jae needed to put a freaking shirt on.

Jae's face was a blend of frustration and irritation, but he maintained his polite demeanor. "I didn't know you were coming by. You could have emailed these documents. I don't normally allow house visits from employees."

"I just wanted to drop these off," she said, holding up the documents as if they were the Holy Grail. "But it seems I'm intruding on family time."

Auntie clapped her hands. "Nonsense! We have plenty of food and you're welcome to join us."

The assistant's eyes flicked to our cat. "I didn't know you have a cat, Jae."

"I don't," Jae said flatly, sneezing again. "I'm allergic to cats."

I chimed in, a mischievous grin on my face. "He hates cats. But I couldn't help it; I had to rescue this sweet baby."

Jae grumbled, "She's the devil."

I shot him a mock glare. "Don't talk about Mina that way."

The assistant looked confused, glancing between us. "The cat's name is Mina, too?"

"Yep," I said cheerfully. "It's a common name in our household."

Assistant Mina's smile faltered slightly. "Oh...okay."

The cat Mina, clearly enjoying the attention, started knocking over utensils, creating even more of a mess. Jae sneezed again, louder this time, causing the cat to leap gracefully.

I struggled to maintain composure as the assistant flirted subtly with Jae, who was oblivious to the dynamics at play.

"Jae, you have a lovely home," Assistant Mina said, her eyes lingering on him a little too long.

"Thanks," Jae replied, rubbing his nose. "Just trying to make it cozy for Verena."

I bit my lip, resisting the urge to roll my eyes. "Yes, very cozy."

Auntie beamed. "Isn't it wonderful to see a couple so in love?"

Assistant Mina's smile tightened. "Yes, quite."

Before the tension could escalate further, Jae's phone rang. He glanced at the screen, his expression turning serious. "Excuse me," he said, stepping aside to take the call.

Cat Mina took this opportunity to knock over the stack of papers, sending them flying across the floor. Jae's sneezes echoed from the hallway as he tried to manage the phone call and his allergies simultaneously.

I moved to gather the scattered documents, but Assistant Mina was quicker, her dress riding up as she bent over. "I'll get these," she offered, giving Jae a clear view of her...assets.

I shot a glare at her, my irritation mounting. "No need, I've got it."

She straightened up, handing me the papers with a saccharine smile. "Of course. Just trying to help."

The door closed behind Jae as he finished his call, his expression grim. "I'm sorry," he said, looking at me and Auntie. "I have to deal with an emergency at work. I'll be back as soon as I can."

Auntie nodded, understanding. "Of course, dear. Do what you need to do."

Assistant Mina shot me a smug look. "Looks like we'll be busy today. I'll try not to keep him out too late."

I forced a smile. "Work comes first."

The door closed behind her, and I sighed, feeling the weight of the situation pressing down on me. This fake engagement was becoming more complicated by the minute, and I had no idea how we were going to keep up the charade.

Auntie looked at me with a concerned expression. "Are you alright, dear?"

I nodded, trying to muster up some enthusiasm. "Yeah, just hard giving up my old job."

Auntie patted my hand. "Don't worry. Everything will work out."

Just then, cat Mina decided to leap from the counter to the table, landing directly in front of Auntie. She giggled and scratched her behind the ears. "Such a mischievous little thing."

I shook my head, smiling despite myself. "She certainly keeps things interesting."

As Auntie continued to fawn over the cat, I couldn't help but feel a mixture of emotions swirling within me. On one hand, I cherished Auntie like family and was grateful for the opportunity to spend more time with her.

But on the other hand, the reality of our situation loomed over me like a dark cloud. Jae's demanding job, Auntie's high expectations, and our own unresolved feelings felt like a precarious balancing act. One wrong step could send everything crashing down, and the pressure was mounting.

Part of me was relieved to be away from the constant grind of work, grateful for the chance to take a step back and breathe. But another part of me felt conflicted, knowing that things weren't running as smoothly without me. I had always been an integral part of the company, and it was hard to just cut that off cold turkey. I cared deeply about the business and the people in it, and that care was what had made me good at my job.

Yet here I was, caught between my responsibilities and my love for Auntie. It was a delicate balance, and I was determined to navigate it as best as I could. I just hoped that, in the process, I wouldn't lose myself or the things that mattered most to me.

27

(CAN)CER

VERENA

Five Years Ago

Jae called me into his office. He was sitting behind his massive mahogany desk, fingers steepled under his chin, looking more stressed than usual. As I walked in, he looked up, his eyes dark and intense.

"We're going to Korea," he said, his voice clipped.

I blinked, taken aback. "Uh, we have all these projects, Jae."

He raised an eyebrow, clearly expecting a fight. "Everything's covered. The team is prepped and ready to handle the workload."

I wasn't convinced. "The McAllister project? The one you've been micromanaging for weeks?"

He waved a hand dismissively. "Derek's taking over."

"And the Martinez proposal? We're supposed to meet with them tomorrow."

"Priya's got it under control."

I frowned, not ready to give up. "The new interns? You've been obsessing over their training."

"Ben will oversee their progress."

I sighed. "What about the quarterly review? The investor's meeting? The charity event next weekend?"

"Handled, managed, and postponed," he replied curtly.

I was running out of excuses. "Jae, I have plans. A trip with you sounds… terrible. Every day you've been worse and worse. Our friendship has changed. You're more like a full-time boss now, not the friend I used to know."

He cut me off, his voice softening. "Auntie was diagnosed with cancer. We're going to Korea."

My breath caught in my throat, and my eyes immediately filled with tears. This wasn't the brusque, domineering Jae I'd been dealing with lately. This was my friend, vulnerable and scared. "Oh my God, Jae, I'm so sorry."

He cleared his throat, clearly uncomfortable with the emotion in the room. "I'll need you there, Verena. I can't do this alone."

I nodded, my voice trembling. "Okay. When are we leaving?"

"Tonight," he said simply.

Without thinking, I crossed the room and gave him a hug, something I hadn't done in a long time. He stiffened at first, then cautiously hugged me back for a brief moment before pulling away and clearing his throat.

"Prepare everything," he said, reverting to his businesslike tone. "We need flights, accommodations, transport, and notify everyone on the team. Make sure they know how to reach us in case of an emergency. Also, get our documents in order, check the visa requirements, and handle any legal issues that might come up while we're gone. Coordinate with Auntie's doctors here and make sure we have all her medical records. And pack a bag for yourself— you'll need professional attire and something comfortable for the plane."

The list was meticulous, typical of Jae. I nodded, absorbing the enormity of the task ahead. "Got it," I said, turning to leave.

"Verena," he called after me. I paused, looking back. "Thanks."

His gratitude was simple, but it warmed me in a way I hadn't felt in a long time. "Of course, Jae," I said softly, walking out of his office with a renewed sense of purpose. This wasn't just a business trip; it was a mission to support the person who had always been there for me, no matter how much things had changed.

28

(PROMISE)D

VERENA

Walking into the tiny boutique with Auntie, I marveled at the explosion of colors and patterns. Every rack was bursting with summer clothes—flowy dresses, bold prints, and, of course, bikinis. Auntie, ever the troublemaker, zeroed in on the swimwear section with a gleam in her eye.

"Alright, darling, today's the day," she declared, grabbing a neon pink bikini off the rack. "I'm going to greet the afterlife looking sexy as hell."

I snorted, trying to keep up with her. "Auntie, you're really going to buy a bikini?"

She shot me a wicked grin. "Why not? I want to be buried in one. Figure if I'm going out, I might as well do it looking fabulous."

I laughed. "You're something else, you know that?"

She held up a fiery red bikini against her chest, examining herself in the mirror. "You know, I was always too scared to wear one of these. Always thought my body wasn't good enough, that people would judge. Now it just seems so silly."

I picked up a sleek black bikini, turning it over in my hands. "I get it. I've always felt the same way."

Auntie's eyes softened. "Well, darling, it's high time we both stop caring about what other people think. Life's too short, especially mine."

I blinked, trying to mask the sting of her words with a smile. "You're right. Let's do this."

We headed to the dressing rooms, Auntie still cracking jokes. "If I'm going to haunt anyone, I want them to remember me in a hot bikini. None of this frumpy ghost nonsense."

I laughed, despite the lump in my throat. "You'd be the sassiest ghost around."

"Damn straight," she said, wiggling into her bikini and stepping out, striking a pose. "What do you think? Ready to make the afterlife jealous?"

"You look amazing," I said, and I meant it. She was radiant, even with the shadow of her illness looming over us.

I emerged in my own bikini, feeling more confident than I expected. Auntie's approval was immediate and enthusiastic. "Verena, you look stunning! See? We've still got it!"

We bought our bikinis, and as we walked out, Auntie's coughing fit returned. She waved me off when I reached out to steady her. "I'm fine, just a little winded. Dying's a real workout, you know?"

"Auntie, you sure you're okay?"

She nodded. "Yes, darling. Now let's get to the car before I drop dead in the parking lot. That would really ruin my plans for a stylish exit."

"Wouldn't want that," I said, chuckling softly. "You've got to save the grand finale for a more dramatic location."

"Exactly," she said with a wink. "Maybe the opera. Or a masquerade ball."

As we strolled towards the car, I tried to keep the mood light. "You know, Auntie, you could make a whole line of ghost bikinis. 'Haunt in style.'"

She laughed, a rich, genuine sound. "And I'd be the cover model, of course. *Ghostly Glamour Magazine*."

"I can see it now," I said, grinning. "You'd be a sensation."

She started coughing again. "Auntie, maybe I should take you to the hospital."

"Oh, hush. I'm just trying to add some drama to my performance."

I shook my head, trying to keep my voice steady. "You don't need to try. You're naturally dramatic."

She leaned on me slightly as we walked, and I held her a little tighter. "Remember, darling, if I collapse, you'd better make it look like a fainting spell from a movie. Elegant and tragic."

"I promise," I said, my voice tinged with sadness. "I'll make sure you go out with all the flair you deserve."

"You know, Verena, I'm not afraid of dying. I'm just sad about leaving you. And about missing out on all the things I wanted to do."

Tears pricked my eyes, but I blinked them away. "I know, Auntie. I'm going to miss you so much."

I forced a smile, but inside, my heart was heavy. With all the fake engagement and the constant hustle of maintaining appearances, it was easy to avoid the why of it all. Auntie was dying. Really dying. And now that we'd walked the mall, the symptoms were impossible to ignore.

She didn't seem sick most of the time—she was full of life and energy, always the first to laugh, always ready with a kind word or a warm hug. But there were little hints, barely noticeable unless you were looking for them. Like how she went to bed earlier than she used to, her once boundless energy fading a little more each day. How she seemed more tired after simple tasks, her steps a bit slower, her breaths a bit more labored.

"Are you okay, Auntie?" I asked, my voice tinged with worry as she coughed, the sound harsh and rattling. "I mean, really okay? You sound like you're struggling to breathe."

"I'm fine," she replied, her words coming in short gasps. "Just a little out of breath. Don't worry about me."

But how could I not worry? Every cough, every labored inhale, was a reminder that our time with her was running out. It wasn't fair. Auntie, with her endless positivity and strength, didn't deserve this.

Cancer didn't care about fairness. It didn't care about how much life you still had left to live, or how many moments you still wanted to share. It's a thief in the night, stealing away the vibrant essence of someone you love, leaving you to grapple with the hollow truth of their mortality. The reality of losing Auntie was like a shadow that darkened every corner of our lives, and no amount of pretending could make it right. This was as bad as it seemed, and it wasn't something that could be fixed or made better. Some things can only be carried.

I wanted to pretend. I pretended when I focused on the humor of my fake engagement, laughing off the absurdity of our situation to distract myself. I pretended when I selfishly thought about my own pain, my own grievances, letting them eclipse the much larger suffering unfolding before me. I pretended when I didn't notice the way Jae was clinging to me because pretty soon he would have no one to cling to.

I pretended because acknowledging the truth meant accepting the inevitable loss, and I wasn't ready for that. Not now, not ever.

But the signs were there, clear and undeniable.

I helped Auntie into the town car Jae had set up for us, her steps slow and careful. She settled into the seat with a sigh, her weariness evident despite her attempts to hide it.

"You didn't buy a lot," she remarked, trying to shift the focus away from her condition.

"I had more fun watching you shop," I replied, forcing a lightness into my voice that I didn't feel.

Auntie shook her head, a twinkle of mischief in her eyes despite her fatigue. "You need photos for the magazine shoot. Didn't Jae's assistant tell you? They want to feature your engagement. There will be an interview."

I blinked in surprise, feeling a surge of frustration. "An interview? Mina didn't mention anything about that." Of course she didn't. I was really starting to not like her.

"Are you okay, Verena?" Auntie asked, her gaze soft and concerned.

"I'm just...worried about you," I admitted, my voice breaking slightly.

"Let's not talk about that," Auntie said gently, her eyes shining with a combination of determination and something else—something that made my heart ache even more. "I want to focus on the wedding. We should plan for something next month."

I sputtered, barely able to contain my shock. "Next month?!"

"Of course," she replied, her tone resolute. "I want to see the wedding."

Guilt and sadness washed over me, threatening to drown me in their relentless tide. Here she was, planning for her death by focusing on the joy of a marriage she didn't even realize was fake. The very thought made my chest tighten, a knot of grief forming in my throat. How could I let her down? How could I shatter her hopes when she was clinging to them so desperately?

Auntie was pouring every bit of her dwindling energy into the idea of seeing Jae and me happily married. She was planning for a future she knew she wouldn't be a part of, and the weight of that realization crushed me. She wanted to see the wedding. She needed to see it, as if it were a beacon of hope amidst the darkness of her illness.

"Don't you think that's a little soon?" I asked, my mind racing.

"You're nervous? Is it your mom?" Auntie's eyes softened with understanding. "Don't worry, I invited Jennifer over for dinner tonight. We're going to smooth this all over."

"You did?" Panic surged through me. I still had about a bazillion missed calls and texts from my mom. "Does Jae know about dinner?"

"I told his assistant. It'll be great," Auntie assured me.

As the car started moving, I glanced out the window, my thoughts a chaotic whirl. We were racing against time, against the inevitable.

Auntie took a deep breath, her voice softening. "Let's cook together, Verena. I want to teach you how to make Jae's favorite meal." Tears filled her eyes, and she blinked them away quickly. "I think it would mean a lot to him. It's a traditional Korean dish—kimchi jjigae."

I nodded, swallowing the lump in my throat. "Of course, Auntie. I'd love to learn."

When we got back to the penthouse, Auntie led me to the kitchen. She moved with a purpose, opening the refrigerator and cabinets and pulling out ingredients: napa cabbage, pork belly, tofu, garlic, green onions, and bottles of red chili paste and flakes, called gochujang and gochugaru. She set them all on the counter, her movements sure and steady despite the fatigue I knew she was feeling.

"First, you need to make the kimchi," Auntie said, her voice filled with warmth and nostalgia. "This is the heart of the dish. Our mother taught me how to make it, and I taught Jae's father after she passed."

We worked side by side, slicing the cabbage and mixing it with the gochujang and gochugaru. Auntie explained each step, her hands moving deftly as she spoke. "You need to massage the spices into the cabbage, make sure it's evenly coated. This is where the flavor comes from."

I followed her instructions, my fingers tingling from the spicy concoction. As we worked, Auntie told me stories about Jae's father, her eyes shining with fond memories. "We used to make this in our parents' kitchen. Jae's father would sneak pieces of kimchi before it was ready. He had no patience."

She laughed softly, a sound that was both joyful and tinged with sadness. "We would sit together, eating kimchi jjigae and talking about our dreams. Those were the best times."

I listened, absorbing the stories and the love that infused her words. Auntie wiped a tear from her cheek, her smile trembling. "I always wanted to make this for Jae's children one day. I imagined us all sitting around the table at my parents' old home in Korea, sharing this meal and creating new memories."

My heart ached at the thought, her unfulfilled dreams pressing down on me. I reached out, squeezing her hand gently. "We'll make sure this recipe is passed down, Auntie. I promise."

She smiled through her tears, nodding. "Thank you, Verena."

We continued cooking, adding the pork belly to the pot and letting it brown before adding the kimchi and water. The rich aroma filled the kitchen, a comforting scent that wrapped around us like a warm embrace. Auntie showed me how to prepare the tofu and green onions, her hands steady despite the tremor in her voice.

"Jae loves this dish," she said softly. "It always reminds him of his parents."

This wasn't just about cooking a meal; it was about preserving memories, honoring the past, and creating a sense of continuity in a world that felt increasingly uncertain.

As the kimchi jjigae simmered on the stove, we took breaks to let the flavors meld. Auntie and I moved to the living room, where she showed me old family photos and shared more stories about Jae's childhood. It was a rare glimpse into a side of him I rarely saw, and my heart ached for the boy who had lost so much.

Hours passed, and we returned to the kitchen to check on the jjigae, adding tofu and green onions, letting it cook a little longer. The anticipation built with each passing minute, the aromas growing richer and more inviting. I couldn't help but feel a deep sense of gratitude for this moment, for the opportunity to share in this tradition.

"Thank you for teaching me, Auntie," I said, my voice thick with emotion. "This means more than you know."

She smiled, her eyes filled with a mixture of sadness and joy. "It's my pleasure, Verena. I'm so glad we could share this."

29

MIS(COMMUNICATIONS)

JAE

Working late at the office was my playground. I thrived on solving problems and managing crises. But tonight was different. As I sifted through contract revisions and financial reports, my mind kept wandering back to Verena. Damn her. I was irritated, distracted, restless. She'd invaded my thoughts, and it was driving me insane.

Mina, my new assistant, had been hovering around all damn day. Efficient, sure, but her constant flirting grated on my nerves. Usually, I'd welcome the attention because it was a welcome distraction from the fact that the person I actually wanted thought I was an asshole, but tonight, I just wanted to get the hell out and go home to Verena.

Mina leaned over my desk, her blouse gaping open a bit too much. "Mr. Lee, I think we might have to pull an all-nighter to get this contract revised properly," she purred, batting her eyelashes.

I sighed, barely glancing up from my computer. "It can wait."

She looked taken aback. "But it's important. We need to get it done tonight."

"Didn't you hear me?" I snapped, my eyes finally locking onto hers with a cold stare. "I said it can wait. Go home."

"I'm just trying to help, Mr. Lee," she said softly, but the tone was artificially pouty, like she was baiting me to comfort her.

"Let legal look over it and send it to me. I can review it at home," I replied curtly, already feeling the pull to leave.

Mina stepped closer, her perfume a cloying cloud that made me miss Verena's subtle, clean scent. Her tone dropped to a suggestive whisper. "Want me to come home with you? We can go over it together, just like you and Verena used to."

I stiffened. "We need to establish professional boundaries, Mina."

Her expression faltered, but she quickly recovered, a coy smile playing on her lips. She placed a manicured hand on my shoulder, leaning in so close I could feel her exhales. "Verena always worked closely with you. I was hoping for that sort of relationship."

"Verena is irreplaceable, and you're out of line. Don't push your luck."

The comparison was jarring. Verena had always been professional, her touches never more than a brief brush of fingers passing a document or a pat on the back for a job well done. Her presence had been comforting, grounding, something I relied on more than I realized.

Mina's touch felt invasive, her intentions too obvious and unwanted.

I pushed my chair back and stood, towering over her. "If you can't be professional, you'll find yourself without employment. Do you understand?"

She recoiled slightly but then pouted again, attempting one last seductive move. She traced a finger down the front of my shirt. "Are you sure, Mr. Lee? Verena always understood your...needs. I thought I could do the same."

Disgust churned in my stomach. The way she tried to manipulate her position, the way she insinuated herself into a role that was never hers to take, made my skin crawl. Verena never used her closeness to me for personal gain. She was genuine, honest, and her loyalty was unquestionable.

I grabbed her wrist, removing her hand from my shirt with a firm grip. "Verena earned her place. You're just overstepping. Don't confuse the two."

Mina stepped back, her face falling into a mask of hurt and confusion. "Yes, Mr. Lee. I understand."

Without another word, I grabbed my briefcase and stormed out of the office. Irritation and guilt gnawed at me. I checked my phone and saw twelve missed calls. My stomach sank as I scrolled through the texts from Auntie.

Auntie: Where are you? We're supposed to have dinner with Verena and her mom.

Auntie: Jae!!

Auntie: Please call me.

How the fuck could I forget this? I never let things slip through the cracks. This was unacceptable. I raced to my car, cursing under my breath. "Mr. Jameson, hurry. We need to get home now," I barked at my driver.

As the car sped through the city streets, dread gnawed at me. Verena's mom was already skeptical of me, and this wouldn't help. I had to be there for Verena, make sure Auntie was okay, be part of this makeshift family we were pretending to build.

But now, I was late. Very late.

I slammed my fist against the car door in frustration. How the hell did I let this happen? The thought of Verena's disappointed eyes made my chest tighten.

Mr. Jameson weaved through traffic with a skill I was grateful for, but the minutes felt like hours. As we neared home, I straightened my tie and steeled myself for the fallout. There was no room for error tonight. I couldn't afford to screw this up any further.

Pulling out my phone, I dialed Verena's number. She picked up on the second ring. "Hey, baby," she said. I knew for damn sure she had an audience and the only reason she'd call me that was if people were listening. But that endearment went straight to my cock. How could just her voice make me hard? Even though she sounded pissed, I wanted her to greet me that way every fucking day. I was already trying to figure out ways to make people stand around her every time I called.

"Where the hell are you?" she demanded.

"I'm rushing home right now," I replied, my tone urgent. "I'm so sorry, baby."

"Dinner is getting cold, and my mother has been here for hours," she snapped.

Guilt churned in my stomach. "I'm sorry. I'm hurrying."

"I'm used to you overworking," she said, her voice clipped.

"I'll make it up to you," I promised, trying to inject sincerity into my voice.

She paused, her tone softening slightly. "H-how?"

A smirk formed on my lips. "More practice."

She cleared her throat, clearly flustered. I could hear her feet padding across the tile as she walked away from any listening ears. "Oh, you had a busy day. Yes...mm-hmm." Then, she started hissing at me. "What the hell are you thinking?! My mother is right there, and you can't—"

"I want to know how you taste," I growled, unable to suppress my desire. "I crave the way your sweetness lingers on my tongue. I want to drown in it, lose myself in you."

"Jae, I don't know what's gotten into you—"

"That makes two of us."

"You can't just...you can't say shit like that."

"You can't deny the heat between us," I whispered. "I want to feel your body writhe with pleasure against my tongue. And I promise you this, baby, when I finally plunge myself inside you, you'll be moaning my name."

She was momentarily speechless. The soft gasp that escaped her lips was unmistakable over the phone line. I knew I had her attention now.

"That's n-not in the contract," she stammered. "You're so wicked."

The word *wicked* rolled around my brain, a promise of the dark, twisted desires that I was about to unleash. My voice was laced with desperation as I spoke into the phone, craving her touch and longing to show just how much I needed her. "Baby, I'll be getting home soon," I rasped, picturing every seductive move I would make once I arrived.

"And when I do, there will be no holding back." My desire for her burned hot and fierce, driving me wild with aching need.

"We have dinner with my mother."

"Then after dinner…"

"I'm moving into the guest room."

"Like hell you are."

"Let me make one thing abundantly clear, Jae. The only way you'll get anything from me is if you're begging on your knees, and even then, I'd be difficult to convince."

I imagined that for a moment. Her in heels, looking down at me as I kissed a trail up her leg, pleading for a taste. "I'd be more than happy to beg. And being on my knees just puts me that much closer to what I want. See you soon, Verena."

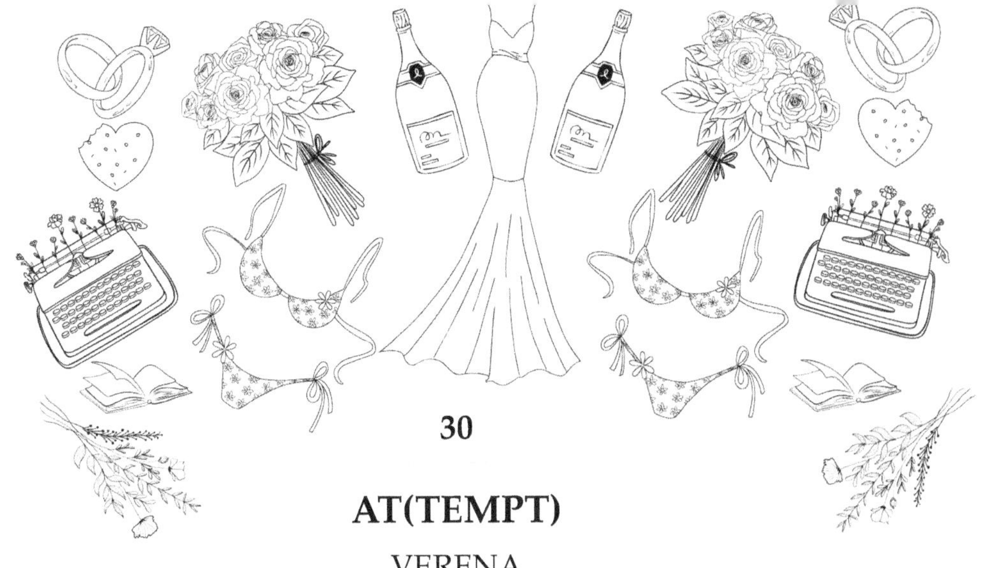

30

AT(TEMPT)

VERENA

I couldn't shake the feeling of Jae's words. *"There will be no holding back..."* They echoed in my mind, making me question everything. What had gotten into him? Maybe it was a weird version of grief, a distraction from the pain of Auntie's illness. Yes, that had to be it. He was using this fake engagement to cope. But still, we needed way more rules. Because this couldn't happen. It wouldn't, no matter what he said.

"Vee?" My mom's voice cut through my thoughts. "Are you even listening to me? Where is Jae, I thought he wanted this dinner."

Auntie cleared her throat. "I'm so sorry, Jennifer. I must have told him the wrong time."

"He'll be here soon," I replied, trying to keep my voice steady.

The door swung open, and in strutted Jae, clutching a bouquet of flowers like he was a doting son-in-law. Really? He found time to pick up flowers while I was stuck here, under the laser focus of my mom's interrogation glare?

"Oh, flowers," Mom said, "This feels familiar."

Jae flashed his award-winning smile at Mom and Auntie before turning his full attention to me. With no warning whatsoever, he swooped in and kissed me, his lips moving against mine with a kind of fervor that made the room spin. For a second, I lost myself in the kiss, forgetting all about our audience. When he finally pulled back, he murmured against my lips, "We have to make it believable, right?"

I narrowed my eyes at him, shooting a silent promise that this wasn't over. "Right."

We sat at the table, the flowers now sitting in a vase that Auntie had eagerly provided. The air was thick with tension as Mom's gaze shifted between us, clearly suspicious.

"So, Jae," Mom started. "Tell me about your intentions with my daughter."

Jae straightened, a charming smile in place. "My intentions are to make Verena the happiest woman in the world."

I almost choked on my water. He was laying it on thick.

"And how do you plan to do that?" Mom's eyes were like lasers, piercing through his facade.

Jae took my hand, his thumb brushing over my knuckles. "By loving her, supporting her, and standing by her side through everything."

Mom raised an eyebrow. "And what about all those late nights at work? How does that fit into your grand plan?"

I felt Jae's grip tighten slightly, but his smile never faltered. "We're working on finding a balance. I want to be there for Verena as much as possible."

"Is that why you were late tonight?" Mom's tone was icy.

"I'm sorry about that," Jae said sincerely. "Work ran longer than expected. But I'm committed to making this work."

Mom's gaze flicked to me, waiting for my input. "We're figuring things out," I said, trying to sound convincing.

"Figuring things out," Mom repeated, her skepticism evident. "It seems to me that you're both rushing into this."

I forced a smile, my heart pounding. "We know it's fast, but sometimes when you know, you just know."

Mom wasn't buying it. "And how did you two get together in the first place? You never mentioned anything about dating Jae before."

Jae jumped in smoothly. "We kept it quiet at first. Wanted to be sure it was real before we told anyone."

Mom crossed her arms. "And when exactly did you start dating?"

"About six months ago," Jae replied without missing a beat.

I nodded, trying to back him up. "It just...it felt right."

Mom looked at us both, her eyes narrowing. "Six months, and you're already engaged? That's quite a whirlwind romance."

"We've known each other for years," Jae said, his voice calm and steady. "Our relationship developed naturally over time."

"But why the secrecy?" Mom pressed. "Why didn't you tell anyone? Why did you lie to me and make it seem like you hated him, Vee?"

"We wanted to be sure," I said, echoing Jae's earlier words. "It's a big step, and we didn't want to rush into anything without being certain. And yes, him being my boss...complicated things. I like him a lot more now that I don't work for him."

Jae forced a playful laugh.

Mom wasn't convinced. "I just want to make sure my daughter is happy. This seems...sudden."

Auntie, always the peacemaker, jumped in. "They're a wonderful couple. You should see them together, so in love."

I forced another smile, feeling my cheeks heat up. "Thanks, Auntie."

Mom's gaze shifted back to Jae. "And you, Jae. How do you see your future together? What are your plans?"

Jae's grip on my hand tightened. "I see us building a life together, a family. I want to give Verena everything she deserves."

"And what about your work?" Mom asked, her tone challenging. "Can you balance that with a family?"

Jae nodded confidently. "Absolutely. Verena's happiness is my priority."

"I still think this is moving too quickly. I just found out about you dating!" Mom said, exasperated.

Auntie patted Mom's hand, her eyes twinkling with a knowing smile. "I think I can explain."

Jae and I exchanged a nervous glance. "What do you mean, Auntie?"

"You two aren't that good at keeping secrets," Auntie said, her tone gentle but firm, a knowing glint in her eyes.

"Huh?" I asked, feeling a sting of panic. My stomach churned as the room's tension thickened.

Auntie took a deep breath, her expression softening, eyes glistening with unshed tears. "They pushed up the engagement for me."

"Auntie, wait, we can—" Jae began, his voice trembling, but Auntie silenced him with a look.

"Jennifer, I'm dying," she said, her voice breaking slightly. "My cancer came back."

The room fell into a stunned silence. Mom gasped, her hand flying to her mouth, tears spilling over her cheeks. "Oh my God, Binna, why didn't you tell me sooner? How long have you known? Are you getting treatment? What can we do?"

Auntie shook her head, a sad smile tugging at her lips. "I've known for a few weeks. I've decided to forgo treatment this time. I want to spend my remaining time making memories, not in a hospital."

Mom's tears flowed freely, her voice choked with emotion. "Binna, no..."

Auntie reached out, squeezing Mom's hand tightly, her eyes shining with love and resolve. "Please, Jennifer, I need you to understand. These two lovebirds...they've been dating for a while, but Jae proposed probably to ease my heart a little, to reassure me that he won't be alone after I'm gone."

I felt a wave of guilt crash over me, a sharp pain that cut through my chest. This wasn't the truth at all. Auntie's belief in our relationship, her faith in our love, was built on a foundation of lies. Her words were a painful reminder of the reality we were pretending to live.

Mom's tears continued to fall. "How could you keep this from me? We could have helped you...we could have been there for you."

Auntie's grip on Mom's hand tightened, her voice steady despite the tears in her eyes. "I didn't want to burden you. I wanted these last moments to be filled with joy, not sorrow."

Jae's hand found mine under the table, squeezing it tightly, a silent promise that we were in this together. His eyes met mine, filled with the same mix of guilt and resoluteness. We had to keep this up, for Auntie's sake.

The enormity of our deception was inescapable.

"Jennifer, I need you to support them," Auntie continued, her voice filled with quiet strength. "They need you now more than ever."

Mom nodded, her tears still flowing, her voice breaking. "Of course, Binna. Whatever you need."

Auntie's eyes softened, her gaze turning to me and Jae. "You two… you have to stay strong. For me."

I swallowed hard, fighting back my own tears. "We will, Auntie."

Jae's voice was steady, but I could hear the strain beneath it. "We promise."

Auntie smiled, a sad, beautiful smile that broke my heart. "Thank you."

As we sat there, I couldn't shake the feeling of impending loss that hung over us. We were racing against time, against the inevitable, and the truth of our situation was more than I could bear.

Mom's tear-streaked face turned toward me. "Let's talk about this more tomorrow, Binna. How about a spa day? I want details and I know some doctors in the city I want you to check in with."

"You might have retired, but those nursing instincts are still strong," Auntie said.

"Damn right. I just want to take care of you." My mother glared at me. "Verena, can you walk me out?"

I stood and followed her, the silence between us thick with unspoken words. We went down the elevator, then stepped outside into the cool evening air, the city lights casting a soft glow around us as we waited for the town car Jae had called.

Mom turned to me, her voice barely above a whisper. "It's all fake, isn't it? For her."

"Due to an ironclad NDA, I cannot confirm nor deny that statement."

Mom's lips trembled as she wiped a tear from her cheek. "I've always loved Binna. When she moved away, she called every week that first year, asking me to check on him. And I love Jae too. He's suffered so much loss and always buries himself in work to escape it. I don't like how he treats you at the job, but no one deserves to be alone."

Her eyes bore into mine. "I don't agree with this. I don't like it, but... I get it. And you're going to need help." She cupped my cheek, her touch warm and comforting.

"Are you going to tell?" I asked, my voice barely a whisper.

She shook her head. "Sweet girl, your heart has always been so big. Just don't lose yourself in this, okay? You've always had big plans for yourself too."

Tears welled up in my eyes as I nodded, the enormity of the situation crashing down on me. "I won't, Mom. I promise."

The town car pulled up, and Mom gave me one last, lingering hug. "Take care of yourself, Verena. And take care of them."

"I will," I whispered, holding her tightly.

As she got into the car, I watched her leave with a hollow pang in my chest. Then, I turned back toward the apartment, my mind racing. I knew what we were doing was for Auntie, but the reality of it was more complicated than I had ever imagined. And now, with Mom's blessing and her warning, I knew I had to find a way to navigate this without losing myself in the process.

Back inside, Jae met my eyes across the room, a question hanging between us. I walked back to him, ready to face whatever came next. We were in this together, for better or worse, and somehow, we would make it through.

31

D(ATE)

JAE

Four Years Ago

Exhaustion had become a constant companion. Another trip to Korea, another grueling round of flights and hospital visits. Auntie had just finished her last round of chemo, and while relief washed over me, knowing she was on the mend, the emotional and physical toll was undeniable. Back in New York, all I wanted was a distraction, and there was only one person who could provide that—Verena.

I dialed her number, craving the sound of her voice. Voicemail. Again. Annoyance twisted in my chest. Where the hell was she?

Scrolling through her social media, I found my answer. There she was, smiling, sparkling eyes, and dressed to kill. But the smile wasn't for me. Some guy was sitting across from her, looking way too comfortable. They were at a chic downtown restaurant. I felt a surge of possessive jealousy. This sorry asshole was definitely not going to take my place. Even if I couldn't have her, that didn't mean this fucker could.

I was in my car before I knew it, navigating through the city streets with a single-minded focus. This date was going to end, and it was going to end badly—for him.

I walked into the restaurant, eyes scanning the room until I spotted them. Verena looked stunning, her laughter echoing in the dimly lit room. Her date, the poor bastard, was eating up every word she said. I settled discreetly at the bar, ordering a drink, and waited for my moment.

When her date excused himself to use the restroom, I followed, timing my entrance perfectly. He was at the sink, washing his hands when I walked in.

"Hey," I said, my tone friendly but with an undercurrent of something sharper. He turned, confusion clear on his face.

"Do I know you?" he asked, brows knitting together.

"Not yet," I replied, a smirk tugging at my lips. "But I couldn't help but notice you're on a date with Verena."

"Yeah, and?" Suspicion laced his voice.

"Just thought you should know," I began, leaning in as if sharing a secret, "Verena's great, but she's got this...thing. She's totally in love with her boss. Talks about him nonstop. It's kind of a deal-breaker for most guys."

His eyes widened. "Seriously?"

I nodded, putting on my best concerned look. "Yeah, it's a shame. She's always mentioning him. I bet she's brought him up tonight already."

He looked even more unsettled. "Actually, yeah. She's brought him up sixteen times."

"See? Told you," I said, patting his shoulder. "Just thought you should know what you're getting into. Good luck, buddy."

I left him there, confusion etched on his face, and returned to my seat at the bar. I ordered another drink, watching the scene unfold with a sense of satisfaction. Her date returned to the table, visibly shaken.

Verena noticed immediately. "Hey, is everything okay?" she asked.

"Yeah, uh, fine," he mumbled, clearly lying. The rest of their conversation was a mess of awkward silences and forced smiles. I almost felt sorry for the guy. Almost.

Eventually, he made some excuse about an early meeting and bailed, leaving Verena alone and looking both confused and annoyed. Perfect.

I waited a few minutes before making my move. I approached her table, feigning surprise. "Verena? What are you doing here?"

She looked up, her eyes narrowing. "Jae? What a coincidence."

I gave her my most charming smile. "Just got back from Korea. Thought I'd grab a drink to unwind. Mind if I join you?"

She sighed, waving at the empty seat. "Why not? My date just left, anyway. But there's one condition—you can sit here, but we're not allowed to discuss work. I'm off the clock."

My heart skipped a beat. Lately, work was the only thing I could talk about with her. It was my safety net, the one thing I knew she'd engage with me on. If I talked about anything else, I might do something stupid, like demand to know why she didn't want me as badly as I wanted her. But I couldn't back down now.

"Deal," I said, sliding into the seat. "So, what are we allowed to talk about then?"

She arched an eyebrow, a smirk playing on her lips. "Anything but work. Surely, Mr. CEO, you can manage that."

I chuckled, trying to mask my nervousness. "I'll give it my best shot. So, what's the latest scandal in Verena's world?"

She laughed, and the sound was like a balm to my weary soul. "Oh, you know, just the usual—terrible dates, gossip at the office I'm not supposed to mention."

"Terrible date, huh? What was wrong with him?"

"He seemed...skittish. And since you don't let me have much of a personal life, I tried to bring up the job, but he seemed...uninterested," she said, rolling her eyes.

I leaned back, a cocky grin on my face. "So, you don't want me to talk about work, but that's your date conversation topic of choice?"

She sighed, looking a bit defeated. "I know. I'm realizing I have nothing of my own these days. No hobbies, I don't write anymore. I don't do anything."

I frowned, feeling a pang of guilt. She was right. I had consumed her life, leaving little room for anything else. I couldn't stand the thought of her feeling so unfulfilled. As much as it hurt to admit it, she needed more than just work, more than just me.

But I could fix this. I was Jae Lee, and I could make anything happen. I started thinking of ways to make it up to her. Maybe I could send her on business trips that were really for her or take her with me when I had special negotiations. Sure, it was work, but a week in Tokyo or a night in Paris might make her life more exciting.

"I don't have a personal life," she admitted after a lingering silence.

I am your personal life, baby.

And I'm going to make it the best damn life you've ever had.

Even if you don't want me back. Even if I had to bury those fucking feelings deep down and hack at them until they were long dead.

32

(SPARK)LING

VERENA

Auntie's revelation cast a shadow over the evening. At least it meant I didn't have to navigate Jae's...peculiar antics that night. He slipped out to work at the crack of dawn, leaving us no chance to talk it over. Part of me longed for him to take a break, to cherish these fleeting moments with Auntie. But I knew he couldn't, and besides, she wouldn't want him to. She hated discussing it or drawing any attention to herself. Yet every time I heard her cough, it was like a jolt of lightning electrifying the whole house, a stark reminder of the storm we were weathering.

When Jae got home from work, Auntie sat us down with a grin on her face. "I'm moving out."

"What?" Jae and I said in unison, our shock evident.

She smiled warmly, reaching for our hands. "I spoke with Jennifer today. Things are going to get more...difficult as things progress. She's a retired nurse and has a spare bedroom. With your relationship being so new and her being so sweet, we think it's best I stay with her. We can spend time together still, obviously, but I think I'll feel more comfortable there. Like a slumber party with a close friend every night."

I felt sadness and relief simultaneously. Sadness because it meant

Auntie's condition was worsening, and relief because it might give Jae and me a bit more space to figure out whatever was happening between us. "Are you sure?"

She nodded. "Yes, sweetie. Jennifer and I had a good talk, and I think it's the best decision for all of us. I don't want you all to see me like...that. Jennifer is a natural caregiver and her cooking is divine. Plus, we enjoy binge-watching the same shows! It'll be fun." Her tone seemed hollow. I knew she'd enjoy it, but I also felt bad, like this fake engagement was stealing time away with Jae.

"Auntie, if you want to spend more time with Jae, I can go—"

"No. Of course I want to spend time with Jae. I love it here, and I'll be over all the time. I just...I don't want you two to remember me as... sick. When I have bad days, I want the option to hide away. I want you to see this version of me. And I want a safe place to be vulnerable."

Jae's jaw tightened, his eyes betraying his internal struggle. "Auntie, we want you to be comfortable. If that means staying with Jennifer, then we'll support you."

She patted his hand affectionately. "Thank you, Jae. And don't worry, I'll be just a phone call away. You two need to focus on each other as well."

Auntie was right; things were going to get more difficult. But her decision to stay with my mom showed just how serious it had become.

"Let's not dwell on it," Auntie said, breaking the silence. "Tonight, we celebrate new beginnings. I've ordered dinner from that fancy Italian place you two love."

I forced a smile, trying to match her enthusiasm. "That sounds perfect."

Dinner arrived, and we sat around the table, the atmosphere a mix of bittersweet emotions. We talked about everything and nothing. Auntie's laughter filled the room, a sound that both comforted and saddened me. She was still so full of life, despite everything.

After dinner, Jae and I helped Auntie pack her things. She insisted on taking only the essentials, leaving most of her belongings behind. "I'll be back to visit often," she assured us, her voice steady.

As we carried her bags to the car, I felt a lump form in my throat.

This was another step towards the inevitable, another reminder that time was running out.

"Take care of each other," Auntie said as she hugged us both.

"We will," Jae promised, his voice thick with emotion.

As Auntie rode off, the reality of our situation settled over us. We stood in silence, watching the car disappear down the street.

Jae sighed, running a hand through his hair. "This is harder than I thought it would be."

I nodded, feeling a tear slip down my cheek. "Yeah, it is."

We walked back into the house, the silence between us filled with unspoken words. I knew we needed to talk, to figure out where we stood. But for now, all I could think about was Auntie and the time we had left with her.

"Do you want to talk about it?" I asked softly, breaking the silence.

He shook his head. "Not right now. I just...need some time."

I nodded, my gaze filled with understanding. "Okay. I'm here if you need me."

"I need...a distraction."

"Okay, how about we watch a movie, then?" I suggested.

Jae nodded, his eyes still clouded with emotion. "Sure. Pick whatever you want."

Without Auntie, the house felt strangely empty, an eerie quiet settling over the rooms. Was this how Jae always felt? The thought made my chest tighten.

And without Auntie, I felt less safe from...Jae. His attention, his heated looks. I shook off the thought, trying to push it to the back of my mind, and settled on the couch. Jae joined me, his presence both comforting and unsettling. He pulled a blanket over us, and I turned on *Casablanca*, hoping the classic would distract me.

"Love this movie," Jae said, his voice breaking the silence. "Bogart and Bergman, timeless."

"Yeah, me too," I replied, trying to keep my tone neutral. My eyes were fixed on the screen, but my mind was elsewhere. What was Jae thinking? Was he as affected by Auntie's absence as I was?

He shifted closer, his arm brushing against mine, sending a shiver down my spine. "You okay?" he asked, his voice soft, concerned.

"Yeah, just...it's weird without Auntie," I admitted, my voice barely above a whisper.

"I know," he replied, clearing his throat and shifting his posture. "You forced this movie on me a thousand times back in college." The subject change was glaringly obvious.

"Because it always cracked you up when you were stressed," I countered, nudging him lightly.

"Yeah, I guess you always had a way of getting me to smile," he said softly, his eyes locking with mine for a brief, intense moment before looking back at the screen.

Without thinking, I reached out and grabbed his hand. His fingers twitched slightly, then relaxed, intertwining with mine. He stared at our joined hands for a moment, his expression unreadable. He shifted his gaze back to the TV, but I could sense his awareness of our touch, the tension between us a constant hum in the background.

The movie played on, but my attention was entirely on Jae. Every breath he took, every subtle shift in his seat, every time his lips curved into a smile at a funny part—it all drew me in. The soft rise and fall of his chest, the way his jaw clenched and relaxed, the way his thumb absentmindedly stroked the back of my hand—it was all so mesmerizing. I found myself committing every detail to memory, savoring the closeness, the intimacy of the moment.

"Are you even watching the movie?" he asked.

I glanced up, meeting his eyes. "Not really," I admitted.

A slow smile spread across his face, his eyes darkening. "Me neither."

I shifted slightly, turning to face him more fully, our knees brushing together under the blanket. The movement brought us even closer, our faces mere inches apart. I could see every detail of his expression—the curve of his lips, the intensity in his eyes.

His gaze flicked down to my lips, then back up to my eyes. "Verena..." he began, his voice trailing off as if he wasn't sure what to say.

"Yeah?" I prompted, my own voice shaky.

He swallowed hard, his Adam's apple bobbing. "I don't know what's happening between us, but...it feels different. More real. Tell me I'm not the only one that wants this."

I could feel his breath on my skin, warm and tantalizing. My own breathing was shallow, my heart racing as I struggled to maintain my composure.

"Can I kiss you?" he asked.

"No," I said, barely above a whisper, feeling a rush of conflicted emotions.

His gaze darkened with something desperate and raw. "Please, Verena," he begged, his voice breaking.

"You've gotten bold in asking."

"That's because I've learned you like it when I'm weak for you," he said, his voice a strained whisper.

"Wh-what?"

"I saw it when we first kissed," he continued, his gaze unwavering. "How your eyes flared when I begged you to touch me. Those pretty lips twisted into a smirk. I've been demanding a lot from you, but you know what gets the sweetest result?"

"What?" I asked, my voice barely audible, the tension between us almost unbearable.

"Please," he murmured, leaning in to kiss my neck. "Please kiss me, Verena." He licked my collarbone.

"Please," he whispered again, his lips trailing kisses along my jawline. "Please, Verena." He kissed the corner of my mouth, his hands trembling slightly.

He moved to my ear, his voice husky and low. "Please." He kissed the sensitive skin just below my earlobe, making me shiver.

"Please," he said once more, his lips brushing against my shoulder, his fingers trailing down my arm. Each kiss, each touch, was a plea, a desperate attempt to bridge the gap between us.

He drew back slightly, his eyes dark with need. "Please, Verena," he whispered, his voice rough with emotion. "I need you."

The room seemed to shrink around us, the air thick with tension and longing. My breath hitched, my resolve crumbling under the weight of his pleas.

Slowly, I leaned in, my lips brushing against his in a soft, tentative kiss. It was all the encouragement he needed. He deepened the kiss, his hands tangling in my hair, pulling me closer as if he could fuse us together. Our tongues fought and he sucked on my bottom lip. It was one of those rough kisses that made your toes curl.

His voice dropped to a husky murmur as he pulled away. "Verena, I need to taste you," he said, his eyes burning.

I bit my lip, feeling the electric tension crackle between us. "Jae…" I started, unsure how to continue.

His hands moved to the waistband of my sleep shorts, his fingers teasing the fabric as his lips brushed against my stomach. "Do you know how many times I've wondered what you taste like?" he growled, his voice thick with need. "Will you be sweet? Or maybe something else entirely?"

"You've thought about it?"

"Too many times to count," he admitted.

What the fuck? "Why am I just now finding out about this?"

He ignored my question and groaned softly, his eyes rolling back. "Just a little taste, hmm? Can I pretty please lick your pussy, baby?"

"Jae…"

"Look at you. You have no idea how much I fucking crave this, crave you. Just give me a taste."

My heart raced as he spoke, his words igniting a fire within me. He kissed the curve of my waist, his lips hot and insistent against my skin. "Keep talking," I rasped. "I…I like this."

I looked down, catching a glimpse of his triumphant smile as he tugged my sleep shorts and panties off. The cool air hit me and—

"Look at that pussy…fucking hell, just…fuck. Let me see how wet you are."

He dragged his index finger along my slit, making me nearly jump off the couch from the zaps of pleasure.

"Can I just appreciate how gorgeous this fucking pussy is for a second? Look at that clit. Makes me want to just wrap my lips around it and…"

And he did just that. It was brief, like he couldn't hold back anymore. Just enough to make my mouth part and a pant escape me.

One little taste. Just one.

I was so fucked.

He looked up at me from between my legs, his eyes dark with hunger. "Can I do that again? I'll do anything, anything you want," he breathed.

My resolve was crumbling. "Mmm. Just one…one more taste," I croaked.

He flicked his tongue against my sensitive nub, teasing me. I twitched from the pleasure.

"Look how that made your leg jump, baby. I could do that again."

"We should…probably maybe stop?" My words sounded like a hollow question.

"Look at me," he murmured against my center, his voice filled with reverence. "I'll do whatever it takes. Beg, plead, get on my knees and worship you. Just give me the chance to fully taste you."

I moaned softly, my hands tangling in his hair, pulling him closer. "Again. Just a little—"

I couldn't even finish my sentence. He wrapped his lips around it and circled his tongue in a rhythm. Once. Twice. Three times. I moaned his name.

His lips were full and soft, molded perfectly around my throbbing clit. His tongue flicked out, circling it in a mesmerizing rhythm, sending sparks of pleasure through me. I watched as he worshiped me, his hands holding my thighs gently but firmly, his eyes locked on mine with hunger.

"Keep going," I choked out.

His eyes flashed with desire, his hands never leaving my thighs, his lips never leaving my aching clit. He knew exactly how to please and torment me at the same time, and I couldn't get enough of it.

"Yes," I gasped, my fingers digging into his hair. "More. I need more."

He chuckled, the sound thrilling as it vibrated through me. "I can do more, Verena. I'd do anything to make you come."

Without warning, he thrust two fingers inside me. I cried out, my hips bucking, and he finger-fucked me harder. His eyes burned into mine as he stroked me with his tongue, the intensity of his gaze making me feel like I was the only person on earth.

"I can give you so much more, baby," he whispered hoarsely against my pulsing center.

"All," I forced out. I couldn't say much. I didn't care if this was a colossal mistake. Or that it wasn't real. My throat was too dry and my heart was pounding in my chest, threatening to burst out of my ribcage.

"All of it, baby. I'll give you everything you want."

The room seemed to spin as his fingers pushed harder, deeper, faster. The pleasure built up, higher and higher, until I thought I'd burst.

"Jae..." I moaned, my voice thin and shaky.

"I'll do anything to make you feel good," he promised, his voice thick with emotion. "Just let me know, and I'll give it to you."

I didn't know what I needed.

"Jae..." I said.

"Yes, baby?" he asked, his voice filled with anticipation.

"Yes," I whispered, my voice shaking. "Make me come."

I was making the demands today.

His lips parted in a smirk as he thrust his fingers in and out of me with renewed vigor. His thumb continued its relentless rhythm, driving me higher, the pleasure building like a wave.

"Just let go, baby," he urged, his voice low and seductive. "Let me show you how good it can feel."

I could feel it building, the pleasure swelling, the wave rising higher and higher.

"Jae..." I moaned again, my eyes fluttering shut.

"That's it," he coaxed, his voice a seductive whisper. "Let go, baby."

And then it hit.

A mind-blowing orgasm washed over me, my entire body tensing and then melting into the couch as wave after wave of pleasure crashed over me. My throat was hoarse from moaning, my breath coming out in labored gasps.

Jae watched me, his face a mix of triumph and satisfaction, his eyes never leaving mine as I rode the high of my climax. He stroked me gently, his fingers slowly sliding out of me as I came back down to earth.

And when the last of the aftershocks were gone, he licked his lips like I was a treat to be savored. Holy shit. Jae was way too good at that.

Holy shit, I let him do, well, *that.*

What now?

Did I say thank you or—

"Let's go to bed, baby."

"What about—"

"It's time to sleep."

He helped me up, his hands gentle but firm, leading me to bed as I felt the remnants of the orgasm still coursing through me. We climbed under the sheets, his body heat radiating against mine as I snuggled close to him.

This was a terrible idea.

I didn't have to sleep in this bed with him. I could have easily gone to the guest room.

But I wanted to.

What did that mean?

Why was I so attracted to him? I thought I gave up on those feelings years ago when he stopped being my friend and started being this relentless boss in pursuit of power.

He kissed my neck and I felt a contentment spread through my body.

"Did you mean what you said earlier?" I asked, my voice barely above a whisper.

"About anything you want?" he asked, and I could hear the genuine curiosity in his tone.

"Yes. What you promised before."

He was quiet for a moment, and I could feel him thinking. Then, he spoke. "I meant everything. I'll do anything."

My heart rate quickened. "Really? Anything?"

"Anything."

I knew my body believed him.

But my heart? My heart didn't.

33

LOOP(HOLES)

JAE

The sun had barely dipped below the horizon when I decided to head home early. I couldn't remember the last time I did that. Usually, I thrived on the demands of my job, but today was different. Today, I *wanted* to be home.

When I walked inside, I found Verena sitting on the couch, chewing on a pencil and staring intently at her laptop. Her legs were bare, and she was wearing a pair of pink lace panties that made it impossible for me to think straight. The curve of her hips, the soft skin of her thighs, and the way the lace hugged her perfectly was a vision I couldn't tear my eyes away from. Her wavy black hair cascaded around her shoulders, framing her face perfectly.

My gaze trailed over her, soaking in every detail. She hadn't noticed me yet, too absorbed in whatever she was working on. The sight of her, so relaxed and unaware of my presence, sent a jolt of desire through me. She had no idea the power she wielded.

"Enjoying the view?" I said, my voice low and rough, a smirk playing on my lips.

She jumped, nearly dropping her laptop. "Jae! What are you doing home so early?"

"I decided to surprise you." My eyes devoured her, and I couldn't hide the hunger in my voice. "And I'm glad I did."

Her cheeks flushed, and she shifted on the couch, trying to cover herself with the laptop. "I was just working…"

I crossed the room in a few strides, towering over her. "Don't stop on my account." My fingers brushed her cheek, trailing down to her neck. "You have no idea how much I've missed you."

"Missed me?"

"Every second," I growled, leaning down to capture her lips in a searing kiss. My hands roamed her body, feeling the soft skin of her thighs. She tasted like home, like everything I'd been missing.

"Jae," she murmured against my lips, her voice trembling. "What's gotten into you?"

"You," I whispered, pulling her closer. "Only you."

She quickly glanced at her watch. "You're home way early."

"I didn't want to be at work," I said, my eyes drifting over her. "What are you working on?"

Her reaction was immediate. She slammed the laptop shut, her cheeks flushing. "Nothing."

My curiosity was piqued. "Nothing, huh?"

She stood up quickly, and I let my gaze travel up and down her body. The way her panties clung to her hips, the swell of her breasts barely contained by her tank top—it all made me ache for her in a way that was becoming increasingly difficult to ignore. Every inch of her seemed to be designed to drive me mad with want. Last night, she let me taste her. And I wanted to do it again. Now.

"Uh, I'll put pants on," she said, moving to leave.

As she turned, I reached out and grabbed her wrist, pulling her towards me. The heat of her skin against mine sent a jolt through my body. "Don't."

She looked up at me, her eyes wide and filled with something that mirrored the craving I felt. "We have to talk about last night, Jae. It can't happen again. Th-this wasn't in the contract."

"The contract?"

She nodded. "When we are here alone, there's no reason to, uh, put on a show."

I smirked, my grip on her wrist firm but gentle. "Well then, I'd be more than happy to take you in public. In fact, it would make me very happy to let everyone watch as I make you—"

"Jae!" She slapped my chest, her cheeks turning a deeper shade of red.

"Get dressed." I chuckled, releasing her wrist. "I'm taking you on a date."

"A date?" she echoed, clearly taken aback.

"You mentioned the contract," I said, my smirk widening. "We need a public appearance, hmm?"

She hesitated for a moment, her eyes searching mine. The tension between us was electric, a force that made my heart race and my body ache for her touch. She was so close, and every second that passed only heightened my desire.

Finally, she nodded and scurried away to her room in those fucking panties I wanted to tear from her body and stuff in my mouth.

I had plans for tonight, plans she couldn't even begin to imagine. I was an expert at loopholes, at getting what I wanted. And tonight, I wanted her.

The thought of seeing her dressed up, the anticipation of being close to her, touching her—it was almost too much to bear. I now knew exactly how to make her unravel. I'd been going about this all wrong before. She wanted me *desperate* for her. And I was more than happy to oblige. The reward was worth it.

She had no idea what she was in for.

When she returned, she was dressed in a simple but elegant minidress that hugged her body in all the right places. Her hair was pinned up, revealing the graceful slope of her neck. The sight of her made my heart skip a beat. I felt a surge of pride and desire as I looked at her.

"You look stunning," I said, my voice low and sincere.

She gave me a small smile, clearly still a bit flustered. "Thanks. So, where are we going?"

"You'll see," I replied, offering her my arm. She took it hesitantly, and we walked out to the waiting car I had arranged earlier.

The drive was anything but comfortable. The silence was thick with unspoken words and simmering tension. I couldn't stop looking at her, every glance a brutal test of my restraint. Her dress rode up slightly, revealing more of her thighs, and I had to clench my fist to keep from reaching out. The fabric clung to her, making my mouth go dry.

I wanted her so bad it hurt, a physical ache that was becoming unbearable. My cock strained against my pants, and I bit my fist, trying to contain how much I needed her. She had no idea what she was doing to me, how close I was to losing control.

The desire to take her right there was almost overwhelming. I was an expert at getting what I wanted, and right now, all I wanted was her.

As we arrived at our destination, Verena looked around in surprise, but I could barely focus on anything other than the raw desire coursing through me. I wanted to pull her close, to kiss her until we were both gasping, to feel her skin against mine.

"Jae," she said, her voice pulling me out of my thoughts.

"Hmm?" I replied, my eyes still lingering on her legs.

"This place is amazing," she said, her excitement evident.

I forced a smile, trying to ignore the throbbing need that seemed to consume me. "Only the best for you," I managed to say, my voice strained.

As we got out of the car, I reached for her hand, needing to touch her in some way. Her fingers intertwined with mine, and I sighed in relief. I wanted more. I needed more.

Leading her towards the entrance, I kept stealing glances at her, every part of me yearning to close the distance between us. The way her dress hugged her body, the way her hair framed her face, the way her eyes sparkled with excitement—it was all too much.

"Jae," she said, stopping suddenly and turning to face me.

"Yes?" I asked, trying to keep my voice steady.

"Thank you for this," she said, her voice soft and sincere.

I nodded, swallowing hard. "You're welcome."

Tonight, I would make her see just how much I wanted her, just how desperate I was to make her mine. But for now, I had to play it cool, even though my body was screaming for hers.

We took the elevator up to the top floor and went outside. "I rented the entire rooftop garden for dinner," I said casually, watching her reaction. "Michelin chef and all."

I watched with satisfaction as she took in the scene. The twinkling lights strung overhead cast a magical glow over the rooftop, transforming it into a wonderland. She gasped softly, her lips parting in awe. The sight of her like this, genuinely surprised and delighted, made my chest tighten.

A million more future dates flashed through my mind, each one designed to elicit this exact reaction. I grinned when we reached the table, noticing the chairs placed side by side just as I'd requested. The server guided us to our seats, and I held my breath, waiting to see her response.

As we sat down, I leaned in close, my lips brushing her ear. "Is this public enough for you?" I whispered, my voice low and teasing.

She rolled her eyes, but I could see the hint of a smile playing at the corners of her mouth. "You really went all out, didn't you?"

Before I could respond, the server approached with a bottle of wine, expertly pouring two glasses. I watched Verena take a sip, her eyes closing briefly in appreciation of the rich flavor.

Unable to resist any longer, I placed my hand on her thigh, feeling the warmth of her skin through the thin fabric of her dress. She gasped, her eyes flying open to meet mine.

"Relax," I murmured, my fingers gently stroking her thigh. "Just trying to make sure we look convincing."

I saw her struggle to maintain her composure. "You're enjoying this way too much," she muttered, but there was no mistaking the way her body responded to my touch.

"Maybe I am," I admitted, my voice husky with desire. "But I think you are too."

She bit her lip, her eyes flashing with a mix of frustration and something else—something that made my pulse race even faster. The server brought out our first course, but all I could think about was how much I wanted to kiss her, to taste her, to make her mine.

As the night went on, I couldn't take my eyes off her. Every smile, every laugh, every shy glance in my direction fueled the fire inside me. I knew I was pushing boundaries, but I couldn't help it. Being this close to her, touching her, seeing her reactions—it was intoxicating.

The server set down our dessert: a beautifully arranged fruit plate with a scoop of creamy ice cream in the center. Verena's eyes sparkled as she looked at it, and I couldn't help but smile.

"We've come a long way from Jake's Pizza Parlor on campus," she joked, her laughter like music to my ears.

I chuckled, remembering that hole-in-the-wall place we used to frequent. "Ah, Jake's. That place was a dump, but they had the best pepperoni pizza. Remember how they'd always forget to clean the tables?"

She grinned, shaking her head. "And the jukebox that only played nineties hits. I swear, if I never hear 'Wannabe' by the Spice Girls again, it'll be too soon."

I laughed, feeling a warmth spread through me that had nothing to do with the wine. "Hey, I still have fond memories of that place. It was where we'd go to de-stress after finals."

"True," she admitted, her eyes softening. "It was our little escape."

We fell into a comfortable silence. The server discreetly stepped back, leaving us alone with our memories and the dessert.

Feeling a sudden surge of mischief, I picked up a strawberry, dipped it in the ice cream, and then, with deliberate slowness, rubbed it along the curve of her neck. She seemed shocked, but she didn't push me away. I leaned in and licked the sweet trail off her skin, savoring the taste of strawberries and her natural scent.

I hesitated for a moment, my eyes never leaving hers as I dipped the strawberry into the ice cream. There was a raw, unspoken desire between us, and I felt my own restraint fading away. I could see the anticipation in her eyes, the exhilaration of being so close to me, so close to a forbidden act. And I wanted her to experience that rush, feel that magnetism as I pushed us closer to the edge.

Gently, I slid the strawberry between her lips. Her mouth opened slightly, and I could feel the warmth of her breath on my fingertips. I watched as the ice cream melting on the tip of the strawberry trickled down her chin, a small trail of temptation being offered by the victorious fruit.

I slowly licked the strands away. Fuck, she tasted good.

"To convince people, hmm?" I murmured against her skin.

She quivered slightly. "Quite the loophole, Mr. Lee," she replied, her voice tinged with amusement and something else—something that made my blood heat.

"Well," I said. "I'm an expert at finding loopholes."

She laughed softly, shaking her head. "You're impossible."

"And yet, you're still here," I pointed out, my hand still resting on her thigh, my thumb brushing gentle circles against her skin.

"Yes," she admitted. "I guess I am."

"But, I think I know something that would taste better..." I reached under the table, easing her dress up. She went stiff for a moment and I took a large strawberry, pressing it against her—

"You're not wearing panties," I croaked. Fuck. Fuck. Fuck. She wasn't wearing any. Shit fuck damn I was lost. Gone. I wasn't going to make it home.

"It showed a panty line!"

"I'm not fucking complaining, baby."

She quickly looked around. "Someone could be watching."

"That's the point. You're the one that wanted to stick to the contract. We need to make it convincing, don't we? I'm a public figure. Newspapers and magazines are writing up stories about our whirlwind engagement. Let's give them something to talk about."

I expected her to push me away, slam her legs shut, and stomp out of here in those heels that would drive me mad for the rest of my life.

But instead, she parted her thighs.

She scooted forward in her seat.

She shuddered when I started thrusting the strawberry inside of her slick pussy. I wanted to taste her, didn't I?

Her nails dug into the table, her eyes locked on mine as I slid the juicy fruit into her, the pulsating sensation of my thumb against her clit making her tremble. I could barely breathe, watching her response to my touch. I was completely undone by this woman, and I knew she was too.

"Can I taste you again, Verena?" I asked.

I waited.

And waited.

Her eyes flared. I knew she was imagining me kneeling under the table, licking that glorious swollen clit of hers like I was a starving man.

I waited some more until finally she said what I'd been aching for.

"Yes."

I pulled the strawberry out of her and lifted it to my lips. She watched with rapt attention as I wrapped my lips around it and groaned.

The sweetness of the strawberry combined with the taste of her arousal sent a jolt of desire through me. I closed my eyes, savoring the moment.

"You taste like heaven," I murmured as I savored the sweet fruit. "I could eat you all night."

Verena bit her lip.

"Were you hoping for something else?" I teased.

"Get the check, Jae," she rasped.

"Yes, baby."

"Hurry the fuck up."

"As you wish."

"Now, Jae."

That was enough to have me picking her up and carrying her to the elevator, the strawberries long forgotten. I'd prepaid for our meal with the reservation. I'd planned for all of this the same way I planned business proposals and schematics. I didn't leave anything to chance or give her a reason to back out of this deal.

The town car parked out front with the driver was waiting for us.

A finish line I'd worked hard for.

"Take a walk," I barked at the driver before gently placing her in the back seat and joining her. Once the door was locked, she clawed at me, feral.

Our teeth clashed. Our lips pressed in fury.

She dug her nails into my neck.

I laid her down on the back seat and rolled her dress up.

Fuck. Her pussy was the prettiest pussy I'd ever seen. I could stare at it all fucking day.

It was a delicate pink, with wetness that glistened beautifully against her smooth skin. It was like a flower in full bloom, inviting and alluring.

Every contour and fold was like a work of art, designed purely for my pleasure and worship. I couldn't resist the temptation to explore every inch of it, to taste and savor and lose myself.

Her thighs were splayed open, inviting me in. I couldn't resist. I dove in, my tongue exploring every inch of her, tasting her sweetness and desire.

And fuck. She tasted so goddamn good. I couldn't even help but groan in appreciation.

Verena arched her back, her breaths becoming ragged as I devoured her. I thrust my tongue deep inside her, feeling her muscles clench and release around me.

The sound of her moans and gasps filled the small space, mingling with the soft rustle of clothing and the occasional squeak of the car suspension. It was a symphony of pleasure.

She grabbed the back of my head, pulling me deeper into her, her hips bucking against my face. My hands roamed over her body, cupping her breasts, teasing her nipples until they hardened beneath my touch. I knew she wanted this as much as I did.

"Fucking hell, Verena. I'll do whatever you want. Just please, please, please, let me taste this every day. I want to live every moment with you grinding your clit against my tongue."

"Stop talking and make me come, Jae."

My heart pounded as I continued to devour her, knowing that she was so close. I longed to feel her orgasm tremors beneath my mouth, the flush of her heated skin against my lips and tongue. I delved deeper, my fingers pulling on her nipples.

Her body started to tremble, and then it happened. A shudder passed through her, and she cried out, her orgasm washing over her. I held her there, letting her ride it out, my mouth still pressed against her core.

Finally, she came back to earth, and I pulled away. Her eyes met mine, and I saw the same hunger and desire that I felt reflected back at me.

"Mmm, thank you," I moaned, my voice husky with desire.

"For what?" she purred, a seductive smile playing on her lips.

"For blowing my mind with that amazing fucking dessert. You're too damn irresistible, Vee." My eyes traveled down her body hungrily, unable to resist the lust coursing through me. "Everything about you is just so goddamn delicious."

She sat up, still breathing hard. Then, when she saw my hard cock straining against my pants, she reached for it, but I grabbed her wrist, stopping her. "Nope."

"That has to be uncomfortable. And last night..."

"You only touch me when I ask, baby. When I beg. Don't even think about giving me the privilege of pleasure until I've earned it."

Her mouth dropped open. "O-oh."

"I'll get the driver. Let's go home."

34

(CARE)SSING

VERENA

It had been days since the car incident.

I was such a fucking coward, hiding from Jae. Running away because I didn't want to talk about what happened during our fake...or maybe not fake...date. It was easy when he went to work.

But at night, I had to use Mina the cat as a shield, his sneezes and red eyes keeping him away.

I couldn't avoid him forever, though.

Every evening was the same routine. Jae would return from work, his presence filling the apartment with a tension that made the air feel thicker. I'd retreat to the guest room, Mina curled up in my lap, her purring a comforting contrast to the turmoil inside me. I'd hear Jae's muffled curses whenever he came near, his allergic reactions to Mina providing a temporary barrier.

But I couldn't avoid him forever. We had appearances to keep up.

Visiting Mom was always an event, but today felt like a spectacle. Jae and I walked up the front steps, hand in hand for the sake of our charade, but the warmth of his grip felt too real. I tried to ignore it as we stepped inside.

Things had been weird since our date night. I didn't know where we stood—what was fake, what wasn't—and I wasn't ready to ask him what we were. How did you define this sort of relationship? Jae didn't seem in any hurry to define it either. Plus, it felt wrong to pressure him into answering when Auntie was so sick.

They'd been spending more time together, which made me happy. She came over for dinner, or he left work early to take her to the park. It was sweet, and the fact that he was relinquishing control at work to prioritize her and...well...me...was a shock. But I couldn't dwell on that now. I had to focus on today.

The smell of freshly baked cookies hit me first. Laura and Luke were in the kitchen, flour on their hands, laughing as they tried to outdo each other with the cookie shapes. Auntie was there too, but her persistent cough cut through the hilarity, a harsh reminder of why we were all gathered here.

Mom's eyes were on Auntie, a worried crease between her brows. "Auntie, you need to check your oxygen levels," she said gently but firmly.

Auntie waved her off, smiling. "I'm fine, Jennifer. Just a little winded from all the baking."

"You didn't tell me Luke would be here," Jae grumbled, his jaw tightening, the veins in his neck pulsing with barely concealed irritation.

I rolled my eyes. Jae always hated him, and I never understood why. "It's not like it's a big deal," I replied, trying to keep my voice light. "He's just a friend."

Jae's eyes narrowed as he watched Luke laughing with Laura and Auntie. "Yeah, just a friend who wants to fuck you."

I sighed, nudging him playfully, though my heart raced at the possessive edge in his voice. "Jealous much?"

Jae's gaze flicked to mine, a flicker of something intense in his eyes that made my breath catch. "I'm not jealous. Just...cautious."

"Cautious?" I raised an eyebrow. "Of what? Luke's cookie-baking skills?"

His lips twitched, but he didn't smile. The tension in his jaw remained, his eyes dark with a mixture of protectiveness and frustration. "Of how he looks at you."

"Oh, please." I waved off his comment, though a small thrill ran through me at the thought of Jae being jealous. "We're here for Auntie, remember? Not to start a war with Luke."

Jae's grip on my hand tightened, pulling me closer until our bodies were nearly touching. The proximity made my heart pound, and I could feel the heat of his breath against my ear as he whispered, "Just remember why we're here. And that I'm not going anywhere."

I glanced at Luke, who was now shaping cookies with Laura, oblivious to the tension between Jae and me. "You're being ridiculous," I whispered back, though my voice lacked conviction.

"Am I?" Jae's eyes bored into mine. "Maybe I just know how guys like Luke think."

"And how's that?" I shot back, trying to keep my tone light, but failing miserably.

"They see something they want, and they won't stop until they get it," he said, his voice low and dangerous. "But I won't let that happen. Not with you."

I swallowed hard, the intensity of his words leaving me momentarily speechless. Before I could respond, Auntie's cough broke through the moment, reminding us of the real reason we were here.

Jae released my hand, his gaze softening as he looked at Auntie. "Let's enjoy our evening," he said, his tone gentler but still firm. "We can deal with everything else later."

As if on cue, Luke looked up and spotted us. "Hey, Verena! Jae! Come join us!"

"Great," he muttered.

We walked over to the kitchen, where Luke immediately stepped closer to me, his eyes lighting up. "Verena, you look amazing! How have you been?"

"Thanks, Luke," I replied, feeling Jae's eyes boring into the side of my head. "I've been good. Just busy with...everything."

Luke leaned in a little closer, his smile widening. "Well, you look fantastic. I read the first chapter of your book, by the way. I know you aren't sure what to write, but it's a great start."

Jae's head whipped around so fast I thought he might get whiplash. "What book?"

I hesitated. "I decided to try writing again."

Luke jumped in, clearly enjoying the moment. "Oh, you didn't know? She asked me to read it and give some feedback."

Jae's jaw tightened, his eyes narrowing. "No, she didn't tell me. Why am I not reading it?"

Luke smirked, sensing the tension. "Uh-oh, trouble in paradise?"

Jae's eyes flashed with irritation, a muscle twitching in his jaw. "No trouble. Just surprised I wasn't included."

I tried to defuse the situation, placing a hand on Jae's arm. "I was going to tell you. I just…I didn't want to distract you."

Luke chuckled. "Well, it's really good, Verena. You've got a gift."

Jae's grip on my hand loosened slightly, but his eyes remained locked on mine. "I would have liked to read it."

"I'm sorry, Jae," I said softly, feeling the sting of his disappointment. "I didn't mean to exclude you."

He took a deep breath, his expression softening just a bit, but the tension in his body was still evident. "It's fine. But let me read it when we get home."

"Okay," I agreed, feeling a pang of guilt.

Luke leaned in even closer, his voice dropping to a conspiratorial whisper. "You know, Verena, you really should have more confidence in yourself. You're more talented than you realize."

Jae's eyes darkened, his hand tightening around mine once more. "I think she knows that, Luke. She doesn't need you to tell her."

Luke raised an eyebrow, his smirk never faltering. "Just trying to be supportive. Something a good friend does."

Jae's glare could have cut through steel. "Well, she has plenty of support from people who actually matter."

Mom, sensing the tension, stepped in. "Verena, why don't you help me with the cookies?"

I nodded, grateful for the distraction. As she and I moved to the counter, I could still feel Jae's eyes on me, a storm of emotions swirling beneath the surface.

As we worked, Mom leaned in close. "Things are different between the two of you," she murmured.

I blinked, caught off guard. "Oh?"

"I sense a disturbance in the force," she said with a knowing look. "There's...tension. Lingering looks."

"Mom, I'm not talking about my sex life with you," I hissed, trying to divert the conversation.

She gasped, her eyes widening. "So you've had sex with him?"

I hesitated. "No. Maybe."

"Oh shit, you went and fell for your fake fiancé."

"Say it a little louder, Mom, why don't you?" I muttered, rolling my eyes.

"Well, he seems more human these days, and you're happier. I could get on board, depending on if he treats you right."

"You were anti-Jae, like, a week ago," I pointed out.

"I'm allowed to reassess and reevaluate," she replied. "Plus, Auntie keeps sharing all these cute stories about him."

"Mom, what do you mean?" I asked, my curiosity piqued and my nerves on edge.

She glanced around, making sure no one was within earshot, then leaned in closer. "I had no idea how much he's built up his business, or all the things he's done for you over the years."

"What are you talking about?" My stomach tightened with unease.

"Well, remember that contract error you made once? The one that lost millions?"

My stomach dropped, the memory flooding back. "Yeah, I came home crying because I messed up a contract, but Jae fixed it. What about it?"

Mom's eyes softened. "I didn't realize he paid for it with his own money."

My heart skipped a beat. "He what?"

Mom nodded. "The board wanted to fire you, but Jae stepped in. He paid the penalty out of his own pocket to keep you on."

I stood there, stunned. I didn't realize he paid for it with his own money, either.

"Why didn't he ever tell me?" I whispered, more to myself than to Mom.

She shrugged. "Maybe he didn't want you to feel indebted to him. Or maybe he just cares about you more than you realize."

I glanced over at Jae, who was arguing with Luke again. The way he spoke, the way he moved—it all seemed so different now. More meaningful. More...real.

My mind raced as I processed this new information. The Jae I knew was arrogant, domineering, and often infuriating, but this revelation painted him in a new light. He had protected me, sacrificed for me, without expecting anything in return.

"Mom, why didn't you tell me this sooner?" I asked, my voice quivering slightly.

She sighed. "I only found out recently. Jae never wanted anyone to know. But I thought you deserved to know the truth."

I tried to steady my swirling emotions. "Thank you."

She gave me a reassuring smile. "Just remember, people often show their love in different ways. Sometimes, it's the things they don't say or do that speak the loudest."

I nodded, my eyes drifting back to Jae. He caught my gaze and gave me a small, playful wink, completely oblivious to the emotional storm brewing inside me.

As I watched him, a flood of memories rushed through my mind— his support, the way he always seemed to be there when I needed him most. And now, this. A sacrifice I never knew he made.

I glanced over at the table where Auntie was watching Jae, who was now engaged in an arm-wrestling contest with Luke. Her smile was wide, eyes sparkling with amusement. It was a rare sight, one that filled me with warmth. But then, her expression changed.

A violent cough erupted from her chest, shaking her entire body. The force of it was terrifying. She tried to wave us off, insisting she was fine, but her body betrayed her. Her eyes rolled back, and she collapsed in a heap.

"Auntie!" I screamed, my voice breaking as I rushed to her side.

Jae was already there, his face pale with fear. He cradled her gently, his hands trembling. "Call an ambulance!" he shouted, his voice tight with panic.

Mom's hands shook as she dialed. "We need an ambulance. Now!"

Laura and Luke hovered nearby, their faces mirrors of shock and horror.

The sound of Auntie's labored breathing was the only thing I could hear. It was shallow, irregular, a horrifying reminder of her fragility. Her face was ashen, the life that usually lit up her eyes dimming.

"Auntie, stay with us," Jae whispered, his voice breaking, the words a desperate plea.

I gripped her hand, my heart pounding so hard it felt like it would burst from my chest.

My mother, a seasoned nurse, was the only calm one in the group, listening to her chest, checking her pulse, barking orders.

Time seemed to stretch endlessly. The seconds dragged on, each one an eternity as we waited for the paramedics. Every breath she took was a battle, and it tore at my heart to see her like this.

When the paramedics finally arrived, the room exploded into a flurry of activity. Urgent voices filled the air as they assessed her condition, their movements quick and precise. They lifted Auntie onto a stretcher, and the sight of her frail body lying there, so still, was more than I could bear.

We followed them out to the ambulance, every step burdensome with dread.

As the ambulance doors closed, sealing her away from us, I turned to Jae. Tears streamed down my face, my vision blurred by the sheer intensity of my emotions. "She has to be okay."

Jae's eyes were red-rimmed, his face etched with fear and helplessness. "She will be," he said, his voice a hollow promise, as if he was trying to convince himself as much as me.

We stood there, watching as the ambulance sped away, the sirens wailing a mournful cry. It felt like a piece of our hearts had been ripped away, leaving a gaping wound in its place.

The world seemed to stand still as we stood there, united in our shared grief and desperation. And as the ambulance disappeared from sight, carrying Auntie away from us, the reality of our situation settled in.

She had to be okay. She just had to be.

35

RE(UNITE)D

JAE

The air was thick with the smell of antiseptic, and the hum of fluorescent lights overhead did nothing to ease the tension twisting in my gut. I glanced over at Verena, her eyes red and puffy from crying, her thin frame shivering slightly as she held Auntie's hand.

The door creaked open, and a doctor stepped inside, his expression somber. He carried a clipboard, his eyes meeting mine for a moment before he took a seat across from us.

"Hello," he began, his voice gentle but firm. "I'm Dr. Patel, the oncologist overseeing Miss Lee's care. I have some updates regarding her condition."

Verena squeezed Auntie's hand tighter, her knuckles white. I placed a reassuring hand on her back, feeling the tension in her muscles.

"Dr. Patel," I said, my voice rough. "Please, tell us what's going on."

Dr. Patel nodded, glancing at his notes. "Miss Lee's lung cancer has progressed more rapidly than we anticipated. The cancer has metastasized to other parts of her lungs, and we're now seeing evidence that it's spreading to her bones as well. This is why she's been experiencing increased pain and coughing."

I struggled to keep my composure, focusing on the doctor's explanation.

"As the cancer progresses," Dr. Patel continued, "we can expect to see more severe symptoms. This will likely include increased pain, shortness of breath, and significant fatigue. As her lung function decreases, she may require supplemental oxygen."

"How much time does she have?" Verena asked, her voice barely more than a whisper.

Dr. Patel hesitated, his eyes full of sympathy. "It's difficult to say with certainty. Based on her current condition and the rate at which the cancer is progressing, we're looking at a couple of months, possibly less."

My world stopped. The air was sucked out of the room, leaving a vacuum of disbelief and impending grief. I felt like a grieving teen again, powerless and lost.

"What can we do to make her comfortable?" I asked, my voice cracking slightly. The usual arrogance, the demanding tone, it was all stripped away in the face of this raw, aching fear.

Dr. Patel's face softened even more, if that was possible. "We'll focus on palliative care. Pain management, ensuring she's as comfortable as possible. We'll provide emotional support as well, for both her and the family."

I nodded, trying to process his words. Palliative care. Pain management. Emotional support. It all sounded so clinical, so sterile compared to the vibrant life my aunt had always lived. "Is there...is there any chance at all?" I hated the way my voice wavered, betraying the desperation I felt.

He sighed, looking down at his notes for a moment before meeting my gaze again. "I'm sorry, Mr. Lee. At this stage, our focus is on quality of life, not cure. We want to make her remaining time as peaceful and pain-free as possible."

My fists clenched, nails digging into my palms. This wasn't how it was supposed to be. I built an empire, conquered a world of steel and glass, but I couldn't do a damn thing to save her. The helplessness was infuriating.

"Thank you, Dr. Patel," I said, my voice hardening slightly as I tried to regain some semblance of control. "I appreciate your honesty."

He nodded, his expression a blend of professionalism and empathy.

Auntie squeezed Verena's hand weakly, her voice barely a whisper. "I don't want to be a burden."

"You're not a burden," Verena insisted, her voice shaky. "We're here for you, Auntie. Every step of the way."

Dr. Patel offered a small, reassuring smile. "We'll work together to ensure she's as comfortable as possible. If you have any questions or need support, don't hesitate to reach out to us. We're here to help."

I knelt beside Auntie and grabbed her hand, feeling the frailty in her once strong grip. She looked at me, her eyes filled with sorrow and regret. "*I must have scared you,*" she said softly in Korean.

I nodded, unable to speak past the lump in my throat.

"*I'm so sorry, sweet boy,*" Auntie continued, her voice trembling with emotion. "*I thought I had more time.*"

The words pierced through me, tearing down the walls I had built to keep my emotions in check. Tears blurred my vision, making everything around me hazy and indistinct. I felt them spill over, warm and relentless, running down my cheeks. Auntie had always been my rock, the pillar of strength in my life. She was the one who held me when my parents died, who whispered soothing words and wiped away my tears. She was the one who never made me be strong when the situation demanded vulnerability, always letting me know it was okay to feel, to grieve, to be human.

I knelt beside her hospital bed, grasping her frail hand in mine, and felt the weight of her love and the impending loss crushing my chest. "*Auntie, I...*"

She squeezed my hand gently, her own eyes glistening with unshed tears. "*You've always been so strong, Jae. Strong for everyone else, but you don't have to be strong for me right now. It's okay to let go.*"

The lump in my throat grew tighter, making it hard to breathe, let alone speak. I bowed my head, the tears falling freely now, mingling with the memories of every time she had been there for me, every moment she had been my sanctuary. *"I don't want to lose you,"* I whispered, my voice cracking.

As I knelt there, holding Auntie's frail hand, a memory surfaced, vivid and poignant. I was six years old, visiting her in Korea for a couple of weeks in the summer. There was a spider in the house. It wasn't particularly big or threatening, but to my young eyes, it was a monster. I cried out for Auntie, and she came rushing in, concern etched on her face. When she saw the source of my distress, she didn't laugh or scold me. Instead, she grabbed a cup and a napkin, gently coaxing the spider into the cup and carrying it outside. She let it walk away, her movements calm and reassuring.

"See, Jae," she had said, her voice soothing, "everything deserves a chance to live."

Now, I wished for that same mercy for her. Cancer was not merciful. It was cruel, unrelenting, and it didn't care about fairness or kindness. It didn't care about how much life Auntie still had left to live or how many moments she still wanted to share. It was a thief in the night, stealing away the vibrant essence of someone I loved, leaving me to grapple with the truth of her mortality.

Now, facing the harsh reality of Auntie's illness, I wished I could find a cup and a napkin, something to make this all more merciful for her. I wished for a way to take her pain and fear and let them walk away, just as she had done with that spider all those years ago.

"I want the two of you to get married before I go," she said, her voice breaking.

I cried harder, the weight of her words crushing me. Memories of my parents' funeral flooded my mind, the way everyone told me to be strong, to be a man, while Auntie had swatted them away and held me as I sobbed.

"I'm sorry," I choked out, my voice barely a whisper. "I'm so sorry."

She squeezed my hand gently. "Jae," she began, her voice firmer now. *"I know you're not really dating."* She spoke in Korean now, so Verena couldn't understand.

My gaze snapped to her, eyes wide in shock.

Auntie smirked, a glint of mischief in her tired eyes. *"I'm smarter than I look. I know you're doing this for me. But you know what? I know you really love her. I know you've loved her for a while. I was hoping I had more time for the two of you to figure this out and fall in love for real. So I need you to approach this like you do every problem. Convince her of what you and I already know. You are meant to be together. I want a wedding, Jae. I want to leave this world knowing you are taken care of."*

I swallowed hard, the lump in my throat making it difficult to speak. "Auntie, I—"

She cut me off, her grip on my hand tightening slightly. *"Jae, you are the type of man who doesn't settle, who always goes after what he wants. You have to do this."*

Her words were like a challenge, one I couldn't refuse. *"But, Auntie, what if—"*

"No 'what ifs,' Jae. When you wanted your business to make a billion in five years, you made it happen. When you wanted to be valedictorian, you made it happen. You want Verena, now make it happen."

I blinked. Auntie had always seen through me, understood the drive that fueled me. She had been there for every major milestone, cheering me on, pushing me to be my best. Now, she was asking me to fight for the one thing I wanted most, the one thing I hadn't allowed myself to fully acknowledge until now.

"You really think I can do this?" I asked, my voice barely above a whisper.

Auntie's eyes softened, and she smiled. *"I know you can. You're Jae Lee. There's nothing you can't do when you set your mind to it."*

I nodded, the determination building within me. "We will get married next week, Auntie," I said, switching to English for Verena's sake.

Verena gasped, her eyes wide with shock. "If it's what Auntie wants," she forced out, her voice shaky.

I looked at Verena with pleading eyes, hoping she could see the sincerity in mine. Auntie knew the truth, and now it was up to me to make Verena see it too. I had to juggle this debilitating grief and give the only family I had left her dying wish. And I had to make the woman I loved finally see that I've loved her for years.

As we all sat there, I knew one thing for certain: Verena was it for me. I just had to make her see it too.

36

A(LONE)

JAE

Three Years Ago

The New Year was supposed to be a time for celebration, but for me, it was a reminder of everything I didn't have. My employees were all on holiday, leaving the office empty and silent. I was alone in my penthouse, the city's distant fireworks mocking my solitude. Holidays intensified my loneliness, sharpening the edges of my vulnerability.

I hated this time of year. It made the void in my life feel more cavernous, the silence more oppressive. My thoughts drifted to Verena. Things had changed between us, grown distant. I'd put her back in the box of "employee" where I could keep her close without feeling the sting of rejection. At least this way, I could see her every day. If I ever screwed up and told her how I truly felt, she'd be gone for good, and that was a risk I couldn't take.

I knew she was at a local bar with Laura and Luke, ringing in the New Year. She never invited me to things anymore. The sting of exclusion was sharp, and I couldn't shake the feeling of being left behind.

Before I knew it, I was grabbing my jacket and heading out into the cold. The air was biting, each breath a reminder of how raw and exposed I felt. I thought about my parents, how their memories were slipping away, growing fuzzier with each passing year. I thought about Auntie, my only family, *thousands of miles away in Korea. Work was my refuge. Surrounded by people, I could ignore the gnawing loneliness. I could pretend that the woman I loved didn't look at me as just her boss. I could avoid the reality that I was utterly alone.*

The bar was packed when I walked in, the noise and warmth enveloping me. I spotted Verena instantly, laughing with Laura and Luke. She looked stunning, her dress clinging to her curves, her hair falling in soft waves around her shoulders. My heart ached seeing her like that, so close yet so unattainable.

The lights dimmed, and an emcee took the stage, announcing the midnight countdown. "Be bold," he encouraged. "Start the year off with an anonymous kiss." I saw Luke's eyes light up, his gaze fixed on Verena.

No fucking way.

The countdown began, and the lights went out. "Ten...nine...eight..." The room was almost pitch black, filled with the excited murmurs of people ready to start the year with a kiss. My pulse raced as I pushed through the crowd, every second ticking away. "Seven...six...five..."

I had to get to her. "Four...three..." I was almost there, the darkness my ally. "Two...one..."

I reached her just as the final second passed, my hands finding her shoulders. I crushed my lips to hers, fast and hard, my heart pounding in my chest. The world fell away, and for a brief moment, nothing else mattered. Her arms wrapped around me, her body pressing against mine. The kiss was quick but intense, a desperate collision of longing and unspoken words.

It was over in a heartbeat, but it was enough. Enough to think about for the rest of my life. Enough to know that the only way she'd ever want me was if I was a stranger, some fool fumbling in the dark.

I fled before the lights came back on, my heart racing as I slipped out of the bar and into the cold night. The cheers and laughter of the crowd faded behind me, and I was alone again, the bitter wind biting at my skin. But for those few seconds, I'd had her. I'd kissed Verena, and it was the best start to the worst year of my life.

37

(SWEET)HEART

VERENA

The bridal gown shop was elegant and pristine, filled with rows of beautiful dresses that sparkled under the soft lighting. I stood in front of a full-length mirror, feeling a mix of emotions that I couldn't quite untangle. I wasn't necessarily mad at Jae. It had been an emotional moment when Auntie asked us to get married soon. He was put on the spot and wanted to give a woman we both loved her dying wish. But that didn't mean I was thrilled about going through with this wedding. The original plan was a nine-month engagement. Now, I was buying a wedding dress. It was too much. Too soon.

The dress attendant, a kind woman named Elise, helped me into a gown that was undeniably pretty. It was an A-line dress with intricate lace detailing and a sweetheart neckline. The fabric flowed gracefully, hugging my curves in all the right places. I stepped out of the dressing room and into the main area where Jae was sitting, looking surprisingly comfortable in a place he clearly didn't frequent.

As soon as he looked up and saw me, I noticed his Adam's apple bob as he swallowed hard. His eyes roamed over me, taking in every detail of the gown. The sexual tension between us was tangible, an electric current that seemed to hum in the air. But then, his expression shifted. He frowned, noticing my lack of enthusiasm.

"You look beautiful," he said softly, his voice filled with genuine admiration. "Why don't you look happy?"

I shrugged, trying to keep my tone neutral. "Well, it's not real, so it doesn't matter what I wear, yeah? Do you like it?"

He sighed, his eyes softening. "I want you to like it."

"I don't have to like it," I retorted, my frustration bubbling to the surface.

Jae's jaw tightened, but he kept his voice calm. "Try on one that makes you smile, then."

I huffed and disappeared back into the dressing room. Elise patiently helped me try on gown after gown, but none of them brought a smile to my face. It wasn't the dress; it was the idea behind it. This wasn't how I envisioned picking out my wedding dress—under the weight of an obligation rather than joy.

Finally, I found a beaded mermaid gown that exposed my entire back. The intricate beading shimmered with every movement, catching the light and drawing attention to the delicate details that adorned the fabric. The gown hugged my curves perfectly, flaring out at the knees into a stunning train that flowed gracefully behind me. It was an astonishing dress, one that made me feel beautiful.

I sighed and said, "Fine, we can try this one."

As I stepped out of the dressing room, I couldn't help but feel a tiny, reluctant smile tugging at the corners of my lips. The reaction was immediate. Jae's eyes lit up with a brightness I hadn't seen in a long time. He stood up, his body language shifting from relaxed to intensely focused. His gaze roamed over me, drinking in every detail of the gown and how it clung to my body.

"That's the one," he said with conviction, his voice steady and unyielding.

I tried to brush it off, forcing a casual tone. "Whatever. If you like it, that's fine."

But Jae wasn't having it. He turned to the shop owner, who had been watching us with curiosity. "I'll give you fifty thousand dollars to let us have the shop for two hours. Alone."

The shop owner's eyebrows shot up in surprise. "Uh, sir—"

"Seventy-five thousand," Jae interrupted, his voice firm.

The owner blinked, then nodded quickly. "Deal."

As she and the other attendants left, giggling softly, I turned to Jae, my confusion turning into irritation. "What are you doing?"

He didn't answer immediately, his eyes still locked onto mine. The shop felt unnaturally quiet, the echo of the door closing behind the attendants leaving a tension in the air. He took a step closer, the commanding presence of the CEO I knew so well radiating from him.

"I needed us to be alone," he said, his voice low but filled with authority. "There are things we need to talk about, and I don't want any interruptions."

I crossed my arms, the voluminous dress rustling slightly. "You didn't have to buy out the entire shop just for that."

"Yes, I did," he insisted. "Because you keep avoiding the conversation we need to have."

I felt a mix of anger and vulnerability welling up inside me. "What conversation, Jae? About Auntie's wish? About how we're supposed to get married when we're not even really together?"

He moved closer, his presence almost overwhelming. "No, Verena. About us. About what's real and what's not. About what I feel for you and what I know you feel for me."

I opened my mouth to protest, but he cut me off, his voice taking on that domineering edge I had come to both despise and crave.

"Stop pretending this doesn't matter," he said, his tone softer but no less intense. "I know you, Verena. I know how you think, how you feel. You've been hiding, running away from this, but you can't anymore. Not when everything is on the line."

He stepped closer, his eyes searching mine with a seriousness that took my breath away. "Tell me what's wrong, Verena. I know this isn't just about the dress."

I could feel the heat radiating from his body, the way his gaze seemed to pierce right through me. The tension between us was thick, a force that made the air around us crackle with electricity. Every inch of my skin felt hyperaware of his proximity, the way his breath hitched slightly as he took me in.

"It's everything, Jae. This wasn't the plan. It's too soon, too fast. And it feels...wrong. I don't know how to make myself feel right about it."

Jae reached out and gently took my hands in his, his touch warm and grounding. "I know it's a lot, and I know it's not how we planned it. But we're doing this for Auntie. And I want to make it as real and as right for you as possible."

I looked down at our intertwined hands, feeling the familiar spark that always seemed to burn whenever we touched. "But it's not real. It's just for show."

He stepped closer. "Do you like me, Verena?"

"I'd feel better knowing if you like me."

He sighed, running a hand through his hair. "If you have to ask that, then I've failed miserably."

My insecurities spilled out before I could stop them. "Can you blame me? We've worked together for years, been friends for years, and not once did things turn...awkward. You never once hinted that you liked me in that way. We've shared beds, we've—"

Jae cut me off, his voice firm but gentle. "Verena, I've been an idiot. I thought keeping my distance would protect our friendship. I didn't want to risk what we had. But that night in the car, it changed everything for me. I've wanted you for a long time, but I was too afraid to admit it."

I stared at him, my heart pounding. "Why now, Jae? Why not before?"

He stepped even closer, his presence overwhelming. "Because I can't keep pretending anymore. I can't keep watching you from the sidelines, wishing you were mine. I need you to know how I feel, even if it scares the hell out of me."

I searched his eyes, seeing the raw honesty and vulnerability there. "And how do you feel, Jae?"

"Hold up," he interrupted, raising a hand. He went to his briefcase, which he carried everywhere, and pulled out that damn notebook—the one I had slammed on his desk in anger. My heart pounded as he flipped through the pages.

"Let's go through this," he said, his voice softer now.

I blinked, taken aback. "What?"

"February fourteenth, the tulips. You love tulips, and Auntie mentioned once that they were your favorite. I wanted you to have them. And you'd been so stressed. I thought...I thought it would be a fun project for you.

"April seventh, Tokyo. I wanted you to see the cherry blossoms. You talked about them all the time."

He looked up, his eyes intense and pleading. "I wasn't trying to control you, Vee. I was trying to make you happy in the only ways I knew how."

My mind reeled as I processed his words, my heart beating erratically. "And the personal dates I missed?"

His expression softened, making his usually composed face look almost boyish. "I was jealous, Vee. Every time you went out with someone else, it drove me crazy. I couldn't stand the thought of you with anyone else."

I stared at him, my heart aching with the importance of his confession. My breath hitched, and I had to look away for a moment, the intensity of his gaze too much to bear. "Jae..."

"I've been too scared to ruin things, so I didn't say how I felt. But I can't deny it anymore."

Tears filled my eyes as the reality of his words sank in. Every beat of my heart seemed to echo with the truth of his confession. "You really mean it?"

He nodded, eyes shimmering with unspoken emotions. "I do. And I want you to know that I will do whatever it takes to make this real. For us, for Auntie."

"Jae, I..."

He reached out, taking my hand in his, his grip firm yet gentle. "Please, Vee. Let me show you how much you mean to me."

The sincerity in his eyes was almost unbearable. The man who was usually so guarded, so in control, was laying his heart bare before me. I could see the fear, the hopelessness in his gaze. It was as if he were holding his breath, waiting for me to either save him or break him.

I closed my eyes. The room seemed to shrink, the air thick with tension and unspoken truths. I could hear my own heartbeat, feel the warmth of his hand and the overwhelming need to believe him, to let go of all the doubts and fears.

And then, without warning, he kissed me. He didn't ask for permission, but the moment our lips touched, it was obvious he'd been longing for this. His hands gripped me with a fervent need. The kiss was intense, raw, and full of unspoken emotion. His lips moved hungrily against mine, and I felt the world melt away.

He sank his teeth into my bottom lip, a guttural groan escaping him as he pulled me even closer. The sound vibrated through me. I could feel the way he poured everything he couldn't say into the connection between us.

I responded in kind, my hands sliding up his chest to wrap around his neck, pulling him deeper into the kiss. The air around us crackled with tension, and I felt like I was drowning in him, in the intensity of his need and the raw vulnerability he was showing.

His grip on me tightened, and he groaned into my mouth again. Every touch, every movement was filled with a need that was almost tangible. It was as if he was trying to make up for all the times he hadn't kissed me, all the moments he'd held back.

When we finally broke apart, we were both breathing heavily, our foreheads pressed together. His eyes were dark with desire.

"If you don't get out of this dress, I'll rip it from your body, baby," he rasped. He pulled me in tight and grabbed the zipper at my back, easing it down. With the zipper undone, Jae slipped the dress off my body, leaving me in my underwear. His eyes lingered on the sight before him, hunger and desire shining in his irises.

He grabbed my hand, pulling me towards the couch in the dressing lounge. In one swift motion, he pushed me onto it. I could tell this was just as much a turn-on for him as it was for me, his every touch eliciting whimpers from deep within me.

As he leaned in to kiss me, I felt the tension in his muscles dissipate little by little. His hands began to explore my body, making me feel desired, loved, cherished. Each touch, each kiss, was filled with a promise that he would never hold back again.

He freed my breasts from the strapless bra I wore and immediately sucked on my nipple, his teeth grazing the hardened peak. I arched closer to him. "These fucking tits." He kneaded my breasts before flicking my nipple with his tongue and looking at me with heavy eyes. "I've never wanted something so bad in my goddamn life."

"Take off your clothes, Jae."

I didn't have to tell him twice.

He stood up and began to undress, his movements slow and deliberate. Each piece of clothing falling to the floor seemed to add to the intensity of the moment. I watched him, my heart pounding in my chest, as he revealed his toned body beneath his clothes.

He stood before me, fully naked and more beautiful than I could have ever imagined. His cock was hard and ready, the tip glistening with precum.

"You're so hard," I whispered. "Do you have a condom?"

He cursed. "I don't. But I'll come wherever you want me to. I'll make a mess on my fucking stomach if it means you'll touch me, baby."

"Then let's make a mess," I whispered, my voice filled with equal parts desire and nervousness.

He looked at me for a moment, his eyes searching mine for consent, for a sign that I was truly ready for this. I nodded, and he grabbed me, pulling me close and kissing me deeply. The warmth of his body against mine was exhilarating, and I could feel his cock pressing against me, a forceful reminder how much he ached for me.

He prodded at my entrance as I bent my knees and opened my thighs. He rested his forehead against mine and rasped, "Tell me I'm not allowed to come yet."

"Why?"

"Because you deserve at least half a dozen orgasms before I do. And my cock might have a mind of its own, but it'll listen to you."

My voice trembled with desire. "Make me feel good, Jae."

He thrust inside of me, slowly at first, stretching me inch by glorious inch, but soon picking up speed.

I moaned and clung to him, my nails digging into his back. This was beyond anything I could have ever imagined. Our connection was primal and raw, our passion insatiable.

Jae's lips trailed hotly down my neck, leaving marks as he nibbled and sucked on my skin. His body never stopped moving, each thrust taking me higher and higher with pleasure.

"God, Vee," he groaned, his voice husky and pleading. "You're driving me crazy. You feel so fucking good."

The scent of sex and sweat hung in the air. Jae's cologne wafted around us, adding to the electrifying atmosphere.

"Vee, I need you to come," he panted. "Please, I need you to come. I need it more than anything."

I gripped his shoulders, feeling his strength beneath my fingertips. Every touch of his skin against mine sent shivers of pleasure through me. His chest pressed against mine, the heat of his breath fanning across my neck.

"Fuck, fuck, fuck, fuck, fuck." Jae's body trembled, his face contorted in intense pleasure as he repeated the word over and over. His curses turned to whimpers. It was as if the words were molten lava, scorching and desperate as they spilled from his lips, melting into a pool of vulnerability and need.

Jae's panting and moaning filled the room. The sounds of flesh slapping against flesh and our bodies moving together in synchronized, frantic fucking filled the room.

And just like that, my body exploded with pleasure. I cried out his name, my body writhing underneath him as I felt the waves of orgasm wash over me. Jae's eyes widened with surprise and delight as he felt me tighten around him, pulling him even closer.

As he neared the peak of pleasure, his body became a coiled spring, his muscles taut and ready to release. With one final thrust, he let out a guttural cry. As he pulled out and spilled onto my stomach, I felt the warmth of his release against my skin, a tingle that spread throughout my body. His eyes, once filled with desire, now rolled back as if overcome by the intensity of it all.

My mouth was dry and my lips were tingling, as if his pleasure was radiating through my body.

We lay there, panting and entwined, our bodies still shaking with the aftereffects of our intense passion. His chest rose and fell rapidly, his skin glistening with a sheen of sweat. I could feel his heart pounding against me, the rhythm syncing with my own. A contented sigh escaped my lips as I savored the warmth of his body pressed against mine.

My breath came in ragged gasps as the now-familiar waves of pleasure slowly subsided. "Holy shit," I managed to say, my voice still shaky with the remnants of my orgasm. I couldn't believe what had just happened—I had just slept with my best friend.

We had crossed a line that could never be uncrossed.

And I wasn't mad about it.

38

(SHOW)ER

VERENA

T hings with Jae were…normal. Or at least as normal as a new couple about to get married could be. We weren't fake dating anymore, but things were now moving impossibly fast for two people who had just accepted their feelings for one another. I didn't even have time to process it, because all the preparations were taking up so much time.

Today was the bridal shower, and Jae had invited all the female coworkers. Auntie was having a bad health day, and Mom had stayed behind to be with her, so I'd be facing the wolves by myself. I just prayed Laura could come.

Stepping into the Crown Jewels Luxury Hotel felt like walking into a palace. The grand chandeliers sparkled overhead, casting a golden glow over the marble floors. Every corner was adorned with fresh flowers, their fragrance mingling with the rich aroma of expensive perfume.

As I approached the front desk, I was greeted by a woman named Danny. She was beautiful, with sleek blonde hair that fell in soft waves around her shoulders, and she wore a perfectly tailored suit that accentuated her slim figure. Her smile was warm and genuine, immediately putting me at ease.

"Welcome to the Crown Jewels Luxury Hotel," she said, her voice smooth and professional. "How can I assist you today?"

"I'm here for a bridal shower," I replied, trying to keep my nerves in check. "The Verena and Jae party."

Danny's eyes lit up with recognition. "Of course, Miss Williams. The event is in the Grand Ballroom. Let me show you the way."

I followed her through the grand hallways, my heels clicking softly against the marble floor. Danny led me to a set of double doors, opening them to reveal the stunning ballroom. It was beautiful. Crystal chandeliers hung from the ceiling, their light reflecting off the mirrored walls. Elegant tables were set with fine china and sparkling glassware, each one adorned with elaborate floral centerpieces.

"This place is amazing."

"Thank you! We strive to make every event special," she said, her tone professional yet friendly. "It's exciting to work on your wedding," Danny said, glancing at me with a smile. "You're the first bride I've had who wanted a wedding in a week but didn't want to plan it."

I blushed, feeling a bit self-conscious. "I'm not that picky."

Danny laughed softly. "I wish more of my clients were like you. Most brides have a very specific vision and can be...well, demanding."

We both laughed, easing some of the tension I felt. "I just want it to be special for Auntie," I admitted.

Danny nodded, her expression softening. "She's a lovely woman. It's clear how much she means to you."

As we walked through the lavish corridors, a sudden commotion ahead caught our attention. A tall, stern-looking man in a suit was berating Danny, his voice loud and sharp. "Danny, I told you the floral arrangements were supposed to be in the ballroom, not here! How many times do I have to repeat myself?"

Danny's smile faltered slightly, but she maintained her composure. "I'm so sorry, Mr. Collins. I'll get it sorted right away."

As Mr. Collins walked away, muttering to himself, Danny let out a small sigh. "Sometimes, things don't go as planned," she said with a wry smile.

I laughed softly. "Trust me, I know the feeling. I used to be an assistant, and my boss drove me nuts."

"What happened?" she asked, her interest piqued.

"I'm going to marry him," I said with a chuckle.

Danny's eyes widened, and she grinned. "Godspeed."

"Will you be in the event hall with us today?" I asked, hoping Danny could be my emotional support human for the day.

"Normally, I just come in if I'm needed," she replied.

"What if the client needs emotional support? Or bodyguards?"

"Bodyguards?" Danny raised an eyebrow. "Are you in danger?"

"No, maybe…kind of, possibly," I rambled. "I'm about to enter a room full of ex-coworkers. Coworkers who I used to complain to about my current fiancé. A fiancé who is their boss. And my old boss."

Danny cringed, then laughed. "Ouch."

"Yeah, you seem nice. I need a buffer."

She grinned. "I can totally be there as a buffer."

We both laughed, the tension easing a bit as I realized she'd be around to help smooth things over.

As I walked further into the room, the awkward tension from my former coworkers hit me. These were the same people who had freely shared their Jae-related office gossip with me, never imagining I was dating him. The surprise and curiosity in their eyes were obvious.

"Hey, everyone," I said, forcing a smile and trying to ignore the heavy silence that followed.

Mina, Jae's assistant, was already there, dressed head to toe in white. She looked like she was trying to upstage the bride, which, in this case, was me. Her eyes narrowed slightly as she saw me, but she quickly replaced her glare with a saccharine smile.

Danny reappeared, now in a new pair of heels. She leaned in and whispered, "Want me to kick her out?"

I chuckled softly. "Nah, it's okay. I can handle her."

"Verena! Congratulations!" one of my former colleagues, Anaya from marketing, said. She had a friendly smile, but her eyes were tinged with disbelief. Anaya was known for her impeccable presentations and her uncanny ability to sniff out office gossip.

"Thank you, Anaya," I replied, trying to keep my smile genuine. My cheeks were starting to ache from all the forced cheer. Anaya and I had spent many a lunch break in the cafeteria, swapping horror stories about Jae's ridiculous demands.

Another colleague, Sofia from HR, approached. Sofia was the queen of passive-aggressive emails and knew everyone's business. "I have to admit, we were all shocked when we heard. We never saw it coming."

I laughed awkwardly, glancing around the room. "Yeah, it surprised me too. One minute I'm filing TPS reports, the next...boom, engaged." I tried to laugh it off, but it came out more like a nervous giggle. Sofia had once caught Jae in a lie about attending a corporate wellness seminar and had shared the gossip with me over drinks.

The room filled with uncomfortable chuckles, my words hanging in the air like a bad joke.

Sofia leaned in, her eyes narrowing slightly. "So, how did this happen? You and Jae?"

I shifted my weight, feeling the heat rise to my face. "You know how it is with office romances, right?"

Danny, sensing the awkwardness, stepped in with a bright smile. "Ladies, why don't we start with some champagne? Let's celebrate Verena and Jae properly!"

As she handed out flutes of champagne, I mouthed a silent "thank you" to her. She winked in response, clearly enjoying her role as my unofficial bodyguard.

Another colleague, Kiara from accounting, sidled up to me. Kiara was infamous for her ability to find mistakes in any expense report and for her penchant for bringing homemade cookies to the office. "So, what's it like being engaged to the boss? Does he make you do overtime at home too?"

I forced a laugh, my mind racing for a witty comeback. "Well, let's just say the benefits package is a lot more interesting."

Kiara laughed, a bit too loudly, and I could feel the eyes of my former coworkers boring into me. This was going to be a long afternoon.

I felt a tap on my shoulder and turned to see Danny standing there. "You okay?" she asked quietly.

I nodded, though my smile was starting to feel like a grimace. "Yeah, just...navigating the awkwardness."

She patted my arm reassuringly. "You're doing great. Just breathe."

Just then, Mina sauntered over, her gaze icy. "Verena," she cooed, her voice dripping with false sweetness. "I must say, I never expected this. Jae just never seemed interested in you."

I resisted the urge to roll my eyes. "Thanks, Mina. Life is full of surprises."

As everyone gravitated towards the refreshment table, I felt Mina's gaze boring into me. "That dress is...an interesting choice," she remarked.

I forced a smile. "I like it."

Mina's eyes flicked over me, her lips curling into a smirk. "I suppose Jae has a...unique taste in women. It's surprising he chose someone like you."

I clenched my jaw, trying to keep my cool. "Well, he did."

She laughed, the sound grating. "You must feel incredibly lucky to have caught his eye."

"Lucky?" I echoed, my voice steady despite the storm brewing inside me. "Sure, if that's what you want to call it."

Danny stepped in smoothly. "Verena, how about we get you some champagne?"

"Great idea," I said, grateful for the escape.

Just as we reached the refreshment table, the door burst open, and Laura came rushing in. "Sorry I'm late!" she exclaimed, her voice bright and cheerful. She was a whirlwind of energy, her long hair flying as she hurried over to me. "Traffic was a nightmare."

Laura's arrival was like a breath of fresh air, immediately lifting the mood. She wrapped me in a tight hug. "Hey, Vee! Miss me?"

I laughed, hugging her back. "Always."

She pulled back, her eyes sparkling. "You look amazing! This place is incredible."

Danny handed Laura a glass of champagne, and Laura took it

gratefully. "Thanks. You must be Danny, the amazing event planner I've heard so much about from Auntie. I'm the maid of honor."

Danny smiled warmly. "Guilty as charged. Nice to meet you."

Laura turned to the room, her voice loud enough to draw everyone's attention. "Alright, ladies, let's get this party started! Who's ready for some fun?"

The awkwardness dissolved as everyone turned their attention to Laura, who had a natural talent for bringing people together. She chatted animatedly with my former coworkers, effortlessly deflecting any lingering tension.

Mina's expression soured as she realized she'd lost her audience. She stalked off to the corner of the room, clearly annoyed.

The atmosphere in the room had significantly lightened, thanks to Laura's infectious energy and Danny's seamless event planning. But as the event started to wind down, I felt a twinge of anxiety nibbling at me. Laura was deep in conversation with a group of my former coworkers, her laughter ringing out above the chatter.

"I need to use the bathroom," I whispered to her. She nodded, waving me off as she continued her animated story.

I made my way through the crowd, aiming for the door, when Mina intercepted me, her smile a venomous curl.

"You know, Verena," she began, "I have full access to all of Jae's contracts. It's so interesting that I came across one recently that caught my eye."

I stiffened, trying to keep my expression neutral. "What are you talking about, Mina?"

She leaned in, her eyes gleaming with a predatory glint. "You're not fooling anyone. This is all fake. He doesn't really like you. He just wants to give his auntie a good memory before she passes away. He's a dutiful nephew, nothing more."

My heart hammered in my chest, and I struggled to keep my composure. "You're wrong," I whispered, my voice shaking.

She laughed, a cold, mirthless sound that sent chills down my spine. "Am I? Jae cares about work. He lives for it. Someone like you could never measure up. You're just a distraction, a means to an end."

Tears pricked at the corners of my eyes, but I blinked them away, refusing to let her see how much she was getting to me. "You're wrong," I repeated, though my voice was less certain this time.

"We'll see once it's all said and done, hmm?" Mina's smile widened, the cruelty in her gaze cutting me. "You'll make a beautiful fake bride, Verena. I took your job, and I'll take Jae too. And if you say a word to him about this little conversation, I'll tell Auntie all about the sham of a marriage. You wouldn't want to break a dying woman's heart, would you?"

I swallowed hard, the lump in my throat making it difficult to breathe. "You're a monster," I whispered, my voice barely audible.

Mina shrugged, her smile never faltering. "Maybe. But I'm a monster who knows how to play the game. And you? You're just a pawn. Jae puts work first, Verena. Always has, always will. You were convenient as his assistant, but now you don't even have that in common. I mean, honestly. Think about the last ten years you worked there. We all saw how he treated you. Do you really think anyone in that room believes you had some whirlwind romance?"

I opened my mouth to argue. "That's not true, Mina. You don't know what we have. Jae cares about me. He—"

She cut me off with a dismissive wave, her smile turning even more condescending. "Oh, please. Just give it a week, maybe a month. He'll go back to the office and eventually forget you, like he always does. Work is his priority. He's just feeling sentimental right now."

"No, you're wrong," I insisted, my voice shaking with a mix of anger and desperation. "Jae and I...it's different this time. He's changed. We've changed."

Mina laughed, a cold, mocking sound that sent chills down my spine. "You really believe that, don't you? You think he's changed because he's with you now? Wake up, Verena. The only thing that man cares about is his career and his aunt. And before, you were tied to both. But then you quit. Now his aunt is dying. Does he really care about you?"

The tears threatened to spill over, but I quickly wiped them away, not wanting anyone to see me break down.

"Just wait and see," Mina continued. "He'll go back to his old ways. Work will consume him again, and you'll be left behind. You're just a temporary distraction, Verena. Nothing more."

I straightened my shoulders, refusing to let her see how deeply her words had cut. "You don't know anything about us, Mina," I said, my voice firm despite the quiver I couldn't completely hide. "Jae isn't like that."

Mina's smile widened, but it didn't reach her eyes. "Keep telling yourself that. But deep down, you know I'm right. You'll see."

She turned on her heel and walked away, leaving me standing there, my heart pounding and my mind racing. Her words echoed in my head, each one a dagger to my already fragile confidence. How could I face Jae now, knowing what Mina had said? How could I pretend everything was okay when my heart felt like it was shattering into pieces?

As I stood there, trying to collect myself, I felt a surge of determination. I wouldn't let Mina's words destroy what Jae and I had. I wouldn't let her doubts become my reality. But the fear lingered, a shadow over my heart, making me question everything I thought I knew about us.

<h1 style="text-align:center">39</h1>

<h1 style="text-align:center">(LONG)ING</h1>

JAE

By the time I got home, it was late. Every day at the office seemed like a never-ending cycle of fires to put out, and I was struggling to balance it all. Auntie's deteriorating health was a constant worry, and the need to support Verena was pulling me in another direction entirely.

Auntie's condition was a relentless shadow over everything. Her health was deteriorating faster than we had anticipated, and every visit was a stark reminder of the limited time we had left. The wedding had become a beacon of hope, something for her to look forward to, a reason to keep fighting. Every detail was planned with her in mind, to bring her a bit of happiness in these dark times.

When I headed to the bedroom, I found Verena lying in bed, staring at the ceiling. She seemed lost in thought, her expression troubled.

"Hey," I said softly, approaching the bed. "What's wrong?"

She quickly composed herself, clearing her throat. "Nothing," she said, but the forced smile didn't reach her eyes.

I sat down on the edge of the bed, sensing the tension in the room. "Sorry I'm home late. I stopped by to see Auntie after work."

Her expression softened slightly, and she turned to face me. "How is she?"

I sighed, running a hand through my hair. "She had a bad day today. But she's so happy about the wedding. She keeps talking about how much it means to her."

Verena's eyes flickered with a mix of emotions, but she forced another smile. "That's good. I'm glad it's making her happy."

I continued, feeling a need to share. "She loves talking about the plans. She lights up every time we discuss the flowers, the cake, everything. It's like, for a moment, she's not sick."

Verena nodded, but I noticed her gaze was distant, and her hands were clenched into fists on the blanket. "It's good she has something to look forward to," she said, her voice strained.

I moved beside her then reached out to take her hand, feeling the tension in her grip. Her fingers were cold, her knuckles white as she clung to me. "Are you okay?"

She hesitated, then nodded, her eyes not quite meeting mine. "Yeah, I'm fine. Just tired."

I squeezed her hand gently, trying to offer some comfort. "I know this is a lot. We're both juggling so much right now." I looked down at where our fingers were threaded together, the contrast between her delicate hand and my larger one stark. "Auntie asked why you don't wear your ring."

She sighed, looking down at her hands. "The one you got doesn't fit. I'll get it resized."

I felt like I'd been punched in the gut, the realization hitting me hard. "I didn't even ask if you liked it."

She hesitated before answering, her voice soft. "It's...nice."

"Nice?" I echoed, feeling a mix of disappointment and guilt settle in my chest.

She shrugged, giving me a sheepish smile that didn't quite reach her eyes. "It's not what I ever would have imagined for myself, but none of this really is."

I could see the weariness in her eyes, the way she was struggling to keep everything together. The ring, a symbol of our rushed engagement, was just one more thing that wasn't quite right.

"Verena," I said softly, my voice thick with emotion. "I'm sorry.

Auntie picked it out because she thought it was perfect. I should have made sure it was what you wanted."

She squeezed my hand back, her grip tightening for a moment before she let go. "If Auntie likes it, then it's fine."

Her words were meant to reassure me, but they only made me feel worse. Verena was always putting others first, even when she was struggling. The situation was taking its toll on her, and I could see it in every line of her face.

"We'll get it resized," I said, trying to find a solution. "Or we can get a new one. Something you'll love."

She nodded, a small, grateful smile playing on her lips. "After the wedding, we can focus on that."

I nodded, feeling a twinge of regret that it had come to this. "Yeah, after the wedding. Are you okay?"

She nodded, but the movement was hesitant. "Maybe tomorrow we can go on a date? Just the two of us?" Her voice held a note of hope, but also an undercurrent of desperation.

Guilt stabbed at me. "I'd love to, but I have a meeting with the board. Mina just called to tell me."

Verena's smile faltered, her eyes dropping to our intertwined hands. "Of course, I understand." She took a deep breath and tried to lighten the mood. "How about the night before the rehearsal dinner?"

"Let me check my schedule," I said, pulling out my phone. I frowned as I saw the messages from some of the guys at work. "It looks like the guys planned a bachelor party for that night."

"Oh," she said quietly.

"Are you going to have a bachelorette party?" I asked, trying to keep the conversation going, desperate to erase the shadow in her eyes.

"Probably not," she replied, her voice barely above a whisper. "I might do something with Auntie and Mom, though."

I nodded, still feeling the tension between us, trying to find the right words. Maybe talking about the wedding would help her feel more assured in me. "I need to check on the marriage license and the prenup. We really don't have a lot of time."

"That won't really be necessary, will it?" Her words made me blink twice, caught off guard.

I paused, processing her words. "I guess not," I said, assuming she meant the prenup. I trusted Verena implicitly, and a prenup seemed unnecessary.

But then she added, "We don't need a marriage license yet. I mean, let's see if this lasts first."

"What?" I asked, my voice barely more than a whisper.

Verena's expression was serious but tinged with sadness. "Look, I get that you like me. Or you think you do. And I don't regret that we slept together, but up until a couple of days ago, work was your priority. I still think it is. All of this is going on with Auntie, and I know you want to give her the world right now." She paused, her eyes searching mine, trying to make me understand. "If you're suggesting a prenup, it means you're planning for what comes after. I know you want me to be happy, but I can't help feeling that this is all for Auntie. You're doing this for her, not because it's what you truly want."

I opened my mouth to protest, but she shook her head.

"Jae, I want this to work too. But I'm not going to put pressure on you or have any expectations. We need to figure out if this is real, if we're doing this for us. If once the pain wears off, you'll still want me…"

I felt like the ground had been pulled out from under me. "Verena, I—"

"I support you because I've always supported you. I'll help you with my whole heart, but I can't expect forever from you. Not when it feels like you're just doing this for her. Because when the dust settles, you'll still be Jae Lee, billionaire workaholic, and I'll still be the girl that no longer works for you."

"Is this because I couldn't go on a date?" I asked.

"Are you listening to me?" she snapped. "It's not just that."

She hesitated for a moment before continuing, "Can you honestly say you'd be marrying me if Auntie wasn't sick? Would you have declared everything? Kissed me if she hadn't been sick? Or would you have let me quit and leave?"

I opened my mouth to respond, but the words caught in my throat.

Had Auntie's illness pushed me to act on feelings I had buried for years? Had I been using her situation as an excuse to finally express what I'd felt all along?

"I don't know," I admitted, my voice barely more than a whisper. "I don't know if I would have had the courage to tell you how I feel if things were different. But what I do know is that I care about you, Verena. I've cared for a long time, and Auntie's illness just made me realize how precious time is. Regardless of Auntie, I wasn't going to let you quit. I had my team of lawyers comb through your fucking contract."

"You would have kept me as an employee, sure," Verena said, her voice low but steady. "But would we have gotten to this point?"

I hesitated, searching for the right words. "I don't know. It's hypothetical."

She crossed her arms, her eyes piercing into mine. "Answer me."

I clenched my jaw. "Probably not. It wasn't even…a possibility I considered. I didn't want to ruin our friendship."

"Jae, let's hold off on the marriage license."

Those words made me sick. It was unacceptable.

"What can I do to prove that I'm in this?" I asked, desperation creeping into my voice.

"Time," she replied, her eyes softening. "Time will show us if this is real. When we don't have a job forcing us together or Auntie's situation or anything else. Will you still want me here? That's what I need to know. Will you still make the effort to see me? To be there for me? To stand beside me."

She took a deep breath, her voice trembling slightly. "Do you genuinely want to be there for me, Jae? Because right now, we have all these things forcing us together, and I don't have a ring that fits, a wedding I'm involved in planning, or even a date night to process this."

I opened my mouth to protest, but she held up a hand, silencing me. "And yes, you should absolutely focus on Auntie right now. I am not the priority. I don't want to be the priority. We have chemistry and love between us, but marriage is so much more than that. And you have so much more on your plate."

She paused, her eyes glistening with unshed tears. "I'm not saying we have to figure this out right now, but I'm saying...please give me the chance to fall in love with you on my own terms once the dust settles."

"Verena, I want this. I want us. And I'll give you all the time you need. We'll take it slow, one step at a time. And I can prove it to you. How about a coed bachelorette party?" Fixing this was what was best for her. For me. For everyone.

"Coed?"

"Let's do something together. And we have the rehearsal dinner too," I said, my voice filled with determination. I was a fixer. I could do it all. "I need to prove to you how important you are to me. I know I've prioritized work, but I don't want you to be just another part of my schedule anymore. I don't want you to feel like someone who has to call me Mr. Lee or wait up late for me to fit you into the corners of my day."

"Jae," she sighed. "I feel like an asshole for bringing this up when you already have so much—"

"Don't. You're important to me. Your happiness is important to Auntie, too."

Her face fell. Apparently, focusing on Auntie wasn't the way to go about this.

"Coed bachelorette party. It'll be fun. We can invite everyone," I rushed out.

"Sure," she replied. "Auntie would love that." She yawned.

I nodded, feeling the growing distance between us like a physical barrier. "Are you sure you're okay?"

She forced another smile, but it was brittle, like it might shatter at any moment. "I'm just tired. I think I'll go to sleep."

Verena turned away from me, pulling the covers up to her chin. She looked so delicate. So perfect. I had to do better. "Verena," I called softly, but she didn't respond, her breathing evening out as if she'd fallen asleep. I watched her for a moment longer. The engagement ring had been a mistake, a glaring symbol of everything we were doing wrong.

I reached out and brushed a stray lock of hair from her face, my heart throbbing. "I'm sorry," I whispered, though I knew she couldn't hear me.

As I lay down beside her, I couldn't shake the feeling that things were slipping through my fingers. Verena was troubled, and I was too wrapped up in my responsibilities to give her the attention she needed. And with Auntie's health declining, the pressure to make everything perfect was overwhelming.

Tomorrow, I promised myself. Tomorrow, I'd make it right.

40

(SPELL)BOUND

VERENA

Bachelorette parties were supposed to be wild, right? Full of scandalous games, risqué outfits, and way too much alcohol. But this? This was...different. More like a family get-together with a twist.

The familiar, cozy chaos of Mom's house greeted me as I stepped through the front door. The living room was decked out with streamers, balloons, and a big "Congratulations, Verena!" banner hanging across the fireplace.

"Vee! You made it!" Laura's voice rang out, and she rushed over to hug me. Her enthusiasm was infectious, and I found myself smiling despite the nerves fluttering in my stomach.

"Of course I did," I laughed, hugging her back. "Wouldn't miss my own party, would I?" I was lying to myself. I absolutely wanted to miss my own party. I was debating on pretending to be sick. But that damn guilt, the one where I had to pretend to put on a brave face for Auntie, kept me from hiding.

Mom and Auntie were bustling around the kitchen, arranging trays of food and pitchers of what looked like dangerously strong cocktails. Auntie looked better today, her face lit up with excitement, but I could still see the shadows of exhaustion around her eyes.

"Hey, honey," Mom said, pulling me into a tight hug. "How's my beautiful bride-to-be?"

"Nervous," I admitted. "But good."

Auntie came over and hugged me next. "You look stunning, Vee. And don't worry, tonight is going to be perfect."

"Thanks, Auntie," I said, squeezing her hand. Her health was deteriorating, and here I was, pretending everything was fine.

Luke strolled in, carrying a large cooler filled with ice and beer. He gave me a lopsided grin. "Ready to party, Vee?"

"Always," I replied, trying to match his enthusiasm.

Just then, the doorbell rang, and I turned to see Jae walking in, followed by a man who could only be described as the epitome of tall, dark, and handsome.

"Verena, you remember Sinclaire Jewel," Jae said, introducing his longtime friend. "Sin owns the Crown Jewels Hotels where the wedding will be."

"Please, call me Sin," he said, taking my hand and pressing a light kiss to the back of it. "It's a pleasure to see you again, Verena. Jae's told me so much about you lately."

I glanced at Jae, raising an eyebrow. "Has he now?"

Jae smirked, a playful glint in his eye. "Only the good stuff."

Sin laughed, a rich, warm sound that filled the room. "I brought a friend, I hope that's okay." He stepped aside to reveal another man, equally attractive, holding several bottles of expensive-looking alcohol.

"More the merrier," I said, trying to keep the atmosphere light.

Sin's friend stepped forward, offering a charming smile. "Hi, I'm Nathan. Nice to meet you."

"Nice to meet you too," I replied, shaking his hand. "Welcome to the coed shower."

As we settled in, I remembered my night at the hotel Sin owned. "Sin, I must say, your event planner, Danny, has gone above and beyond for us. She is wonderful."

A shadow crossed Sin's expression, his charming demeanor faltering for a split second. "I'll be sure to keep that in mind," he said, his tone cool and measured, but there was an underlying tension that hadn't been there before.

Nathan glanced at Sin, then back at me, his smile not quite reaching his eyes. "Danny is exceptional at her job," he said diplomatically. "Sin is lucky to have her."

I noticed the brief exchange, sensing there was more to the story, but decided to let it drop for now. "Well, she's made everything run so smoothly. Please thank her for me."

Sin nodded, his expression softening slightly. "I will, Verena. Thank you for letting us join your celebration."

As everyone mingled, I caught snippets of conversations. Luke and Laura were deep in a debate about which game to play first, while Mom and Auntie were discussing the latest episode of their favorite TV show. Sin and Nathan were fitting in effortlessly, charming everyone with their wit and stories.

"Hey, are we going to play a game or what?" Luke called out, breaking the moment.

"Let's get started!" Laura said, her voice brimming with excitement.

We gathered around the living room, forming a loose circle on the plush carpet. Laura took charge, pulling out a stack of cards with a gleam in her eye. "Alright, everyone, teams of two! Let's see who can guess the most movie titles. And no cheating!" she declared, pointing a finger at Luke, who feigned innocence.

Sin stood up first, his presence commanding attention. With a devil-may-care grin, he pulled a card from the stack and glanced at it before dramatically dropping to his knees. His face contorted in fierce concentration as he mimed an intense, life-or-death struggle, his movements precise and powerful.

"*Gladiator!*" Luke shouted, but Sin shook his head, continuing his elaborate performance with unwavering intensity.

"*Pirates of the Caribbean!*" Auntie guessed, her eyes twinkling with excitement.

Sin nodded vigorously, and everyone cheered. Nathan gave him a hearty slap on the back. "That was spot on, man."

"Thanks," Sin said with a wink, his smile causing Laura to practically swoon. "I have a flair for the dramatic."

Nathan stepped up next, his chiseled features and confident demeanor making him equally captivating. He grabbed a card and immediately started an intense and fluid movement, mimicking the precise and deadly skills of a master assassin. His eyes were sharp, and his movements were controlled and deadly.

"*John Wick!*" Laura guessed, her voice filled with excitement.

Nathan shook his head, continuing his performance with a relentless focus.

"*Mission Impossible?*" Mom ventured, her eyes wide with anticipation.

Nathan shook his head again, his expression remaining intense. He then pretended to pull off an elaborate heist, his actions smooth and calculated.

"*Ocean's Eleven!*" I shouted, finally catching on.

Nathan pointed at me with a grin, the room erupting in applause. Auntie was wiping tears from her eyes, unable to contain her amusement.

Meanwhile, Luke was taking every opportunity to outshine Jae, clearly trying to impress me. During his turn, he performed an over-the-top impression of King Kong, complete with chest beating and roaring.

"Come on, Jae, you can't let him win!" Laura teased.

Jae rolled his eyes but couldn't hide his competitive grin. He reached for a card just as his phone buzzed in his pocket. Pulling it out, he glanced at the screen, his expression darkening. "One sec," he muttered, stepping away to take the call.

Luke, seizing the opportunity, sauntered over to me with a cocky smile. "Looks like Jae's a bit distracted. Maybe he's realized he can't compete with the King Kong performance."

I forced a smile, not wanting to encourage Luke's antics. "You certainly went all out, Luke."

He leaned in closer, lowering his voice. "You know, Verena, some people are all about talk, but I'm about action. I'm here, giving it my all, while others...well, they're busy with their phones."

Before I could respond, Jae returned, his expression stormy. "Everything okay?" I asked, trying to defuse the tension.

Jae's eyes flicked to Luke, then back to me. "Just business," he replied curtly, but I could see the jealousy simmering beneath his calm exterior.

Luke chuckled, clearly enjoying the shift in dynamics. "Don't worry, Jae. We kept the fun going in your absence."

Jae's jaw tightened, his eyes narrowing. "I'm sure you did, Luke."

Sensing the brewing confrontation, I stepped between them, placing a hand on Jae's chest. "Let's get back to the game, okay?"

Jae's gaze softened slightly as he looked at me, but his competitive edge was still sharp. "Alright," he said, his voice low and controlled. He turned to face Luke, his demeanor all business. "Ready to lose, Luke?"

Luke smirked, unfazed. "Bring it on, Jae."

Jae picked up a card, his eyes never leaving Luke's. With a dramatic flourish, he began an intense, spot-on impression of a famous movie scene, his performance both captivating and commanding.

"*Terminator*!" Laura guessed, laughing.

Jae shook his head, continuing his performance with unwavering intensity. He mimed the intricate actions of the character, every move calculated and precise.

"James Bond!" I guessed, my heart racing.

Jae pointed at me, a triumphant grin spreading across his face. "Correct."

Luke's smile faltered slightly, but he quickly recovered, giving Jae a grudging nod of respect. "Well played, Jae."

Jae's eyes gleamed with satisfaction. "Thanks, Luke. Looks like you'll have to step up your game."

As the evening wore on, the rivalry between Jae and Luke added an undercurrent of tension to the festivities. Jae's protective nature and Luke's persistent attempts to impress me created a dynamic that was both thrilling and exhausting.

At one point, Auntie leaned over to me. "They're quite the showmen, aren't they? Do you think Sin and Nathan would strip? It's a bachelorette party; we need strippers."

I snorted, trying to stifle my laughter. "Auntie! You can't just ask them that."

Auntie shrugged, a playful smile on her lips. "Why not? It's all in good fun. Besides, look at them. They'd make fantastic strippers."

"They do look the part," I admitted, grinning.

"Exactly," Auntie said, patting my hand. "Let's just enjoy the view for now. But if things get dull, we know who to ask."

"Should we do our next game?" Laura asked.

Jae held up a finger, signaling for a moment. He moved to the corner of the room, his voice low and tense as he spoke. "Mina? I told you only to call for emergencies. Yes? Shit. I told them that's not acceptable."

I tried to keep my smile. "Guess it's time for a drink," I said, forcing a laugh, but the heaviness in my chest was hard to ignore.

Time passed, and I couldn't help but notice Jae still on the phone. His words drifted over to me, fragments of his conversation painting a picture of chaos. "No, Mina, they can't just override the system... Yes, get IT on it now."

The laughter around me became background noise as I kept glancing his way. Auntie's eyes flickered between him and me, concern etched on her face. I took another sip of my drink, letting the alcohol blur the edges of my disappointment.

"Alright, what's next?" Luke called out, oblivious to the tension.

"Cake," Laura said, jumping up with a giggle.

I tried to match her enthusiasm, but I could feel the weight of Jae's absence settling in the pit of my stomach.

Work. It was always work.

Jae finally returned, but his phone buzzed again almost immediately. He sighed, frustration evident, and turned away to answer it. Auntie caught my eye, her brow furrowed. I shrugged helplessly, downing the rest of my drink.

"Vee, let's cut the cake," Laura suggested, handing me another glass. I smiled gratefully, feeling the warmth of the alcohol spread through me.

Luke leaned in, clearly trying to distract me. "Hey, remember that time in high school when we tried to cook Thanksgiving dinner and almost burned the house down?"

I laughed, the memory brightening my mood momentarily. "Yeah, and we had to call the fire department. That was a disaster."

Just then, Jae returned, his expression serious. "Sorry," he said, looking around the room. "We've got a major issue at work. Our servers went down, and there's a huge security breach. I need to get to the office and handle this personally. It's a complete mess."

Sin gave him a pointed look. "Really? No one else can handle it?"

Jae turned to me, his eyes filled with regret. "Would you mind, Vee?"

I forced a smile for Auntie's sake, even though I was miserable. Wasn't this what I feared? That work would take priority. I understood, but it still stung. "Of course, it's fine."

He leaned in, pressing a quick kiss to my cheek. "Thanks. I'll be back as soon as I can."

As Jae turned to leave, Luke seized the moment, stepping up to me with a smirk. "Looks like the knight in shining armor has to ride off to save the day. Again."

The tension in the room spiked as Jae paused mid-step, his shoulders tensing. He turned slowly, his eyes narrowing as they locked onto Luke. "You have something to say, Luke?"

Luke didn't back down, his smirk widening. "Just seems like you're always leaving her hanging for work. Maybe you should learn to prioritize."

Jae's jaw clenched, his eyes flashing with anger. "This is a critical issue, Luke. Something you wouldn't understand because you've never had to handle real responsibility."

The air grew thick with the charged silence that followed. I could feel the intensity radiating from Jae, his domineering presence almost suffocating.

Luke crossed his arms, his posture challenging. "Funny, I seem to remember being pretty responsible back in high school when Verena needed someone to rely on. I was there."

Jae took a step forward, his voice low and dangerous. "You think you're a better man for her, Luke? Think you can do what I do?"

Luke shrugged nonchalantly, but there was a glint of challenge in his eyes. "I'm just saying, maybe she deserves someone who's actually present. Someone who doesn't always put work first."

I stepped between them, placing a hand on Jae's chest to calm him down. "Enough, both of you. This isn't the time or place."

Jae's eyes softened slightly as he looked at me, but his anger was still simmering beneath the surface. "I'll deal with you later, Luke."

With that, he turned and walked out, leaving an oppressive silence in his wake. I turned to Luke, frustration and disappointment swirling within me. "Why do you always have to provoke him?"

Luke shrugged, his smirk fading. "Just trying to remind him what he's got. Maybe he needs a wake-up call."

I shook my head. "This isn't helping, Luke."

He sighed, running a hand through his hair. "I know. I'm sorry. I just...hate seeing you hurt."

I glanced towards the door where Jae had disappeared, my heart heavy with the conflict between them. "We all have our ways of dealing with things, Luke. But this...this isn't the way."

Luke nodded, his expression softening. "I get it. I'm sorry."

I forced a smile. "Let's just focus on enjoying the rest of the evening, okay?"

He nodded, his demeanor more subdued. "Okay."

The room felt emptier without Jae, the laughter and warmth a little dimmer. Auntie's worried gaze followed Jae out the door, then turned to me. I swallowed hard and raised my glass.

Laura nudged me playfully. "Hey, let's make a toast. To Vee, the most amazing bride-to-be!"

My voice was steady despite the turmoil inside. "To all of you, for making this night special."

We clinked glasses, and I downed my drink, the alcohol a welcome distraction from the ache in my chest. As the night wore on, I felt the tension ease slightly, the love and support from my friends and family a soothing balm. But underneath it all, the worry for Jae and Auntie lingered, a constant reminder of the fragile balance we were trying to maintain.

41

(SIGN)IFICANT

JAE

The office was a war zone. Papers were scattered across my desk, monitors flashed with endless streams of data, and the hum of frantic activity filled the room. I'd been here all night, grappling with the havoc of the server breach. Mina had been by my side, bringing me food and tea, her flirty demeanor a constant presence only adding to my stress.

"You're running on fumes," she said, walking in with another tray. Her perfume, a heady mix of vanilla and something spicy, preceded her. It was overwhelming, almost cloying in the already tense atmosphere. She placed the tray on my desk, her hand lingering on my shoulder, fingers lightly trailing down my arm. Too familiar. Too much.

"You need to eat something, Jae." Her voice was soft, almost seductive, as she moved the tray closer to me. A steaming cup of tea and a sandwich sat there, tempting me. I was too exhausted to argue.

"Thanks, Mina," I replied, picking up the tea and taking a sip. The warmth spread through me, momentarily easing the tension that had coiled in my muscles. I needed that, at least.

She perched on the edge of my desk, crossing her legs. Her skirt hiked up a bit too high, a deliberate move. "You've been working nonstop. Maybe you should take a nap."

I shook my head, my focus back on the screen. "I can't. There's too much to do." My voice came out sharper than I intended, but I couldn't help it.

"Just a short one," she insisted, her voice coaxing. She leaned in closer, her hand brushing my arm again. "You'll be no good to anyone if you collapse from exhaustion."

I rubbed my temples. She wasn't wrong. The exhaustion was making it hard to think straight, and I knew I was no good to anyone in this state. "Fine. But wake me up in time for the rehearsal dinner."

Her smile widened, satisfaction glinting in her eyes. "Of course, Jae. I'll take care of everything."

I pushed back from my desk, standing up and stretching. My muscles protested, and I winced at the stiffness. I needed this nap more than I cared to admit. "I'll crash on the couch in my office. Just an hour or so."

"Good idea," she said, her gaze following me as I walked away. "You deserve a break."

I sank onto the couch in my office, the soft cushions a welcome relief. Closing my eyes, I willed myself to relax, but my mind wouldn't shut off. The server breach, the rehearsal dinner, Verena. Everything swirled in a relentless spiral.

My phone buzzed, and I pulled it out, seeing a message from Verena.

Verena: How's it going?

I sighed, typing a quick response.

Jae: It's a mess here. I'll be at the rehearsal dinner though. I'm sorry about last night. I know I need to make it up to you.

Her reply was almost immediate.

Verena: It's okay. I understand. We'll talk later.

Guilt gnawed at me. She said she understood, but I knew I had let her down. Again. I set my phone aside and closed my eyes, letting the exhaustion take over.

Just as I began to drift off, I felt a pair of hands on my shoulders. Startled, I opened my eyes to see Mina standing over me, her fingers pressing into my tense muscles.

"What are you doing?" I snapped, shrugging off her hands.

"Relax, Jae. You need this," she said, her voice low and soothing. "Just let me help you."

I pushed her away, my patience wearing thin. "No, Mina. This isn't appropriate. I need you to handle things out there, not in here."

Her expression shifted, a hint of annoyance crossing her features before she masked it with a sweet smile. "Yes, sir. Whatever you need. I'm here for you."

She backed away but not before giving me a lingering look that made my skin crawl. As she left the room, I tried to shake off the unsettling feeling. Mina was becoming more of a problem than I had realized.

I closed my eyes again, but sleep wouldn't come. My mind was too busy, too tangled with worries about Verena, the rehearsal dinner, and the work disaster unfolding just beyond my office door. Mina's behavior was the last thing I needed to deal with right now.

Verena's understanding text played on a loop in my mind, her patience and support making me feel even guiltier. I owed it to her to be there, to show up and prove that I could balance everything. But right now, all I could do was wait for the minutes to tick by, hoping for a moment of rest before I had to dive back into the storm.

Hours later, I jolted awake, my phone buzzing insistently. I grabbed it, squinting at the screen. It was Verena.

Verena: Jae, where are you? The rehearsal dinner is halfway through.

I jolted upright, my heart pounding. How could I have slept so long? I bolted to my feet, grabbing my jacket. I stormed out of my office and saw Mina leaning casually against the doorframe, a smug smile on her face.

"You forgot to wake me up," I snapped, pushing past her.

She blinked, feigning innocence. "Oh, did I? I must have gotten distracted. So sorry, Jae."

Her nonchalance stoked the flames of my frustration. I didn't have time to argue. I needed to get to the rehearsal dinner. I glared back at her. "This can't happen again, Mina."

She tilted her head, her smile never wavering. "What does it matter? It's not like it's a real marriage," she said, her tone dripping with condescension.

That was it. Something in me snapped. I turned back to her, my eyes blazing with anger. "It is real, Mina. As real as it gets. And your attitude and behavior are completely unacceptable."

She straightened, her smile faltering for the first time. "I know it's not real, Jae. You're doing this for your aunt. Everyone knows it."

"Even if that were true," I said, my voice cold and steady, "it doesn't give you the right to undermine my relationship or sabotage my responsibilities. You've been a hindrance rather than a help, and I won't tolerate it anymore."

Mina's eyes widened, and she opened her mouth to speak, but I cut her off.

"Pack your things. You're fired."

She stared at me, stunned. "You can't be serious."

"Dead serious," I replied, my tone leaving no room for doubt. "I need someone I can trust, someone who respects my decisions and my relationships. You're not that person."

She stood there, speechless, as I turned on my heel and walked out of the office. Relief and anxiety churned in my gut. Firing Mina was long overdue, but now I had to face the repercussions. More importantly, I had to get to the rehearsal dinner and make things right with Verena.

As I hurried to my car, my phone buzzed again. It was another text from Verena.

Verena: Jae?

I glanced at the time and cursed. I quickly typed a response.

Jae: I'm on my way. Sorry, I overslept. Be there soon.

As I slid into the back seat, I told my driver to hurry. The engine roared to life, and we sped through the city, the streets blurring past me. My mind raced with a thousand thoughts. Verena had every right to be upset. I had promised her I'd be there, and now I was running late again, caught up in the endless demands of work.

Every second felt like an eternity. I thought about Auntie, her frail frame and the way her eyes lit up when she talked about the wedding. I was missing precious time with her, time that was slipping through my fingers like sand. The guilt gnawed at me. I was letting everyone down —Auntie, Verena, myself.

We hit a traffic jam, the car lurching to a stop. Wall-to-wall cars surrounded us, the cacophony of honking horns and frustrated drivers filling the air. I clenched my fists, my nails digging into my palms. "Fuck," I muttered.

I thought about Verena's face when I'd last seen her, the hope and frustration mingling in her eyes. I couldn't keep doing this to her. She deserved better than a fiancé who was always late, always distracted. She deserved someone who could be there, fully present, not torn between responsibilities.

Mr. Jameson, my driver, glanced back at me, concern in his eyes. "We're stuck in traffic, sir. It looks like it might be a while."

Auntie was dying. I was losing Verena. My job was a constant source of stress. It was all too much. I pressed my hands to my face, trying to hold back the rising tide of panic.

The honking horns grew louder, the noise drilling into my skull. My breath came in short, ragged gasps, my chest tightening with each inhale. I couldn't do this. I couldn't be everything to everyone. The pressure was suffocating, a vise tightening around my heart.

"Fuck!" I shouted, slamming my fist against the seat in front of me. The driver flinched, but I barely noticed, lost in my own spiraling thoughts. Tears stung my eyes, and I let out a choked sob, the floodgates opening. "I can't do this," I whispered, my voice breaking. "I can't."

The realization hit me hard. I had been avoiding it, pushing it down, pretending I could handle it all. But I couldn't. Auntie was slipping away, and I hadn't even accepted it. Verena was slipping away, and I was too caught up in everything else to see it.

The car moved forward a few inches, then stopped again. The futility of it all washed over me, and I broke down, my shoulders shaking with sobs. I buried my face in my hands, the tears flowing freely now. I was failing. Failing everyone I loved, failing myself.

Mr. Jameson's voice broke through the haze of my panic. "Mr. Lee, we'll get there. Just breathe, okay?"

I nodded, unable to speak, the lump in my throat making it hard to swallow. I took a shaky breath, then another, trying to calm the storm raging inside me. But the weight of everything was too much. I couldn't think, couldn't move.

I had to pull myself together. For Auntie, for Verena, for myself. But as I sat there, trapped in traffic and my own despair, I didn't know how.

42

(DISAPPOINT)MENT

JAE

Two Years Ago

The news hit me like a freight train. Verena had messed up a major contract when relaying information to legal. A million-dollar mistake. The board was livid, calling for her termination. As I listened to their accusations, my mind spiraled. If she was fired, it wasn't just about the money or the contract. It was about losing her, losing the chance to see her every day, to hear her voice. She would disappear from my life, and I couldn't let that happen.

In the boardroom, the tension was thick enough to cut with a knife. My heart pounded in my chest as I stood at the head of the table, trying to keep my composure. "We can't just fire her," I said, my voice tight with barely controlled panic.

One of the board members, a gray-haired man with a stern expression, leaned forward. "Jae, this is a million-dollar mistake. Think of the investors. Think of the company's reputation."

"I don't give a damn about the investors!" I snapped, slamming my hand on the table. "Verena is an essential part of this team. We can't afford to lose her."

"She's jeopardized a major contract. We have to consider the implications," another board member chimed in, her voice cold and pragmatic.

"I'll pay it," I said, the words out before I could think them through.

"What?" The room went silent, all eyes on me.

"I'll cover the cost," I repeated, my tone defiant. "No one mentions this outside of this room. No one does anything to jeopardize Verena's job. Are we clear?"

They exchanged glances, shock and disbelief written across their faces. "Jae, that's—"

"Are. We. Clear?" I growled, daring anyone to challenge me.

After a tense silence, the gray-haired man nodded reluctantly. "Fine. But this stays between us."

"Good," I said, my voice hard. "Meeting adjourned."

I stormed out of the room, my mind racing. How could I fix this? How could I make sure she stayed? As I walked into the main office area, I spotted Verena at her desk, looking dejected. She glanced up as I approached, her eyes filled with resignation.

"I guess I'm fired, huh?" she said, a small, bittersweet smile playing on her lips. It was like a punch to the gut, seeing her almost relieved at the thought of leaving. Anger flared up inside me, irrational and fierce.

Without thinking, I grabbed her wrist and pulled her towards my office. She stumbled slightly, caught off guard by my sudden movement. Once inside, I pushed her against the wall, my hands braced on either side of her.

"You're not going anywhere," I snarled, my face inches from hers. "It's fixed. The board is fine. You're not leaving."

She looked up at me, sadness flickering in her eyes. "Jae, I—"

"Do you have any idea what you've done?" I cut her off, my voice a harsh whisper. "Do you think you can just waltz out of here after making a million-dollar mistake? You think you're that indispensable?"

Her eyes widened in shock, but I pressed on, my words laced with venom. "You're lucky I didn't throw you out on the spot. The only reason you're still here is because I can't afford another screwup. You've been sloppy, Verena. Unfocused. If this is your idea of dedication, maybe you should reconsider your priorities."

She flinched, her expression hardening, but I could see the hurt in her *eyes. It cut through me, making me want to take it all back, but I couldn't stop. "You think anyone else would put up with your mistakes? You're here because I fought for you. Because I cleaned up your mess."*

"Jae, please, I—" she started, but I couldn't let her finish.

"Get back to work," I barked, my tone leaving no room for argument. "And don't think for a second that your job isn't hanging by a thread. You screw up again, and you're gone."

Her face hardened, her eyes turning cold as she pushed past me, heading back to her desk without another word. I watched her go, my chest tightening with a mix of anger and regret. What I wanted to say was, "You can't leave me. I need you." But all that came out was cruelty, masking the fear that, without her, I'd be lost.

43

(VOW)EL

VERENA

The remnants of the rehearsal dinner lingered around me, a harsh reminder of how things were supposed to be. The twinkling lights, the elegant decorations, the carefully arranged centerpieces—everything designed to be perfect—felt like a cruel joke. The pitying looks from the departing guests only deepened the ache in my chest.

The night had started so differently. Auntie had been here, her presence a beacon of warmth and love. But as the evening wore on, I saw the toll it was taking on her. She moved slower, her laughter quieter, her smiles tinged with exhaustion. It broke my heart to see her that way, but she insisted on staying as long as she could.

"Verena, sweetheart," Auntie called softly as she prepared to leave, leaning on Mom for support.

I hurried over, my eyes filling with concern. "Auntie, are you okay?"

She gave me a weak smile, her eyes full of love and sadness. "I'm fine, just tired. But I need to get home and rest."

I hugged her gently, afraid to squeeze too tight. "I understand. Please take care of yourself."

She nodded and then whispered in my ear, "Have grace for Jae. He's doing his best."

Her words were a balm and a burden. I knew she was right, but it didn't make it any easier. As she and Mom left, I stood there, feeling helpless. This entire thing was what Auntie wanted, and I was trying so hard to make it perfect for her.

The room felt emptier without Auntie and Mom, their absence a gaping hole in the evening. Danny, the wedding planner, approached me with a sympathetic smile.

"Everything looks beautiful, Verena. I'm sure the wedding will be just as magical."

"Thank you, Danny," I replied, trying to muster a smile. "You've done an amazing job."

She gave my hand a reassuring squeeze before heading off to coordinate with the staff.

An hour later, the door swung open, and Jae walked in looking disheveled and frazzled. His suit was wrinkled, his tie askew, and his hair a mess. Dark circles under his eyes betrayed his exhaustion, and his entire demeanor screamed stress and fatigue.

My heart ached at the sight of him. He looked so lost, so burdened. I wanted to be angry, to yell at him for being late again, but all I felt was a profound sadness. This was supposed to be our night, a celebration of our commitment, but it was clear that commitment wasn't to me.

"Where is everyone?" Jae asked, his voice strained and tired.

"They left," I replied softly, unable to hide the disappointment in my voice.

He let out a heavy sigh. "I'm so sorry, Verena. Mina didn't wake me up when I fell asleep. I was so busy with the server breach, and I just... lost track of time. Where is Auntie?"

"She left, she was tired," I replied, my voice barely above a whisper.

"Fuck!" he roared, the sound echoing through the empty restaurant. His face contorted in frustration, and before I could react, he kicked a nearby chair, sending it skidding across the floor. "The whole point of this was for her to have a memorable night, and I ruined it."

I flinched at the sudden violence, my heart pounding in my chest. The raw pain in his eyes was almost unbearable to witness. He stood there, breathing heavily, his fists clenched at his sides.

"Jae," I began softly, taking a tentative step toward him, but he cut me off.

"No, Vee," he snapped, his voice breaking. "I don't need your pity right now. I don't need you to tell me it's okay, because it's not. I fucked up. Again."

I swallowed hard, the lump in my throat growing by the second. "I'm not trying to pity you, Jae. But you need to understand—"

"Understand what?" he interrupted, his eyes flashing with anger. "That I'm failing everyone around me? That no matter how hard I try, I can't be there for the people I love when it matters the most?"

"You're not failing," I insisted, my own voice rising. "You're dealing with so much, Jae. Auntie knows that. She knows you're trying your best."

He shook his head violently, his frustration palpable. "My best isn't good enough! Do you get that, Vee? It's never fucking good enough!"

The intensity of his self-loathing cut deep, and I could feel tears welling up in my eyes. "Jae, you're here now. You can still make things right. Auntie understands—"

"But do you?" he shouted, his voice raw with emotion. "Do you understand? Because I don't think you do. You keep telling me it's okay, but it's not."

I tried to steady my trembling hands. "I'm not mad, Jae. I'm hurt. You left the bachelorette party. You made this big declaration and put all your attention on me and then...nothing. I feel like an asshole even demanding, well, anything from you. This was so much easier when it was fake, because I knew where I stood."

His eyes softened slightly, the anger giving way to a deep, aching sadness. "I know, Vee. And I'm sorry. I know I've let you down. But I need you to hold on a bit longer. Please."

"Jae, what am I even holding on to?" I said, my voice trembling with emotion. "I don't even have the chance to see if you can put me first, because you're being pulled in so many directions. I shouldn't be a priority right now even though I want to be, and it's so fucked up.."

He opened his mouth to speak, but I pushed on, the words tumbling out in a rush. "Now that feelings are involved, I don't know where we stand. Part of me wants you to treat me right, to make me feel like I matter. Part of me understands that doing this for Auntie is important. And part of me wants this to be real and done the normal way—dating, figuring this out. Not diving headfirst into marriage."

I looked up at him, searching his face for answers. "I need to know where we stand, Jae. I need to know if there's a future for us that isn't just about convenience or obligation."

His eyes were pleading. "I get it, Vee. I do. And I want all of that too. I don't want to fuck this up, especially when I've wanted this for so long. But right now, I just need you. I need you to help me get through this."

I shook my head, tears spilling over. "You can't keep asking me to be strong for both of us, Jae. I'm breaking too. And I need you to see that." I took a deep breath, feeling the weight of what I was about to say. "Jae, you have to understand something. This...this fake marriage, this charade—it's tearing me apart. I can't keep pretending that everything's okay when it's not."

"You think it's easy for me?" he shot back, his voice rising, his eyes flashing with anger. "You think I don't see how hard this is for you? For us?"

"Then why do you keep doing it?" I demanded, my heart pounding. "Why do you keep pushing me into this role? What if we just—"

"I'm doing my best!" he yelled, fists clenched, his body trembling with frustration. "You don't understand the pressure I'm under. Auntie is dying, Vee."

"And what about me?" I fired back, my own anger bubbling up, hot and fierce. "What about what I need? You think this fake marriage is enough for me? You think I'm happy pretending?"

His eyes widened, but I continued, unable to hold back the torrent of emotions any longer. "I'm not even mad for me, Jae. I'm mad for you. You have this precious time with Auntie, and you're still putting work first. Every day, you choose the office over the moments you could be spending with her. Do you even realize what you're missing out on? She needs you, Jae. And you're not there."

I took a step closer, my voice shaking with a mix of frustration and sadness. "You keep leaving for work, letting it consume you. And it's not just hurting me—it's hurting you. You're missing out on these precious moments with her. Moments that you won't ever get back. And for what? A deal? A contract? Money?"

He looked away, guilt flickering in his eyes, but I wasn't done. "I understand that work is important. I understand that it's a part of who you are. But, Jae, you're losing sight of what really matters. You have this limited time left with Auntie, and you're wasting it. You'll regret this one day. You'll look back and realize that while you were busy making deals and signing contracts, you missed out on the last memories you could have made with her."

I felt tears welling up, but I blinked them away, refusing to break down. "I'm hurt for myself, yes. Because I love you, and I want to be a priority in your life. But I'm also sad for you. Because I see you drowning in your work, and it's tearing you apart. And I'm terrified that when it's too late, you'll realize what you've lost."

My voice dropped to a whisper, raw with emotion. "I want to be there for you, Jae. I want to help you through this, but you keep pushing me away. You're so focused on work that you're blind to what's happening right in front of you. I don't want to be the one to say 'I told you so' when you realize what you've sacrificed."

"You agreed to help me!" he accused, pointing a finger at me, his voice filled with bitterness. "You agreed to be there for me."

"Yes, I agreed to help you," I said, my voice shaking with emotion, my vision blurring with tears. "But I didn't sign up to watch you destroy yourself. I'm giving you everything, Jae. My time, my energy, a damn wedding. What are you giving in return?"

"I just need you to understand!" he pleaded, desperation replacing the anger in his eyes. "I need you to be patient."

"Patient?" I laughed bitterly, wiping at my tears with the back of my hand. "I've been patient. I've been standing by your side, supporting you, loving you. But I can't love someone so blind to what really matters right now."

His face twisted in frustration, his body rigid with tension. "So what? You want out? You want to leave me when I need you the most?"

"I want you to figure out your priorities!" I yelled, my voice echoing in the empty banquet hall. "I want you to deal with what's happening instead of hiding at the office. You can't love me properly until you do."

"I can try," he said, his voice breaking.

"Trying isn't enough," I snapped, my heart aching with the intensity of my feelings. "You need to prove it, starting with Auntie. And you have to do it on your own."

"Fine!" he shouted, his face contorted with rage. "You want me to suffer alone? You want me to push you away? Then go! Leave!"

"I just want you to understand that I'm worried you'll regret this, Jae. She's dying."

"You think I don't know that?" he yelled back, his eyes blazing with anger and hurt.

"Then do something about it!" I shouted, my voice raw with emotion. "Face your grief. Stop going to the office and spend time with her. That is what she wants. And maybe then, we can talk about us."

He looked at me, his chest heaving, and for a moment, I thought he might actually listen. But then his expression hardened, his eyes narrowing. "Fine. You want me to face it? I'll face it alone."

"Maybe that's what you need," I shot back, my voice icy, my heart breaking.

I turned on my heel, my steps quick and determined as I stormed out of the restaurant. The door slammed shut behind me with a resounding bang, leaving Jae standing there in the empty space. I turned back for one last glance, the shock and despair on his face nearly destroying me.

As I walked away, the cool night air hit my face, mingling with the hot tears streaming down my cheeks. My mind was a whirlwind of emotions—anger, sadness, frustration, and a sliver of hope that maybe, just maybe, this would be the wake-up call Jae needed.

I needed him to heal, to face his pain, and to come out on the other side stronger. And until then, I needed to find my own strength, to stand on my own two feet. Only then could we have a chance at something real, something more than just a fake marriage built on lies and desperation.

44

(RUN)AWAY

VERENA

Lying in bed at my apartment felt strangely alien. After spending so much time at Jae's house, this place felt like a forgotten corner of my life. The sheets smelled like lavender instead of his cologne, and the silence was deafening compared to the hum of his late-night pacing.

I never thought I'd find out the wedding was called off through an online tabloid. It was clickbait, and Laura sent it to me with a "WTF?" as the subject line. My mother pounded on my door at six in the morning, and Auntie had called me an hour ago.

Jae sent me one text saying *It's done.*

And I was mad. I was livid. I was also sad.

I needed to talk to Auntie. So I wrapped a scarf around my head like a celebrity trying to dodge paparazzi and threw on oversized sunglasses. Because, really, why not? At this point, I might as well embrace the drama.

The subway ride to my mother's house was a blur of grimy seats and indistinct announcements. When I finally knocked on the door, my mother opened it with a look that was part worry, part exasperation.

"What the hell happened?" she demanded.

"Where is Auntie?" I asked, ignoring her question.

"Jae was just here," she said, eyes narrowing as if trying to read my mind.

I walked past her to the guest room. Auntie looked frail, but there she was, painting her nails a bright red. Because what else would she be doing, I suppose?

"I expected you," she said, wiggling her fingers at me. "Come here, let me paint your toenails."

Leave it to Auntie to make me feel comfortable despite it all. I kicked off my shoes and sat down, sticking my feet out toward her.

"Red?" I asked. "Feeling bold today?"

"Always," she replied with a wink. "A woman should never lose her sense of style, no matter what."

As she carefully applied the polish, I felt a wave of calm wash over me. Auntie had that effect. She made everything seem a little less daunting, a little more manageable.

"So," she said casually, "how are you holding up?"

I let out a bitter laugh. "I don't know, Auntie. How am I supposed to feel after finding out my wedding was called off from a tabloid?"

She paused, looking up at me with a serious expression. "You're supposed to feel however you feel. And right now, you look like you could use a stiff drink and a good cry."

I nodded, tears welling up in my eyes. "Jae just sent me a text. One text. *It's done.* That's all I got."

Auntie sighed, capping the nail polish. "Men can be such idiots sometimes. But you know Jae loves you, right? He's just...lost right now."

I shook my head, tears welling up again. "I don't know, Auntie. I don't know anything anymore."

"I guess it was always supposed to happen this way," Auntie said with a sad smile.

"Do you know?" I asked, the question hanging heavily between us.

"That it was all fake?" she replied. "Of course I knew. Why else do you think I encouraged it?" She muttered a curse in Korean and laughed to herself.

I blinked, taken aback. "What do you mean?"

Auntie looked at me with a knowing smile. "I know my nephew better than anyone. He needed a distraction, and I needed an excuse to spend time with him. He *also* needed an excuse to admit to you how he was feeling. I never expected that wedding to happen, but I had so much fun planning it. I told Danny I wanted the decor to be used for my funeral!"

My eyes widened in shock.

She shrugged. "Why not? Those centerpieces are too gorgeous to go to waste."

I cringed. "Auntie, that's morbid."

"It's practical," she countered, waving a hand dismissively. "And stylish. I intend to go out with a bang, darling. You should know that by now."

"Only you could make planning a wedding and a funeral sound like a fabulous event."

"Exactly," she said, nodding sagely. "Life is too short to be boring. Or to not have red toenails."

I wiggled my newly painted toes. "Thanks for this. I needed it."

Auntie leaned back, admiring her work. "Anytime, sweetheart. Now, tell me more about what's going on in that beautiful head of yours."

I sighed, running a hand through my hair. "I feel like an idiot, Auntie. I knew from the beginning that Jae was avoiding things. That this was just...fake. But when he started to...treat me like it was real, I wanted it to be real. But Jae...he's so caught up in his own world. Rightfully so. And now...it's all so complicated."

She nodded, her expression softening. "Love is always complicated. But you and Jae have something special. It's just...buried under a lot of mess right now. It'll pass."

Auntie started coughing, the fit making her tiny body shake and my chest clench with worry. I reached out, steadying her until the coughing subsided.

"I don't know if we can dig our way out of it," I admitted, my voice breaking. "Tell me what I should do."

She looked at me with a gentle but firm expression. "You do what you've done for the last ten years, darling."

I let out a choked laugh. "Assist him?"

She shook her head, her eyes narrowing. "Don't diminish your role in such a way. You managed him."

I frowned, ignoring the ache in my chest. "What do you mean?"

"You march yourself into that office. You tell him he's taking the next two months off, and you coordinate his schedule. And then..." A shadow crossed her expression, a hint of sorrow in her eyes. "The hardest part."

I swallowed hard, my heart pounding. "What?"

"You leave."

I stiffened. "Auntie, you need me."

She shook her head gently. "I need Jae, and I have your mother. I need you to leave so he can stop using you as a crutch. I need you to leave and write that book you've told me you want to write for the last ten years. I need you to leave and focus on you. Jae needs to accept his grief, and you need to accept yourself."

Tears streamed down my cheeks, and she reached out to wipe them away, the familiar smell of nail polish hitting me as she smiled warmly. "I want you to give me the gift of knowing you're finally chasing your dreams. That was always the goal. Not the wedding. Not the rehearsal dinner. I wanted Jae to realize if he doesn't want to be alone, he has to be still for a while, and if you want your dreams, you have to stop running on someone else's path."

I looked at her, her words sinking in, and for the first time, I saw the strength behind her frail exterior. "But, Auntie, what if he falls apart without me?"

She shook her head again, more firmly this time. "He won't. He'll learn to stand on his own, and you...you'll finally learn to soar. It's time, Verena. It's time for both of you to find your own way."

I nodded slowly, the realization dawning on me. "And what if I fall apart?"

Auntie squeezed my hand, her grip surprisingly strong. "Then you pick up the pieces and build something even more beautiful. You deserve to live your own life, not just be a part of his."

The tears flowed freely now, and I didn't try to stop them. "I'm scared, Auntie."

"I know, sweetheart," she whispered, pulling me into a gentle hug. "But sometimes, the bravest thing you can do is let go. Let go of him, let go of the fear, and hold on to yourself."

I clung to her, the scent of her familiar perfume mingling with the nail polish, creating a sense of comfort and home. Auntie always knew how to make everything seem okay, even when it felt like the world was falling apart.

"Today," she continued, her voice soft but steady, "I want you to hold me for a little while. Smile with me. Let's do facials and giggle and enjoy these precious moments."

I nodded, tears still streaming down my cheeks. "Okay, Auntie. We can do that."

"But then," she said, her tone turning more serious, her eyes locking onto mine with an intensity that pierced through my heart, "I want you to leave. And please, darling, don't come back. Remember me just like this—full of life and sass, painting my nails red. I want you to remember me in my big hats and bikinis at the beach, not as someone wasting away. Think of me laughing too loud and spilling expensive wine on the couch without a care in the world."

She paused, a wistful smile touching her lips. "I want you to hold on to the memories of us giggling during late-night facials, of me insisting on wearing the most outrageous outfits just because they made me feel fabulous. Remember me as the woman who always had a wicked comeback, who loved fiercely and lived boldly."

I could feel the tears welling up again, but she squeezed my hand, grounding me. "Don't return for the funeral, don't come in my final days. My real wish, my deepest desire, is for you to stay away until Jae finds his strength. Let him come to you when he's ready, when he truly deserves you. Only then will he have earned the right to stand by your side."

She took a deep breath, her eyes shining with unshed tears, but her voice steady. "I want this to be our goodbye for now. I want you to remember me just like this, painting my nails red and dishing out sass. Let this be the image you carry with you. Promise me, Verena."

I nodded, the lump in my throat making it hard to speak. "I promise, Auntie."

"Good," she said, her smile returning, warmer and softer. "Now, let's make today a beautiful memory to add to your collection. And always, always remember that I love you, and I'm proud of the woman you are and the one you're becoming."

We forced ourselves not to cry. Instead, we giggled like conspirators in a secret club. We did sassy things, eating store-bought cake straight out of the box with our fingers in bed, smearing icing on our lips like war paint. We snuggled in her thick, fur robes, those extravagant, impractical things she loved, and we listened to old records that crackled with memories. We drank wine out of plastic cups, toasting to everything and nothing, savoring each stolen moment as if it were the last drop of precious joy. Auntie's laughter was a bright melody, a defiant stand against the encroaching darkness.

We lay back, our heads touching, sharing secrets and dreams under the canopy of her fading strength. She told me stories from her wild youth, adventures and loves and losses, painting a vivid tapestry of a life lived with passion and without regret.

As the night grew darker, so did the pressure in my chest. Finally, when the words we'd avoided could no longer be postponed, she turned to me.

"It's time to say goodbye," she whispered, her voice steady but filled with unspoken emotion. "Write your own story, Verena. Live it boldly, fiercely."

I could feel the tears streaming down my cheeks, a silent testament to the promise I was making. "I promise, Auntie."

She pulled me into a weak hug, her frail arms still managing to convey all the love and strength she had left. "Good," she murmured. "Now, go. Be brave. Be you."

45

(HONOR)ARY

JAE

Keep busy. Keep busy. Keep busy.

I barked orders at my board members, the echo of my own voice ricocheting off the sterile walls of the conference room. The wedding had been called off, the PR nightmare was unfolding, and Verena hadn't replied. Auntie was frail. The only thing keeping me sane was work. *Keep busy. Focus on the tasks. Ignore the pain.*

"Jae, the stockholders are concerned about the recent developments," one of the board members started.

"I don't care about their concerns," I snapped. "We have a product launch in two weeks. All efforts should be focused on that."

I could feel their eyes on me, heavy with judgment and silent disapproval. They didn't understand. They couldn't. The tangled web of my life was unraveling at the seams, and all I could do was cling to the one thing I could control—work.

My PR person looked like she wanted to throttle me. Her frustration was a tangible presence in the room. "Jae, this is a disaster. We need to release a statement about the wedding."

"Draft something," I said curtly. "I'll approve it later. Right now, we need to concentrate on what matters."

Keep busy. Keep busy.

I looked down at the reports in front of me, the figures swimming before my eyes. Revenue projections, market strategies, growth potentials—all meaningless numbers that were supposed to anchor me. I had to stay focused. The world outside this room could fall apart, but in here, I could maintain the illusion of control.

"Jae," another board member ventured cautiously, "perhaps we should postpone the launch. Given the circumstances—"

"No," I cut in sharply. "We stay the course. Delays cost money. We need to keep moving forward."

Keep busy. Keep busy.

My phone buzzed with incoming messages, each one a potential landmine. I ignored them. If I stopped to read, to engage with the outside world, the fragile dam I had built to contain my emotions would burst. I couldn't afford that. Not now. Not ever.

"There's also the issue with the marketing campaign," someone else chimed in. "We need your input on the new direction."

"Send me the proposals," I replied, my tone clipped. "I'll review them by the end of the day."

Keep busy. Keep busy.

I forced myself to focus on the next quarter's targets, outlining our goals with a precision that felt like grasping at straws. The words came out mechanically, devoid of the passion I usually brought to these meetings. But it didn't matter. Passion was a luxury I couldn't afford right now.

"Q2 is crucial," I continued, my voice steady. "We need to hit our targets or we risk losing investor confidence. I expect everyone to double their efforts."

They nodded, jotting down notes, but their eyes betrayed their uncertainty. They were used to my intensity, but this was different. This was desperation masquerading as determination.

Keep busy. Keep busy.

I glanced at the clock, the minutes ticking by with agonizing slowness. Every second felt like an eternity. I had to keep going, keep pushing forward. It was the only way to drown out the noise, the turmoil that threatened to consume me.

The door swung open. The sudden motion startled everyone, and I looked up, my breath catching in my throat.

Verena walked in.

She looked exactly like she did when she used to work for me—tight pencil skirt hugging her curves, her heels clicking against the polished floor with a confidence that demanded attention. Her hair was pulled back in a sleek ponytail, revealing the graceful lines of her neck. She held an iPad with an air of authority, her movements sharp and precise.

The room fell silent, confusion etched on every face. But all I could see was her.

My heart twisted painfully at the sight of her. It hurt, a deep, gut-wrenching ache. I longed for her, missed her presence, her laughter, the way she could calm the storm inside me. I wanted to reach out, to pull her into my arms and apologize for everything, but I was frozen, stuck in a web of my own making.

Her eyes met mine, and for a brief moment, the world narrowed down to just the two of us. I saw the resolve in her gaze. But there was something else there now—something harder, more unyielding. She was here on a mission.

"Thanks for coming to my meeting, everyone," she said, her voice cool and authoritative.

Each word cut through the silence. The board members exchanged bewildered glances, their confusion evident. But I couldn't tear my eyes away from her. Every detail of her appearance was a painful reminder of what I had lost. The way her skirt clung to her hips, the confident stride of her heels, the steely resolve in her eyes—it was all too much, too overwhelming.

"Good to see you all," Verena continued. "I appreciate you making time for this on such short notice."

She paused, her gaze sweeping across the room, meeting each board member's eyes with an intensity that brooked no argument. "Today, we're going to address some immediate changes that need to happen within this company. Changes that will ensure we move forward efficiently and effectively."

There was a murmur of confusion, a rustling of papers as the board members tried to make sense of what was happening. I felt a knot tightening in my stomach, a mix of anger and something I couldn't quite name. Longing, perhaps. Or regret.

"Verena," one of the board members ventured, his voice tentative, "what exactly is going on here?"

She turned to him, her expression calm but unyielding. "What's going on is that we need to reorganize our priorities. Effective immediately, Jae will be taking a leave of absence to spend time with his aunt. In his stead, I will be overseeing operations."

Her announcement hung in the air. The room buzzed with disbelief.

"Excuse me?" another board member interjected, his tone incredulous. "On whose authority?"

"On my authority," Verena replied smoothly. "I've worked with this company for ten years. I know its ins and outs better than anyone here. And right now, Jae needs to step away, and I'm here to make sure this transition is as seamless as possible."

She turned her attention back to the rest of the room. "I've already prepared a detailed schedule for the next four months," she said, tapping on her iPad. "Each of you will receive your roles and responsibilities via email within the hour. Any deviations will not be tolerated."

She began delegating tasks, stripping them away from me with an efficiency that was both impressive and heartbreaking. It was like watching a master sculptor, each command shaping the future of my company, leaving me with nothing to hold onto.

One of the board members tried to protest, but she cut him off with a look that could freeze fire. "Two years ago, I stood in line at Christmas for four hours to get your son that limited edition toy."

The man paled and sank back into his chair, his defiance crumbling. She turned her gaze to another member, her eyes narrowing to slits. "And you, if you even think about disagreeing, I'll make sure your wife knows about your mistress."

Silence. Absolute silence.

"Jae is taking four months off to spend time with his dying aunt, who is like his mother. If anyone has a problem with that, remember, I was with this company for ten years and have enough dirt on all of you to ruin you."

She walked over to me, each step echoing in the stillness of the room, her presence overwhelming. "I have changed all your passwords. Canceled all your appointments. Changed the locks on everything. You can't access the building. Your phone is turned off. You have nothing. No one."

She stalked up to me, her face inches from mine, her eyes blazing with a fire that both scared and thrilled me. "You will be staying with my mother. She got you an air mattress. I hope your billionaire sensibilities can handle it."

"What?" I stammered, trying to process everything. "What about you?"

She smiled, but it was a smile that held no warmth. "Laura is watching our cat, and I'll be staying at your house in the Hamptons."

And with that, she turned on her heel and stormed out, leaving the room in stunned silence. For the first time in what felt like forever, I had nothing to keep me busy. Nothing to focus on. Just the emptiness she left behind and the realization that I needed to face the pain I had been so desperately trying to avoid.

Keep busy. Keep busy.

But now, there was nothing left to distract me. It was time to face my reality.

46

(SOFT)EN

JAE

I showed up at Jennifer's house in New Jersey feeling like I was walking into an ambush.

Jennifer greeted me at the door with a knowing look in her sharp eyes. "Hello, Jae," she said, her tone neutral yet welcoming. "Follow me."

She led me through the cozy living room filled with family photos, mismatched furniture, and the scent of freshly baked cookies. The walls were adorned with eclectic art and trinkets from her travels. I half expected her to hand me an apron and put me to work in the kitchen, as she had done so many times before. Instead, she showed me to a small room in the back of the house where an air mattress was set up on the floor, neatly made with a set of floral sheets.

"Here you go," she said, patting the mattress. "Home sweet home."

Before I could respond, Auntie's voice rang out from the next room. "Hello, darling! We're getting tattoos today."

I moved to see her, a frail but fiery figure, standing in the bedroom. "Auntie," I started, my frustration bubbling over, "did you tell Verena to change my locks and log me out of everything? I can't even access my bank account."

She giggled, a sound that was both endearing and exasperating.

"Maybe I did, maybe I didn't. Now, did you hear me say we're getting tattoos?"

"Wait," I said, the absurdity of it catching up to me. "Did you say tattoos?"

"Yes, darling," she replied, as if it were the most natural thing in the world. "I feel like it. My doctor said I can basically do whatever the hell I want to. So let's go."

"Auntie, this isn't funny. I can't get into my email, my accounts, anything. How am I supposed to work?" I demanded, running a hand through my hair in frustration.

"Work? Is that all you think about?" she shot back, crossing her arms over her chest. "You need to live a little, Jae. You're wound tighter than a drum."

"This is serious! I have responsibilities!" I argued, feeling my control slipping.

"And I have cancer," she retorted, her tone suddenly fierce. "And right now, my responsibility is to make memories with my nephew. So, we're getting tattoos."

"You're impossible," I muttered, exasperated.

"And you're stubborn," she countered. "Now, are you coming, or do I have to drag you there myself?"

I sighed, realizing I was arguing with a woman who had always gotten her way, one way or another. "Fine. But if this is some elaborate prank—"

"It's not," she said, cutting me off with a laugh. "I promise, you'll enjoy it. Besides, when was the last time you did something spontaneous?"

I opened my mouth to protest, then closed it again. She had a point. I had been avoiding everything, burying myself in work to escape the reality of our situation.

"Alright, let's go," I said finally.

"That's the spirit!" she cheered, linking her arm with mine. "Now, let's get a move on. The tattoo artist won't wait forever."

As we walked out of her room and down the hallway, Auntie leaned on my arm, her steps slow but determined. "You know, Jae, you didn't fail me," she said softly.

"I feel like I did," I admitted, my voice tight with emotion. "You were so excited about the wedding…"

"I'm using the centerpieces for my funeral," she insisted.

"That's so morbid."

"That's what Verena said," she giggled.

"So you *have* talked to her."

"Don't change the subject. I was just giving you a little time to focus on something else. Putting something in your head before it got bad. Now, let's go get matching tattoos."

"You're serious?" I asked, still trying to wrap my head around the idea.

"Absolutely," she replied without missing a beat.

"Really?"

She didn't answer. This felt like more than just an outing with my aunt. This felt like goodbye.

"My car is still parked out front," I said, guiding her carefully. "Auntie, wait, what is going on?"

"We're facing this together, baby," she said firmly.

"And what exactly are we facing, Auntie?" I choked out. "Tattoos?"

She looked at me with those wise eyes that always gave me grace. "The end, Jae. We're going to face the end."

We rode to the tattoo shop, and I was still bewildered, the events of the day swirling in my mind. On her phone, Auntie pulled up the design she wanted—a beautifully detailed illustration of the traditional Korean home where she and my father had grown up. Seeing it made my throat close up. The hanok, with its curved tiled roof and wooden beams, nestled in the serene countryside of Korea, was a place of memories and deep familial roots.

"I always want you to remember you have a home, Jae," she said, her voice softening. "And it's the people that make it, not the place."

The tattoo artist looked up from her work, her eyes lighting up with recognition and warmth.

"Hello, Quincy Nichole," Auntie said with a broad smile.

"Auntie!" Quincy exclaimed, stepping around the counter to give Auntie a warm hug. She was a striking figure, with her fiery red hair, multiple piercings, and sleeves of intricate tattoos that told stories in ink.

"You two know each other?" I asked, bewildered by the scene unfolding before me.

"Know each other?" Quincy laughed, pulling back from the hug but keeping a hand on Auntie's shoulder. "We're practically family now."

Auntie nodded. "We've been emailing back and forth to select the design for months."

"Months?" I echoed, the realization dawning on me. "This has been planned for weeks?"

"Of course, darling," Auntie said, patting my hand. "You think I do anything on a whim? Where do you think you get your organizational skills from?"

Quincy grinned. "Auntie here has been very particular about every detail. We've exchanged so many emails I feel like we're old friends."

"It's true," Auntie confirmed. "I knew exactly what I wanted, and Quincy Nichole has been amazing. She's an artist, Jae, not just a tattooist."

Quincy rolled her eyes playfully. "Oh, stop it, you're making me blush. Now, let's get started, shall we?"

As Quincy prepared her equipment, Auntie and she continued to banter like old friends. "I hope you're ready for some pain, Auntie," Quincy teased. "This isn't going to tickle."

Auntie laughed, her voice strong and full of life. "Pain? Please, I've been through worse. Besides, it's nothing compared to the joy of getting this tattoo with my favorite nephew."

I watched them interact, my bewilderment giving way to a reluctant smile. It was so on-brand for Auntie to make friends with everyone she met, to turn even the most daunting experiences into something filled with warmth and laughter.

Quincy glanced at me. "So, you're Jae, huh? Auntie's told me all about you. Ready to get inked? My friend John is going to do yours. We have similar styles."

John appeared, a tall, tattooed man with a bright smile. "I've been briefed on the design, and Quincy gave me very detailed demands."

"As she should," Auntie teased.

"Uh," I said, still trying to process everything. "Let's do this."

We settled into the chairs, side by side. Quincy began working on Auntie first, her skilled hands moving with practiced ease. John glared at me, as if daring me to chicken out. "You know, Auntie has quite the eye for design," she said, her voice carrying over the buzz of the tattoo machine. "She picked out this beautiful hanok. It's going to look amazing."

I felt my throat tighten. "Auntie, I don't know what to say."

"Don't say anything," she replied softly, her voice a soothing balm to my frayed nerves. "Just be here with me. That's all I need." She paused, her gaze growing distant for a moment before she continued. "I loved how peaceful the old home was. It was the kind of place where time slowed and you could just...settle. I want that for you, Jae."

Her eyes were shining with both wisdom and a hint of sadness. "It doesn't have to be a place, it can be a person. But when you look at it, I want you to remember that it's okay to pause. To breathe. To find peace in the midst of everything."

Her words hit me hard, the weight of them sinking deep into my soul. Auntie had always been my anchor, and now, even as she faced the end, she was trying to give me the guidance and solace I so desperately needed.

"Auntie..." I started, but my voice cracked, emotion overwhelming me.

She squeezed my hand again, a gentle, reassuring pressure. "You work so hard, Jae. You've built this incredible life, but don't forget to live it. Don't forget to find those moments of peace. Promise me you'll try."

I nodded, tears blurring my vision. "I promise, Auntie. I'll try."

Her smile was soft, filled with love and pride. "That's all I ask. Just remember, it's okay to pause and find your peace. You deserve that."

As I sat there, holding her hand, I felt a profound sense of clarity wash over me. Auntie's words were a reminder that no matter how chaotic life became, it was essential to find moments of tranquility and connection. And in that moment, I vowed to honor her wish, to seek out that peace, and to cherish the people who brought it into my life.

As Quincy and John worked, the buzz of the tattoo machines filled the small studio, a constant hum that seemed to sync with the rhythm of our conversation. Auntie and I began to reminisce, our words weaving a tapestry of memories that spanned decades.

"Do you remember the summer we spent at the hanok?" she asked, her eyes distant as she recalled the past. "You and your father would wake up early to help with the garden, while I made breakfast with your grandmother."

I smiled, the warmth of the memory pushing back the present's cold reality. "I remember. The air was always so fresh in the morning, and the birds...they sang the most beautiful songs."

"And the apricot tree," Auntie continued, her smile growing. "You used to climb it every day, even though you were terrified of heights. But you wanted those apricots more than anything."

I laughed, the sound mingling with the hum of the tattoo machines. "Those apricots were worth the fear. They were the sweetest I've ever tasted."

Her grip on my hand tightened, a silent agreement. "It was a simple life, but it was beautiful. Those days were filled with love and laughter."

The pain of the tattoo was a sharp, burning sensation, but it paled in comparison to the warmth spreading through my chest from these shared memories. "I miss those times, Auntie," I admitted, my voice barely above a whisper. "I miss how close we all were."

"We still are, Jae," she said gently. "Distance and time can't change that. Family is always with you, in your heart, in your memories. This tattoo, it's just a reminder of that."

The artist paused to wipe away the excess ink, giving me a moment to breathe through the discomfort. Auntie's eyes met mine again, filled with a mixture of love and determination. "You're my greatest joy, Jae. I am so thankful I had the chance to raise you. I miss your parents every day, but I'll always thank them for the beautiful gift they gave me. *You.*"

My eyes stung with unshed tears. "Thank you, Auntie. For everything."

She smiled, a tear slipping down her own cheek. "Thank you, Jae, for being the amazing man you've become. Your father would be so proud."

As Quincy resumed her work, Auntie and I continued to share stories, each one a thread in the fabric of our family's history. We talked about the first time I rode a bike, the festivals we celebrated, the nights spent under a blanket of stars. Each memory was a balm to the pain, a reminder of the love that bound us together.

And in that small studio, amidst the hum of the tattoo machine and the scent of antiseptic, I felt a profound connection to my past, to my family, to the roots that held me firm even as life pulled me in different directions.

"Done," John finally announced, stepping back to admire his work. "What do you think?"

I looked at the mirror he held up, my eyes tracing the intricate lines of the hanok, the place that symbolized so much of my past and present. "It's perfect," I said, my voice barely above a whisper.

Auntie beamed. "Good. Now you'll always have a piece of home with you."

47

(WARM)TH

VERENA

I pulled up to Jae's house in the Hamptons, the imposing structure looming against the clear blue sky. The sprawling estate was an extreme difference from the cozy, cluttered home of my mother's in New Jersey. I cut the engine and took a deep breath before grabbing my bag and stepping out of the car. The gravel crunched under my feet as I walked up to the front door and let myself inside.

The house was quiet, almost eerily so. I stood in the foyer, unsure of what to do first. The place was immaculate, of course. Jae had always kept a clean house, probably because he was rarely here to mess it up. I wandered through the rooms, the luxurious decor and expensive furniture a testament to his success, but it all felt so lifeless.

I made my way to the kitchen, the heart of any home. The stainless steel appliances gleamed, and the countertops were spotless. I opened the fridge, intending to clean it out, but stopped myself. This wasn't my job anymore. I wasn't Jae's assistant. I wasn't anything to him now.

Shaking off the urge to organize his life, I decided to go shopping instead. I needed groceries, something to ground me in this unfamiliar place. The local store was quaint, with friendly staff who greeted me warmly. As I wandered the aisles, I found myself reaching for Jae's favorite foods out of habit—filet mignon, his favorite brand of coffee, the artisanal bread he liked. I paused, my hand hovering over a jar of imported olives.

No. This was my time now.

I turned my cart around and picked out the things I loved instead. Fresh strawberries, brie cheese, a bottle of my favorite wine. I grabbed ingredients for a pasta dish I hadn't made in years and felt a small spark of excitement.

This was for me.

Back at the house, I decided to take my dinner to the beach. I packed a picnic basket with my groceries and a blanket and made my way to the shore. The sun was beginning to set, casting a warm golden light over the water. I found a secluded spot and spread out my blanket.

The first bite of pasta was like a revelation. I had forgotten how much I loved cooking for myself, for the joy of it, not out of obligation. I savored each bite, the flavors bursting on my tongue. I poured myself a generous glass of wine and looked out at the horizon, the waves gently lapping at the shore.

And then it hit me—everything I had been holding back. The job I had quit, the one that had consumed so much of my life. Auntie's illness, and the inevitability of losing her. The ten years I had spent in a role that wasn't truly mine. The writing career I had postponed time and time again. The uncertainty of the future, the embarrassment of a canceled wedding, the mess of a fake marriage turned real disaster.

I cried. I cried for all of it, for everything I had lost and for everything I was afraid to lose. But most of all, I cried for Jae. I cried for the man I had loved in silence, the man who was too wrapped up in his own pain to see mine. I cried for the dreams we had built on shaky foundations, and for the love that never had a chance to flourish.

The tears came hard and fast, and I didn't try to stop them. I let myself feel every bit of the pain, the sorrow, the regret. It was a cathartic release, a necessary purge of emotions I had kept bottled up for too long. As the sun dipped below the horizon, the sky painted in hues of orange and pink, I finally felt a strange sense of calm.

As I sat there, staring at the ocean, an idea for a book hit me. It was like a spark in the darkness, a beacon of hope. I quickly packed up my things and hurried back to the house, my heart pounding with excitement. I pulled out my laptop and sat down at the kitchen table.

The draft I had been working on seemed so trivial now, so disconnected from what I really wanted to say. I deleted it without a second thought. I needed to start fresh, to write something that truly came from my heart.

The first line flowed effortlessly, as if it had been waiting for me all along: "In the ashes of a life unraveled, she found the strength to rise again."

I stared at the screen, a sense of satisfaction settling over me. This was it. This was the start of something new, something real.

The story I needed to tell.

I spent the next few hours writing, the words pouring out of me with a fervor I hadn't felt in years. The characters came to life on the page, their struggles and triumphs echoing my own. It was a story of loss and love, of finding oneself amidst the chaos, of rising from the ashes stronger than before.

When I finally closed my laptop, I felt lighter, freer. This was my time now.

And for the first time in a long time, I felt like I was exactly where I was meant to be.

I climbed into bed, exhaustion settling over me like a blanket. But it was a good kind of exhaustion, the kind that comes from doing something meaningful. As I drifted off to sleep, I thought of Jae and hoped that he, too, would find his way. That he would find his own strength, his own path.

Tomorrow was a new day, and for the first time in years, I was ready to face it head-on. I was ready to write my own story.

48

CL(AIM)

JAE

Two Months Later

Auntie died on a Tuesday morning.

The news came quietly, a soft knock on the door of my consciousness, but its impact was seismic. Grief is a wild, untamed thing, and it swept through my life with the force of a hurricane. There was no preparing for it, no way to brace myself against the wave that would follow.

Her final days were spent in Jennifer's house, a place filled with the clutter of a life well-lived. I learned how to cook. How to care. How to be still.

Photographs lined the walls, bookshelves overflowed with stories, and every corner held a memory. Jennifer's warmth filled the house with comfort, an anchor in the storm of sorrow. My back ached from the air mattress that deflated every night, a minor inconvenience in the face of the profound loss I was experiencing.

Auntie passed in her sleep, her battle fought with grace, and in the end, she embraced death like an old friend. I found her that morning, her features serene, as if she had merely drifted off to a place free of pain. I sat beside her, numb, my hand still clutching hers. Jennifer found us like that, her face crumpling in sorrow as she gently closed Auntie's eyes.

"She loved you so much, Jae," Jennifer said, her voice thick with emotion. "You were her world."

The funeral was a testament to Auntie's vibrant spirit.

I hadn't invited anyone.

It felt too personal, too sacred to share with those who wouldn't understand. Instead, I focused on making it a celebration of her life. I used the wedding centerpieces she had loved so much, repurposing them into a fitting tribute. The irony wasn't lost on me, but it felt right, as if Auntie would have appreciated the twist.

A jazz band played sultry tunes as they lowered her casket, the mournful notes weaving through the air, telling stories of love and loss. She wore a bright red dress, the ink of her tattoo still fresh, a symbol of her defiant spirit even in death. The casket was adorned with flowers, each petal a silent farewell.

Jennifer stood beside me, her hand resting gently on my arm. "She would have loved this," she said quietly.

I nodded, my eyes fixed on the casket. "I hope so."

The band played on, their music a bittersweet symphony that mirrored the emotions swirling inside me. Tears streamed down my cheeks, the dam of my grief finally breaking. I cried for Auntie, for the life she had lived and the life she had lost. I cried for the emptiness her absence left behind, a void that seemed too vast to fill.

Jennifer pulled me into a hug, her embrace warm and solid. "Let it out, Jae. She wouldn't want you to hold it all in."

I clung to her, the tears flowing freely. For Auntie, for the time we had lost, for the future that felt so uncertain. I cried for the love that had been taken too soon, and for the woman who had been my anchor in a stormy sea.

As the funeral came to a close, I stayed behind, unable to leave her side. The sun dipped below the horizon, casting long shadows over the cemetery. Jennifer stayed with me, her presence a comfort in the gathering darkness.

"She told me once," Jennifer said, breaking the silence, "that she wanted to be remembered for her spirit, not her suffering. I think you gave her that today."

I looked at the casket, the final resting place of the woman who had been like a mother to me. "I hope so," I repeated, my voice barely above a whisper.

Jennifer squeezed my arm. "You did, Jae. You did."

I thought about calling Verena again, but the words still wouldn't come. I wasn't ready to face her, to explain the mess of emotions tangled inside me. Instead, I focused on the promise I had made to Auntie—to live my life, to find a way to move forward.

The drive back to Jennifer's house was quiet, the only sound the hum of the engine and the soft jazz playing on the radio. Jennifer didn't say much, sensing my need for silence. When we arrived, she wrapped me in another hug, her strength a balm to my wounded heart.

"Jennifer?"

"Yes?"

I looked at the woman who stepped up to care for us these last two months. "Can...can I stay here a little longer?"

Her eyes filled with tears. "Take your time, Jae," she said. "Grief isn't something you rush through. It's a journey."

I nodded, knowing she was right. Grief was wild, alive, and untamed. It's a testament to the love we have for those we lost.

Back in my room, I lay on the air mattress, staring at the ceiling. The pain was still there, a dull ache that would never fully go away. But there was also a flicker of hope, a glimmer of light in the darkness.

Auntie had taught me to embrace life, to cherish the moments, the memories, the love. As I drifted off to sleep, her words echoed in my mind, a comforting reminder of the promise I had made.

"Live your life, Jae. Promise me you will."

And I would. For her, for me, for the future that awaited. Grief was sacred, but so was life. And eventually, it would be time to start living again.

I realized then that, while Auntie had stolen my todays with her passing, she had left my tomorrows untouched. Those tomorrows were mine to reclaim, one by one. And I would. For her, for me, and for the promise of new beginnings.

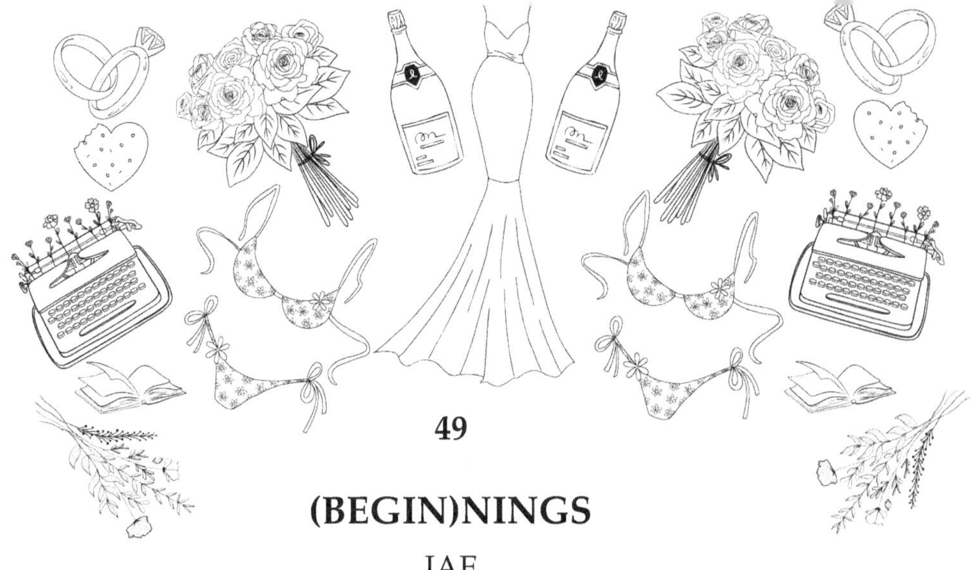

49

(BEGIN)NINGS

JAE

Two Months Later

My days at Jennifer's house had become routine. I woke up with my back fucking hurting because of this goddamn air mattress. I had half a mind to just refurnish the room, but Jennifer told me I wasn't allowed to take over her house. Even though it needed new windows. An updated bathroom...I was already planning on gifting her the remodel of her dreams for helping out so much.

And like every other day at her house, Jennifer burst into my room, the no-nonsense nurse, coaxing me out of bed by tempting me with an update on Vee.

"Jae, get up! You can't sleep your life away on that deflating piece of plastic," Jennifer announced, flinging open the curtains with a flourish.

I groaned, rolling over and glaring at her. "I'm considering buying you a new house just so I can sleep in a decent bed."

She laughed, shaking her head. "Not necessary. But I do have news about Verena."

I sat up instantly, ignoring the protest from my aching back. "What about her?"

Jennifer smiled knowingly. "Get up and I'll tell you. Maybe even let you in on how she's doing these days."

I grumbled but swung my legs over the side of the air mattress. "Fine. But this better be good."

"It's great," she said, tossing me a pair of jeans. "Now, come on. The kitchen floor isn't going to sweep itself."

"Yeah, yeah," I muttered, pulling on my jeans. "You know, this place could use some serious upgrades."

"Nice try," Jennifer shot back. "But I'm not letting you take over. You can't fix everything with money, Jae."

I smirked, grabbing the broom she handed me. "Wanna bet?"

Jennifer chuckled, patting my shoulder. "Sweep the kitchen, and then we'll talk."

With a sigh, I started sweeping, feeling a strange sense of comfort in the routine. Jennifer hovered nearby, offering unsolicited advice on my technique.

"You know, Verena always hated cleaning too," she said, a hint of teasing in her voice.

Mina, my cat, lazily walked through the piles of dirt I just swept up.

Fuck, that was weird to say. I had a cat. I wasn't planning on having a cat, and I even surprised myself when I had Jennifer ask Laura to bring Mina here. But...she was comforting. When I wasn't sneezing at the sight of her. And when she graced us with her presence.

I paused, looking up. "How is she?"

Jennifer's smile softened. "Why don't you see for yourself?" She pulled out her phone and showed me a photo. "She finished her book."

I froze, my eyes locked on the image of Verena on the beach. She looked so at peace, so happy. Her hair blew gently in the breeze, and she had that serene look I hadn't seen in a long time. My heart ached with longing and regret. "She did? She finished her book?" I whispered, unable to tear my gaze away from the photo. "I should've taken her to the house in the Hamptons more often. Always too busy with work."

Jennifer nodded, a knowing smile on her face. "She did. And she looks so proud. Now, let's get to work. I'll teach you how to make another one of her favorite dishes. Let's talk."

The past two months, Jennifer had made it her personal mission to teach me how to cook. It was something to do, a way to keep my mind occupied. We pulled out ingredients, and she started showing me the steps.

"Jae, it's time for you to leave," she said softly as she showed me how to chop vegetables.

My heart sank. "I'm not ready," I said, the thought of leaving the safety of her home overwhelming.

She placed a hand on my arm, her eyes kind but firm. "You are. The purpose of you staying away from Verena was to find your footing and let her shine. My baby is bright as the sun, and I haven't seen you log on to read news updates for your company in a couple of weeks."

I nodded, knowing she was right. Jennifer had a way of cutting through the bullshit. "I guess I've been distracting myself with everything else."

She smiled, shaking her head. "Sometimes, being still is the hardest thing to do. But it's necessary. You have to go for what you want, Jae. You can't keep running."

I sighed, looking down at the chopping board. "I know. I just...I miss her so much."

Jennifer's expression softened. "I used to think I was so smart. But there you were, suffering right under my nose. I think of you as part of the family, and I didn't include you because the lines got blurred. I didn't know what part of you was my daughter's boss and who was the goofy kid in college that I had to literally beg to stop calling me Mrs. Williams."

I chuckled, remembering those days. "You'll always be Mrs. Williams to me."

She rolled her eyes playfully. "Just call me Jennifer, for heaven's sake. And remember, you're stronger than you think. It's time to face Verena and figure things out."

I was about to ask where to begin when the most annoying motherfucker in the world walked into the house like he owned the place.

Luke.

I hated him. Genuinely. The ease he had with Jennifer, the cocky way he'd update us on Verena. This man showed up every goddamn day, and I was two seconds from murdering him.

He trudged in and hugged Jennifer while sneering at me. "You're still here?"

Jennifer clicked her tongue. "No dick-measuring contests in the kitchen, children. Jae is welcome to stay here."

Luke shrugged, giving me a smug smile. "Just surprised he's still around. Thought he'd have run back to his office by now."

I clenched my jaw, trying to keep my cool. "I've got more important things to deal with than work."

Luke's smirk widened. "Like trying to win Verena back? Good luck with that."

I took a step closer, my fists clenching at my sides. "What are you implying?"

"Nothing," he said innocently. "Just that I'm driving out to see Verena tonight. Thought she could use some company to celebrate finishing her book."

My heart stopped. "What?"

Luke's eyes gleamed with mischief. "Gonna surprise her. She finished her book, so we should celebrate."

"You can't go," I snapped, the words out before I could stop them.

"And why not?"

Jennifer rolled her eyes, clearly tired of our antics. "Boys, enough."

I ignored her, my gaze locked on Luke. "Because she's staying at my house, and I forbid it."

Luke laughed, shaking his head. "Then I'll just meet her at the bar she's going to."

My blood ran cold. "She's going to a bar?"

He nodded, a smug grin on his face. "Yep. Told me herself."

The jealousy rolled through me, and I had to resist the urge to punch him. "You have no right—"

Jennifer's voice cut through the tension like a knife. "Enough!"

We both turned to her, the authority in her voice undeniable.

She turned to Luke, her eyes narrowing. "When are you going to stop pretending to be in love with my daughter?"

Luke looked nervous, shifting on his feet. "What are you talking about?"

Jennifer sighed. "You pretend to like Verena because it's easy. You automatically know she'll reject you, so you use it as an excuse to avoid the elephant in the room."

Luke's face paled, and he opened his mouth to protest, but no words came out.

Jennifer softened. "It's time to stop running, Luke. You never settle, because you're afraid. For once, be honest with yourself."

I stood there for a moment, letting Jennifer's words sink in. Then, a thought hit me, and I said, "I'm going to the Hamptons."

Jennifer's face lit up with a smile, while Luke's expression darkened into a glare.

Luke crossed his arms, trying to look nonchalant but failing miserably. "You should stay, Jae. You're just going to mess things up."

I shook my head. "No, I'm done with running. Verena deserves better."

Luke scoffed, his jealousy evident. "You think you can just waltz back into her life and everything will be fine?"

"Yes, because I'm not going to run away anymore. I'm going to fight for her."

His face twisted in frustration. "You're making a mistake."

I chuckled. "You can fight this and I'll tie you to Jennifer's kitchen chair, or you can back down. I think we both know Jennifer is right and you're pursuing someone that will never be yours, Luke."

Luke's face turned a shade of red I'd never seen before. "I-I don't like Laura," he protested weakly.

"Sure you don't, dear," Jennifer said, patting his shoulder. "Why don't you stay here tonight and help me with a few things. Vee doesn't need your pestering."

Luke pouted like a fucking puppy, clearly torn between his jealousy and his loyalty.

I turned to Jennifer, a grateful smile on my face. "Thank you. For everything."

She nodded, her eyes warm. "Go get your girl, Jae."

I headed upstairs to pack a few things, feeling a sense of purpose I hadn't felt in months. As I threw clothes into a bag, my mind raced with thoughts of Verena—her smile, her laugh, the way she made everything brighter.

By the time I finished packing, I felt ready. Ready to face her, to tell her everything, to fight for what we had. I took one last look around the room, then headed downstairs.

Jennifer and Luke were in the kitchen, Luke sulking while Jennifer busied herself with some task.

"I'm ready," I announced.

Jennifer looked up and smiled. "Good luck, Jae."

I nodded, then turned to Luke, who was still pouting. "Don't worry, Luke. You'll find your own path. Just stop trying to sabotage mine."

With that, I walked out the door, ready to reclaim my future and the woman I loved.

50

(TEMPT)ATION

VERENA

I finished writing my book two months after Auntie died.

I still felt weird saying that.

Auntie was dead.

And I wasn't there to say goodbye. I knew it's what she wanted. What Jae needed. What I was supposed to do.

But I did what she asked.

I finished the fucking book.

The moment I typed "The End," I felt a rush of emotions—pride, relief, sadness—all mingling together in a way that left me breathless. I had poured everything into those pages, writing it for Auntie, for myself, for the future she wanted me to have. I stopped waiting for Jae to call. I stopped asking my mother for updates, though I knew he was still at her house. Somehow, my mother went from hating him to taking care of him, and it eased my heart to know that.

Laura was coming to visit and celebrate my finished book, and I wanted to remember Auntie in my own way. The book had been my refuge, a place to pour all my emotions, my grief, my love, and my memories of Auntie. But in my frantic race to finish it, I realized I hadn't taken the time to properly celebrate her life. The guilt gnawed at me, a constant reminder that I was failing to honor her as she deserved.

Yes, I was sad. Losing Auntie was devastating, leaving a gaping hole that ached. But I knew Auntie wouldn't want me to wallow in sorrow. She had always been a beacon of joy and vitality, embracing life with a kind of fearless abandon that I envied. She wanted me to live my life fully, to chase my dreams, to find happiness even in the darkest times.

No one tells you how to navigate the endless waves of sadness, the moments of numbness, the sudden bursts of anger and regret. I felt like I was stumbling through a fog, trying to find my way back to a place where I could breathe again. Feeling sad almost felt like it went against Auntie's wishes, like I was betraying her memory by succumbing to the darkness.

Auntie had always said, "Life is for the living, darling." It was her mantra, her way of reminding me to seize the moment, to find joy in the little things, to dance even when the music was too quiet to hear. So, I decided to celebrate her life the way she would have wanted—by living mine.

Laura arrived in the late afternoon, her eyes bright with excitement and a bottle of champagne in hand. "You did it, Verena! You actually did it!"

"I did," I said, my voice tinged with both pride and melancholy. "And now, I want to celebrate. For Auntie."

Laura gave me a knowing look. "What do you have in mind?"

"I want to go to a club. Auntie loved wild things. I want to buy expensive drinks and dance. I want to wear a risqué dress and feel human and sexy."

Laura grinned. "Now you're talking!"

We spent the next hour getting ready, our movements almost ritualistic as we transformed ourselves from grieving friends into vibrant women ready to seize the night. I stood in front of my closet, my fingers trailing over fabrics and textures until I found it—the slinky black dress that always made me feel powerful. The fabric was smooth and cool against my skin as I slipped it on, the dress hugging my curves in all the right places. It had a plunging neckline that flirted with the edge of propriety and a hemline that teased just above the knee, allowing me to feel both sexy and sophisticated.

I looked in the mirror, adjusting the straps and smoothing out the fabric. My dark hair cascaded in loose waves over my shoulders, and I carefully applied my makeup, accentuating my eyes with smoky shadows and adding a bold red lip for a pop of color. I wanted to feel alive, to embody the spirit Auntie had always admired in me.

Laura, on the other hand, chose a sparkly silver number that shimmered with every move she made. The dress was a mini, ending mid-thigh and adorned with tiny sequins that caught the light, creating a dazzling effect. Her blonde hair was styled in soft curls, and she opted for a more natural makeup look, with just a hint of shimmer on her eyelids and a glossy nude lip.

We stood side by side in front of the full-length mirror, taking in our transformed appearances. The disparity between us was striking—me in my sleek, black dress, radiating a sort of edgy elegance, and Laura in her sparkling silver, emanating a playful, carefree vibe. Yet, in our reflections, I saw the same tenacity in both our eyes, the same readiness to embrace the night ahead.

"Wow," Laura said, adjusting a curl of her hair and turning to give me an appraising look. "You look incredible, Verena. Auntie would be so proud."

I smiled, feeling a swell of affection for my friend. "Thanks, Laura. You look amazing too. Ready to show the Hamptons how it's done?"

She laughed, the sound light. "Absolutely. Let's do this."

With one last look in the mirror, we nodded in approval, our outfits a testament to our resolve to celebrate, to remember Auntie in a way she would have loved. We grabbed our clutches, mine a sleek black leather, hers a sparkling silver to match her dress, and headed out the door, ready to take on the night.

"Tonight, we're celebrating you, Auntie, and living life to the fullest," Laura said.

We arrived at the club in the Hamptons, the neon lights reflecting off the dark water nearby. Inside, the music was loud, the bass thumping in my chest. The crowd was a blend of locals and weekend visitors, all dressed to impress. The atmosphere was filled with laughter and the clinking of glasses.

I turned to Laura, feeling a rush of excitement. "We're buying expensive drinks, and it's on Jae," I said, holding up his card.

Laura's eyes widened in delight. "Auntie would have loved that!"

We made our way to the bar, and I found the top shelf liquor that was fifty dollars a glass—something most in the Hamptons wouldn't blink at. I started ordering with Jae's card, feeling a naughty thrill. Laura cheered me on, and soon enough, we had a selection of the finest drinks in the house.

"To Auntie," I said, holding up my glass.

"To Auntie," Laura echoed, clinking her glass against mine.

As the night wore on, the club became a swirling sea of lights, laughter, and music, each beat of the music syncing with the pounding of my heart. Laura and I had downed several rounds of drinks, our spirits high, our inhibitions low. The world around us blurred into a kaleidoscope of colors and sensations, and for the first time in a long while, I felt truly free.

Amidst the thrumming bass and the pulsing crowd, a group of guys caught our attention. Their tailored suits and expensive watches were a stark contrast to the casual attire of many others in the club. They had the polished, easy charm of men who were used to getting what they wanted, their smiles bright and their eyes sharp.

One of them, a tall guy with dark hair, made his way over to us. His hair was slicked back in a way that looked effortlessly stylish, and his piercing blue eyes twinkled as he leaned in close to me. The scent of his cologne—something woodsy and expensive—mingled with the alcohol on his breath.

"Can I buy you a drink?" he asked, his voice smooth and inviting.

I glanced up at him, feeling a heady mix of boldness and curiosity. "No need," I replied with a playful smile. "I'm buying tonight. What do you want?"

He raised an eyebrow, clearly intrigued. "Surprise me," he said, his smile widening.

Beside him, his friends were equally striking. There was a sandy-haired guy with an athletic build and a catching grin, his green eyes dancing as he chatted animatedly with Laura. He wore a crisp white shirt that clung to his muscular frame, the sleeves rolled up to reveal strong forearms. Another, slightly shorter but with a lean, toned physique, had a mop of curly brown hair and dark, brooding eyes. He leaned against the bar with a casual elegance, watching the scene unfold with a knowing smirk.

I ordered more drinks, the alcohol making me feel light and free. We danced, the music pulsing through us, our bodies moving in sync with the beat. I felt hot, alive, and for the first time in a long while, I felt like I was truly living.

Laura danced beside me.

I smiled, thinking of Auntie cheering me on. "I wrote the fucking book, Laura. And now, I'm celebrating."

We danced and drank, the world spinning around us in a blur of lights and music. The bass thrummed through my veins, and the alcohol made everything seem more vivid, more alive. I felt a guy's hands on my waist. He whispered something, but I was too far gone to make sense of it. All I knew was that I was happy, and for tonight, that was enough.

Suddenly, a voice cut through the music, loud and unmistakable. "Where is my fiancée?!"

I spun around, my vision fuzzy from the drinks. Standing there, looking frantic and completely out of place in his suit, was Jae. His presence was a shock to the system, a jarring contrast to the neon lights and thumping beats of the club. My heart skipped a beat, and I blinked, trying to focus on the man who had suddenly turned my world upside down.

"Jae?" I slurred, swaying slightly, my head spinning as I tried to reconcile his appearance with the havoc around me.

He marched over, his eyes locking onto mine with an intensity that made my breath catch. His clothes were slightly disheveled, his hair mussed as if he'd run his hands through it a dozen times in frustration. The worry etched into his features was bleak, making his normally composed demeanor crumble.

The guy dancing with me laughed, clearly amused by the sudden interruption. "Whoa, dude. Calm down. Who are you?"

Jae's eyes blazed with a fierce protectiveness I hadn't seen before. "Her fiancé. Get your fucking hands off her."

51

(CLING)ING
VERENA

I woke up with a pounding headache, the room spinning slightly as I tried to make sense of my surroundings. The sunlight streamed through the curtains, too bright, too harsh, piercing my skull like a thousand tiny daggers. I squinted and realized I was in the main bedroom of Jae's house in the Hamptons.

Groaning, I sat up, the events of the previous night a hazy blur of neon lights, loud music, and too many drinks.

Stumbling into the living room, I stopped short when I saw Jae. He was sitting on the couch, my laptop open on his knees, tears in his eyes. The sight of him like that sent a jolt through me.

"What happened last night?" I croaked, my voice hoarse and raspy from a combination of too much alcohol and too much yelling over the music.

He looked up, his eyes red-rimmed and glossy, ignoring my question. "You wrote the book," he said, his voice thick with emotion.

I frowned, my brain struggling to catch up. "What are you doing here, Jae?"

"I saw the charges on my card and showed up," he explained, closing the laptop and setting it aside. "I was already on my way and then came to the club. But more importantly, this book, Verena. It's...it's fucking good."

I blinked, my hangover making it hard to process his words. "You stayed up to read it?"

He nodded, a tear slipping down his cheek. "It's really good. The way you wrote about her growth... It's incredible." He stood up abruptly, crossing the room to me in a few quick strides. Before I knew it, he had wrapped me in a tight hug.

"You did it," he murmured, his voice trembling. "You really did it."

I stood there, stunned, feeling his warmth seep into me. This was Jae, but it was a side of him I hadn't seen in years. I saw glimpses of the boy who used to cheer me on in college, the guy who supported me and wanted me to chase my dreams.

"How did I get home?" I asked, my voice muffled against his chest.

"I brought you home," he said, pulling back slightly to look at me. "I sent Laura back to Jersey."

I pulled back, frowning. "Jae, that's rude."

"We're staying here for a while," he said firmly, his tone brooking no argument.

I gaped at him. "What?"

He smiled, a boyish grin that made my heart skip a beat. "I'm making breakfast. Jennifer taught me a few skills I want to test out. So go shower."

I stared at him, bewildered. "What?"

"Shower," he repeated, gesturing towards the bathroom. "Get ready. I'm making your favorite."

I stood there, open-mouthed, trying to process this new, unfamiliar version of Jae. He looked at me expectantly. "Verena?"

"Yeah?" I managed to say.

"I'm ready for us now," he said softly, his eyes full of sincerity.

"Oh," I replied, my heart racing.

He leaned in and kissed me softly, his lips warm and gentle against mine. When he pulled away, he smiled. "Now go shower. You taste like really expensive whiskey and vomit."

I laughed, the sound surprising even me. "Okay," I said, still a bit dazed.

As I turned to go to the bathroom, I glanced back at him. He was already heading to the kitchen, whistling softly. For the first time in a long while, I felt a glimmer of hope. Maybe, just maybe, we could make this work.

I STOOD UNDER THE HOT SPRAY OF THE SHOWER, LETTING THE WATER wash away the remnants of last night's debauchery. My head still throbbed, but the fog was beginning to lift. I couldn't stop thinking about Jae—about the way he had looked at me, the way he had spoken about my book with such raw emotion. It was like seeing a different person, a glimpse of the man I had befriended years ago.

After showering, I wrapped myself in a towel and stepped out, feeling somewhat human again. I dressed quickly in a pair of comfortable jeans and a soft sweater, my mind still reeling from the morning's revelations.

As I walked into the kitchen, the smell of cooking bacon greeted me. Jae stood at the stove, flipping pancakes with a practiced ease. He looked over his shoulder and smiled when he saw me, his eyes lighting up in a way that made my heart skip a beat.

"Good morning," he said, his voice warm and inviting.

"Morning," I replied, my voice still a bit shaky. "What's all this?"

"Breakfast," he said simply. "Your favorite. Bacon, pancakes, and eggs."

"You remember."

"Of course I do," he said, turning back to the stove. "I remember everything about you."

I watched him for a moment, marveling at this unexpected turn of events. This was the Jae I had missed, the one who knew me better than anyone. The one who cared.

"So," I said, leaning against the counter, "you stayed up all night reading my book?"

He nodded, his expression serious. "I couldn't put it down, Verena. It's incredible. The way you wrote about her growth, her struggles...it felt so real."

"Thank you," I said softly, my heart swelling with pride and emotion.

He turned off the stove and plated the food, setting it on the table. "Come on, sit down. Eat."

We sat across from each other, the silence between us filled with unspoken words. I picked at my food, my mind racing with questions.

"Why did you come here, Jae?" I finally asked, looking up at him.

He sighed, running a hand through his hair. "Because I'm ready to prioritize you, Verena."

I looked down at my plate, my appetite suddenly gone. "You can't just waltz back into my life and expect everything to be okay."

"I know," he said quietly. "I don't expect that. But I want to try. I want to make things right."

I sighed, feeling the weight of his words. "Jae, it's not that simple."

"I know it's not," he said, his voice earnest. "But I'd regret it for the rest of my life if I didn't do everything in my power to get you back."

I met his gaze, searching his eyes for any sign of doubt. But all I saw was sincerity, a raw honesty that took my breath away.

"Oh," I said softly, my mind struggling to catch up with my heart.

He reached across the table and took my hand, his touch warm and reassuring. "I'm not asking for everything to be perfect. I just want a chance. A chance to show you that I'm here for you. That I want us to work."

I squeezed his hand, feeling a surge of hope. "Okay," I said, my voice barely above a whisper. "But it's going to take time. And we have a lot to work through."

"I know," he said, his grip tightening. "And I'm ready for that."

"How have you been, Jae? Really?"

"It was hard for a while. Really hard. But I have to thank you for forcing me to be there, to settle, to sit still. It was the first time in ten years I was really still."

He rolled up his sleeve, revealing a tattoo on his forearm. I stared at it, recognizing the intricate design immediately. It was a traditional Korean hanok, the same one Auntie had chosen and showed me the last night we'd spent together. The detail was incredible—the curved roof, the ornate patterns. It was as if a piece of history had been etched into his skin.

I laughed despite the lump forming in my throat. "You and Auntie got matching tattoos?" I asked, shaking my head in disbelief.

"Yeah," he said, smiling. "It was her idea. Said it would be a reminder of home, of family. Of taking time to be still. It was...it was special."

My eyes watered, the significance of his words hitting me hard. "I can't believe it. You, getting a tattoo."

Jae laughed, the sound rich and warm, sharply contrasting with the seriousness of our conversation. "Yeah, neither can I. But it felt right. She wanted to do it, and so did I. It was a way to honor everything she stood for."

I looked at him, tears threatening to spill over. The gesture, the commitment, it was all so deeply meaningful. "Thank you for being there for her, Jae. It means more than you know."

He reached out, wiping a tear from my cheek with his thumb, his touch gentle and comforting. "She was strong, Verena. Right up to the end. And I needed to be the one there with her. You gave me that chance."

I nodded, my heart heavy with gratitude and sorrow. "I'm sorry I wasn't there."

He shook his head, his expression softening with understanding. "It needed to be me. She wanted it that way. And she'd want this book to be out in the world. She'd want her story to be told."

I took a deep breath. "I wrote Auntie's story. This incredible woman who adopted her nephew as a single woman. Whose fiancé left her when she found out she would be taking on a teenage son. Who still built a life and found fulfillment despite it all."

Jae's eyes softened. "She was amazing, wasn't she?"

"She was," I agreed, my voice thick with emotion. "Writing her story was my way of honoring her, of keeping her legacy alive."

Jae squeezed my hand, his grip firm and reassuring. "You did a beautiful job, Verena. She'd be so proud of you."

I felt a swell of emotion rise in my chest. "I just wanted to do her justice. To tell the world how incredible she was."

"You did," Jae said softly. "Every word, every page. It's a testament to her strength and her love."

For a moment, we sat in silence, the memories of Auntie filling the space between us. It was a comfortable silence, one that spoke of shared grief and mutual understanding.

"What now?" I asked, afraid of the answer.

He smirked. "I'm taking you on a date, baby."

52

(KIND)LING

JAE

This wasn't just any date—it was the date that should have happened long ago. A night picnic on the beach, complete with a carefully selected assortment of her favorite foods. My nerves were shot from pure anxiety and lack of sleep, every detail feeling like it held the weight of the world.

I secured the best picnic essentials: a large blanket, plush cushions, and a selection of gourmet foods. I oversaw every detail personally, wanting everything to be perfect. I had lanterns and candles placed strategically to add a soft glow, creating an intimate atmosphere as the sun set over the water. The picnic basket was filled with fresh strawberries, gourmet sandwiches, artisanal cheeses, and a bottle of her favorite vintage wine.

As I arranged everything, my hands were slightly shaky. I couldn't remember the last time I had felt this nervous. I was used to boardrooms and billion-dollar deals, not romantic picnics on the beach. This was how it should have been from the beginning—real dates, real moments, real connections.

When I heard her footsteps approaching, I turned and saw Verena walking toward me, holding her wedges in one hand and a bright smile on her face. She looked stunning in a summer dress that flowed around her like a soft breeze, its pastel colors complementing her radiant skin. Her hair cascaded in loose waves, and her eyes sparkled with a mix of excitement and curiosity.

"Hey," she said softly, her voice carrying over the gentle sounds of the waves.

"Hey," I replied, trying to keep my nerves in check. I reached out and took her hand, feeling a rush of warmth as her fingers intertwined with mine.

"You went all out," she said, glancing around at the setup. "It's beautiful."

I smiled, feeling a bit of the tension ease. "I wanted it to be special. This is how it should have been."

She squeezed my hand and looked into my eyes. "I'm glad we're doing this now."

We settled onto the blanket, the plush cushions giving us a comfortable spot to relax. I reached for the picnic basket, my fingers brushing against the woven fabric as I opened it. Inside, the assortment of gourmet foods I had carefully chosen gleamed under the soft glow of the lanterns.

I pulled out a container of fresh strawberries, their vibrant red color catching the light. Picking one up, I held it out to Verena.

"Open wide," I said, my voice playful.

She opened her mouth, her lips parting slightly, and I gently placed the strawberry between them. She bit down, the juice dripping onto her chin, and she laughed, the sound mingling with the rhythmic crash of the waves against the shore.

I chuckled, reaching out to wipe the juice away with my thumb. "Messy eater," I teased.

She wrinkled her nose at me. "Says the man who once spilled an entire glass of wine on his white shirt during a business dinner."

I laughed, the memory flooding back. "Touché. But I've gotten better since then."

"Oh, have you now?" she challenged.

"Absolutely," I replied, picking up another strawberry. "Watch this."

I fed her another strawberry, and she took it with a smile, her eyes never leaving mine. There was something incredibly intimate about the act, a connection that felt deeper than words.

She reached for a piece of cheese, her fingers grazing mine as she did. "You really did go all out," she said, her tone softening.

"I wanted it to be perfect," I admitted, my voice low. "You deserve perfect."

Her expression softened, and she leaned in closer, her gaze intense. "This *is* perfect, Jae. Just being here with you."

I swallowed, feeling a lump form in my throat. "I'm glad," I said, my voice barely above a whisper.

I couldn't stop staring at Verena. She looked stunning in her summer dress, the fabric flowing gracefully around her. But my mind kept drifting back to a different outfit.

"You look beautiful tonight," I said, unable to tear my eyes away from her. "But I must say, I'm still daydreaming about your power suit from the day you yelled at the board members and bossed them around."

She playfully slapped my chest, a teasing smile on her lips. "Oh, come on, Jae. That's what you're thinking about?"

I laughed, catching her hand and holding it against my chest. "I'm serious. You were amazing. I've never been more attracted to you than at that moment."

"Really? More than right now?"

I leaned in, my voice dropping to a conspiratorial whisper. "I thought I liked being in charge, but it was nice to...have someone take over and force me to not be."

Verena laughed, the sound light and infectious. "So, you're saying you like a woman who can boss you around?"

"Absolutely," I said, grinning. "The way you just told them what was happening, no hesitation, no second-guessing. It was...hot."

She shook her head, still smiling. "I was just doing what needed to be done. Those guys were completely lost without direction."

"And you gave it to them," I replied, feeling a surge of admiration. "You stepped in and took control. It was impressive. Sexy as hell, but also impressive."

She rolled her eyes playfully. "Well, I'm glad my bossy side is appreciated."

I squeezed her hand, my gaze serious for a moment. "It really is, Verena. Seeing you like that, seeing you step up and take charge...it made me realize how much I need you. Not just at work, but in my life."

She softened, her teasing demeanor giving way to something more vulnerable. "I needed to do it, Jae. For the company, for you. But also for me. It showed me what I'm capable of."

"And you're capable of so much," I said, my voice filled with conviction. "I'm happy you quit. I never thought I'd say that, but you were meant to be a writer, Verena. Watching you follow your dreams, it's incredible."

She looked down, a blush creeping up her cheeks. "Thank you, Jae. That means a lot."

I couldn't stop myself from rambling. "You know, I've been thinking. We should send your book to a publisher. I have contacts; I can help you get a great deal. Or, if you prefer, we can self-publish. I can fund it, get a graphic designer, handle the marketing..."

Verena cut me off with a gentle laugh, placing a finger on my lips. "Jae, I want to do this myself."

I blinked, slightly taken aback. "I just want to prove I can support you."

"How about just letting me continue to use your beach house when I need some writing inspiration?"

I laughed, feeling a warmth spread through my chest. "You can come here whenever you'd like."

She nodded, looking thoughtful for a moment. "I guess your four months off work is almost up."

"It is," I admitted. "But I can go back when I'm ready. They have it under control, and I hired a new assistant."

"Things are changing, Verena. I'm going to be still more. I've realized I need to slow down, to enjoy life and the people in it. I'm done being a workaholic."

She looked at me, her expression softening. "I want to spend one more week here, then head back to New York. I need to find a new apartment."

"You can move in with me," I offered without thinking, my heart pounding at the prospect of having her close all the time.

She shook her head gently. "No. I want to take this slow."

Her refusal hurt, but I wasn't a man that was used to giving up. "Okay," I said, nodding. "Slow I can do."

We finished eating, the conversation light and filled with laughter. As we walked back to the beach house, the moonlight casting a gentle glow on everything, I felt a sense of peace.

At the door, I paused, looking at her. "Can I kiss you?" I asked.

Her eyes softened, and she stepped closer, her breath mingling with mine. "Yes," she whispered.

I leaned in, capturing her lips in a kiss that was both tender and filled with longing. I wondered if I would always feel this desperate for her, but it was different this time. Before, I craved the distraction, the escape. Now, I craved *her*. Her taste, her skin, her perfume, the strawberries on her tongue, the buzz in my veins.

She pulled me inside after opening the door, but I stopped her, pressing my forehead to hers. "We're going to take this slow," I murmured.

She pouted, her eyes dark with desire. "Jae..."

I enjoyed seeing her panting for me, the tables turned for once. I kissed her forehead, then her nose, savoring every moment. "Goodnight, Verena," I said softly, stepping back.

As I walked off to the guest room, every step felt like a battle against my own desires. Regret gnawed at me for walking away from her, but I knew it would be worth it in the end. For once, I was looking forward to the slow, steady burn of something real, something lasting.

53

(SLOW)BURN

VERENA

I spent the entire week in a state of high alert, every nerve ending tingling with anticipation. It was as if I was starring in my own personal version of *Fifty Shades of Torture*, where the leading man had perfected the art of edging. Seriously, the man was trying to kill me softly with his kisses. Long, slow, toe-curling kisses that made my eyes roll back in my head and my knees buckle. And that's all he was doing. Kissing. Teasing. Taking me to the brink and then pulling back like some kind of sadistic romantic.

Let me give you the rundown of my week in paradise (or purgatory, depending on how you look at it).

Monday started with a sunrise picnic on the beach. Jae had made mimosas and croissants, and we watched the sun come up over the water. It was idyllic. Romantic. And then he kissed me senseless right there on the blanket. Just when I thought we'd be taking things further, he pulled back, grinning like he'd won the lottery. We spent the rest of the day building sandcastles and collecting seashells while I tried not to strangle him with seaweed.

Tuesday, he brought me breakfast in bed. Pancakes with fresh berries and whipped cream, my favorite. He lounged next to me, feeding me bites and kissing me every time I opened my mouth to protest his maddening restraint. By lunchtime, I was ready to throw the plate at him. Instead, we went for a bike ride along the coastline, stopping at a little café where he flirted outrageously with me, making me blush and curse his very existence.

Wednesday, he took me sailing. Yes, sailing. We rented a boat, and he somehow managed to steer it expertly while simultaneously driving me insane with his touch. Every time he adjusted a sail or pulled a rope, he'd brush against me, sending a jolt of electricity through my body. We anchored in a quiet cove for lunch, where he made sandwiches and, of course, kissed me until I was squirming. Torture. Pure torture.

Thursday, we had a cooking class. He found a local chef to give us a private lesson in making seafood paella. There I was, chopping vegetables while he whispered dirty promises in my ear, his breath hot against my neck. By the time we finished cooking, I was ready to throw him onto the counter and have my way with him, but no, we had to sit and enjoy our meal like civilized people. Torture, I tell you.

Friday, he booked us a spa day. Massages, facials, the works. And let me tell you, there's nothing quite like being relaxed into a puddle of goo by a professional masseuse only to have Jae kiss you stupid the moment you're alone. Every. Single. Time. The sexual tension was so thick I could have cut it with a butter knife.

Saturday, we went on a hike through a nature reserve. It was beautiful and serene, with the sound of birds chirping and leaves rustling. And then there was Jae, holding my hand, helping me over rocks, and stealing kisses every chance he got. By the time we reached the waterfall at the end of the trail, I was ready to push him into the water just to cool off my raging hormones.

Sunday was the grand finale—stargazing on the beach. He set up a telescope, and we spent the evening lying on a blanket, looking at the stars and talking about everything and nothing. And, of course, kissing. Lots and lots of kissing. It was romantic and sweet and just about drove me to the edge of sanity.

So, here I was, at the end of a week of pure, sweet torture, lying on the couch in the beach house, staring at the ceiling and wondering how I was going to survive the long drive back to the city. The man had made all my favorite meals, taken me on fantastic dates, done the sweetest things imaginable, and somehow managed to keep things PG-13 the entire time. It was enough to drive a girl mad.

I heard the door open and close, and a moment later, Jae walked into the room, looking like he'd just stepped out of a *GQ* magazine. His shirt was unbuttoned just enough to be distracting, his hair tousled in that perfect way that made me want to run my fingers through it. He smiled when he saw me, that infuriatingly sexy smile that made my heart skip a beat.

"Hey," he said, sitting down beside me and leaning in for a kiss.

I pulled back, narrowing my eyes at him. "If you kiss me one more time without following through, I swear to God, Jae, I'm going to lose it."

He chuckled. "Lose it, huh? That sounds interesting."

I groaned, covering my face with my hands. "You're enjoying this, aren't you?"

"Maybe a little," he admitted, pulling my hands away and kissing my knuckles. "But I promise, it's all part of the plan."

"Plan?" I echoed, raising an eyebrow. "What plan?"

He grinned, leaning in to whisper in my ear. "The plan to make you mine. Completely."

My resolve melted under his touch. "You're already driving me crazy, Jae. I don't think I can take much more."

"Ready for the drive back to the city?" he asked, pulling out his suitcase and giving me that devastating smile. "I'm having our cars transported so we can ride together in a little surprise I rented for you."

I nodded, though my mind wandered to the long drive ahead. We walked out to his car, and my jaw nearly dropped. He had a sleek, sexy convertible that looked like it was made for beach drives and city escapes. The kind of car that made heads turn and hearts race.

As we got in, I couldn't help but admire the smooth leather seats and the gleaming dashboard. Jae slid into the driver's seat with an easy confidence that made my pulse quicken. He reached over, placing his hand on my thigh, his fingers warm against my skin. As he started the engine, he began to inch his hand up my leg.

I groaned, the tension from the past week bubbling up to the surface. "Jae, you've been teasing me all week."

He glanced at me with a sly grin. "Oh? Have I?" I shot him a look, half-exasperated, half-amused. "Good things come to those who wait," he teased, his voice a low rumble.

I rolled my eyes, trying to keep my cool. "I miss the good old days when you were begging me for a taste."

His grin widened, and he leaned in slightly. "We can go back to that if you'd like."

"Really? Yes. Absolutely."

He chuckled, his hand continuing its slow journey up my thigh. "How about we compromise?"

"Compromise?" I squeaked.

"Stay at my place, and I'll go back to begging," he said, his fingers dancing along my thigh, making my pulse race.

I bit my lip, considering his offer. "Stay at your place, huh?"

"Yeah," he said, his voice dropping to a low, seductive murmur. "You're trying to get your new book up and running. You don't need to spend money on a new place. Spend it on getting your book out there."

I squirmed in my seat, trying to focus on his words despite the way his touch was driving me crazy. "You're serious?"

"Dead serious," he replied, his fingers tracing tantalizing circles on my skin. "I want you close, Verena. And if it means I have to beg, then so be it."

"I'm just...not sure that I'm ready, Jae," I whispered.

We drove in a charged silence, the tension between us crackling like a live wire. As we pulled up to a red light, Jae leaned in, his breath hot against my ear. "Maybe you need a taste of what that could be like," he whispered, his voice rough.

He inched his fingers higher up my thigh, his touch making me tremble. "Please, Verena," he murmured, his voice a low, pleading whimper. "Stay at my house."

"Jae..."

"Please," he whispered again, his lips brushing against my earlobe. "I need you. I need to feel you close. I'll beg, Verena. I'll do whatever it takes. Just stay with me."

His fingers moved higher, teasing the edge of my skirt

. "You don't know what you do to me," he groaned, his voice breaking. "I've been aching for you all week, and it's driving me insane. Please."

The sound of him begging, his voice filled with such longing, sent a thrill through me. I could feel his need, and it mirrored my own. I hesitated, the words on the tip of my tongue.

"Verena," he continued, his voice cracking with emotion. "I can't stand being apart from you. I need you. I need this. Stay with me. Let me take care of you."

My resolve melted under his touch, his pleading tone unraveling me. "Jae..."

His hand moved higher, his fingers brushing against my inner thigh. "I'll make it worth your while," he promised, his voice a whisper. "I'll do anything. Just say you'll stay."

"I...can't. I need you to prove to me first that you've changed."

The light turned green, and Jae's hand moved back to the wheel, leaving my thigh tingling with his touch. I tried to steady myself as we drove deeper into the city. The familiar skyline loomed ahead, and I tried to focus on anything other than the way his fingers had felt against my skin.

We hit a patch of traffic, and Jae took the opportunity to slide his hand back onto my thigh. His touch was warm, his fingers tracing slow, teasing patterns. "What's going on?" I asked, my voice barely steady.

"Let me prove myself, baby."

His fingers moved higher, and I could feel the heat radiating from his hand. "Every second away from you is pure hell, and I can't take it," he murmured.

The traffic started moving again, and Jae pulled his hand away, gripping the wheel with a white-knuckled intensity. I let out a frustrated sigh, the ache between my thighs growing unbearable. My mind was a tumultuous combination of desire and doubt, each touch of his fingers a reminder of the precarious edge we balanced on.

When we hit another red light, his hand was back, more insistent this time. His fingers danced along the edge of my underwear, teasing and torturing me. My breath hitched, my heart pounding as I fought the urge to give in completely.

"Jae, you're killing me," I whispered.

"I want you just as badly, believe me."

I turned my head slightly, our lips almost brushing. "You're the one who's been teasing me all week," I reminded him.

His fingers pressed more firmly against me, and I bit back a moan. "Maybe I was wrong," he admitted, his voice rough with desire.

The light turned green again, and he pulled away, the car jerking forward as he accelerated. The tension in the air was obvious, each touch, each glance driving me closer to the edge. I struggled to keep my thoughts coherent, to focus on anything other than the way his touch made me feel.

We stopped for gas, and as he filled the tank, he leaned in through the window. "I bet you'd like it if I got on my knees and begged right here," he said, his voice a rasp.

I looked around the crowded gas station, the buzz of people moving around us oblivious to the charged moment unfolding inside our car. A thrill shot through me, electrifying my senses. The very idea of Jae, this powerful, commanding man, being so desperate for me, made my pulse race and my breath hitch.

He straightened up, the muscles in his arms flexing as he replaced the gas nozzle and twisted the cap back on. My eyes traced the lines of his body, the way his shirt clung to his chest, the confident way he moved. Everything about him screamed control and dominance, yet here he was, offering to beg for me, to lower himself to his knees in a public place, all for me.

As he walked back to the driver's side, I felt my heart pound harder. My mind raced, caught between the propriety of the moment and the allure of his words.

Jae slid back into the car, his hand immediately returning to my thigh. The warmth of his touch seeped through the fabric of my dress, setting my skin on fire. His eyes held an intense, silent promise in their depths.

"Does that turn you on, Verena?" he whispered, his voice husky. "The thought of me on my knees for you, right here?"

"Why does the idea of you being so...desperate for me turn me on?" I managed to whisper back, my voice trembling with a mix of excitement and fear.

"Because you know how much power you have over me," he replied, his hand inching higher, teasing the edge of my underwear again. "And it drives you wild, doesn't it?"

I couldn't deny it. The thought of Jae, the man who seemed unbreakable, willing to break for me, was addictive. It made me feel powerful, desired, and utterly alive.

He leaned closer. "I'd do it, you know," he murmured, his voice a tantalizing caress. "I'd crawl to you just to feel your breath on my skin."

I closed my eyes, trying to steady myself against the overwhelming tide of emotions. "Jae, you're driving me crazy."

"Good," he whispered, his lips brushing against my neck. "Because that's exactly what you do to me. Every second I'm not touching you is pure torture."

"Fuckkk."

"See, baby? You could have this all the time. You just have to say yes."

He turned the car on and pulled back onto the road, the tension between us thick and electric. My heart raced, each touch of his fingers sending waves of heat through my body. We drove in a charged silence, the city lights casting a warm glow around us as we neared his penthouse.

The sleek penthouse building loomed ahead, a symbol of his power and success. As we pulled into the valet area, he looked at me. "I'll stay tonight," I said, my voice trembling.

"Stay forever," he countered, his fingers tracing patterns on my thigh.

"Tonight," I insisted, my heart pounding.

"Forever," he repeated, leaning in close. "And I'll make it worth it."

He sucked on my earlobe, his teeth grazing the sensitive skin, sending a jolt of pleasure through me. "Tonight," I rasped, my resolve crumbling.

"Fine," he whispered, his voice thick with desire. "I'll settle for tonight."

He tossed the keys to the valet and practically dragged me out of the car, his grip on my hand firm and unyielding. The city buzzed around us, but all I could focus on was the feel of his hand in mine, the promise of what was to come hanging in the air.

We entered the building, the cool marble floors and high ceilings a stark contrast to the heat building between us. The elevator ride was a blur, my mind spinning with anticipation and desire. As the doors opened to his penthouse, he led me inside, his touch never leaving mine.

The door closed behind us with a finality that made my breath catch. This was it. The beginning of something new, something real. And as Jae pulled me closer, his lips capturing mine in a searing kiss, I knew.

I knew he had me right where he wanted me.

54

CLI(MAX)

JAE

I dragged her through the penthouse, my grip firm on her wrist, my heart pounding with anticipation. The city lights spilled through the floor-to-ceiling windows, casting a soft glow over everything. But I couldn't focus on that. All I could think about was her —Verena—standing here in my home, agreeing to stay the night.

As we reached my bedroom, I pushed the door open and pulled her inside, my hands already reaching for the zipper of her skirt. The fabric parted under my fingers, revealing her smooth skin, and I felt a growl of desire rumble in my chest. "You have no idea how long I've wanted this," I whispered, my voice rough with need.

Verena's eyes were wide. "You always were impatient," she teased, a smile tugging at her lips.

"Impatient?" I echoed, a grin spreading across my face. "When it comes to you, yeah. Impatient doesn't even begin to cover it."

I tore at her clothes, the fabric slipping from her shoulders and pooling at her feet. She stood there in her lingerie, looking like a goddess, and I felt my knees go weak. "Fuck, you're beautiful," I murmured, my hands trembling as I reached for her.

"Keep saying things like that," she replied, her voice a sultry purr, "and I might just decide to stay forever."

I laughed, the sound mingling with my heavy breathing. "I'll make sure of it."

As our lips met in a desperate kiss, I tasted the salt of sweat and the sweetness on her tongue, my senses overwhelmed by the intensity of our connection.

My hands roamed over her body, fingers fumbling with the clasp of her bra. I cursed, my clumsiness making her giggle. "Need some help there?" she asked, arching an eyebrow.

"Always," I admitted with a sheepish grin. "But only from you."

She reached behind her and unclasped her bra, letting it fall away. The sight of her bare skin, the way she looked at me with those eyes—hungry and playful—made my breath catch. "You're killing me, Verena," I whispered, my hands sliding down her sides, tugging at the waistband of her panties.

"That's the plan," she quipped, her fingers threading through my hair and pulling me closer. Our lips met in a frantic kiss, all tongue and teeth and desperate need.

I felt her hands tugging at my shirt, yanking it over my head. The cool air hit my skin, but it was nothing compared to the heat between us. "You know," I said between kisses, "I always thought I'd be the one in control."

"Turns out you're a softy," she teased, her hands sliding down my chest. "But I kind of like it."

I laughed, the sound raw. "Yeah? You like seeing me beg?"

"I do," she admitted, her voice low and seductive. "Now show me how good you can beg, Jae."

My fingers hooked into her panties, pulling them down her legs as I dropped to my knees. "I need you, Verena," I murmured, my lips brushing her thigh. "I'm a wreck without you, and I hate it. I've changed. I'm going to put you first in every way."

Her hand cupped my chin, lifting my gaze to meet hers. "Then prove it."

I kissed a path up her leg, my desperation growing with every inch. "I'll shatter for you and cherish every broken piece," I promised, my voice thick with emotion. "You're my obsession, and I don't care who knows it."

She pulled me up, her lips crashing against mine as she guided me toward the bed. We tumbled onto the sheets, a mess of limbs and laughter, the intensity of our need tempered by the joy of finally being together.

"You're really bad at this," she teased as my hand got caught in her hair.

"I'm just distracted by how gorgeous you are," I replied, untangling my fingers and kissing her neck.

I paused, the words I'd wanted to say lingering on my tongue.

I needed just one moment of bravery.

"I love every part of you, Verena. Every single part."

Her eyes widened. "L-love?"

I trailed kisses down her collarbone, pausing to nibble gently at her skin. "I love the way your hair smells like lavender," I murmured against her skin. "And the little birthmark on your hip that looks like a tiny heart."

She laughed, the sound sending a thrill through me. "You noticed that?"

"Of course I did," I replied, pressing a kiss to the spot. "And I love the way your freckles get darker in the summer. They make a little constellation on your cheeks."

"You're such a nerd," she said, but her eyes were soft, her fingers threading through my hair.

"Maybe," I admitted, kissing my way down her stomach. "But I also love the scar on your knee from when you fell off your bike in college. It reminds me of how brave you are."

She quivered under my touch. "Jae…"

"I love the way your eyes light up when you talk about something you're passionate about," I continued, my lips brushing against her skin with each word. "And the little wrinkle you get on your forehead when you're thinking hard about something."

"You're ridiculous," she whispered, pulling me back up to kiss her deeply.

"Ridiculously in love with you," I corrected, kissing the corner of her mouth. "And I love the way your lips taste like strawberries."

She laughed, the sound turning into a gasp as I kissed her again, deeper this time. "You're really laying it on thick," she teased, her fingers tracing patterns on my back.

"I mean every word," I said, my voice low and serious. "I love the way you laugh, the way you move, the way you make me feel like I'm the only person in the world when you look at me."

"Jae," she whispered, her eyes shining with emotion.

"I love the way your toes curl when you're excited," I added, smiling against her lips. "And the way you sigh when you're really content."

"You're not missing anything, are you?" she asked, her voice trembling with laughter and emotion.

"Not a thing," I promised, kissing her softly. "Because every part of you is perfect to me."

Her eyes sparkled with a mixture of amusement and desire. "I don't just love how you look," I said, my voice dropping to a husky whisper. "Because, fuck, I love how you feel."

I let my hands roam over her soft skin, reveling in the way she shivered under my touch. "I love the way your skin feels against mine," I murmured, kissing the hollow of her throat. "So soft, so warm. And the way it blushes red when I suck on your neck."

She gasped as my lips found her pulse point, her fingers digging into my shoulders. "Jae..."

"And your eyes," I continued, my voice thick with need. "The way they flare when you feel good, when you're on the edge of losing control. I'm addicted to seeing how you respond to me."

I moved lower, trailing kisses down her chest, savoring the taste of her skin. "I love the way your body arches into mine," I said. "The way you moan my name when I hit the right spot."

She tangled her fingers in my hair, her breath coming in short gasps. "I...I l-love you too, Jae." she whispered, her voice trembling with need.

"Good," I growled, my hands gripping her hips. "Because I want to spend my life deserving that love. Begging for that love. Doing right by you. I want to make you feel things you've never felt before."

I kissed a path down her stomach, my hands exploring every inch of her body. "I want to hear you demand for more," I said, my voice a low rumble. "I want to feel you tremble beneath me."

"Jae," she moaned, her hips lifting to meet my touch.

"Tell me what you want," I demanded, my voice rough with desire. "Tell me how to make you feel good."

"I want you," she whispered, her eyes dark with longing. "I want all of you."

I moved back up, capturing her lips in a searing kiss. "You have me," I promised, my voice filled with raw emotion. "You have all of me, Verena."

We moved together, our bodies a perfect match, the heat between us building with every touch, every kiss. "I love you," I murmured against her lips, my hands gripping her tighter. "Every part of you."

"Show me," she whispered. "Show me how much you love me."

"Move in with me, baby," I begged.

"Fuck me, Jae." She adjusted her position, her legs wrapping around my waist as I stood between them. "Don't you want me?"

I groaned, my body trembling with need. I looked down at my straining cock. "Look at how hard I am for you, baby. Aching."

Her hands gripped my hips, guiding me closer. "I need it."

I thrust forward, her body enveloping me as we fell back on the pillows. Our skin met in a slick embrace, the world falling away as we surrendered to the wildness of our passion.

"Harder, Jae. Fuck me harder," she demanded.

I knew she needed this, needed to feel me inside her, to know that I was hers and she was mine. My heart pounded in my chest, matching the rhythm of our movements as I drove myself deeper into her, taking her with every thrust.

"I love you," I groaned, my voice hoarse with need. "Say it. Say you'll live here."

"Stop"—she paused to moan—"demanding shit and fuck, fuck, *fuck* me."

I grinned, my hips bucking harder as I felt her clench around my cock. "Live here, Verena. Say it," I demanded, my voice a low growl.

"Fuck me, Jae!" she cried, her body shaking with need. "I'll move in, I'll live here with you, just fuck me!"

The words sent a flood of pleasure through me, and I thrust harder, my body responding to her demand. I let loose a low moan, the sound muffled by her skin. "I love you, Verena. I need you. I need you here with me."

"I love you too, Jae," she gasped. "Fuck, I need you too."

"Say it again," I demanded, my voice rough with need. "Say you love me."

"Love..." A sigh, a moan, a scream. She fell apart and I built her back up with more thrusts. Orgasms built and crumbled. I didn't stop. I couldn't. I wanted rolling pleasure and declarations and muddled promises of forever.

Verena's body trembled, her cries filling the room as she met my every thrust. Her pleas for more, for harder, fueled my own desire, and I knew I would give her anything she wanted, anything she needed.

As pleasure built within us, words tumbled from my lips, full of love and longing. "I need you, Verena. I need you so much."

"I need you too, Jae. All of you."

I buried myself deep inside her, our bodies trembling together as we reached the peak of our pleasure. Our bodies moved in perfect sync, our skin slick with sweat and our fingers digging into each other's flesh as we clung to one another.

Verena was moving in.

I was a fucking goner for this woman.

55

(BOSS)Y

VERENA

I woke up with apprehension coursing through me. This was it—the moment of truth. Jae had quite literally fucked me into convincing me to stay. His dick could be used by the CIA as a tool for extracting information from terrorists. It was lethal, and now, here I was, about to live with him again.

Today was his first day back at work, and it felt like a crucial test. Our time at his vacation home had been a bubble of bliss where I didn't think he'd go back to his old ways, but now we were back to reality. I woke up alone in bed, a pang of sadness hitting me. Had it all been a dream?

I dragged myself out of bed and wandered into the kitchen, half expecting to find it empty. Instead, there was Jae, standing by the stove, flipping pancakes with an air of casual domesticity that almost made me do a double-take.

I checked the clock. 7 a.m. "You always go to work at six," I said, confused.

"I go in at nine now," he replied, glancing over his shoulder with a smile.

"Really?" I asked, suspicion lacing my voice.

"I want to have breakfast with you every morning," he said, leaning over to kiss my cheek. "Sit down."

I sat, staring at the plate he set in front of me like it was a UFO. "Can you join me for lunch?" he asked, his tone casual.

"You always have lunch meetings," I pointed out, narrowing my eyes.

"Not anymore. I told my new assistant to always block them off," he said, sliding into the seat across from me.

"New assistant?" I echoed, raising an eyebrow.

"I fired Mina the night of the rehearsal dinner," he admitted.

I nodded. I knew this, but hearing him say it felt...good. Like a closure I didn't know I needed.

"In the future, I won't tolerate anyone who undermines our relationship or makes you uncomfortable," Jae said, his tone so familiar, that bossy man who built an empire and made billions.

"I...appreciate that," I croaked out.

"Will you meet me for lunch? I want to talk more about your book and your plans. I won't interfere, but I want to know what you're going to do. It's so good."

I was floored. "Really?"

"Yes, really. And I'll be off at six. Why don't we go pick out some new furniture and decor for the place? I want it to be comfortable for you here."

I couldn't hold back the tears. They came out of nowhere, surprising both of us. Jae got up immediately and wrapped his arms around me. "Are you really going to be here?" I asked, my voice cracking.

"Yes, baby," he whispered, his hand stroking my hair. "I'm here."

"Okay," I said, sniffling into his shirt.

He pulled back slightly, looking into my eyes. "We also need to visit your mom and pick up our cat. I had Laura bring me Mina a month ago."

I paused. "*You* requested Mina?"

He blushed. "When I take my allergy medicine, she's not too bad. And once she settled, she was nice to have around."

I let out a laugh through my tears. "You're kidding."

"Nope," he said, grinning. "But be warned, she likes me more now."

I rolled my eyes. "Keep dreaming. I'll see you at lunch."

He kissed me softly before grabbing his briefcase and heading out the door. As I watched him leave, I marveled at how much he'd changed. The man who used to leave for work before dawn was now making me breakfast and adjusting his schedule to spend more time with me.

I spent the rest of the morning thinking about all the little ways he'd shown he was serious. The way he'd talked about my book, his new schedule, firing Mina. It was all so...different. And good. And it made me hopeful.

Walking into Jae's office building felt like stepping into a different lifetime. The sleek lobby, the polished floors, the hum of productivity—it all brought back memories of when I used to work here. Back then, I was the efficient, invisible assistant, making sure everything ran smoothly while keeping my own dreams on the backburner.

I remembered the day I quit. It felt like jumping off a cliff, exhilarating and terrifying all at once. But it was the right decision, a necessary step to reclaim my life and pursue my passion for writing. Now, walking through these familiar halls, I felt a sense of closure rather than trepidation.

People whispered as I passed by, their curious eyes following me. But I didn't care. Let them talk. I was here for Jae, and nothing else mattered.

A cheerful voice broke through my thoughts. I turned to see a bubbly guy with a wide smile heading toward me. "You must be Verena. I'm Connor, Jae's new assistant."

"Nice to meet you, Connor," I replied, smiling back at him. His enthusiasm was contagious, a refreshing burst of energy in the otherwise polished and sterile office environment.

"Mr. Lee is just wrapping up a meeting," Connor said, gesturing for me to follow him. "But he's already ordered your favorite lunch. He said you love the chicken avocado salad from that place down the street."

I raised an eyebrow, impressed. "He remembered."

Connor led me to Jae's office, chatting animatedly. "I was so nervous to work for Mr. Lee. I heard he's really strict. You were his previous assistant, right?"

"Yeah, I was," I said, smiling at the memory. "And he can be strict, but he's fair. Once you get to know him, you'll see he has a soft side."

"Really?" Connor's eyes widened in surprise. "I haven't seen that side yet."

I laughed, shaking my head. "It takes a little while, but trust me, it's there."

Connor's curiosity seemed piqued. "Any tips on handling him? I mean, besides the obvious."

I leaned in conspiratorially, grinning. "Oh, I have a few tips. First off, never let his coffee sit for more than five minutes. He's convinced it loses its optimal temperature and flavor profile after exactly five minutes and thirty-two seconds."

Connor chuckled, nodding. "Got it. Coffee—five minutes, thirty-two seconds. What else?"

"Don't ever, and I mean ever, let him run out of those little imported sugar packets from Italy. I had to beg a customs officer once to release a shipment because they were stuck in transit."

"Seriously?"

"Oh, it gets better," I said, laughing. "He has this thing about the blinds in his office. They have to be at a twenty-three-degree angle. Not twenty-two, not twenty-four. Exactly twenty-three. I used a protractor for months."

Connor burst out laughing. "That's insane."

"And then there's his Post-it notes. They have to be the recycled kind, but only in pastel colors. No neon. He says neon colors distract him from serious thought processes."

"Wow, he really is particular," Connor said, shaking his head in amazement.

"Oh, and let's not forget the office supplies," I added, warming up to my theme. "His pens must be fountain pens with black ink—blue ink is a mortal sin. And every notepad he uses has to be leather-bound. I once had to drive three hours to get him a specific brand because it was out of stock locally."

Connor looked like he was struggling to keep up. "Is there anything else?"

"Well, he has this thing about meetings. If they start even a minute late, he's grumpy for the rest of the day. I used to set all the clocks in the office five minutes ahead just to make sure no one was late."

"Smart move," Connor said, laughing.

"And if he's had a really stressful day, he likes to unwind with a specific playlist. It's all eighties power ballads. He claims they're the ultimate de-stress music."

Connor was practically in stitches by this point. "I can't believe you had to deal with all that."

"Yeah, well, it kept things interesting," I said with a grin. "And it was worth it. He's a great boss once you get used to his quirks."

As we arrived at Jae's office, I couldn't help but feel a strange sense of nostalgia. The memories of my time here, the challenges and the triumphs, all came rushing back. Connor opened the door and motioned for me to sit down. "Make yourself comfortable. He should be out any minute."

I sat in the plush chair, glancing around the office. It was the same as I remembered—minimalistic and efficient—yet there were new personal touches that reflected Jae's transformation. A framed photo of us from a recent beach trip sat on his desk, making me smile. It was a small reminder of the love and commitment we had built together.

Moments later, Jae walked in, his face lighting up when he saw me. "Hey, you," he greeted, crossing the room to kiss me. "Sorry to keep you waiting."

"It's fine," I said, smiling against his lips. "Connor kept me entertained."

Jae laughed, glancing at his assistant. "He's good at that. Did he tell you I ordered your favorite?"

"He did," I replied, touched by the gesture. "Thank you."

We sat down to eat, the atmosphere comfortable and relaxed. Jae listened intently as I talked about my book and my plans. He seemed genuinely interested. It was a pivotal moment, seeing how supportive and invested he was without being overbearing.

"So, what's next for you?" Jae asked, taking a bite of his sandwich.

"I think I'm going to self-publish," I said. "I want to have control over the process."

Jae nodded approvingly. "I think that's a great idea. And you know I'm here to help if you need anything."

"I appreciate that," I said, my heart swelling with gratitude. "But I really want to do this on my own."

He reached across the table, taking my hand in his. "I understand. Just know that I believe in you, Verena. You're going to be amazing."

Connor walked in, carrying a stack of files. "Mr. Lee, here are the reports you asked for."

"Thanks, Connor," Jae said, taking the files. "And call me Jae."

Connor blinked in surprise. "Oh, sure...Jae."

Once Conner was gone, Jae turned to me. "Why did my new assistant look at me like I had two heads when I told him to call me Jae? Is my reputation really that bad?"

I laughed, shaking my head. "You're doing just fine. But if you want some advice, maybe don't yell at him if he forgets to charge your smartwatch."

Jae grinned. "Noted. Anything else?"

"Listen to Connor's ideas," I suggested. "He seems bright and enthusiastic. Encourage that."

Jae nodded thoughtfully. "Anything else?"

I leaned back in my chair, considering. "Well, let's start with the basics. For instance, don't freak out if he accidentally uses regular paper instead of recycled for your daily reports. I remember that happening once and it was like the world was ending."

Jae's eyes widened. "Got it."

"And maybe ease up on the binder clips," I continued, smirking.

"You have a tendency to treat them like gold. Let the man use them without fearing a lecture about resource conservation."

Jae chuckled, rubbing the back of his neck. "Okay, okay. Anything else?"

"Yes, actually. If he ever needs to reschedule a meeting, try to be a bit more flexible. I know your schedule is tight, but life happens. Give him some leeway."

"I won't be flexible when it comes to my time with *you*," he argued, making my stomach flutter.

"And for the love of all things holy, please don't make him run across town to get those specific pens you like. Remember that time I almost missed a conference call because I was hunting down the last Montblanc in the city?"

Jae laughed, the sound filling the room. "I remember. You were pretty mad."

"Mad? I was ready to quit on the spot," I teased, shaking my head. "Seriously, though, it's the little things. Show some understanding and flexibility, and it'll go a long way."

As we finished our lunch, the conversation flowed easily, filled with laughter and sweet moments. Jae kept asking about my book. It was so different from the days when I felt like a cog in the corporate machine. Now, I was a woman on the brink of achieving her dreams, supported by the man who had become my biggest champion.

"I can't wait to see your book on the shelves," Jae said, squeezing my hand.

"Neither can I," I replied. "It's going to be incredible."

By the end of the meal, I felt a renewed sense of purpose and hope for the future. The anxiety that had been gnawing at me earlier that day had dissipated, replaced by a warmth that spread through my entire being.

As we left the office, I couldn't help but marvel at the journey we'd taken. I used to be the girl who felt invisible, drowning in the shadows of my own doubts and insecurities. But not anymore. It was surreal, a blend of the unbelievable and the inevitable.

Somewhere, I knew Auntie was smiling. Her faith in us, in Jae, had been resolute. She had seen the potential in him, the strength buried beneath his grief. She knew he could emerge from the storm of despair and become the man she always believed he could be.

Strong. Settled. Still. And so, so loved.

Grief had tried to drown us, but instead, it forged us into something unbreakable. Jae had become everything Auntie had hoped for, and more. His transformation was proof of the power of love and resilience.

As Jae pulled me close, whispering promises of forever, I felt the most beautiful sense of certainty. This was just the beginning of our story. The road ahead was filled with promise, not because it was free of challenges, but because we were ready to face them together.

And in that moment, I knew—our story would be one of hope, of unyielding love, and of countless mornings spent wrapped in each other's arms. This was our new beginning, and I couldn't wait to see where it would lead us.

EPILOGUE

JAE

Six months later

It had been six months since Verena moved in with me, and life had taken on a rhythm that felt both familiar and exhilaratingly new. Every morning, I woke up next to her, feeling a sense of peace and contentment that I hadn't known I was missing.

Today was a special day. Verena's book launch. The culmination of all her hard work, her dedication, and her dreams was finally coming to fruition. I had taken the day off to be with her, to support her, to witness the moment when her words would be shared with the world.

As I stood in our kitchen, making breakfast, I couldn't help but reflect on how much had changed. The man I was before—obsessed with work, driven by a need to prove myself—seemed like a distant memory. Now, my priorities had shifted. Verena was my anchor, my inspiration, my everything.

"Good morning," Verena's voice broke through my thoughts. She walked into the kitchen, her hair tousled from sleep, wearing one of my shirts. She looked beautiful, as always.

"Good morning," I replied, smiling as I handed her a cup of coffee. "Excited for today?"

She took a sip, her eyes lighting up. "Nervous and excited. But mostly excited."

I pulled her into my arms, kissing the top of her head. "You're going to be amazing. I'm so proud of you."

She leaned into me, her arms wrapping around my waist. "Thank you, Jae. For everything."

"Anything for you," I whispered, holding her close.

Later that morning, we arrived at the bookstore where the launch was being held. The room hummed with anticipation, filled with people—friends, family, and eager new readers—gathered to celebrate Verena's moment. The air was thick with excitement and the scent of freshly printed pages. I couldn't help but feel a bit smug. Maybe I had booked out the entire bookstore, hired people to attend, and bought copies for everyone in the office. So what? What use was being a billionaire if I couldn't support the woman I loved in every possible way?

Verena had realized how challenging indie publishing was and graciously accepted this extravagant gesture. She took the stage, radiating confidence and grace. Her eyes sparkled as she spoke about her journey, the trials and triumphs that had led her here.

"And most importantly," she said, her gaze locking onto mine, "I want to thank Jae. For believing in me, for supporting me, and for loving me through it all. I couldn't have done this without you."

My heart swelled, and I had to blink back tears. Her words held more weight than she could ever know.

Verena settled into a chair at the front of the room, her book in hand. The cover, an illustration of the tattoo Auntie and I had gotten, painted by Quincy Nichole, was a tribute to the love and legacy Auntie left behind. Verena opened the book, her fingers trembling slightly as she began to read aloud.

"The way a person leaves says more about them than how they enter your life. My brother and his wife departed this world in a sudden, tragic car crash. The police report said they were holding hands, united even in death. My fiancé left when he found out I was going to raise my teenage nephew. Beginnings are often a matter of happenstance and cosmic alignment. My beginning happened when my brother died—a cruel fate no one saw coming. But my ending, the way I made my exit was a decision I made. That choice defined me. It revealed my true character and laid bare the essence of who I am."

I listened, each word a vivid stroke on the canvas of memory. Verena's voice, steady yet laced with emotion, brought Auntie's story to life. The pain and strength, the love and sacrifice—it was all there, woven into every line.

"Endings are like that. They are deliberate, often painful, and irrevocably shape the course of our lives. My brother's exit was beyond his control, a cruel twist of fate. My fiancé's exit, however, was a conscious decision, one that left me to navigate the uncharted waters of guardianship alone."

The room was silent, each person drawn into the narrative. I thought about Auntie, the woman who had shaped my life, and the profound impact she had on both of us. She had faced unimaginable challenges with grace and resilience, her love steadfast even in the darkest times.

Verena continued reading, her voice a melodic blend of sorrow and hope. "But in the wake of their departures, I discovered something profound. Endings, while often devastating, also make room for new beginnings. They force us to confront our fears, to adapt, and to grow in ways we never imagined."

Tears welled up as I absorbed the gravity of her words. This book was more than a story; it was a legacy, a testament to Auntie's enduring spirit and the love that bound us together.

When Verena finished reading, the room erupted in applause. She looked over at me, her eyes shimmering with tears and pride. I knew what she was feeling—an overwhelming sense of gratitude and accomplishment.

After the launch, we returned home, the excitement of the day still buzzing in the air. We celebrated with a quiet dinner, just the two of us, savoring the moment. As we sat on the couch, sipping wine, Verena leaned her head on my shoulder.

"Today was perfect," she said softly.

"It was," I agreed, kissing her forehead. "You were perfect."

She smiled, looking up at me. "You know, I think Auntie would be proud of me."

I nodded, feeling a lump form in my throat. "I think so too."

We sat in comfortable silence for a while, just enjoying each other's presence. The future was still uncertain, filled with unknowns and challenges. But for the first time in my life, I felt ready to face it all. With Verena by my side, I knew we could handle anything.

I reached for her hand, intertwining our fingers, feeling the warmth and the undeniable connection that bound us together. "Verena," I began, my voice trembling with emotion, "there's something I've been wanting to ask you."

She turned to me, her eyes wide with curiosity and a hint of nervous anticipation. "What is it?" she asked softly, her voice barely above a whisper.

I took a deep breath, my heart pounding in my chest like a drum, each beat echoing the gravity of this moment. I pulled out a small velvet box from my pocket and opened it to reveal the ring. It was delicate and beautiful, with a vintage design she had once admired in a shop window. The center stone was a sapphire, her favorite, surrounded by a halo of tiny diamonds.

"Verena," I said, my voice steady but filled with a depth of feeling I could barely contain, "I love you more than words can ever express. From the moment we met, you've been my anchor, my light, my everything. We've been through so much together—the highs, the lows, the moments of joy and the depths of sorrow. And through it all, my love for you has only grown stronger."

Her eyes filled with tears, and she squeezed my hand tightly, her fingers trembling.

"I want to spend the rest of my life with you," I continued, my voice gaining strength. "I want to be there for you, to support you, to cherish you, and to build a future together. No more fake engagements, no more pretenses. Just us, forever, with all the love and honesty we can give each other."

I slipped the ring onto her finger, where it fit perfectly, as if it had always belonged there. "Will you marry me, Verena? Will you make this promise of forever with me?"

For a heartbeat, the world seemed to stand still. Then, tears welled up in her eyes, sparkling like diamonds. Her radiant smile spread across her face, lighting up the room, and she nodded, a tear slipping down her cheek. "Yes, Jae," she whispered, her voice choked with emotion. "Yes, I will."

In that moment, everything else faded away—the past, the pain, the uncertainties of the future. All that mattered was this beautiful, incredible woman standing before me, saying yes to forever. I pulled her into my arms, holding her close as a wave of overwhelming joy and love washed over us, sealing our promise to one another with the strength and clarity of a thousand unspoken words.

As we held each other, I felt the ring on her finger—a symbol of our love, our commitment, and the future we would build together. It was more than just a piece of jewelry; it was evidence of the journey we had taken and the endless possibilities that lay ahead.

"I love you, Verena," I whispered into her ear, my voice filled with reverence and awe. "And I promise to spend every day showing you just how much."

THANK YOU SO MUCH FOR DIVING INTO MY STORY! IF YOU ENJOYED THE journey, I'd be thrilled if you could leave a review – it means the world to me and helps other readers find their next favorite book. For more behind-the-scenes glimpses, writing shenanigans, and a sprinkle of daily inspiration, follow me on Instagram @authorcoraleejune. Let's keep the adventure going together!

AFTERWORD

Thank you so much for reading *The End in Friends*. This book was truly a labor of love and a story that's been on my heart for a very long time.

When I first started writing this book, I thought it was just going to be a quirky love story with lots of humor, but it evolved into something much deeper. The story of losing Auntie was unexpected but necessary. It opened up a space for exploring how we navigate mortality and grief in our own unique ways. I wanted the characters to dive into those feelings with authenticity.

Jae's relationship with his job is something I deeply relate to. When I first started writing, I felt the pressure to work myself to the bone, constantly striving to be noticed. In this industry, it can seem like if you're not always doing something, you'll be forgotten. Jae is trying so hard to build a legacy, but he's losing sight of the precious moments right in front of him. I found myself in a similar place, realizing a year ago just how precious time is. With three young children and a wonderful, adoring husband, I wanted to be present in my life for them.

Jae's journey to finding stillness and Verena's journey to writing her own story both mirror my path into this new genre and brand. I wanted to create characters facing battles that resonate with me, particularly the struggle with the idea that time and life are precious. You never know how long you have, and it's crucial to cherish every moment.

I hope this story resonated with you as much as it did with me. Thank you again for being part of this journey.

ACKNOWLEDGMENTS

First and foremost, I want to extend my deepest gratitude to my editor, Helayna Trask. A couple of weeks before the book's release, she called me and said that the book felt very surface level and needed flashbacks. In the midst of signings and chaos, I wrote an additional 30,000 words. This added so much depth to the story, and without her bravery in telling me I could do better, I probably wouldn't have written the story you're reading today. It would have fallen flat, so I truly owe her a lot.

I'd also like to thank my amazing team of beta readers. They are wonderful, encouraging, and honest. Honest feedback is crucial when crafting a story, and their insights have been invaluable.

My heartfelt thanks go to my business manager, Brittany Franks, and my assistants and PR team at Chaotic Creatives. Your dedication and hard work have been instrumental in bringing this book to life.

To my husband, my rock and support system, thank you for understanding that when I go into the writing cave, sometimes I'm just a little gremlin that needs food thrown at her. Your patience and love mean the world to me.

A special thanks to my kids, who were absolute troopers staying at home during the first couple weeks of their summer vacation while I was in the trenches of adding additional words.

Lastly, to the readers who have stayed by me and encouraged me to take this new journey into writing a different genre, thank you. Your support and enthusiasm have been my driving force, and I am endlessly grateful for each and every one of you.

ABOUT THE AUTHOR

CoraLee is a romance author who crafts heartfelt stories that make you laugh and provide a delightful escape from the chaos of everyday life. A former librarian and English major from Texas State, she has a deep love for the written word and storytelling. Cora is passionate about creating narratives that linger in your heart long after you've turned the last page. When she's not weaving tales of love and connection, she enjoys spending time with her family in the Lone Star State.

ALSO BY CORALEE

GET HIM BACK

WIN HIM OVER

LEVEL HIM UP

www.ingramcontent.com/pod-product-compliance
Lightning Source LLC
Chambersburg PA
CBHW071443140726
47997CB00005B/1577